TWISTED

SILVER

SPOONS

TWISTED

SILVER

SPOONS

KAREN M. WICKS

atmosphere press

Published by Atmosphere Press

Cover design by Ronaldo Alves

atmospherepress.com

I would like to thank my husband Les, my sister Joyce Dalton, and my friend Debby Chambers for their thoughtful comments on early versions of *Twisted Silver Spoons*. Above all, Les' encouragement over the years has encouraged me to find my voice and pursue my dreams.

Part 1

But Love has pitched her mansion in
The place of excrement,
For nothing can be sole or whole
That has not been rent.
—W.B. Yeats

Prologue
1985

"Y-Yes. I'm just feeling a little hemmed in, I guess. A passing fantasy."

The silver spoon lodged in George's throat was choking the life out of him.

She beckoned across the dunes toward the spangled house, still filled with Fritz and Belinda's guests.

"Yes, I see what you mean."

Her eyes peeled back his ambivalence.

Chapter 1
1986

Daggers of Caribbean sunlight pried open George's eyes, as a continent of stifling duty constricted his view. He arose, unsteady, his patrician mouth curled around the scum of filial duty. An approaching shadow rescued him.

"Mr. Leibnitz, may I offer you some refreshment?"

"No, thank you. I am meeting Father for lunch shortly."

"Very good, sir."

George watched the steward retreat down the teak stairs. His eyes moistened with inevitability. Ten days in the Grenadines on his father Fritz's one-hundred-ninety-foot Feadship yacht, *Aleksandra*, had held such promise. No loathsome stepmother and stepsiblings. But Fritz's frequent disparaging remarks threaded rancor through George's shock of black hair. How ironic that the motor yacht had been named for his *Gran'maman* when it was one of Fritz's seats of power.

He lumbered down two steps to the lavatory. Fritz wouldn't fail to notice a hair out of place. The placid demeanor and bold, aquamarine eyes staring out from the antique beveled mirror masked his angst. He fingered the well-worn Cartier tank watch *Gran'maman* had given him for his fourteenth birthday, each compulsive stroke attacking his dread. Jerking his head toward the open door, he tightened the knots in his stomach and launched toward the dining room.

12:33.

Striding through the salon, he straightened to his full six-foot-four height, poised to tower over his father. But with each step he shrank a few inches under the uniform of obsequiousness. Even seated, Fritz's tall, muscular frame, the jut of his square chin, and his penetrating, electric-blue eyes commanded obedience. If only they had sailed on the Morgan, where his youth would have given him the advantage.

Each step prickled sweat on his neck. Fritz would needle him about graduating from New York University School of Law a year late. Preparation for the New York bar would be a perfunctory requirement, and recriminations that he had not gone to Yale Law School along with new expectations would be served for lunch. The intrusion of the fond memory of his childhood father withered in the tight bud of his heart.

"Good afternoon, Mr. Leibnitz."

George's skin quivered. His head turned. "Bruce."

"Are you alright, sir?"

"Tell Father I will be along directly," he snapped.

"Very good, sir."

As the steward moved off, George bit the inside of his cheek and the metallic taste of blood propelled him back to his grandfather Rainer's death and Fritz's quick rise to power over his brother Guenther. George had been sent off to Phillips Exeter Academy, and in time his mother—an exquisite doll who had lost her sheen—had been replaced.

He scurried into the nearby lavatory to collect himself. The face of a child lost in memories accosted him in the gilded mirror.

Clenching his jaw, he embraced his twenty-four years and wheeled toward the dining room. As he shortened the remaining expanse, a scowling Fritz tapped his Rolex. His steeled gaze refused the expected apology, and Fritz's face morphed into a smile.

"Have a nice nap, did we? The stone crabs and the *salade frisée* look delectable. I have ordered you a glass of Chardonnay and an iced coffee for our meeting afterwards."

George sat down, pique tightening his shoulders.

"*Papa*," he began in French as the wait staff began serving them, "*J'ai des questions. Je voudrais savoir si Ol'papa...*"

Fritz raised his eyebrows. "Your grandfather?"

"I-I have questions about his death."

Fritz's eyes sharpened as he dangled a crab in mid-air.

"Marcus said something sinister hap..."

"Your cousin?"

A smirk crossed Fritz's face.

Tearing into the crustacean, he deposited the shell onto an empty plate and patted his mouth with a linen napkin.

"*Ol'Papa's* death was his own doing. I was preoccupied with securing the foreign divisions. The strain of our conversation must have affected him. But you must understand, he used every weapon at his disposal to wound me."

George sipped his wine.

"He seduced the first girl I loved when I was seventeen to prove he was the better man."

The golden liquid scalded his throat.

Bitterness flickered across Fritz's face, darkening his jowls.

"It gives one a sense of the lengths to which your grandfather would go to keep his family in line, *n'est-ce pas?*"

George's tongue congealed.

"Arrogant fool. Not a scintilla of humility. If it had not been for Aleksandra, Rainer would have been some mid-level functionary in the bowels of Austrian bureaucracy."

"*Gran'maman?* Wh-What do you m-mean? I know *Gran'maman* and Great-Uncle Sergey fled Russia, but..."

"You remember so little while your cousin makes a point to know everyone's affairs."

George lined up his knife and spoon.

"Aleksandra's fortune started Leibnitz Enterprises. Rainer was a mere engineer with a modest inheritance. She had the means and the intellect to..."

"I thought..."

"*She* was the visionary. And as LE became successful, Rainer grew to resent her."

Contempt etched his face. "He tried to limit her influence. By the time I was fifteen, he particularly detested me, her *favorite* son."

His lips pursed as he looked out across the expanse of ocean. "Fortunately, your grandmother was shrewd enough to insist on maintaining majority ownership. She shipped me off to Paris to Uncle Sergey..."

"You are saying *Gran'maman* favored you?"

He stared at his son.

"Your supercilious grandfather believed she favored me to justify his jealousy. I was capable of succeeding him, not dear brother Guenther, and he pitted us against each other. Such hubris!"

He waved his hand in disgust.

George's lip quivered. "H-He actually..."

"*Absolument.*"

A steward approached.

"He would have succeeded if Aleksandra had not steered Guenther and me into the roles for which we were born."

George's eyes brightened. "Is that why Uncle Guenther leads the engineering and manufacturing divisions, and you are the CEO?"

"*Bien sûr, Georges.* You can thank your grandmother and Uncle Sergey for the cordial relationship between Guenther and me, and for LE's success."

Fritz sipped his wine and picked up his fork.

"I-I thought you took the chairmanship away from Uncle Guenther."

Fritz exhaled a sinister laugh. "Marcus feeding you misinformation?"

George blinked and arranged his food by color.

"Do not be so gullible. Papa hated me because Mummy was preparing me to succeed him. She was guiding Guenther, of course. A rather blunt instrument, but he came along."

George raised his eyebrows. Fritz scattered the leaves of the lettuces to the edges of the plate.

"Papa marginalized my role in the company. He may have succeeded if he had not died."

A wistful look crossed his eyes. "I loved him, you know."

His face hardened. "And I despised him. Nothing can erase what he did. Especially to Mummy."

George's back straightened. "What do you mean?"

"Uncle Sergey discovered another well-cared for family in London—a wife and daughter."

George's fork thudded against his plate.

Fritz's voice bristled. "And a long string of mistresses. In his will, Rainer provided generously for all of them. I had every reason to wish Papa dead. However, a brain hemorrhage killed him."

George leaned forward.

"I was leaving the room when I heard a noise at the door, and, of course, you know the rest."

George nodded. "How could I forget? You tumbled into me as you left." His eyes sharpened. "Was he breathing when you returned to the study?"

Fritz's eyes darkened. "No."

George contemplated the irony of the father Fritz described with such bitterness to the father he had become. As he sipped his Chardonnay, the wine swirled with the past.

Chapter 2
1968

The Saturday afternoon before his grandfather's birthday party, George was looking for his Labradors at the stables, where they often played, when he heard the caustic voices of his father and grandfather as he approached the stable door.

"Fritz, you lack what it takes," Rainer hissed as he mounted his Arabian. "You barely showed yourself adequate as the Paris *Chef de Bureau*, and your negotiations on the Russian and Greek pulp deals have amounted to little."

Fritz cinched the saddle. "Clearly, withholding key information and upstaging me at every turn has not helped."

George peeked around the corner, his heart pounding. The chiseled physique and steel bearing of the two men tightened his chest. He detected a hint of vulnerability mixed with guarded respect behind his father's fiery blue eyes. But in Ol'Papa's icy glower lay raw contempt, the eagle advancing on his prey.

Rainer picked up the reins. "Always ready with the excuse. By your age, Guenther was managing a fleet of engineers."

As shame flooded George's face, he slinked away.

The weekend of Ol'Papa's party, George's family had been staying in the guest house that overlooked the pool at the Wilton, Connecticut estate, with Uncle Guenther's family in the cottage abutting the clay tennis courts. George kept alert on nearby paths so cousins Marcus and Wilhelm would not capture him for their spy games. Marcus, two years older than

George and the leader of the three, modeled himself after their Great-Uncle Sergey, a former French Resistance spy. Wilhelm, a year younger than George, played the double-agent, and George the Soviet operative whom his cousins hunted. He would seek escape in the dense stands of pine, oak, birch, and elm trees against the thick stone walls that secluded the 300-acre property. When he tired of the games, he sought refuge with his cousin Georgina, who shared his interests and precocious talents. On the rare occasions when his family visited Wilton without his cousins, he rode with his father or meandered alone down the wooded trails with his chocolate Labs.

Setting off for his pets now, he walked to the paddock and riding ring, where they often frisked with the horses. Not finding them, he circled back to the octagonal hay barn on the north side of the eight-stall oak stable to see if the veterinarian or stable hands had seen them. Not finding them, he exited the rear door toward the riding master's cottage to be greeted by slobbers of affection from Sabrina and Basil just outside. His heart melted. He threw a twig into the wind, jettisoning his fear of *Ol'papa*. The thought of his family being exiled again to Paris without his cousins and *Gran'maman* frayed his nerves.

To quiet his heart, he focused the memory of racing Marcus on the circular track of the fitness center the previous day.

"Hey, cuz, you'll never keep up with me today," Marcus taunted.

"Ha, if you're so fast, I'll give you a head start."

George's heart lurched.

"Go on, George. Show'im," pudgy Willie urged from the sidelines.

He sighed, then set off against Marcus, who won by a nose-length on the seventh lap.

"Told you," Marcus crowed, sweat rolling down his beet-red face. "Maybe next time, Georgie?"

He thumped George's back.

"You-can-count-on-it," George wheezed.

After a few stretches, they padded off to the pool-house.

"I think Willie and I'll head for the whirlpool. If you're taking a swim, see you in what, twenty minutes?"

George stepped up his pace. "No, I am tagging along."

The boys were rough-housing in the entertainment area when their nannies arrived an hour later.

"*Vous voilà!*" Martine panted as she spotted her charges, Marcus and Willie.

"You laddies're wanted in the third floor sittin' room in thirty minutes. No more time for games," Florida, George's nanny, scolded. "Lisbeth and Fiona're waitin' for you lot to start your lessons. You'll need proper attire, o'course, so be quick about it. No dawdling."

She glowered at George's cousins, then turned to him. "I'll be fetchin' you from your lessons at 5:30 sharp for a change of clothes. You're to meet Father Thomas in the libr'y at 6:30, 'n dinner'll be served promptly at 7:30. Understood?"

"Yes, Miss Florida," he simpered, shifting from one foot to the other.

While he enjoyed discussing religion and philosophy with the family priest, he preferred games with his cousins.

Marcus stuck out his tongue as the nannies turned to leave. The boys shuffled their feet, then padded toward the main house. Yews and hedges hid access from the manor to the fitness center. Marcus dashed behind a bush as soon as the nannies were out of sight, and Wilhelm grabbed George's arm, pulling him behind his older brother.

George took in the bucolic scene and smirked at his cousin's pedestrian tastes. He savored the rolling acres of sprawling lawns and ponds, colorfully splashed with patterned plantings and bedding gardens that attracted all manner of butterflies and birds. Spring through fall, the stone garden paths and parterre blazed with a rainbow of redolent blooms. He often tagged along with his mother and grandmother as they picked flowers and chatted about matters few eight-year-olds would have understood.

Earlier that morning, he and *Gran'maman* had strolled through the gardens. When they reached a carved wooden bench in the parterre, they sat down under the shade of a tulip tree.

"*Liebchin,* Aberforth tells me your oils are coming along nicely. *Du arbeitest schwer, ja?*"

She pursed her lips.

His eyes brightened. "Yes, *Gran'maman*, I work hard. I enjoy the oils, but *Meister* says I am ready for watercolors."

Her eyes twinkled. "You will enjoy the challenge, *ja?*"

His face broke into a broad smile. "Look, *Gran'maman*, butterflies!"

A rainbow of colors alighted on the butterfly bushes.

"Are they Heliconiuses?"

"*Sehr güt.* Look closely. You may see some Metalmarks and Jezebels."

"Beautiful, like you."

She breathed in the redolent air. "Ah, *Leibchen*, you warm a grandmother's heart."

She patted his knee, her gray-blue eyes moist.

His heart blossomed.

As she arranged the flowers in her basket, his thoughts meandered through the main house, where the cousins often played hide-and-seek. Three floors of fifteen-thousand square feet of inlaid oak-parquet were offset by Sardinian basket-woven textured loop carpet and colorful Persians on a variety of Italian and Portuguese tiles. Rooms with ten-foot ceilings were warmed with textured wall coverings and hand-woven French and Italian fabrics on oversized Chenille and silk velvet sofas and chairs.

His mind wandered down the long, expansive gallery where, if he were clever, he could find an alcove or a large piece of furniture or urn behind which he could elude his cousins. Alone, he would sit for hours, sketchbook in hand, to study the extensive collection of Pieter Breughel the Elder, Caravaggio, and Albert Dürer that graced the hallways or the Rembrandts in the main dining room. A massive hand-carved oak table and sideboard reflected the formality of this ornate room. On the south side lay a modest conservatory beyond French glass doors.

He basked in the memory of *Gran'maman* making sure the chef prepared his favorite foods in the rustic French country kitchen of oak timber frame construction and built-in furniture of hand-rubbed white pine with antique finish. On the east side of the kitchen, a door led to a large rectangular mud room. A covered breezeway extended to the six-car garage, where he often hid from his cousins on the floorboard of one of the antique cars. He had memorized every inch of *Gran'maman*'s domain. He often read in the floor-to-ceiling library with faux-bois walls and Beauvais wall-to-wall carpeting. And when his cousins especially tormented him, he retreated to the mezzanine level, accessed at the far right of the stone fireplace, to hide and explore the stories of strangers, whose lives were so different from his secluded world of protective servants and bodyguards who cloistered him. How many times he had longed to join a game with his peers in Central Park or *les Jardins de Luxembourg* in Paris. Denied, he imagined a life filled with siblings. He was Peter in *The Chronicles of Narnia* or Charles Wallace in *A Wrinkle in Time*, surrounded by brothers and sisters who shared his triumphs and disappointments. He was brave Nikolas in *Die Geschichte von den Shwarzen Buben*.

Gran'maman's voice interrupted his musings. "I leave you now." She patted his knee. "You will find a book on the fireplace mantel in the library."

He helped her to her feet.

"We should broaden your horizons, *ja*?"

"Should I have started at the A's...?"

She ruffled his thick hair. "What silly ideas has Lisbeth put in your head? You must read the most interesting authors first."

"*Ja, Gran'maman.*"

"At your age, I spent hours in the *Buecherein Wien* with the authors who matter."

He peered up at her. "The Vienna Library?"

"When Sergey and I arrived in Vienna, I was almost eight, Sergey eleven. It was many years before we had our own *bibliothèque*. I kept most of the collection when I married, but we had to leave many books behind when we came to America. I have filled this library over many years with books that feed the soul."

Contentment graced her ruby smile.

"You and Great-Uncle Sergey moved to Vienna? *Où étaient vos parents*?"

Sadness clouded her eyes. "Your great-grandparents— Vasily Georg Marcus Sergey and Nadja Katerina Zerbst— died to save Sergey and me."

He gasped.

"We lived in Petrograd when Lenin..."

"Petrograd?"

"St. Petersburg, my beautiful Petrograd."

She frowned. "You do not know Russian history. I must speak to Lisbeth about your instruction. St. Petersburg is the land of your forefathers. It was Petrograd during my youth. Then Lenin changed it to Leningrad in '24? Stalin, another tyrant, renamed it..."

"St. Petersburg."

She smiled. "*Sehr güt.*"

He screwed up his face. "What happened?"

Her lips turned down. "*Ach.* The *Cheka*, Lenin's secret police, discovered our ancestry."

"Catherine the Great."

Her pale eyes brightened as she ruffled his pitch-dark hair, then smoothed it in place. "*Oui.*"

"*Qu'est-ce qui s'est passé?*"

Her eyes knitted together. "*Papa avait des amis importants.*"

She squeezed his hand. "He had been paying these 'friends' while discreetly shipping paintings and jewels to his brother in Vienna. He planned to send *Maman*, Sergey, and me to Vienna, then he would follow. But the *Cheka* discovered his plans."

Darkness shrouded her face. "He loaded *Maman*, Sergey, and me with silver, diamonds, and emeralds sewn into our clothing. He planned to hand us to his contact at the train who would escort us to a trusted friend in Estonia who would then deliver us to Uncle Sergey-Marcus in Vienna."

Her eyes pooled. George's heart raced.

"Papa was betrayed."

He gasped.

"We were entering *Katya's Little Garden*. We heard a loud popping sound. *Maman* was shot protecting me."

Her eyes crinkled into tiny crow's feet. "Papa and his friend pushed us on and dragged her into the trees. Gunfire came from all directions. Papa and his friend were riddled with bullets."

Her beautifully maintained face aged. "Sergey shielded me and followed Papa's instructions to go to the train. But we saw *Cheka* everywhere, so we had to run on foot through the forest. What we had to do to survive."

A dark shadow aged her face, then vanished. "Enough of that. It is time to introduce you to other wonderful adventures by *St.Exupéry*. You enjoyed *Le Petit Prince, ja?*"

He nodded. Her eyes brightened.

"For discussion tomorrow. I left Hugo's *Notre-Dame de Paris* in French for you, *n'est-ce pas?*"

"*Je veux l'essayer.*"

15

"*Magnifique.* Now, Christine is waiting to tame this unruly head of hair."

She threaded her fingers through her perfectly coiffed, wavy auburn tresses.

"Please tell me more."

Her smile enveloped him. "*Ein bischen.* It took many months, but we found our contact in Estonia. He drove us to Uncle Sergey in Vienna."

George released the tension in his shoulders. "What a relief to see you!"

Her eyes crinkled.

"What was he like?"

"A tolerable guardian. He provided a governess, servants. Uncle taught Sergey the manufacturing business, which he left to us when he died. He schooled me in finance. We had the means to start our lives."

She stood and stepped to the door. He followed.

"*Gran'maman*, do you ever speak Russian?"

"That language died with my parents."

Hardness lined her face. She turned, gesturing for him to follow. "Another time we will speak of such things."

She directed him toward the double-wide mahogany doors of the library.

"Now, you have your lessons with Father Thomas, and Christine awaits." Her face relaxed. "Tata, for now."

He basked in her adoration. *Ol'papa*, however, terrified him.

It was, therefore, with a tightened jaw that he approached the study the Monday morning after his grandfather's party, before his family returned to their Gramercy Park townhouse on Manhattan's Upper East Side. His father had promised to ride with him after meeting with *Ol'Papa*. Meanwhile, George roughhoused with his cousins.

After two hours of chasing collaborators, the boys were making their way toward the kitchen for refreshment when they overheard voices. George's mother Racquel was talking to Florida and a servant near the limousine. Marcus shoved George toward Wilhelm and the kitchen door.

"So the meeting must be over," he whispered.

He flicked George on the arm.

"Georgie's a sissy. So worried that *Ol'papa's* study is *verboten* he won't even check it out, Willie."

"Georgie's a goody two-shoes, afraid of his own shadow. Probably thinks *Ol'Papa'll* give him a smack."

"Right you are. Let's tar 'n feather'im. Isn't that what they did in the old days to chicken shits?"

George's mind ping-ponged between his cousins' taunts and facing *Ol'papa*. Bracing the unknown, he slinked down the hallway past the family room toward the study. The temptation of the music room beckoned as he limped by. He looked hungrily up the swooping staircase as he inched toward the massive mahogany door, small and foolish.

Hands slick, he stepped one throbbing foot at a time. A sound at the top of the stairway threw him behind one of the large Chinese Ceylon urns that framed the massive door. His foot knocked against the urn on his right. The sound reverberated against the parquet floor. He melted against the wall.

Waiting for silence, he tip-toed in front of the door and put his ear against the wood, but the thickness of the dark mahogany sealed the study. As his moist hand touched the brass knob, a body bounded through the door and collided into him. Both fell, legs tangled together. As he pulled himself up, he glimpsed *Ol'papa,* slumped in the sumptuous Moroccan leather chair behind his desk. Goya's *Saturn Devouring His Son* loomed on the wall. His father snapped up and yanked the massive door shut with a thud.

"*Merde! Qu'est-ce que tu fais là, Georges* Rainer Vasily Leibnitz?!"

George's tongue froze.

"*Viens*!"

Fritz clamped down on his right shoulder and steered him down the hall toward the kitchen. Still pulsing from the collision, he squirmed. Fritz's grip loosened. Upon entering the kitchen, he wheeled George around.

"Papa was especially impossible this morning. I-I did not mean to be so cross. Y-You startled me. Are you hurt?"

"N-no, sir."

"Good. What were you doing? Snooping? Someone put you up to it? One of your cousins? Their father, no doubt."

A distant muffled scream emanated from the hallway.

He gripped George's arms. "Wait here! Do not move," he snarled.

The image of his slumped grandfather and his father slamming the door rattled around in his head. He scanned the kitchen for his cousins, who surely waited to pounce. Within moments, he heard the voices of servants and his mother in the hallway. As he was straining to make out the words by leaning close to the swinging doors, a body bounded into him.

"*Autsch! Scheisse!*"

Lightning erupted in his head, and the thunder of footsteps running onto the kitchen's African slate floor split his brain. Through sparks of light, he recognized the downstairs maid, Tina, lying on her left shoulder, her arm beneath her. Bits of broken china and dented silver lay strewn between them.

His hand recoiled from his viscous, flooding nose. Tina's moans and muted voice buzzed like bees.

Nauseating waves swatted his brain into darkness.

He awoke to his parents' whispers, the touch of scratchy sheets, and a vile antiseptic smell.

"If I had not been so forceful, *Papa* would not be dead. I should have capitulated, as usual. But not this time, Racquel."

"You did nothing wrong. It was a hemorrhage."

"But I could see his blood vessels bulging. If I had not

turned away, I may have noticed his pallor. I would have summoned Dr. Mensch..."

"You are too hard..."

As if suddenly aware of George staring up at them, the conversation ended. His mother smothered his cheek in kisses.

"Florida, stay with Mrs. Racquel. I must speak to Mr. Guenther and Mrs. Aleksandra at once," Fritz commanded. He squeezed George's hand and left.

The emergency room doctor released him to Dr. Mensch, the aged Austrian doctor who lived in a cottage on the estate.

Once Florida had tucked him into bed, his head reverberated with bits of china congealed on *Ol'Papa*'s profile. His mother's vanilla scent faded into Florida's gardenia smell. Goya painted his father as he choked *Ol'Papa*.

A familiar voice batted his head. "Impressive. So what did you do—kill him, scare him to death, or what?"

Marcus's cynical laugh bonged. "More likely your father did him in, right?"

George's brain screamed.

"No matter. Now that *my* father will be in charge, you'll be packed off to Paris."

His brain thickened into darkness.

Chapter 3
1986

"George!—are you listening?" Fritz thundered.

He gritted his teeth. "Y-Yes, sir."

"Daydreaming, are we? As I was saying, Parker Gibson and Gregory Putter will prepare you for the bar exam while you become Parker's apprentice in the Legal Department. He is an old curmudgeon, but his legal expertise has served this family brilliantly for many years. You will learn the ins and outs of our business. He will set your schedule. Since Gregory passed the bar six months ago, he should be extremely useful."

George planted his hands on either side of his plate. "I have already hired a tutor."

Fritz's fork dangled in mid-air. "Without consulting me? Fire him. Surely, an NYU Law School graduate does not need a tutor."

George's neck flared. "I disagree."

"We will discuss this later. We have more pressing issues."

His eyes drilled into George's resolve, and his tongue congealed.

"It is a great honor to be selected to lead the family business. My father wanted nothing more than to frustrate my advancement, while I will do everything in my power to prepare you for leadership."

"I was never asked!"

Fritz shot him a withering look. "It means nothing to you that your grandparents endured countless hardships to give you the wonderful life you have done nothing to earn. Need I remind you that only a few months before the Nazis marched into Vienna in 1938, they fled Austria."

His lips pouted that Fritz harangued him with this familiar story.

"They had to endure a year-long separation as Rainer tied up business matters from London while Aleksandra brought Guenther and me with the household staff to New York. Your grandparents had the foresight to secure their assets long before their departure. If not for their circumspection, you would not be sailing on this floating mansion."

He waved his hand, dismissing their surroundings. "Some tawdry job might be waiting for you somewhere. I should think you would consider it a privilege to do your part in maintaining the lifestyle which LE affords you."

George's pride injured, his eyes sought purchase. "Of course I want to contribute, Father, but in a more suitable role."

Fritz's gaze steeled. "Are you suggesting you would happily cede leadership to Marcus, the one who uses every opportunity to upstage you? Just last week he implied that he was more capable than you."

George's fork clattered against his plate.

Fritz's eyes softened. "Son, you are capable. With experience, I assure you that you will be prepared the day you become chairman and he will report to *you*."

He picked at his food as his father described his increasing level of roles and responsibilities.

"I would like to pursue my artistic talents and-and champion the underprivileged by..."

Fritz flicked his right hand. "Not now. We can discuss that once you have passed the bar and master LE operations."

He scowled. "Besides, you have not touched the fruit and camembert."

George's arguments withered with his appetite.

On the last day of the vacation, as the two made their way to the helipad on the upper deck, he formulated irrefutable reasons Fritz could not deny, but courage eluded him. They approached the twin jet-engine Bell Ranger, which would ferry them to San Juan, Puerto Rico. From there Fritz's Boeing 737 Business Jet would fly them to New York. Fritz touched his arm.

"I want to congratulate you for achieving yet another milestone. I know Yale was rough, and NYU was a nightmare, but what matters is that you pulled through with the help of that specialist, Dr.?..."

"Dr. Stanley," George muttered.

"Of course. Despite what you think, I am proud of your desire to engage in philanthropic work. It is just not the right time."

"I..."

Fritz put up his hand. "You will have ample opportunities to make significant contributions through the Leibnitz Foundation after you have honed your management and leadership skills."

"I would like to make a name for myself on my own, not be the next Leibnitz to increase the family's wealth for what? How *can I*...?"

"As you learn the business, you will understand. You owe it to me, to your grandmother. None of us is getting any younger."

He fingered his graying temples. "I am doing what is best for you. You will see."

His tender gaze embraced George. "The foundation has millions that you can earmark for your projects once you have done your share of making LE more prosperous. It will happen at the proper time."

He patted George on the shoulder and turned to the chopper.

"It is settled then. We must not keep the pilots waiting."

George trudged on board and berated himself for not consulting *Gran'maman* first. Then shame flared his cheeks. She would expect him to accept the mantle, too. Mummy might be able to convince them. Not with her life secure with the Gramercy Park mansion, the French country estate, the Azimut yacht, anything she wanted.

His eyes brightened. Dr. Stanley would know what to do.

Chapter 4

George arrived home and made an appointment with Dr. Stanley. Her office was four blocks north of his Fifth Avenue apartment. He had bought the penthouse, which overlooked Washington Square Park, before starting law school. Once his grandmother had approved the purchase from his trust fund, he had engaged her designer to create an intimate atmosphere befitting a young bachelor.

As he stepped into the marble foyer, he surveyed his domain, relieved to be beyond Fritz's control. Old-world handicraft harmonized with splashes of oriental and modern, reflecting his eclectic tastes. He stepped out onto the wraparound terrace of flagstone mixed with brick and breathed in the floral scents of multicolored flora and fauna. After a few moments, he returned to the living room of Victorian toile and soft velvet floral couches and Edelman maroon leather chairs, offset by a combination of Moroccan and modern cubed accent furniture and Mansour carpets over oak parquet. He remembered the shop where he had purchased the tapestries when he and his boarding school roommate, Laurence, had vacationed in Morocco the summer after starting law school.

He continued to survey every possession devoid of Fritz's imprint. An inviting kitchen with terra-cotta countertops, antique oak cabinets, a La Cornue range, and Sub-Zero refrigerator wrapped around his bruised ego. He opened a bottle of *Pouilly-Fuissé* and poured it into a Baccarat goblet. Sipping the liquid, he ambled to the library down the hall from the living room. Two oversized Moroccan leather chairs faced the stone fireplace. Four Stickley high-backed chairs with floral cushions surrounded a six-foot Steinway grand piano, on which silver-framed pictures of Leibnitzes sat atop a pale pink, embroidered silk throw. Blue-blooded faces shot accusing stares back at him.

Averting their gaze, he ran his fingers over the ivory, recalling how he had found the rare Steinway in a West 69th Street *klavierhaus*, where the artisans rebuilt nineteenth century pianos. He turned his gaze upward above the rosewood mantle, where a large Braque hung against the backdrop of the Delaware stone. The round, elongated edges, cube-like shapes, and brooding figure of *Patience* mirrored his pensiveness. His thoughts tumbled over what he should have said to Fritz, then swallowed his obsequiousness in a sip of wine. He luxuriated a few moments longer under the recessed lighting and natural rays that splashed through the gilded French doors that led to the terrace. Cozy acceptance bathed him here.

Still, Fritz invaded his thoughts, and a strong need to walk through his apartment to shake off the feeling of being a marionette bending to his father's will propelled him. He stepped into the master bedroom suite, accessed down the long east gallery of Expressionist and Cubist paintings from the white marble entrance hall. He ran his fingers across the pale blue linen-covered chairs, chaises-longues, and couches that offset the royal blue wall-to-wall carpet. A rosewood and leather king-size sleigh bed with large round side tables accented a massive Louis XIII walnut-ebonized armoire and matching secretary in the sitting room. He fingered the antiques as he continued around the room, recalling his delight in finding them in an eclectic shop in Avignon, France. A sixteen-by-ten-foot expanse of gilded windowed doors leading to the terrace offset a black marble fireplace purchased in a *bric-à-brac* shop in *L'Isle-sur-la-Sorgue*, near Avignon. Thick linen drapes lined with silk sheers closed the room from outside light with a touch of a button from a remote pad.

Despite the comforts of home, his shoulders stooped and his heart sank into inevitability. He trudged toward the two 400-square-foot walk-in closets on either side that led to the bath. One day, the woman of his dreams would fill the second empty closet—a sharp reminder of a failed romance. If only he had brought Kat here instead of the Martha's Vineyard house, then his vile stepmother's meddling would have been thwarted.

He discarded the thought with a gulp of wine and an abrupt detour into the lavatory. The dusty white marble and mirrored bathroom had the sharp edges of ultra-modern design softened by a colorful oriental rug and a view through the framed windows of the lush perennials on the terrace. He stroked a large Ming urn until his mirrored reflection accosted him and retreated from the Leibnitz staring back at him.

His feet fled impotence and headed toward the two guest bedroom suites and baths. He increased his pace down the west gallery of southwestern and southern antebellum charm, venturing a smile. Everything here was ordered according to *his* design. He entered his place of refuge, the art studio, situated between the bedrooms and the servants' wing. Fritz, who orchestrated everyone's life, could not touch him here.

Draining his glass, he turned on his heel and set off for the kitchen, where he filled another glass with the golden liquid and headed for the library. Tomorrow the warmth of Dr. Stanley would heal his wounded ego. He turned on the Bose, nestled within the cabinetry that surrounded the fireplace, and selected Vivaldi's *Four Seasons*. Settling into his favorite chair in front of the fireplace, he picked up Stendhal's *Le Rouge et Le Noir* from the ottoman to immerse himself in the world of Julien Sorel—one of the many flawed heroes to whose stories he returned time and again—and then he would spend a few hours painting the Caribbean sky. But the face of Kat shattered his equilibrium on page one.

Chapter 5
1985

George met his mother at the Skyport Marina for a day on her yacht. To his dismay, a New York real-estate mogul joined them. Lucas hinted that George should meet his daughter, a third-year resident at New York University Medical Center. Racquel insisted that George call Lucas the following week, but he demurred.

Two weeks passed. George received a call from Lucas. He had no intention of meeting his daughter, Kat. He loathed blind dates and disliked having his ordered world disrupted. Yet the thought of his mother nagging him propelled him to acquiesce to an invitation for dinner at Tavern on the Green the following week.

To his surprise, he met a no-nonsense, mature 26-year-old who put him at ease within moments. The evening passed all too quickly. He would have loved to see Kat again, but she had weekend plans with friends at their Fire Island house and would return to Manhattan to an intensive schedule.

He invited her to a weekend at his Martha's Vineyard home the last weekend in August. He planned every detail of their itinerary, determined not to repeat the mistakes he had made with previous failed relationships. As the weekend of their date approached, second thoughts about her actually showing up invaded his thinking. When he called her to confirm, she put him at ease with noticeable excitement about the weekend.

Despite her enthusiasm, within hours his inadequacies invaded his thoughts. He vacillated between having his housekeeper prepare a meal for Kat's arrival or reserving a table at his favorite French restaurant. Fritz ended up making the decision for him by informing him that he and Belinda were hosting a party to celebrate George's law degree to start off the weekend. He countered every argument, and George ended up convinced a party would ease his nerves and usher Kat into the weekend with a flourish.

By the time guests started arriving Friday evening, George had asked Belinda four times to see the guest list. When she barked at him, he gulped a glass of champagne to silence the butterflies floating in his stomach. When his friend, Laurence, and his entourage arrived, his anxiety eased. Laurence and his Exeter friends, John and Anthony, introduced their girlfriends. The six were staying at Laurence's parents' house on the island and were delighted Fritz had invited them. Laurence regaled his friends with his Wall Street triumphs. John and Anthony crowed about "top-secret" projects at Microsoft, and the four friends reminisced about old times in boarding school.

George and Laurence were playing chess when Kat arrived. George saw her as his father's booming voice caught his attention. She glanced around, a skittish colt. When he introduced his companions, her intoxicating smile settled his nerves. As the evening progressed, her comfortable aura embraced George with hope. When he invited her for a private walk on the beach, her eyes sparkled. They set out down the winding path to the water's edge.

"I understand from your friends this is your house. It's gorgeous. When did you buy it?"

She slipped her hand into his.

"Actually, *Gran'maman* gave it to me for my 21st birthday."

His voice trailed off as his face heated up, despite the nipping ocean breeze.

"How generous. You must be rather special."

They reached the sand and turned their backs against the wind as they glided across the beach.

He tittered. "Not really. She's generous to my three cousins also."

She peered up at the house.

"I see. Well, if it were me, I'd like some say in the furnishings at least. But it's lovely. Your grandmother has impeccable taste."

"Yes, everything about her is exquisite."

He smiled and cocked his head, leading her along the packed sand. He wanted to say that he had chosen the furnishings with *Gran'maman*'s recommendations, but words eluded him. Kat snuggled her shoulder against his.

"She's rather special to you, isn't she? A good buffer between you and your parents, no doubt."

"Y-Yes, she is."

He stopped and turned to face her.

"Where do you think you'll practice medicine?"

"I'd really like to work in pediatric oncology, but my father thinks I should be some high-paying surgeon." She grimaced. "It's quite annoying."

"Fathers think they know best."

She laughed and moved against his side as they continued their walk. "True. But I'll decide for myself and ease him into it."

"Wouldn't it be nice to sail away where no one makes any demands, where you could be anything you want, follow your dreams?"

She screwed up her face. "I suppose."

He averted her gaze to follow the moonlight's dance on the waves. As his body stiffened he guided them further down the shoreline. She turned to face him.

"It would be boring to make no difference in the world, don't you think?"

"Y-Yes. I'm just feeling a little hemmed in, I guess. A passing fantasy."

The silver spoon lodged in George's throat was choking the life out of him.

She beckoned across the dunes toward the spangled house, still filled with Fritz and Belinda's guests.

"Yes, I see what you mean."

Her eyes peeled back his ambivalence.

"I-I think this weekend has started off on the wrong foot."

"No, it's fine." She smiled. "What do you think you'll do after you've taken the bar exam?"

"I'd really like to find my own path, explore my interests in art, philanthropy, something outside the family business. But that will never happen."

She squeezed his hands between hers and looked into his eyes. "Why not?"

"M-My future's been carved out. I'm a Leibnitz, after all."

"You have no say then?"

Her penetrating gaze shattered his defenses. He looked out at the fierce waves bruising toward the shore. "Not really."

After an eternity of icy silence, she withdrew her hands.

"I'm chilly. Shall we head up?"

She advanced, then turned and grabbed his hand. They made their way up the long pathway to the house, his words still in his chest. Once inside, he zeroed in on his friends, and she excused herself to the lavatory. He bantered with Laurence and his entourage, on edge, seeking equilibrium. When he saw her in his peripheral vision cornered by Belinda, he scampered toward them. She slipped off toward Fritz, and he joined them just as she was saying goodnight. She asked George to walk her out.

"You're not staying?"

"I'm sorry. I have a massive headache and promised Mom to check on the house while I'm here."

"Oh."

They walked to her Corvette in silence. His heart knocked; words died on his tongue. As the glistening cherry red car peeled out the driveway, his heart stopped. He awoke the next morning besotted with Kat, convinced he could explain away last night's temerity. He waited until 8:oo and called, his heart pounding. Her voice sounded half-asleep. She promised to call him later in the day. He moped around all morning, insufferable to the housekeeper when she brought his vegetable omelet and coffee as the minutes turned to hours. Kat called just after eleven.

"Hey. I'm sorry I didn't call sooner, but I have to get back to the city."

"But I..."

"Mom insists. Something that can't wait, I'm afraid. I'm really sorry. Maybe we can have dinner sometime."

"Sure."

He moped around his room, hope cratering with each step. When he finally lumbered down to the kitchen, his parents were eating lunch. His face flared.

"What did you do, Belinda?" he barked.

"I only suggested I could have my stylist give her a makeover," she smirked.

Rage filled his chest.

"Besides, no reasonably intelligent *und* attractive voman vould be interested in someone as indecisive as you."

His shoulders slumped. Fritz's eyes shot darts.

"Stay out of George's affairs. You are not his mother. If you know what is good for you, you will leave the room."

She glared at him. "I vill do no such thing!"

"No, I want to hear it all," George squawked.

"George, you and I need a walk."

"No, I have a few pithy words I have been saving for her."

Fritz stormed out.

George paced back and forth across the plush Ushak living room carpet.

"How dare you? You have gone too far. I'm leaving, but I want you out of my house, and you are never to set foot here again!"

She sneered. He turned on his heel and bolted for his bedroom to pack. When he trudged downstairs, Fritz and Belinda were yapping at each other. George stomped out to the garage. He loaded his weekender into the back seat of his Maserati and flopped into the driver's seat. Even his favorite Italian sports sedan with hand-tooled leather and wood interior provided no joy. Gritting his teeth, he turned the ignition and pressed the garage door button.

A rap on the driver's window intruded.

"Now what?" he bellowed.

He turned to face Fritz and lumbered out of the car.

"I have called Alton and arranged for Étienne and the crew to fly you back to New York. Raul here," Fritz gestured to one of the bodyguards just walking up, "will take you to the FBO and fly with you to New York. The Hawker will come back to collect us tomorrow. If you have no objection."

His pent-up rage swooshed out like a deflated balloon.

"Th-Thanks, Father."

"No need to mention it. By the way, good show, standing up to Belinda like that. She respects strength, you know."

He mustered a smile.

"Well, have a good flight."

Fritz pulled him in a quick embrace and spun toward the house. He glanced back and uncharacteristically waved. Nonplussed, George cantered to the waiting car and watched Raul transfer his bag from the Maserati. By the time the Rolls had pulled out of the long driveway heading toward General Aviation, his heart plummeted and his head slumped. Kat would not call, and he would not have the courage to pursue her.

The bitter taste of unrequited love engulfed him now, a year later.

Chapter 6
1986

As George settled into the plush armchair across the small, round, cherry conference table from Dr. Stanley, his fingers rubbed his watch.

She bathed him in a warm smile.

"You're tanned and fit. A good vacation?"

"All things considered."

He averted her gaze and shuffled his legs. His fingers drummed his legs.

"Your father wasn't enthusiastic about your launching out on your own?"

"You could say that."

She raised her eyebrows.

"I never had a chance," he mumbled, eyes downcast. "He managed me, just like always."

"I see."

Her susurrant, honeyed voice soothed his battered ego.

"How did that make you feel?"

"L-Like I am not a man, I'll never make it on my own, I don't have *a right* to choose my own future, I am obligated to carry on the family name, outmaneuver Marcus, become Father. But what about who I want to be?"

"Who do you want to be?"

"I-I do not know."

"That's the problem."

His face sagged. He fidgeted with the crease in his pants.

"Where do you see yourself six months from now?"

"Six months? I can barely see tomorrow."

He rubbed his nails back and forth.

"A-A big part of me wants to beat Marcus. Another part wants to prove myself outside of LE. But I can't disappoint *Gran'maman*." His brows wrinkled. "She is like *Ol'Papa*, in her own way."

Her eyes widened. "Go on."

A cataract of unsettling memories dribbled out. "I-I was just remembering Aunt Tatania's 50th birthday party at Wilton and *Gran'maman*'s assignment."

"Tell me about it."

He exhaled the pain.

"It was a big party. *Gran'maman* and Aunt Tani have always had a wonderful relationship, and *Gran'maman* said everyone needed to behave. Aunt Tani's mother was there from Prague, her brother, Henri. *Gran'maman*'s brother, Sergey, her close friends, U.N. Secretary-General Kurt Waldheim and his wife, Sissy. Father's friends, Senator Gary Hart and Governor Gaston Caperton, a number of Aunt Tani and Uncle Guenther's friends from New York, Father Thomas, of course."

She smiled. "You have quite a memory."

"My peculiar curse," he groaned.

"A rather political crowd."

"The usual Leibnitz affair."

He rolled his eyes. She chuckled.

"Who's Father Thomas?"

"An elderly Jesuit priest who has served the family since long before I was born. My family supports his many charitable projects and provides for his living expenses. He often stays in Wilton to rest when he is not saving children in Third World countries. A truly holy man."

"Fascinating. So at this party how old were you?"

"Maybe twenty-one. I had just graduated from Yale.

Anyway, I was already uncomfortable with Belinda's attempts to make Mummy and me look bad..."

Her eyes widened. "Your stepmother *and* your mother were there?"

"*Gran'maman* has always had a negative view of Belinda. She invites Mummy to family events out of affection. And to spite Belinda."

"I'd think both your stepmother and your mother would find that arrangement uncomfortable."

She made a notation.

"I've never really thought about it. Anyway, Father, Marcus, and Belinda were orchestrating their little plots, as usual. Of course, no one dared openly squabble. *Gran'maman* would not have stood for that. But I knew what was going on."

She frowned. "They were *all* plotting?"

"The celebration was held outside on the terrace. There were five round cast-iron tables with glass tops, eight people at each. A spray of lilies centered each table. Lilies are Aunt Tani's favorites."

She shook her head. "It amazes me that you have such vivid recall of detail. I don't think I'd remember what the tables were made out of, much less the floral arrangements."

"Is that bad?"

"Not necessarily. I suspect not much gets past you."

"I am not so sure. I ruminate about the past to see what I missed, what I should have done differently."

"Like..."

"*Gran'maman*, for example. A lot of orchestration of events I'm only now figuring out. At Aunt Tani's party..."

He sighed.

"Go on."

"Belinda was trying to change the seating arrangements when I came outside. I overheard Father snap at her to mind her manners. She started arguing, and he told her that what she wanted did not really matter, what *Gran'maman* and Aunt

Tani wanted, what *he* wanted was all she needed to know."

Dr. Stanley's lips puckered. "I assume the tension escalated from there?"

He grinned. "Father glared at Belinda, then walked over to me a few feet away. I became fixated on a procession of tiny black ants making their way across the stones. They had a large many-veined leaf that seemed to weigh down on them with every step."

She looked up from writing. "The weight of the tension perhaps?"

He grimaced, his hands tight. "Father told me I should talk with our guests and went over to *Gran'maman*. When it was time to eat, he motioned me toward her table to sit with Aunt Tani's mother. Then he went to Uncle Guenther's table and sat between Mummy and Henri. Belinda dared not budge. I felt a particular satisfaction at her discomfort."

He cocked his head.

"You really hate her, don't you?"

He nodded. "Absolutely. The stories I could tell. You know how she ruined my relationship with Kat."

A wistful look crossed his face.

"I'm sure that's still a sore spot. Go on."

"Father had placed Marcus and me at *Gran'maman*'s table with Father Thomas. To keep the peace, I suppose. But Marcus tried to bait me from the beginning."

"Oh?"

"*Gran'maman* always told me not to trust Marcus, so I was on guard. I was annoyed that I hadn't devised a suitable plan to counter his deviousness. But I didn't want to bring myself down to his level either. He was a master at cunning, and our boyhood camaraderie had completely disappeared. He used every opportunity to belittle me. Still, I admired his accomplishments and facile ability to talk with anyone. Not like me. I am an observer, not a talker, as you know."

She smiled.

"Marcus has some of my friend Laurence's traits. You remember him?"

"You've spoken of him before. A particularly good friend, as I recall at Phillips Exeter?"

His mouth turned up. "Yes. He helped me immensely in school, what with Father's insane expectations and then telling me he was divorcing Mummy and marrying Belinda in the same breath. Laurence and Marcus are alike, but Laurence's motives are not vicious. Marcus tries to gain control through innuendo and intrigue."

"Tell me about Laurence. I don't think you've actually shared very much about him or about boarding school for that matter, except some obsessive-compulsive tendencies that emerged around that time."

Pain clouded his eyes.

"It can wait until another time if you're not ready."

"It's okay."

The unwelcome memories resurfaced. "It was a Saturday morning, as I recall. I remember the autumn rain pelting the windows of my dorm room, because the stormy weather matched my mood. I had been having more panic attacks and compulsions. I remember needing to line up the items on my desk. I had to shower right after passing a classmate in the hallway. Otherwise, I would become agitated. If two foods on my plate were touching, I lost my appetite."

"Has that changed, George?"

"Somewhat."

"Tell me more about that weekend."

"I loathed encounters with Father. I could never please him. He barged into my room that morning without warning, as usual. He shook my hand, said good morning and then launched in about my academic inadequacies. Dean Thompkins had called him. Father said my achievements in the arts and sports were commendable. I had A+s in most of my classes, but he said I was headed for B+s in World

Civilization and Biology. And that was totally unacceptable."

His ears reddened.

"That must have hurt," Dr. Stanley interjected.

"It bruised, yes. He said he had assured the dean I would not let everyone down. He had taken matters in hand since Mummy was not up to the task."

George pouted. Dr. Stanley waited.

"I told him I was really trying, but I just needed a different school. I mentioned a school for the arts in New York City, but he scalded me with his eyes and said, '*You* think? Your mother's idea, no doubt. I will *not* have my son embarrass *me* because he cannot cut it at my *alma mater*! Do you want Marcus to outshine you? He is a straight A student at Choate, in line to be valedictorian. No, I will not have Guenther gloating over his accomplishments at my expense!' or something like that."

Tears stung George's eyes.

"I tried to defend myself, but Father said he would have a talk with the house prefect and Dean Thompkins, who would provide the necessary assistance."

He bit the inside of his lip so hard he tasted blood. A ball of prickly pears attacked the lining of his stomach. His shoulders fell limp, his palms moistened.

"I-I remember that I waited for him to point out that the crease in my dark-gray flannel trousers were not crisp and my regimental striped tie was askew. I felt the coiled ball that was my stomach tightening with excruciating intensity. Every corpuscle in my body screamed to run away into the safety of Mummy's arms. Vile inadequacy clung to my fingertips. I swallowed blood and nauseous disgust."

"How awful!" Dr. Stanley reached over to squeeze his arm. "We can stop if..."

"No, it's better I remember why I don't trust Father. He-he told me that Dean Thompkins would set me on the straight and narrow. Not to put a fine point on it, but I just needed a guiding, grandfatherly hand. He tried to make it better, I suppose, by saying I had enormous talent and he knew I would not want to disappoint *Gran'maman* and him. I seem to recall he patted me on the back and told me he was confident my performance would be stellar. But then he really undid me. He said he would send one of the chauffeurs to pick me up the following weekend because he wanted me to meet Belinda, that he and Mummy were not working out."

An earthquake rumbled in George's heart, remembering. "I had no idea who he was talking about and struggled to take in what he was saying."

"That's how you learned about your parents' breaking up and...?"

"Yes, and he seemed oblivious to the impact on me. I was barely standing when he said Chauncey would pick me up the following week to have me fitted for my tuxedo, because the wedding was less than a month away."

"Incredible insensitivity to..." Dr. Stanley began, her eyes dark.

"Well, par for the course. He left without ever noticing my horror-stricken face trailing behind him. I can still recall how I rushed to the bathroom to wash the inadequacy off my hands. Laurence found me later, my hands blood-red. I knew he manipulated people, but panic overrode caution. I could have cared less if he pitied me. I was desperate for an ally."

He squirmed. "He was among a few of us who had to endure taunts because of our valets, who were also bodyguards. He validated my feelings and shared that he too suffered from demanding parental expectations. Both his parents berated him for his grades. His mother even told him he was a disappointment to her. But he just shrugged it off and said I should do likewise. He said I could not trust adults and that we had to figure it out for ourselves. We would work together. I didn't share his cynicism, but I envied his charismatic, carefree style. He affected an earnest look to hide the scheming that went on behind the innocuous face. He used his brilliance to manipulate the system, since rules were made for other people, not him. He boasted that he could care less whether he had a B average, but his parents did. Rather than lose privileges, he schmoozed other boys into doing the grunt work for him."

"I can see why Laurence and you became fast friends."

"Yes. To get Dean Thompkins off our backs, he devised a plan. He developed a study schedule with our classmates, John and Anthony, to benefit from each other's strengths and round out the weaknesses. And he advised me to play my parents against each other at every opportunity. He said to 'suck up'—his words exactly—to Belinda."

"I do not..."

"He reminded me that we were both going to inherit a fortune if we behaved, so we could not afford to get into trouble. He advised me to ingratiate myself with everyone I despised."

"Who did you despise, George?"

"Father and Belinda. He knew I loved *Gran'maman* so I had to be careful to play the game. And when no one was watching, have fun, fun, fun."

His eyes twinkled.

"I would never have knowingly deceived *Gran'maman*, but I had no problem being disingenuous with Belinda. Laurence was a real friend, so I went along with any ploy to maintain the A's that would keep me off Father's radar. And I took full advantage of every opportunity to vacation with *Gran'maman*. She took me to Europe to paint with master artists and spend time with her at her Viennese estate. My parents were consumed with their own lives. Belinda had a baby in short order, and Mummy bounced among paramours and had little time for me. *Gran'maman* distracted me from their self-absorption and bolstered my self-esteem."

He smiled.

"I can understand why you gravitated to her, and to Laurence." She made notes. "Your family relationships are quite complicated."

"I buried that memory of Father. I guess I never told you."

"No, you..."

"It's-it's related to what happened at Aunt Tani's party. My father. *Gran'maman*. Marcus."

"Continue."

"At the party, I didn't know how to deal with Marcus. I was so naïve. I thought I could hold my own by just being myself. I mean, I'd mastered the art of deflecting most darts with charm and graciousness. I ended up feeling foolish and weak."

His lips trembled.

"Oh?"

"Father Thomas sat with Marcus and me. He has always shown great affection for us. He is a wonderful, humble man with great insight."

"I'm sure."

We were talking about inane things, like the various languages spoken around the table. Then Marcus told Father Thomas that when we were mere tykes I went out of my way to do my cousins favors and wheedle extra treats from *Gran'maman*."

He chuckled. "I never tattled on my cousins when they put me up to some dastardly deed, like putting toothpaste in Georgina's underwear."

She smiled.

"Or like the morning *Ol'papa* died. He said I was too modest to tell anyone that I had been the hero. Even getting a broken nose and a concussion in the process."

"You've never mentioned this."

"I was perturbed and asked what he meant. He said I was too modest. I had heard arguing, barged in past Father, saw *Ol'papa* having a heart attack and tried to get help, but he wouldn't let me, and I got all tangled with the maid—or something like that. I should have been proud that my courage to defy Father *almost* saved *Ol'papa*'s life. I told him he had it all wrong. We started arguing, Father Thomas intervened. Then Marcus winked at me and switched to talking about some sports team. And, just like that, a bomb burst in my head."

"What do you mean?"

"He was implying that Father had caused *Ol'papa*'s death. I looked at Father, who was busy holding court in his usual charismatic, domineering way. And Marcus' comment transformed him into a monster..."

"Your father's guilt or innocence deeply troubles you."

"I keep dreaming about it. I talked to him about it on vacation, and I-I thought I cleared it up. But I-I am not so sure. He was hiding something."

He strummed his fingers against his knees. "And *Gran'maman*."

"Go on."

"*Gran'maman* made a point to call me over and tell me to distract Uncle Guenther from his conversation with Senator Hart and ask him to work in his office over the summer."

He furrowed his brows, crossed his legs, and fingered the crease of his pants.

"She said he was very fond of me. She told me I could learn some important lessons from him. I was happy to get away from Marcus, but not too sanguine about talking to my uncle. I-I feared him."

She looked up from writing. "Why?"

"I was always a bit nervous around him because Father said Uncle Guenther had always tried to get him in trouble, and I could see *Ol'papa* favored Uncle Guenther. I had spent no alone time with him, and Marcus was devious, so I assumed Father was right. I wanted to please *Gran'maman*, but I doubted Father would want me spending time with his rival. All I wanted to do was go wash my clammy hands. I can still see the crease in my slacks two inches off-center. I could not imagine how I hadn't noticed it before."

Her eyes widened. "You remember the tiniest details, don't you?"

"Oh, yes. Father might have noticed."

He shifted in his seat.

"It sounds like you were more worried about your father than your uncle."

"Both, actually. I just wanted to go change and then I would have been able to avoid both of them."

He uncrossed his legs, crossed his arms.

"Did you?"

"No. I asked *Gran'maman*, but she insisted it could wait. Then she asked me to take a note to Father on my way to Uncle Guenther. I slinked to his table, avoided Father's gaze, and slipped the note to him on my way to Uncle Guenther. To my relief, Father went to sit next to *Gran'maman* at her table. I waited for Uncle Guenther to talk first. I saw Senator Hart turn to talk to Belinda, who had just sat down beside him, flirting."

Dr. Stanley's eyes narrowed. "Your stepmother was flirting with the Senator?"

"She did that sort of thing all the time when she thought Father or *Gran'maman* wouldn't notice."

"Really?"

"Uncle Guenther wasn't at all what I expected. He complimented me on how I looked, on choosing NYU Law School. He talked about the sizable donations *Gran'maman* had made when he had attended NYU."

"He's a lawyer, too?"

"No. He was in the business and engineering programs."

"I see."

"He said *Ol'papa* had insisted he go to Wharton after NYU against his wishes. He really liked NYU and his life in the city. I felt foolish that I knew none of this."

He inhaled and exhaled slowly.

"You really didn't know him?"

His lips pursed. "Exactly! And I had all these misperceptions."

"Like?"

"That he was trying to take Father's place."

"Was he?"

He shook his head. "I doubt it. He was genuinely nice to me. There was an immediate kinship. He made a comment that number one schools were highly overrated, but, of course, one must impress one's peers and world leaders. I was intrigued. I wanted to get past the formal, stilted conversation that is so much a part of my family to really get to know him."

He straightened his back.

"That seemed highly unlikely?"

"Father made sure of it." His mouth set in a hard line. "You would have to know Father to appreciate how he controls people."

She raised her eyebrows. "What happened?"

"Uncle Guenther talked about me interning in his office to learn how the engineering and manufacturing sides of our business work. He said we would need to clear it with Father first. Then, I understood why *Gran'maman* wanted me to get to know him. Although I didn't trust Marcus, his father seemed genuine."

"You have a love-hate relationship with your cousin, don't you? Have you ever wondered if it clouds your judgment?"

He bristled, putting his hands face down on the table.

"I-I don't hate Marcus. He is like an older brother, but I cannot trust him."

"So the rivalry?"

"Father set up this competition between us. Now, I see *Gran'maman* did too. She must have known Uncle Guenther would jump at the chance to influence me."

"And that you would welcome it?"

"Yes."

"Did he?"

"No."

George sharpened the crease of his pants with his fingers.

"Just as Uncle Guenther was suggesting I join him the next day for horseback riding, Father showed up and said I was boring my uncle with stories of my exploits at his *alma mater*. Then, I realized Uncle Guenther had gone to Yale."

"And no one had ever told you."

He harrumphed. "As usual. I asked Father what else he had been hiding from me. He laughed and said he needed to steal me away for a matter that needed my immediate attention."

He gripped the curved corners of his armchair with both hands.

"He told Uncle Guenther that it was too soon for Marcus to intern in the chairman's office, again, news to me. He said Marcus was a bit presumptuous for someone of his age and modest talents. He suggested Marcus would do better with the junior engineers. I felt only slightly sorry for my cousin, but embarrassed for my uncle. For one split second, I would have much preferred him as my father."

His hands relaxed and dangled over the sides of the armchair. "What Father did was to gain control at his expense, at my expense."

"Your father might have realized Marcus was not ready yet or your uncle was..."

George brought his hands to his lap and clasped them tightly. "No, it was about control, because when I said to Uncle Guenther that I very much enjoyed our chat and was looking forward to our ride the following day, Father told me I would not have time. It was clear there would be no internship or any opportunity to develop a meaningful relationship with Uncle Guenther."

Dr. Stanley's eyes went soft.

The acrid pang of bitterness surfaced in George's mouth.

He had a strong need to rinse out the pungent taste of autocratic rule. His body slumped in the chair.

"Father had to make it worse. He waited until we were out of earshot of the party-goers to whisper that he didn't know what game I was playing, but to not even think about cozying up to Guenther like that again. It was as if he slapped me across the face."

His back retreated into the armchair.

"All I could think about was running to the lavatory and changing my trousers. As Father and I made our way through the conservatory into the dining room, I attempted to defend myself with cynicism but ended up looking foolish and petulant. He was quick to diffuse my tiny show of bravado. He told me I could learn nothing from my uncle and not to be so naïve. Guenther was not interested in helping me. If he could get revenge through me, he would jump at the chance. Then he went on to say I had hurt him to the quick by second-guessing his intentions, that he was saving me from falling into my uncle's trap and was acting out of love. He steered me down the hallway, told me to change my trousers, they were disgusting, I needed to spend some time with *Herr* Waldheim, Mr. Caperton asked to chat with me, at my age it was important to learn how to cultivate the right friendships, Mr. Caperton was planning to run for West Virginia governor, we would be building pulp mills in that state, on and on. Then, he shooed me off with a flick of his hand, turned, and went down the hallway."

George looked up for support.

"You must have been devastated."

"A punch in my ego so hard it sent me reeling in front of the door of *Ol'papa*'s old study. Father never looked back, not once. I left behind any illusions I had any worth in his eyes as I hurried up the stairs."

"You thought your father didn't value you?"

He frowned. "I felt I was nothing more than one of those

ants just carrying the expected load."

"Hmmm..."

His eyes filled. "I went into the bedroom and closed the door behind me. It was all I could do not to crumble right there on the floor."

"How did you manage?"

He looked away. "I-I looked out onto the festivities below the windows and felt compassion for the boy he once was, a pawn on *Ol'papa*'s chessboard. Ironic."

His back straightened. "I-I still remember, ominous clouds gathering on the horizon might disrupt the festivities. And here I was in Father's old bedroom, where he must have come time and again to lick his wounds, determined to get the better of *Ol'papa* one day. I wondered what it was that gave him the resolve and the shrewdness to make revenge a reality, because success was revenge."

A prickly pang shot through his chest. "I realize now *Gran'maman* knew what would happen. How could she betray me like that? To set in motion a chain of events that would ensure her legacy? Was all this to keep Father in power, or *Gran'maman*? Was it to show me how power was won and maintained, where the vulnerabilities were? Was it to make me tough? And could Uncle Guenther be as disingenuous as Father said? He seemed so-so kind and caring. And that was such a low blow, the comment about the pants."

His hands lay limply in his lap. "He succeeded, you know."

A surge of competitiveness flushed his face. "I practically screamed, *Marcus will not displace me. I will make Gran'maman and Father proud. I will!*"

Tears pooled, and his hands balled into fists.

"Let it out."

"*Gran'maman* knew what would happen. She was orchestrating..."

"Oh?"

He turned up his nose. "Every family event follows a

pattern. *Gran'maman*, Father—they orchestrate everything. I-I don't want to be that kind of person."

"You don't know why your father or your grandmother felt a need to do what they did. They may have had reasons you couldn't see. Nevertheless, it seems they have given you mixed messages."

He grimaced. "I-I guess so."

"The challenge is to sort out who they are from the person *you* want to be, which may be different, even incompatible."

"B-But I don't know who I want to be."

His honesty enveloped him in calm.

"That's a start. Think of the traits you most admire in others. What's the first admirable trait that comes to mind?"

He smiled. "Strength."

"What kind of strength?"

His back straightened. "The strength to stand up for what I believe."

"What do you believe?"

An imperfection in the patina of the conference table in front of him captured his attention. He became lost in the sea of obsession for perfection, drowning in inadequacy.

"George, tell me what you're feeling."

"Wha-What?"

"Are you feeling trapped in some notion of who someone has said you should be and you've been found wanting?"

He nodded, biting his lip.

"Your family has engendered in you a feeling that a certain kind of strength is superior?"

"*Gran'maman* has always valued and promoted my passion for the arts, strength of character, my sensitivity to matters of the heart, long before she talked about duty and competition. I-It's confusing."

He shook his head.

"She was obviously trying to help you be well-rounded and prepare you for the future. But more may have been going on.

I suspect at that party you started to see a side of your grandmother you had never seen before. She was schooling you in ways that seemed to contradict earlier training. Is this the part you can't resolve? Her methods to help you grow into the heir apparent? Her imperfections? Needing her approval without knowing how to achieve it? Is this what you're still doing?"

Strangled words locked his throat.

"It's your grandmother you really want to please, isn't it?"

"I have always wanted her to be proud of me," he sniffled. "To measure up. I'm still the frightened boy outside *Ol'papa*'s study door discovering the ugly truth about my ancestry. Love sacrificed at the altar of power."

He wiped his eyes with the back of his hand and straightened his back.

"Marcus is my rival, but Father is my enemy."

Her eyebrows shot up.

"We were brought up to be rivals, just like our fathers. *Gran'maman* never seemed to take to him. Even I know she favors me. The next CEO of Leibnitz Enterprises has always been slated to be either Marcus or me. But she has chosen me. Obviously, Father wants me at the helm someday, but I see now that it is more than Father. Marcus and I were set up to continue a family legacy built on an ethical framework that-that goes against my nature. I can't meet Father or *Gran'maman*'s expectations. Something in me resists being carved in this-this Leibnitz mold."

"Your grandmother comes out looking better than your father. Why?"

"Her love is so obvious. She has such good intentions."

"And he doesn't?"

He examined his nails. "He probably means well."

She smiled. "His style is just different?"

"I suppose. I have tried to please my family for so long I couldn't see the real problem. They have saddled me with a role that may not suit me."

"Go on."

"Father may be right that I need to learn the ins and outs of the Leibnitz business. I cannot continue taking everything for granted. Someday someone will have to take over for the brothers. But in the process I have to be who I am, not who someone else thinks I should be. I know it sounds crazy, but I want Marcus to join me in a partnership instead of one of us beating the other. But that will never happen. He enjoys making other people squirm."

He crossed his legs.

"You're sure of that?"

"Absolutely. I've never admitted this, but I-I feel guilty about my lifestyle. I have never worked for any of it. I would fail at anything beyond the protective walls of LE."

"Why do you say that? You're a very capable young man."

"I have never had a job."

"Are you trying to talk yourself into or out of something?"

"I-I need to talk to *Gran'maman*. I refuse to become another tyrant orchestrating everyone else's life."

She leaned toward him. "You can't resolve everything today, but I caution you not to let anyone talk you into something that doesn't feel right."

He uncrossed his legs, his jaw set. "I just need to sort out a few things with my grandmother."

"If that's what you want to do. I'm here when you need me."

He smiled. She peered into the pool of his eyes. "Above all, remember, I believe in you."

His eyes filled. As he rose to leave, he knew what he needed to do.

Chapter 7

George slowed his steps upon entering his grandmother's Wilton study and stepped down into her spacious sitting room. The Chanel-clad *Grande Dame* was dismissing her personal assistant.

While he waited for Marthe to leave, he reflected on the many occasions *Gran'maman* had invited him into her private suite. He remembered one of the first times he had come, when he was maybe four or five years old. Florida had brought him at his request. He blushed, remembering it was only a bloody knee from falling on the wooden barn floor. It seemed so silly now that he had needed her to hold him, take off the bandage, and kiss it. At first, he had been frightened. The room had seemed cavernous, but she had made it cozy and had bathed him with love. He felt a pinch of guilt about what he needed now.

She beamed as she rose to greet him. "*Liebchen*, come give your old *Gran'maman* a kiss."

He rushed to embrace her.

"*Qu'est-ce qu'il y a*? You seem troubled."

"I-I just had some questions about taking my place at LE…"

"*Was fragst du, liebchen*?"

His eyes looked down. "I-I just want you to be proud of me. You know I want to refine my artistic talents…"

She continued in German, "Excelling in one's talents is important. But, we have obligations to others who depend on us."

As she peered into his eyes, he flinched.

"But I am not..."

"You do not think you are ready? Come, sit with me."

She led him to an overstuffed toile couch, guided him to a seat next to her, and squeezed his hand.

"I am not sure I want..."

"You would prefer Marcus take Fritz's place someday?"

His heart wilted. "I-I am not sure I want to lead LE."

His eyes pleaded.

Her eyes embraced him. "Ah, you are caught between what is comfortable and what is your destiny."

The bluntness of her statement punctured his armor.

"Is it that then? My destiny?"

Her mouth hardened. "I could tell you what you want to hear. I could kiss you and make you feel better and send you on your way to play at art or philanthropy or whatever momentary fancy. I cannot let you do what you will one day regret. That would be irresponsible."

His frown deepened. "But what if I want to sell my paintings, become a *maestro,* support the poor...?"

"You can always have the finest *maestros* at your beck and call. Hobbies can be very rewarding. And philanthropy is not a profession. Rather, it is part of who we are. The choice is yours."

The well of her eyes filled. Her voice became a whisper. "Yet it is not. No more than it was for me when I had to choose between what I wanted, *needed* even, and what was required."

Sadness clouded her eyes. "I have had to make hard decisions. Some I hope you never have to make."

He flinched.

"I had to choose to take a man's life to save my brother's."

He gasped. Her eyes hardened.

"I had to choose to put my faith in a faithless husband."

He focused on her eyes.

"I had to choose to fight for my sons. They deserved the opportunity to discover the areas in which they are best suited, not work against each other."

She pursed her lips. "I have kept secrets for the greater good. I had to choose who will best lead LE into the next century. A person of integrity and humility, full of heart, passion, sensitivity. One who doubts who he is capable of becoming."

His face flushed. She patted his hand.

"I do not suggest the path will be easy, but you *must* be true to who you are. You are a Leibnitz. You are meant to lead. So much has been invested in you. I would do you no favors to allow you to continue to enjoy what you cannot yet produce or keep, on your own. *Where much is given, much is required,* yes?"

He nodded in resignation. She smiled.

"After you have been mentored and have given your best for five years, if you still wish to pursue other ventures, then so be it. But not now! In fairness to you. You have no foundation on which to stand in the world."

She moved her fingers as if sifting through sand. He squirmed. Her jaw stiffened.

"I will *not* allow you to become a dilettante."

His lips quivered. She patted his hand.

"You do not really know what you want. That is good and that is bad."

Her hands moved upward, then down.

"Fortunately, you are a sponge. I remember at seven and eight, how precocious you were. Do you recall when I selected books to test your reading ability?"

He smiled.

"*Notre-Dame de Paris* among others challenged me."

She patted his arm.

"But you were up to it. Now, you must move to the next plateau. You are no longer a child. You will find your purpose at LE and use your talents to anticipate and fill needs—this is what we do. Successfully, I might add. Fritz took a big risk by diversifying. Some failures, more successes. New areas are emerging every day. Resource recovery. Consumer electronics. Mobile communications. Technological innovations in numerous nascent fields. You have much to contribute to LE."

Her steely eyes pinned him. Shame burned his cheeks.

"Let me be plain regarding Marcus. Unlike you, he has never responded to my attempts to mentor him. I have not played favorites, despite what he thinks. I saw what you both were capable of becoming when you were youngsters. I saw who was developing a strong character that would make me proud. You have proven your worth. Your cousin, however, gives me pause. He does not understand what he wants, except power. I will not abide another Rainer Leibnitz running *my* empire!"

Her searing eyes choked the arguments hidden in the pocket of his heart. His lips quivered. "I-I will not disappoint you."

Chapter 8

The first day that George reported to Parker Gibson, life changed overnight. The lawyer barked that George had been coddled too long to eventually control a vast financial empire. Within a month he spiraled under the pressure of reporting to a demanding boss every day and conducting tedious research and analyses that had significant financial ramifications. Preparation for the bar intensified his anxiety.

His doctor diagnosed Obsessive-Compulsive Disorder, which created more feelings of inadequacy and fears that he would disappoint his grandmother. He met with Dr. Stanley weekly.

When his anxiety escalated, concentration eluded him. Parker accused him of shoddy workmanship, and his tutors questioned his readiness for the bar exam. He succumbed to pressure and finally began the low dosages of a beta-blocker and Paxil the doctor had prescribed. Within days his focus sharpened, and his work product improved.

When the first day of the two-day exam arrived, he strode from his apartment for the short walk to the exam room on Washington Street. But once he sat down, fear flooded his mind. He perseverated on each question. By the time he had returned to his apartment, the sweat of failure clung to his skin. After a long, scalding shower, he called Dr. Stanley.

"I was the last one to leave the room. I spent so much time on the first half I ran out of time and guessed on the last ten questions. Tomorrow I will not be able to make up the difference. Essay writing is my weakest ar..."

Her soothing voice interrupted. "Take a deep breath and move on from here."

"But how will I get through tomorrow?"

She took him through mental exercises of visualizing taking the exam and seeing the results he wanted.

"I believe in you. You need to believe in yourself. You have a unique contribution to make in life. Let my belief carry you until your belief propels you forward. Tomorrow will be your best performance ever."

After an hour of visualization exercises, his heart pulsed with renewed self-assurance.

He centered his mind during the exam the next day. Afterward, he debriefed with his tutors. Exam results would not be available for two months, so he immediately started planning what he would do if he failed. Doubts plagued his thoughts. Fritz suggested that for at least a week he relax and go out with his friends. He called Laurence, but he was out of town. Fritz suggested he accompany him to an event in the Village at *La Maison Française* the next evening. At first, he demurred, but finally succumbed to his father's insistence.

A reception for faculty members, students, and donors followed the concert of French arias. The singer Marianne Staunton captivated him. She carried her tall, regal bearing with grace. Her dark blond hair coiled around her shoulders, her heart-shaped, opalescent face radiated warmth, and her sapphire-blue eyes crinkled as she sang. Her melodious voice stirred the chords of his heart.

He turned to Fritz and beamed. "I will not leave without securing a date with that exquisite woman."

Fritz clapped him on the back. "Excellent. We will go at once to speak with her."

He took the lead. The vocalist was surrounded by well-wishers and friends, so it was difficult in the small reception area to catch her eye. He maneuvered to the forefront, and within moments, they had her all to themselves.

They learned that M, as she preferred to be called, was an NYU doctoral student of French and Russian. She had just completed her qualifying exams and had started writing her dissertation on the grotesque and the sublime in the works of Victor Hugo and Franz Kafka.

George joked, "I would love to see an artist's rendering of Quasimodo metamorphosed into a large beetle."

She laughed.

He listened with fascination as she described how her fluency in French, German, and Russian had given her an appreciation of different cultures, and Spanish and Italian had improved her musical repertoire. When he told her that he spoke French, German, and Spanish, she clapped her hands together with glee. She waxed on about singing as a child and studying voice with Joy Koslowski at the Metropolitan Opera for the last two years. She had considered a career as a professional singer, but had chosen to pursue other areas of interest such as art, music, architecture, and gourmet cooking. His heart beat with the rhythm of her voice. He was holding her silk-draped body on the deck of the *Aleksandra,* as she looked deeply into his eyes when Fritz's voice shattered the dream. "Our family donates millions to NYU."

She grinned. "Yes, Mr. Leibnitz, I know. Your name is quite familiar to me."

His eyebrows shot up.

"Your signature is on my paychecks."

George's head spun, but Fritz, who was never lost for words, asked for details. She described her duties in the executive suite working for three vice-presidents who coordinated with the London office on engineering projects and with Guenther's senior vice-president for pulp-and-paper machinery.

"Fascinating," he remarked, his eyes brightening. "What a

versatile young woman you are."

She laughed. "Well, one must eat and have a roof over one's head. Living in the city *is* rather expensive. But in truth I have worked my way through school since ninth grade with my secretarial skills, so that's what I'm doing now."

George found his tongue. "Amazing!"

She pivoted her face toward him.

"I was fortunate enough to take typing and shorthand in middle school. I was good at both, like foreign languages and music. Anyway, I competed in tournaments and won the state championship twice in high school for both typing and shorthand."

"Incredible! How fast do you type?" he asked, his eyes widening.

"Let me see. About 155 words-a-minute in typing and, sadly, only 135 in shorthand for lack of use."

His eyes filled out. "I had no idea anyone could type that fast. What is shorthand?"

Fritz smiled and interjected, "Our secretaries use shorthand as a quick way to notate what is dictated."

George's eyebrows shot up. "Oh."

Fritz then turned to her. "You mean to tell me, young lady, that someone of your talents is stuck in the vice-president's suite rather than in the CEO's office?"

She blushed. "Well..."

His eyes bore in. "How much do you earn?"

She stiffened. "Sir, I am just happy for the job."

George's face flushed.

"*Je suis désolé. Pardonnez-moi.* I had visions of a struggling student slaving away in the bowels of my business at a pittance of a salary." Fritz's voice trailed off.

An uncomfortable silence ensued.

"I should not have pried. *Je m'excuse milles fois, mademoiselle.* Let me mingle so you two young people can become better acquainted."

He gave George an encouraging look and kissed her hand. Seeing someone he knew, he moved off. George looked down at his feet. She touched his arm.

"I think we have talked enough about me. I'm interested to know about you. Please, tell me about yourself."

His face lit up, and he launched into a description of law school and his preparation for the bar.

"Vous voilà! Mar-i-anne, il vous faut..."

He grimaced as she introduced him to Professor Gérard, who was polite, but insistent. She gave George a mewling look and handed him a card from a pocket of her gown after grabbing a pen from her professor's pocket and writing on the back. He followed her fluid movements as she greeted the well-wishers. After a few moments, he examined her card. The design featured the shadow of an artistically rendered singer in profile and *Marianne Staunton, Lyric Soprano.* He turned it over. She had written her telephone number and *"Love to hear from you, M."* He stood at a distance with a glass of Chardonnay, following her every move.

"George, you are staring. Ms. Staunton will think you are a stalker."

He turned to Fritz, who had just walked up.

"She is really quite unusual, you know. I will see her again," he replied, his face aglow.

Fritz grinned.

"Yes, I think you shall. She does seem quite special. I must find out exactly how she gets on at LE and if she is in the right department. I would hate to see someone that exceptional stuck in Guenther's division."

George's thoughts swirled with her in his arms on the *Aleksandra*, wrapped in romance.

Part 2

Growth is betrayal.
   —John Updike

Chapter 1

Two weeks later, M began working alongside Frederick Metz, Executive Assistant to the CEO of LE, with two times her previous salary. Her head swam at the turn in fortune and the expectations that came with the raise.

Guenther Leibnitz called his brother while she was taking dictation. To her chagrin, her boss put the call on speaker phone.

"Well, Guenther, with Marcus now working in the executive suite of the main office, the workload for Mr. Metz will increase. He needs an able assistant. Ms. Staunton's move makes it possible for Marcus to remain in the executive department. You wanted him to have this opportunity."

"Of course. But I understand she was doing the job of three people and not easily replaced."

"Well, surely personnel can send up whomever you need," Fritz clipped.

Silence.

"So, then, it is settled."

"As you say."

She ignored the heavy-handedness of her boss and turned her attention to the challenging new position. When George did not call within days, a twinge of disappointment clouded her sudden advancement at LE.

Her phone rang several weeks later as she was walking into her apartment after a jog.

"George, you remembered me," she exclaimed at the sound of his voice.

"H-How did you know who it was?"

"You must remember. Singers are good at memorizing sounds, especially ones they like."

Her flattery set the right tone, and the rest of the conversation sailed.

Within a week, they had arranged a Saturday afternoon visit to an Edward Hopper exhibit at the Whitney Museum on Madison and 75th. Afterward, they strolled to 57th Street and Fifth Avenue for dinner at the Russian Tea Room.

He looked her way.

"You said you have been here before, so what do you recommend?"

"Well, we could do a smorgasbord. I save up to come here every couple of months to enjoy the best."

He smiled.

"Lovely. You choose."

"Let's see. Salted cucumbers, herring in sheepskin coat—no, salmon caviar, that would be better. As a main course, pelmeny."

His eyes widened.

"Not the healthiest, but delicious."

"Exactly. No one has Russian food because it's low-fat. And for dessert, blini or pirozuky."

He simpered.

"I doubt anyone in my family appreciates Russian cuisine as much as I do."

She leaned in.

"I'm dying to hear all about your ancestry. You mentioned Catherine the Great."

"Oh, that. *Gran'maman* was a descendant."

Not wanting to reveal her shock she turned the conversation to France and her summer experiences studying at the *Sorbonne*.

"Where did you stay?"

"A little *pension* on the south side of *les Jardins de Luxembourg*," she replied between bites.

His face lit up as he arranged his food.

"One of my favorite gardens in Paris. *Gran'maman* and I have strolled through the Luxembourg Gardens countless times. I may have been within inches of you yet never made your acquaintance."

She grinned and watched him eat one morsel at a time. To relieve the annoying flutters in her stomach, she rambled about how her interests had taken her to Moscow, where her great-great-grandmother was born, thus the interest in Russian language and literature.

He wiped his mouth with the linen napkin.

"So when did you come to New York?"

Their attention was distracted as the waiter brought pirozuky and black tea mixed with cream.

"I moved to New York six years ago, after I completed my master's degree."

Her fork wandered all around her dessert.

"What major?"

"French and Russian."

"Impressive."

George rubbed his index finger over his thumb several times, then broke into a smile.

"And your doctorate...?"

"In progress."

She curled her fingers around her teacup.

"Hopefully within the year I will have my doctorate in French and Russian language and literature."

He put down his teacup.

"Lovely."

Talking kept her butterflies in formation.

"I fell in love with the city the moment I arrived. Of course, a poor grad student like me can't do everything I want, but I've haunted the halls of every museum, concert hall, and Broadway theater at every opportunity, bad seats and all."

He templed his fingers, hardly touching his dessert.

"You said you have a small studio in Greenwich Village. How long have you lived there?"

"I started out in the law school dorm on Washington Square Park, but it was hard to study because of the noise. I was working that first year as an office manager in a doctor's office, barely surviving, so I had to find a better paying job to afford an apartment."

He leaned forward.

"What did you do?"

"I went through an employment agency and found the position at LE. It paid considerably more than the doctor's office. I was able to move into a tiny apartment within a few months. Crowded, but it's mine. Peace and quiet."

His eyebrows shot up.

She stumbled on, explaining that her goal was to pursue a career in international cultural studies.

His eyes lit up.

"Fascinating."

She glanced around her.

"Everything interests me, which slows me down. I have tons of credits in music, art, foreign affairs. Gosh, I almost have enough credits for multiple degrees."

"How wonderful!"

He fingered the dessert fork several times.

"All the extra classes, working fifty hours a week at my job, and doing concerts every few months slows down getting my Ph.D." She laughed to calm her fluttering heart. "Professor Béjart told me to finish the degree now and pursue my other interests later. He thinks I'll be the perennial ABD."

"Sorry?"

He sipped his tea.

"All-But-Dissertation student."

He patted his mouth with the napkin.

"Is he right?"

"Gosh, no. I want to finish as soon as possible. It's just that I have such catholic tastes."

Her eyes twinkled.

"There's so much to learn. Enriching my education with multidisciplinary courses will help me far more than just taking courses in my department."

"How amazing you can do all that."

He brushed aside a lock of hair that had fallen out of place, examined his nails, and rubbed his index fingers with his thumbs.

"Don't make too much of it. I have *no* social life. Besides, as Gramma always said, 'Where much is given...'"

"'...much is required,'" they finished in unison and laughed.

He relaxed his hands as she shared that halfway through her preparation for her qualifying exams, she had been sure she would fail. She had been meeting with one of her professors and three other students for mock oral exams and sleeping three to four hours a night to meet her work, study, and rehearsal obligations. Fearing she would buckle under the pressure, she met with Professor Béjart to tell him she would not be able to sit before her committee and answer the countless questions they would ask about every century of French and Russian literature and civilization.

"He assured me I'd do fine and he wouldn't allow me to give up. That didn't help. I was just getting up to leave his office, disgusted with myself, when he pushed me against the wall."

George choked on his tea and coughed.

"I knew the reputation of French professors making sexual advances to their students was legend, so I was prepared to fend him off. But he pushed his right index finger into my chest and told me I wanted everything to be perfect, and I was unrealistic. He said I had to trust myself. I was the most ready student he had seen in his twenty-plus-year career. As a performer, I should appreciate the fact that the orals were no more than a performance. And a few other pithy words I don't remember."

George picked up the teacup, then set it down.

"What an unorthodox way to make his point."

She smiled and cocked her head to the side.

"It registered."

"By physically manhandling you? Pretty strange tactic."

He lined up his knife, fork, and spoon.

"Yes, but I left his office knowing I couldn't disappoint his belief in me. From that moment, I worked even harder." The reservoir of tears behind her eyes filled. "I've always had someone to believe in me, even when I've felt the lousiest about myself. I'm extraordinarily blessed."

"You sound just like Dr. Stanley."

"Who?"

His face turned pink, and he looked down at his lap. She threw him an earnest smile.

"I wish I'd been smart enough to go talk with someone about my feelings. Good for you. I'd love to hear about her."

He described the ordeal of law school and the bar exam and Dr. Stanley's help.

"You know, George, I've had my own academic problems."

She swallowed a bite of pirozuky.

"That's hard to imagine."

"In my master's program I realized too late I'd taken on too much. I was unprepared for the level of difficulty of the material and the unhelpful attitude of several of my profs. I had always succeeded academically, but I didn't have the background in synthesis and the level of writing mastery in foreign languages that I needed."

He templed his fingers again.

"What did you do?"

"I struggled. One professor made it worse by telling me I

wasn't smart enough to be in graduate school. I felt like I didn't belong. "

His eyebrows shot up.

"He actually said that?"

"Yes, *she* did. I had always been a star student—not that I didn't have to work my tail off to get A's. To be so summarily dismissed was devastating. I almost quit. I considered scaling back to pursue only one degree. But I'm not a quitter, and I can tell, neither are you."

She could see the burden of inadequacy lift from his shoulders. As they began to reveal details of their individual struggles over more tea, it became obvious they would see each other again.

Chapter 2

Two months into the relationship, the phone rang as M was climbing into bed near midnight.

"Ha-Have I disturbed you?"

She eased herself onto the bed to brace herself.

"Are you alright?"

"I am a failure!"

"What do you mean? What's happened?"

"I-I failed the bar exam! By-by twenty points!"

"I am *so* sorry."

"I-I did really well on the essay section but I missed too many multiple-choice questions because I ran out of time."

Disappointment laced George's voice.

Her heart twisted in empathy but balked at taking on this burden with a concert of French arias on Sunday and another chapter to write for Professor Béjart by the following Friday.

"How can I help? How about if I talked with the doctor you mentioned?"

"No!" he barked.

She sat up straight with rising pique.

"Maybe we should limit our time together for a few months so you can get help and focus on your studies and work." The ticking clock tugged at her heart that she didn't have time for him. "If it would help."

Guilt washed over her.

"I'm greatly touched by the gesture," he replied. "It's a

tempting offer, but I think we should just keep everything the way it is now, okay?"

"Sure."

A whisper of doubt brushed against her face. His perfectionism nagged at her. Maybe he needed an excuse to break off the relationship. He had mentioned that his last girlfriend had quickly exited his life. His privileged life also needled her. How would he handle this setback? Clearly, such a defeat would daunt him. He was charming, bright, and creative, but also stubborn, myopic, indecisive, and entitled. How many people had a high-powered support team yet struggled this much? Did she really want to risk her future with arrogant elitists like Fritz Leibnitz? She'd met George's uncle and grandmother a few times, and his cousins once. Although polite, ultimately she worked for them. She had fielded a few calls from his stepmother and mother and didn't look forward to meeting them. The Leibnitz family enjoyed staggering wealth and privilege, so why was he interested in her? He could never understand the struggle of surviving on one's own. The new job and now the new relationship unsettled her equilibrium, and excited her. The last time she hadn't listened to her heart despite serious misgivings and danger signs had left her devastated. She couldn't survive another betrayal.

What would Grammy Mir say? It had been so many years since her death.

M's eyes brimmed with tears, as the past buffeted her thoughts. She had never known her father, and her mother had abandoned her by running off with a man twice her age when M was two. Pop-Pop and Grammy Mir had raised her as their child.

She settled her blanket around one of her fondest memories of Pop-Pop as a little girl—sitting on his knee in the screened porch of the old farmhouse, while he peeled a Yellow Delicious apple grown right on the farm, cored it, and scraped flesh with his whittling knife, bringing the sweet dripping flesh up to her lips to eat.

"M, who d'ya wanna be when you're grown?" he had asked when she was maybe six or seven.

"A farmer, just like you, Pop-Pop."

"Oh, no. My Princess will have the whole world at her feet. She'll do whatever she sets her heart to. She'll find her passion and foller it."

He had instilled in her the ability to dream big and believe she could achieve anything. Her heart smiled. Grammy had been the disciplinarian who had broken her temper tantrums. A long talk about the importance of learning to follow the rules had always prefaced a quick spanking. The discussion had been the painful part, because she'd known she'd disappointed Grammy.

Her beloved grandfather died of colon cancer when she was ten, and Grammy had a fatal cerebral hemorrhage when she was sixteen. From that day, she had shortened her name in memory of Pop-Pop's nickname for her. How quickly she had needed to grow up. With her modest inheritance and the proceeds from the sale of the farm, she had worked part-time as a freelance typist and funded her undergraduate education. Her determination now at twenty-six to become successful on her own merits had grown immeasurably since her grandmother's death. She suspected her life experiences had given her an advantage over George. After all, she didn't have Fritz Leibnitz for a father, stressful family dynamics, and all the expectations of being a Leibnitz. She had worked at LE long enough to imagine he would consider himself a failure in his father's eyes. And what little she knew of Aleksandra Leibnitz suggested that this formidable woman could make or break him.

His voice broke into her musings.

"M, did you hear me?"

"Sorry. Do you want to come over? I know it's late, but if

it would help."

"I think I need to talk to Dr. Stanley. It was too late to call her, so I thought if I could just talk to you."

She turned away from the phone, her cheeks flushed.

"So you're saying I haven't helped."

Her mouth turned down.

"No. I just think it is unfair to... C-Can I call you tomorrow sometime? I should not have called."

Her eyes hardened. He didn't recognize that he was gravitating to the familiar. She would not lose sleep over him. Her heavy eyelids mirrored her emotional fatigue.

"No problem. I might suggest one thing. At least it helps me when I'm unsure of myself. Try writing three pages on the topic 'Something I Cannot Deny.' It might sort out your thinking."

"Thanks. I promise to call tomorrow morning, if you are free."

"Until 8:00. I have a lot to do."

"Goodnight, then."

She brooded for a moment as she nestled her head into the pillow.

What have I gotten myself into?

Chapter 3

The phone rang a few minutes after 7:00 as she was eating breakfast.

George's voice exuded confidence.

"I took your advice and made some discoveries."

"Great!"

She smiled and sipped her herbal tea.

"I cannot deny a certain warmth in my relationship with Father, but I do not like him very much. I cannot deny I want his position when he retires, but I question if this is the path for me."

He had no idea what being CEO entailed. She forked a strawberry and dipped it in yogurt.

"I wonder if I will fritter away the family fortune. I mean, am I capable of becoming a shrewd wheeler-dealer? Or is Marcus the one to lead LE?"

She wanted to suggest he had the ability to be successful outside the family umbrella if he applied himself, but maybe he wouldn't be successful on his own. She sighed and ate her breakfast.

"I cannot deny I mistrust my cousin. Part of me wants to outmaneuver him and keep him from becoming the next CEO. But I am no match for his ambition and tactics. He feels Father cheated Uncle Guenther. How can I possibly defeat such a formidable opponent? D-Do I really want to?"

She shifted in her chair.

"Good question."

"I-I feel love, jealousy, even contempt for him. What must it have been like all these years for Uncle Guenther to be in Father's shadow and for *Gran'maman* to favor me over my cousins?"

"From what you've said, your grandmother provides generously for all of you."

She wiped her mouth with a cloth napkin.

"Yes, but she picked me to lead LE. I am ashamed to say, I am bitter that Marcus has warm and loving parents, not like mine."

She bristled.

"Some might call you jaded and spoiled."

"I know."

She arose from the table, pacing.

"What advantages?"

"Marcus carries himself with a swagger I couldn't possibly imitate. He can turn the head of any woman and capture her with his charm and witty personality."

She laughed and sat down on her brushed-cotton Macy's fold-out couch.

"Like you couldn't?"

"It is different," he whined. "He has a superior intellect. He is quick on his feet."

"I think you're selling yourself short. You have far more going for you than he does. I've been around him enough to see that your attributes are far greater than his, and he knows it."

"What do you mean?"

"Isn't it obvious that what he lacks and wants the most is what you have—your grandmother's favor?"

"Oh."

She sighed.

"Isn't that the real crux of the problem between you two? You've told me how growing up Marcus and Wilhelm were like brothers to you."

She stretched out her sore hamstrings across the length of the couch.

"That changed. Marcus looks down on Uncle Guenther for having lesser abilities than Father's, and he would love to supplant me in Father's affection. I just lack their devious mindset and consuming ambition to rule."

"Quit torturing yourself."

She leaned her head back. His negativity drained her energy. She couldn't afford to get embroiled in family intrigue.

"You should probably talk with Dr.-Dr. Stanley. I mean, you can't separate what you want from what other people want from you."

She moved her feet onto the floor.

"I'm not sure how to tell you to work through this. I can support you. But at times, you wear your insecurity like-like rosary beads. You finger each area where you don't measure up, rubbing each bead over and over until your emotions become raw. From what you've said, all your self-doubts, your double- and triple-checking every minute detail, your memory of minutiae is because you're trying to be the ideal son and grandson. But you need to find out what *you* want, who *you* want to be."

She stood up and stretched. She really needed to start vocalizing and work on her dissertation.

He sucked in air.

"I want to fight for position. I have tried. But my heart is just not in it. I-I am like a two-headed monster going in different directions, but not belonging in either world. The urge to create perfection around me becomes inexorable. But some things I cannot fix. I look at my cousins, my friends, so strong. I am so weak. I compartmentalize my feelings. I know why I have not allowed anyone to get too close."

"Go on."

She sat down again. Danger signs lit up her forehead. She longed to escape, but her feet planted themselves on the floor.

"You talk about your true self, like Father Thomas told me when I was young. We read the story of David before he faced Goliath. The king made him put on his armor, but David took them off."

"Right, because they weren't right for him."

"He did what worked for him—five stones and his slingshot. I am looking for what is right for me. You-you are a free agent. Not me. What do you know about family pressures to conform? Or what I would have to give up? Sorry, but you cannot possibly understand what it is like to live in my skin." He let out a troubled breath. "You must think me weak. I will never be able to measure up to your expectations. Maybe it is better if we take a break until I sort all these feelings out."

She bolted from her chair. Anger arose in the back of her throat.

"You are so entitled. You don't know what you want."

She walked into her bedroom sanctuary toward her small, antique mahogany desk nestled in the corner.

"Y-yes. I cannot deny I am a Leibnitz and my destiny has been set from birth. I have to admit *Gran'maman* is right. I do not know how to survive outside the protected confines of my family's wealth."

She shook her head and started pacing.

"I am not like my friend Laurence, taking on the world on his own terms, thumbing his nose at his family, creating his own wealth. I cannot imagine drudging away my days in some entry-level legal position earning barely enough to survive. I am trapped. I *am* highly attuned to aesthetics and order. But so is my family. And they have flourished in business. So what is my problem?"

She stopped, her heart leaping with caution. The silence lengthened. She exhaled and rubbed her heavy eyes.

"M, you know where my focus is? The pears and apples on the oval crystal platter, you know, the one on the kitchen counter, are touching and the pomegranates and avocado are positioned at the wrong angle. I have been trying to figure out who rearranged my fruit."

Her throat constricted. In two months she'd yet to enter his private domain.

"You know what I cannot deny? I have lost the big picture. No wonder law school was so hard and passing the bar is torturous. No wonder I cannot stand up to Father and tell him to back off. That is what he did, you know. He earned the right to lead by daring to oppose *Ol'papa* and proving his worth to *Gran'maman*. I have to do the same. I have to insist on doing things my way and live with the consequences. But, first, I have to reorganize the fruit."

M giggled and shook her head as she sat down at her desk. She could see him fixated by the lack of symmetry, his sense of self-worth tied to the appearance of harmony. Of course, he hadn't thought about how she fit into his world. His emotions were running rampant, and she couldn't let herself get wrapped up in them. She should bow out of his life despite her heart throbbing with love for this exasperating and adorable man. Her equilibrium shattered. She sighed the despair of the trapped. She would not spend the day rehearsing and writing. She needed to meditate and write in her journal to find herself again.

"I suggest you do nothing precipitously. There's time to deal with your father. The first thing is to clarify your thinking. Talk with Dr. Stanley. I'm sure you'll think more rationally then."

"Of course. Thanks for listening. I-I am so sorry. Can you be patient with me?"

Her heart fluttered.

"I-I'll try."

"Are we still on tomorrow for brunch and *42nd Street*?"

"Of course, *chéri.*"

Deep inside the shelf behind her heart an insistent voice echoed, "Run! Run as far and as fast as you can!"

Chapter 4

Saturday unraveled. Singing and writing dragged on. By Sunday her nerves were tightened violin strings. She would have canceled their outing, but she had been anticipating the Broadway show for weeks. She put aside the nagging feeling that her needs would become more and more subsumed by his. The afternoon lifted her spirits and settled her nerves.

*****

Monday started at 7:00. A 9:00 meeting of the executive committee required helping Frederick finish preparations. Their boss was notorious for making last-minute changes. Only two weeks earlier, he had rewritten an entire speech thirty minutes before the opening ceremonies of a pulp mill dedication in Alabama.

Her thoughts swirled with how Frederick and she had both been required to see that every detail was carried out to his liking. Frederick had chartered a 747 to take bankers, politicians, engineers, and other staff from New York. The company's three King Airs shuttled guests between the Florida resort and the grand opening ceremony in Alabama on Friday. Then, she orchestrated several sporting and entertainment events at the resort.

Guenther and his family flew from New York in the Hawker 900XP. Fritz and his family traveled in the Boeing

Business Jet 737. M and Frederick accompanied the guests on the 747. At the last moment Fritz asked her to sing the *National Anthem* at the beginning of the opening ceremonies to set the tone for the audience of 5,200 pulp mill employees and their families, local dignitaries, congressmen, senators, the governor, and the guests and staff flown in.

Twenty minutes before the event, he called for her before she had a chance to rehearse with the local school band. She hid her pique and rushed to the computer. She realized it would take at least thirty minutes to make extensive changes before the ceremony. He stood over her while she typed, as if his presence would quicken her pace. He threw out changes while she typed. With racing fingers, she gritted her teeth and focused so hard that her head started pulsating. With one minute to spare, the printer spit out the speech to his waiting hands. Beads of sweat trickled down her hairline; she sucked in her exhaustion and rushed to the stage.

The band had its own pace, so her sole focus was keeping in sync. After the rousing applause, her nerves relaxed. She sat down, her skin coated with tingling sweat.

As she congratulated herself now on how well the celebratory weekend had unfolded, the robe of pride clothed her. She had made the Leibnitz family look good, despite Mrs. Belinda's summoning her during the barbecue when she was conversing with the governor. She would relish the thought of lording over her once she became Mrs. George Leibnitz.

Chapter 5

At 8:22 Mr. Fritz buzzed. As M entered his office, he beckoned.

"Ms. Staunton, I have a top secret project that requires your immediate attention. No one else must know about it, understood?"

Her eyes widened.

"Of course, Mr. Leibnitz."

"My son."

Her stomach dropped.

"Parker needs to direct his studies to ensure he passes the bar this time. A bonus awaits you if you convince George. You understand, *n'est-ce pas*?"

His steely stare returned her steady gaze.

"Yes, but your request puts me in a compromising position."

"You do not appreciate that it is for his good. We will not help him by letting him flounder. This bar exam business has gone on long enough. If he is going to run LE, he must get past this nonsense. His future, and yours, I might add, if you are seriously interested in him, are at stake."

Pique hardened her eyes.

"Mr. Leibnitz, I am not remotely interested in your family's fortune."

He threw her a condescending look.

"My dear, no one is suggesting you are interested in

George for the money. Obviously, you are well equipped to take care of yourself."

She blushed.

"He is his own worst enemy, too stubborn and proud to accept help without some subtle steering. I believe you are perfect for the job, but if you are not up to it, I have other means at my disposal."

She blanched. He offended her sense of integrity and loyalty.

"I will see what I can do," she snapped.

His face softened.

"I respect your principles. My intent is genuine, I assure you. I would appreciate anything you can do."

He smiled. She recognized the practiced sincerity of the gesture. Taking this job had been a mistake. Yet her heart melted for George, and her pride begged for the position. She had become accustomed to the generous income and challenging international environment.

She would help him—her way.

*****

She suggested he talk with Dr. Stanley about Mr. Gibson's offer to help him prepare for the bar. His facile agreement surfaced unanticipated jealousy.

A few days later, he called to confirm that he would take her advice. Suspicion increased when he suggested they only spend weekends together and call each other during the week so they could focus on their many obligations. She relented, uncertain of their future.

As the day of the exam approached, he sought reassurance.

"I'm going to do for you what Professor Béjart did for me. I'm going to push you up against the wall and...kiss you! No, he didn't do that!"

She laughed.

"But I *am* going to kiss *you* and tell you how wonderful you are and that you can take that test standing on your head if you have to."

She steered him up against the wall of her living-dining room and kissed him full on the mouth.

"*Alors, mon chéri,* how are you going to do, knowing *I'll* be waiting for you afterwards?—*Moi!*"

If he didn't pass, his father would surely blame her.

*****

The night before the bar exam George stopped by her apartment asking for her support. Before she could do more than tell him how much she believed in him, he left. The morning of the exam, he called to hear her tell him the exam was no match for him. She sent him off with the promise of a special dinner. The day crawled, and she found it difficult to concentrate. Mr. Fritz seemed out of sorts and barked at everyone. She left the office early and arrived home in time to prepare dinner.

When George limped into her apartment, she was putting the garlic roaster in the oven. She ignored his downcast demeanor and threw him her cheeriest face.

"So, *chéri,* how did it go?"

"I am afraid to guess. I refuse to think about it," he groaned as he joined her in the tiny kitchen. "The second part tomorrow will be the clincher."

"You're at your best on essay writing."

"I guess. So, what are you cooking?"

He pecked her cheek and looked over her shoulder at the two raw tuna steaks on a platter.

"A spinach and arugula salad with roasted garlic and mustard vinaigrette. I'm ready to pan fry the tuna, so I'm gonna shoo you off. There's only room for one of us in here."

He chortled, squeezing past her into the living-dining area.

"You could open the Merlot. It's on the table with the corkscrew."

He walked four steps to the antique oak table, which occupied one side of the area.

"So what is your schedule over the next couple of months?"

She turned the tuna and ground the pepper on the second side.

"Quite full. How long until bar exam results are posted?"

"Couple of months. In the meantime, I will work full time with Parker on several projects. Pretty hectic."

"For sure. The second draft of the first five chapters of my dissertation is due in six weeks, I have several concerts coming up, and your father and Frederick have a full load of assignments for me to do. I'm drowning."

"And you took time to make me this special meal. That wasn't necessary."

"But I wanted to, *chéri.*"

She threw him a seductive smile. He grinned.

"For dessert?"

"Well, I hope my company is enough, with some raspberries and sabayon."

She batted her eyelashes.

"Divine!"

He decanted the wine and threw her a kiss. She swallowed her fears and savored the moment.

Chapter 6

The Saturday night before Mr. Fritz's Paris trip, her cell phone rang at 11:00.

"Ms. Staunton, s-so sorry. Pardon the intrusion. Would you... Please meet me at Mt. Sinai at once."

Her heart seized.

"Mr. Leibnitz, has something happened to George?"

"No, *Mütter* is dead. I-I need you."

She released the tension in her body.

"I will leave immediately."

"Cerebral hemorrhage. One minute she was alive and vibrant, hosting the fundraiser you organized at the Metropolitan Opera. Then she was gone."

"I am *so* sorry."

"She collapsed in the grand foyer of Lincoln Center just as I was turning to thank the few remaining guests. There was nothing anyone could do. The ambulance was too late."

M's mind went blank.

"She thought very highly of you, you know. Aleksandra was an excellent judge of character. I-I cannot imagine life without her."

"What can I do?" she asked in a susurrant tone.

"Leave immediately. George will need you. *I* will need you."

"Of course."

The line went dead. She frowned. The impact of the

matriarch's death would absorb their lives. She was heading to the elevator when George called her cell phone.

"I never got to say goodbye."

"I'm on my way to the hospital right now. I know this must leave a deep crevice in your heart. You were so close to her."

She dropped her keys in her purse and tapped the down elevator button, her mind racing.

"She seemed so healthy. She can't be gone. She didn't even see me pass the bar. No more walks in Hyde Park, the *Burggarten.*"

She listened to his rush of grief on her way into the elevator. His voice dragged on with the nine flights down and out of the apartment building. She exited the elevator and motioned for the bellman to hail a cab while she listened to him reminisce. Memories of losing her own grandparents pricked her heart. She could only imagine how hard the next months were going to be for him. His grandmother was his bulwark. He would feel lost without her. Either they would grow closer or this crisis would break them apart. She exhaled the negative thoughts and set her mouth. She would help him through this tragedy, and he would turn to her alone for comfort.

Chapter 7

Over the next two weeks she shuttled between the Park Avenue office and Wilton. While Frederick rescheduled the Paris trip and countless appointments, she juggled the arrangements for a private wake at Wilton, the funeral at St. Patrick's Cathedral, a memorial service at NYU, and a special celebration of Aleksandra Leibnitz's life at Lincoln Center. Supporting George and his father halted the rest of her life. The expectation that she would sing at the various events with a small chamber orchestra added to her stress. Her head spun with Mr. Fritz's need to use the occasion to exert his authority. The number of dignitaries from various countries who came to pay their respects increased her workload as she needed to sort out seating arrangements and the proper address for each dignitary. She would have been enthralled to be rubbing shoulders with so many important people if her body didn't ache from exhaustion.

To her chagrin, Mr. Fritz summoned her to witness the reading of his mother's will. The Leibnitz brothers, Mr. Gibson, and an older, rather menacing-looking gentleman in an Italian silk suit and cravat awaited her arrival in the Wilton library. By the context of the will, she deduced that the stranger was Aleksandra Leibnitz's brother, Sergey Zerbst.

As Mr. Gibson read the will she studied the faces of the men. They seemed to already know the will's contents. Mr. Fritz would take possession of the Wilton estate, the Paris townhome, and Lieb Island in the Grenadines, and Mr. Guenther would own the Vienna estate, the Roman villa, and the London townhouse. Mr. Zerbst would arrange for the sale of the French Riviera villa, the Indonesian plantation, and the South African farm and deposit the funds in a Swiss account along with the money in the New York and Connecticut bank accounts. The will enumerated the many personal items, works of art, yachts, and other properties that had been given to various family members and the millions that had been added to the grandchildren's trust funds. The immense wealth detailed in the will staggered her imagination.

Over the next few weeks she saw a lot of George's Great-Uncle Sergey. He exuded the formidable nature that she had observed in his sister, but without her warmth and graciousness. He left her with a sense of foreboding. When she asked George about his great-uncle, he brushed aside her concerns.

"Uncle Sergey was a spy long before he made a fortune in the manufacturing business. Father worked with him in Paris when he was younger. He was here for a while after *Ol'papa* died. Parker says that he helped orchestrate Father's rise over Uncle Guenther. Odd since he has always been closer to Uncle Guenther than to Father."

She catalogued this detail.

When the month of mourning and celebration of Aleksandra Zerbst Leibnitz concluded, the family wrapped up their grief and buried it with her. Relief washed over M. She could get back to some semblance of her own life.

Chapter 8

Two weeks after LE business resumed, George stopped by M's desk while Frederick lunched in the employee dining room. When he invited her to his home for the weekend, she recognized the significance of this gesture.

Butterflies hovered in her stomach over the course of the day on Friday. Frederick cleared his throat.

"You've seemed out of sorts all afternoon. Is everything alright? A big date tonight, I wager."

She smiled.

"How did you guess?"

"Let's just say, I recognize first-date jitters. It's about time you had some fun. You will wow him."

Entering George's private domain signaled a big step. When Terence met her at the bank of elevators a few minutes after 6:00, her heart fluttered. It took every bit of her sense of decorum not to drill the chauffeur with questions about the location of George's apartment. When they arrived at One Fifth Avenue, she swallowed hard. She had jogged past this Art Deco building on her morning run around Washington Square Park and up Fifth Avenue countless times. George hadn't even hinted that he lived within a fifteen-minute walk of her six-hundred-square-foot apartment. Her irritation turned to excitement as the doorman appeared at her limousine door.

"Ms. Staunton, Tobias, at your service. How are you this fine spring day?"

"Very well. Thank you."

He helped her exit the car.

"Mr. Leibnitz is expecting you."

The doorman escorted her to gold-plated elevator doors. When he inserted a key and pressed the button marked P for penthouse, her stomach flip-flopped.

"I almost forgot. My bag," she started as Terence appeared with her weekender bag.

"I've got it. Go ahead."

Her pulse quickened.

He was heading toward another bank of elevators to her left when she turned to suggest to the doorman that Terence could accompany her.

"Oh, no, ma'am. He's taking the staff elevator. Don't worry. Everything's being taken care of."

She stepped into the private elevator abashed. Her mind raced up the twenty-seven floors. When the elevator doors opened, her eyes widened. The marble foyer and living room beyond bathed her in a riot of colors and a cozy elegance. Before she had a moment to recover, Terence appeared from the hallway to her right.

"I've taken the liberty of handing your valise to the housekeeper. She'll put them in your room."

"Th-Thank you."

She had fallen into Alice's rabbit hole.

"I'll take my leave now, ma'am."

He turned and went the way he had come.

"There you are," George chirped as he made his way from the kitchen with two glasses of bubbly in his hands.

She rushed to him with such awkwardness that he almost spilled the champagne.

"Sorry," she cooed as she kissed him full on the lips.

"Mmm, you taste delectable."

"So do you."

She took a sip of the proffered champagne.

"I-I feel like this is our first date. I realized as I was coming up on the elevator that..."

"...it's a big step to finally invite you into my kingdom."

She nodded, taking in the expansiveness around her.

"Kingdom indeed."

His eyes smiled.

"I wanted to do it sooner, but ..."

"You don't need to explain."

"Thanks. How about a tour while the chef is putting the finishing touches on our appetizers?" He gestured with his hand.

"You didn't need to go to all this trouble."

"Please, let me do this for you. You have done so much for me."

She smiled, slightly overwhelmed by the gold-plated service and the opulence. As they ambled through the gallery of paintings in and out of the exquisite rooms, his aesthetic taste met her around every corner. They walked into the master bedroom, dizzy with love. They chitchatted about the demanding work in light of the upcoming, re-scheduled trip to Paris, with tidbits about where he had found pieces of furniture and *objets d'art* thrown in. He took her hand to step down into the sitting area when the wraparound terrace came into view.

"I asked Father to borrow Chef for this evening. He'll serve our *hors d'oeuvres* on the terrace, so let's check out Greenwich Village?"

He led her out through the French doors to a panoramic view of Washington Square Park and the skyline beyond.

"It's lovely. You must enjoy coming here to relax."

"I do."

She nestled her head into his shoulder.

"*Vous viola!*"

Chef's booming voice stole the moment.

"*Pardon. Je revenirai en quelque moments.*"

91

"*Non, ça va. Nous sommes prêts, n'est-ce pas, chérie?*"

George turned to her.

"*Bien sûr. Allez-y.*"

Indeed they were ready. The couple's eyes devoured each other a moment more. Then they sat down to enjoy *milles-feuilles* of crab and mushroom, escargots swimming in butter, freshly made baguette, and asparagus wrapped in prosciutto and goat cheese. Promise impregnated the air.

Chapter 9

The week before the Paris trip, tension mounted between the Leibnitz brothers. M took notes by Mr. Fritz's side in his conference room as he met with his brother and senior staff several times a day. The subtle jabs between the Leibnitzes highlighted an ongoing rivalry. Her boss kept looking at her to nod in agreement with his views.

George showed up at her desk when Fredrick was at lunch and invited her to join him on the trip.

"I'm behind in my research. If I had just one day at *la Bibliothèque Nationale*, I could actually get most of what I'm missing on Hugo, but that's out of the question. Hugo would be a great excuse, but Frederick is counting on me to complete the Bonn documents, I haven't rehearsed with my accompanist this week, I haven't written one line on my dissertation since Tuesday, and Professor Béjart is breathing down my neck. I am sooo behind."

"Obviously, you need a vacation."

He sat down next to her.

"Could I ever! But it's the wrong time. I already asked Frederick if I could take a week off, and he emphatically said no."

She turned to her computer screen. He screwed up his face.

"Really? I could ask..."

She glanced at him.

"No, I don't want any favors. It wouldn't be fair to Frederick. If he needs me, I can't let him down."

She put his hands in hers, her eyes pleading.

"He depends on me. Think of what it's like to work for your father. Frederick's blamed far more than he's praised. I don't want to cause him any grief. He's a dedicated, remarkable person. Your father is lucky to have him."

"I have never given him much thought. He arranges my appointments with Father and organizes my trips and such. He seems nice, but I'm less interested in how devoted he is than in how loyal you are to someone whose permission you do not need."

"George, really!"

"I was just thinking of you."

She dismissed the matter until his father called her into his office two days later.

"Ms. Staunton, I need you to accompany me on the Paris trip. New developments require, shall we say, discreet skills. I need someone who can speak French and German fluently. Frederick's German is serviceable, but not his French. The work is too sensitive for the Paris staff, and with so many players involved, I need both of you. And should you need to do research for your dissertation, fine, as long as you are available when I need you. The Paris staff can assist you. Frederick can organize everything. No doubt, he will want you to cover for him while he visits his favorite *couturier*."

He chuckled and rolled his eyes.

Indignation pricked her heart.

"I..."

"So, it is settled."

He grinned. She swallowed her arguments and smiled.

Chapter 10

The trip to Paris coincided with the posting of bar exam results.

George showed up at her desk the day before the trip with a flat face and sagging shoulders. He motioned her to the conference room. When she had closed the door behind them, he mumbled that he had failed the bar by five points and wasn't going to Paris. Her heart sank. Before she could formulate a reply, his father burst through the door.

"Parker tells me you are not going to Paris. Out of the question!"

George's face set.

"I am not going."

"We will not risk millions because you are sulking over an exam."

She watched them volley back and forth. She could have been invisible so little did they acknowledge her presence.

"You are behaving selfishly. This is not some school project. If you were anyone else, you would be fired for this-this insolence. You cannot leave others in the lurch. I will not allow it!"

He tapped his foot.

The minutes ticked.

"You are such a disappointment to me," he spit.

Her eyebrows shot up, and George's shoulders slumped.

"Just like your mother. Weak. Selfish. Unreasonable."

George looked at the floor, fingers limp.

"George Leibnitz, the world does not revolve around you!"

He glared at his father. The grandfather clock in the corner ticked off the minutes. His father's face finally softened.

"You are devastated. I sympathize. You have worked hard. But you have to move on. Believe it or not, you *will* survive. I have survived worse."

Surprise and incredulity flickered across George's face.

"You?!"

"I will not bore you with the details, but once I was caught up in my own problems and cost the company several million. Papa always held it against me."

Pain shadowed his face.

"But I recovered and moved on. You will, too."

George shook his head. His father moved toward him, his lips pressed down.

"Let me be clear. If you do not go to Paris and we lose this deal, you lose your inheritance. I will not have a son of mine, and an employee I might add, jeopardize the consummation of this deal. I will not have it!"

George's eyes darkened.

"If need be, I will give Marcus the chance to prove himself. Is that what you want? Your cousin to make you look bad in front of everyone? Answer me," he bellowed.

George's face paled.

"I need to talk to Dr. Stanley."

"*What?*"

Mr. Leibbnitz's eyes bulged.

"Fine! Call her."

George remained immovable.

"Give me her number. Now!"

George hesitated, then relented.

"Ms. Staunton, dial the number and put it on speaker phone."

She complied. Dr. Stanley was unavailable and could not

be interrupted. Mr. Leibnitz insisted that he needed to speak to her at once. Her voice finally came on the line. She explained that she was with a client and could not speak with him for another thirty-five minutes. His face darkened, then softened. He turned to see George exit the room. He looked at M as if nothing had happened and had her make calls from the day's schedule. Her emotions numbed as she focused on the calls.

At 6:54 he instructed her to call Dr. Stanley and put the call on speaker phone. Once she answered, he explained the situation and asked her to convince George to go to Paris. She agreed to do what she could with the suggestion that it would be better to allow him to come to the decision on his own.

"Well," he declared as he hung up the phone, "I suppose the good doctor is right, *n'est-ce pas,* Ms. Staunton?"

Without waiting for a reply, he started moving papers around on his desk.

"Clearly, we cannot help him stand on his own two feet if we tell him how to think. He really is stubborn. *Comme moi.*"

He laughed and shook his head. She refused to smile.

"I suppose I have not been a very good father."

His eyes bore in.

"Aleksandra. Dr. Stanley. He has never been able to come to me. Or his mother. God knows she would have no sound advice."

He straightened his back.

"No matter. Dr. Stanley may be a good surrogate parent. Clearly, she believes I have unfairly thrown up Marcus as a foil and that I am too tough on George."

His voice became steel.

"But she has no idea what is at stake. And neither does George. Parker is right. Marcus should be given the chance. Let the chips fall where they may."

He turned back to the papers strewn across his desk.

"Ms. Staunton, send for Marcus at once."

Her heart cratered.

Chapter 11

George went to Paris claiming that he had come because of M. She had little patience for his growing pains and his perfunctory performance in the Paris meetings. As doubts about him grew, she immersed herself in her duties and avoided him as much as possible. On their last evening in Paris, he broached the subject she had sought to avoid.

"I am truly sorry for my behavior. I got so caught up in failure that I couldn't see clearly. Then Father hemmed me in and all reason left. Only the thought of Marcus getting the better of me brought me to my senses."

Her cold heart softened.

"I'm glad you came around."

"When I realized I needed to complete what I had started to beat Marcus, everything came into perspective. And the threat of being disinherited got me thinking. It is time I launch out on my own with or without Father's blessing and support as soon as possible."

She grabbed his hands.

"How exciting! The possibilities are endless. Find a cause you can get behind. I'll love you no matter what you choose."

She kissed both his cheeks.

"I wanted to think so, but I had to ask. I have been acting like an ass. I-I didn't want to mislead you. If I leave LE, it will not be easy. I may no longer have the trust fund. You never know with Father, but I doubt he could actually undo the inheritance *Gran'maman* left me. I guess what I'm saying is we will not starve, but I have to find my way, and, who knows how long it will take?"

"It doesn't matter."

He pulled her close.

"Father won't take this very well."

"I dunno. He might be expecting it, and, maybe, he'll even be relieved."

He pulled away.

"What do you mean? You believe he doesn't think I *can* lead the company?"

"Don't get your ego all bruised. I don't *know* anything. It's just, well, he's your father. Don't you think he's figured out by now that you have different priorities? Don't you think he'd be proud to see you make your own way?"

His mouth pouted.

"He can be quite selfish."

She pulled him toward her.

"Why does it matter what he thinks?"

"Because he-he is my father. I want him to be proud of me, and maybe he won't be if he thinks I am taking the easy way out."

She looked into his eyes.

"It's actually the harder route. You won't have all these namby-pambies around who *have* to do your bidding because you own their paychecks, will you? You'll have to prove yourself to people and earn their respect."

"Maybe I fear I won't be able to, that I will fail."

"I see." She stood. "Every single time I audition, I know I can be rejected."

"But you are stronger than I am."

"I'm not so sure. I *have* been accused of being a *prima donna,* not that I've understood exactly why." She screwed up her face. "Anyway, I've learned to become more confident by risking everything time and time again. You just don't have enough practice yet. I'm not saying it's easy and of course this is much harder than an audition, but it becomes easier over time."

"I get your point. Just knowing you are in this with me makes all the difference."

He stood up and kissed her hard on the lips.

"Hmm, I could use some more of that."

She wrapped her arms around his neck and luxuriated in his embrace.

*****

When they returned to New York, she waited until Saturday morning to broach a subject she had been avoiding. After she dressed for their morning run, she looked around his apartment at what could one day be hers.

"I've been meaning to ask you something, but there never seems to be a good time."

She pulled him toward her. He looked into her limpid eyes.

"I just have a few questions."

Her hands sweated, her stomach tightened.

"What kind of relationship do you have with Dr. Stanley? Why haven't I been introduced to your mother or any of your friends? Why haven't you invited me to any family event as your girlfriend? Why haven't you come to hear me sing since the first time you and your father came to *la Maison Française*?"

His face reddened as he squirmed loose.

"I feel like I'm an adjunct to the rest of your life. I'm wondering if it's something about me, or is it because I'm an employee, or am I just a fling and you're not serious about me, or are you having second thoughts so you leave me in only one small part of your life, or are you just screwed up and willing to let other people run your life?"

Tears spilled down her cheeks. He looked down and

shuffled his feet.

"What is there to say? That I am weird? That I compartmentalize everything for emotional survival? That I want to keep you all to myself? I will admit that part of me wants to avoid the answers, but, in truth, I-I care too much about you."

He moved closer, took her hands in his, and peered into her bleary eyes.

"I have no good excuses, except that I-I have been trying to protect you, protect myself, from my family. What I want to say is, they can be rather difficult."

"I know that, but you've never introduced me to anyone as your *girlfriend*, except your personal staff."

"You are better off. If Belinda knew we were together, she would be vicious. And the others, I-I really don't know."

"I can handle myself," she barked.

"I do *not* want you to have to handle anything, to-to deal with snide, insensitive comments or insinuations. You think it won't hurt you."

"I didn't say they couldn't hurt me, but that I could handle it." Her face set. "I get it. I realize you thought you were being noble. But that still doesn't explain your mother, your friends, Dr. Stanley."

She withdrew her hand.

"I-I feel sure Mother would love you. At least, I think she would, but I hardly see her and, I guess I just haven't felt ready to tell my mother about you. After all, she knows practically nothing about my life anymore."

He cleared his throat and looked down at his fingernails. She gently lifted his chin toward her gaze.

"I'm sorry, George. This is painful for you. I feel insensitive for having asked..."

"No, I should have told you. I-I just didn't want to think about it, I guess. There has been so much going on. *Gran'maman*'s death. The bar. I just wanted you all to myself."

He looked away.

"Dr. Stanley does what you wish your family would do. Affirm you for who you are."

He looked at her with stinging eyes.

"I never would have put it like that, but I guess so. *Gran'maman* was my anchor, but she is gone now. And Dr. Stanley. I-It is strictly professional. I don't see her the same way as my mother or grandmother. I mean, maybe I have some affection. I don't know. She is a wise, caring person who allows me to vent and clarify my thinking without judging me. I respect her opinion. But what does it matter?"

"I j-just thought it might be more than that."

His shoulders bristled.

"Why, are you jealous?"

He bolted and glared at her.

"*Chéri*, I wasn't suggesting anything. It was just puzzling. I-I just want to understand you better. Everything's so different from what I'm accustomed to."

"Why? Don't you trust me? Are you looking for a reason to break things off?"

Hot fear covered his face.

"No," she mumbled.

Scalding tears ran like lava down her face.

"It's just that I've been emotionally in this place before. I'm sure I'm misjudging everything. I love you so deeply I just had to know."

Sobs caught in her throat. He rushed to her.

"What is it, *chérie*?"

He led her to the loveseat and wrapped his arms around her.

"M, I live in a small, controlled world. It-it makes me weird. I'm sorry if I was on the defensive. I-I need to trust you more with my feelings. I thought I did, but maybe I need to be more transparent."

Her face throbbed.

"*Chérie*, what is it?"

She fidgeted and wrung her hands.

"Is it something you have not told me?"

He stiffened. She sat upright.

"It has nothing to do with you. I once loved a man, heart and soul, and there are things in our relationship that are too reminiscent of..."

She debated whether to tell him about the ordeal her first love, Donald, and graduate school had put her through, but some things were best left unsaid.

"I-I just needed to know that we'll be okay. We will be, won't we?"

Her eyes sought purchase.

"Of course. But who has broken your heart?"

"It was a long time ago and I'm way over him. It doesn't matter if you and I are alright. We are, aren't we?"

His body relaxed.

"Of course. I'm sorry I did anything to make you doubt me."

"Are you sure?"

He nodded. Her shoulders relaxed, and her rigid jaw turned to butter. He pulled her toward him, took her hands in his, and scooped her into his arms.

Chapter 12

Mr. Leibnitz started working out of his home office on Fridays. One of the chauffeurs picked up M at 8:00 for the hour and a half drive to Wilton and brought her home at the end of the day. One Friday after dictating a letter, Mr. Leibnitz peered into her eyes.

"You know, Ms. Staunton, I envy George."

She bristled.

"Look at this room. My father made brave men tremble by bringing them here."

She followed his gaze, taking in the raw power in the violence of the Delacroix paintings, the brute force of the muscular Rodin sculptures, and the virile quality of the dark leather and mahogany furniture and bookshelves.

"H-He turned every screw to dominate us all."

He turned, his eyes piercing through her as if she were a ghost.

"George will have options I never had. He does not understand what I have sacrificed for him. What I will do for him alone."

Sadness filled his eyes. He turned his head to the window.

"I was so driven to prove my worth, to rid myself of Papa's domination, to wrest control from Guenther after his death. I never once considered another path. And now it is their turn. George and Marcus must learn the ways of men and make hard decisions about who they will become, about who the next CEO will be."

His voice softened.

"By all rights, it should be George. He should have it all. Ah, but will he, Ms. Staunton? Will he?"

He fingered the curves of the leather chair behind the massive desk, eyes frowning.

She wondered if he was seeing his father take his last breath in that chair and his freedom from domination.

"We are at a difficult crossroads."

His head jerked in her direction.

"I want my son to become all he is capable of, but I must consider carefully the future of my company. And my legacy."

She held his gaze with a fluttering heart.

"I will do all I can for George."

He paused, inhaled slowly, exhaled, and slumped in his chair.

He cocked his head and said, "Perhaps, it is time for a rapprochement with Guenther. I must talk to him about Marcus. He has been working full-time in the executive suite since he received his engineering degree from M.I.T and the MBA from Wharton so..."

He turned away and stood, as if looking for some long-sought-after friend outside in the sun-drenched parterre. She followed his gaze.

He touched his lips. "I see a lot of myself in him. Ambition, intelligence, cleverness. He obviously needs mentoring to smooth out the rough edges and tone down some of his need for power. We *cannot* have another Rainer Leibnitz."

He sighed. "Marcus has no idea what leading entails."

She nodded. He looked at her with tender eyes.

"In time, George may come around," he whispered. "You understand me, *n'est-ce pas*?"

She swallowed hard.

Chapter 13

The next few months blurred with work, writing, rehearsals, and performances. M had no time for George.

The cousins' offices were down the executive suite hall, so her orbit included run-ins with Marcus. His arrogance and unbridled ambition needled her. If only George would exhibit more backbone, he could succeed his father in five to ten years. He needed to have the drive and conviction to make the kinds of decisions his father made every day. She would not allow Marcus to fill that role. She would embolden George.

Her spine tingled at his dinner invitation to the Box Tree on East 49th Street one Friday morning. She and George had spent so little time together that she relished the thought of an evening alone.

The *maître d'* escorted them to a quiet corner.

Once seated, George turned to her.

"I can't tell you how relieved I am to be able to get on with my life. I have so much I want to say."

"Take your time."

The *maître d'* interrupted with two glasses of champagne cocktail. With each sip her eyes encouraged George to continue. She set down her champagne glass when a sparkle at the bottom of the fluted crystal caught her attention.

"Something wrong?"

As the bubbles swirled and she tilted the glass, her eyes caught more sparkles.

"Here, let me see."

He slithered his knife down into the liquid and pulled out a dazzling silver-gold ring with an array of three large stones.

"I-I-I, wha-diamonds? They're soooo big!"

"3.65 carats each. Van Cleef & Arpels' finest, made for you."

"Y-You don't mean..."

Her eyes enveloped him as he kneeled at her side.

"Will you marry me, despite all my peccadilloes and shortcomings?"

Her heartbeat raced, and her eyes brimmed with happy tears.

"Yes!"

The restaurant erupted in applause.

The evening became a blur. Confidence in his voice could only mean that he had sailed through the bar exam. Captured in the moment, she barely touched the exquisite repast. When they had finished dessert he escorted her upstairs to an Art Deco suite. He twirled her round and round in his arms until they fell onto the king-size bed and luxuriated in their love.

The next day he burst unannounced into his father's office when he was in the midst of dictating a letter to her. When they shared their exciting news, Mr. Leibnitz broke into a wide smile.

"Finally. I am glad for you. I wish you much happiness."

His face bloomed with pride.

"Thanks, Father. I have more news. I passed the bar and I have decided to start my own business."

Mr. Leibnitz smiled, then frowned.

"You should have consulted me."

M's stomach knotted.

George fumbled, "I-I was afraid you would not approve."

His father's mouth curled. "Indeed. What business could you possibly have in mind? Do you have a business plan? A location? You have a responsibility to your family that cannot be thrown away on a whim." He flicked his wrist. "What makes you think you can be successful in business when you have not even learned enough about one readymade for you? Granted, you now have the bar under your belt, but how do you expect to support a wife and family?"

His mouth set.

"We shall discuss this another time."

George's face caved in. He took M's hand and turned to leave.

"George, you may go. Ms. Staunton, sit down. We have work to do."

She obeyed.

"Where were we? Ah, the arrangements must be..." He frowned. "I simply do not understand George. How can I possibly persuade him to leave behind his naïveté, his idealism, and see the world as it is? Papa's approach was cruel but effective."

He drummed his fingers on the edge of his spacious desk. The wings of her heart quivered.

"Papa was foolish, however clever he might have been. With Guenther at the helm, LE would have become stodgy, and our wealth would be long gone by now. Even he will admit that. I diversified into land development, resource management, and telecommunications."

He sniggered.

"Could my father possibly have thought my phlegmatic brother would risk everything to increase our wealth and position three-fold in only ten years? It was Aleksandra, not Rainer, who had the vision of a greater empire and the foresight to put her energies into orchestrating the right successor to expand into new territories. What would she say now about her beloved grandson?"

She watched the wheels of his mind turn.

"Aleksandra shared with me her plans for him. She knew he would become so dependent on his lifestyle that he would never be able to leave it behind. He would grow into his role with time and training."

He stared at her.

"Perhaps, her vision was clouded by love. She was certain he would make us proud. That remains to be seen, *n'est-ce pas?*"

He sucked in his teeth.

"His trust fund has certain conditions."

He smiled with the smugness of a victor counting his spoils.

"His beloved *Gran'maman* would never allow him *not* to fulfill his assigned role. He has no experience of what life is like outside the family. Imagine, a middle-class lifestyle. How-how repugnant."

Her cheeks reddened.

"He has never had to sacrifice. The very concept would be anathema to him. Has he given any thought to needing to save money, create budgets, earn a paycheck? Does he realize how much everything costs? Anything he has ever wanted has been his for the asking. With his driver's license came the Maserati. For his twenty-first birthday, his island home and staff. For graduate school, partial access to his trust fund, a limousine with driver, and a tony condo on Fifth Avenue with staff. Access to aircraft, yachts, houses on four continents, bodyguards, and vacations around the world. He has no concept of even an upper-middle-class existence."

He frowned and crossed his arms.

She understood all too well what their life would be like without LE.

"He wants to make a difference."

"I beg your pardon."

He uncrossed his arms and turned toward her as if he hadn't known she was there all along. Her eyes brightened.

"He wants something of his own to be passionate about."

He smirked.

"I see. Then we must make sure he has that chance."

He picked up the phone.

"Don't be fooled by his idealism. He *is* a Leibnitz."

A flick of his wrist dismissed her. Her heart shivered. As the future Mrs. George Leibnitz, she couldn't afford to antagonize the family patriarch, but his manipulation bittered her heart.

Chapter 14

The following week M accompanied her boss, Parker Gibson, one of the French vice-presidents Marcel, and Mrs. Belinda on the second trip in two months from New York to Miami on the 737 to oversee negotiations on a telecommunications deal.

Mrs. Leibnitz beggared a private conversation with M while her husband conversed with the men. The ladies sat in the plush leather armchairs at the far end of the spacious lounge while the men huddled together at the oblong conference table of dark veneer in the center of the cabin. M's stomach knotted. Mrs. Belinda never traveled with her husband when M accompanied him, so she prepared herself for the usual condescension.

As soon as the plane reached altitude, Mrs. Leibnitz turned to her.

"*Fraulein,* how often do you travel vith my husband?"

"Quite often, with a cadre of senior staff."

"I understand you are a singer and zat you speak several languages."

"Yes, Mrs. Belinda. Would you prefer we speak German?"

Her sloe eyes examined M.

"My English is *güt* enough. Remember your station."

Her voice lowered as she impaled M with a penetrating stare.

"*Und* I vould remind you, *Fraunlein,* zat vhile you may

spend more time zan I do vith my husband, zee bedroom belongs to me, *und* I take no prisoners."

M's stomach thudded to her knees.

"Excuse me?"

"*Zie verstehen.*"

"Mrs. Belinda, you don't know me very well to suggest that I..."

She hissed, "You vould not be zee first. *Und* do not botzzer to deny it."

She glared.

"You are young and impressionable, *und* it is all understandable. Ve all are taken in by Fritz's charm, but I vill not tolerate..."

Her voice trailed off as she became aware that he was glowering at her.

M would have relished revealing that she was engaged to George to put Mrs. Belinda in *her* place.

Mrs. Leibnitz asked her what she thought about Kathleen Battle's recent Met performance. When they had exhausted that topic, she asked if M bought her suits at Brooks Brothers.

"Paul Stuart, actually."

She sneered.

"I did not realize ve paid you zat much."

M's eyebrows shot up.

"Lovely Italian voolen-silk combination. Zose are Bally shoes, *ja?*"

"Bottega Veneta."

She frowned and fingered the toe of one shoe.

"You have a good eye."

"Thank you."

M swallowed a comeback: *Nice St. John knit dress but too tight, too short, too much of a plunging neckline. But the diamond and emerald tear-drop earrings, matching bracelet, and choker provide a touch of class.* She returned a professional smile instead.

The mood lightened as Mrs. Leibnitz prattled on about her thirteen-year-old son, Claude, and her eight-year-old daughter, Brianna.

When the plane landed, M wanted to tell George about the conversation, but swallowed the thought.

Chapter 15

Work consumed most of M's mental energy. She started losing focus on her dissertation and upcoming Carnegie Hall concert with the New York Choral Society as her life became subsumed by the demands of her position. Her loyalty vacillated between George and his father. Legacy pervaded everything and trapped the entire family. She couldn't ask for advice from anyone she knew, as they would have personal agendas. Perhaps Dr. Stanley would help her. M called her with trepidation. George needed to give his blessing before Dr. Stanley would set the appointment.

M's heart trembled when she approached him after fixing a sumptuous meal in her kitchen.

His eyes flashed.

"Why do you want to see *her*?"

She started clearing the table.

"I thought she could help me sort out some issues."

He stood to help her.

"What issues?"

She moved away.

"I feel torn in many directions. I had a *very* unpleasant conversation with your stepmother two weeks ago on the trip to Florida. My work is suffering. I don't want to hurt you or your father, and it's unfair to unload it on you."

He smiled as he handed her a plate.

"Oh, is that all?"

"What do you mean, is that all?" she snapped, moving toward the dishwasher. "Are my problems of no real importance?"

Tears clouded her vision.

He touched her arm.

"I-I didn't mean it like that. I-I'm just a bit paranoid."

She pushed past him to collect the cloth napkins.

"The world doesn't revolve around you, George Leibnitz."

He followed behind her.

"I'm sorry. Please forgive me."

His eyes sought hers.

"Of course, I'm dying to know what foul thing Belinda said, but I want to help you."

She moved toward the laundry basket in the cramped lavatory.

"I-I think I need a more objective opinion."

He called after her, "Sure. What about your thesis advisor?"

She glared at him as she rounded the corner into the living area.

"I've already considered everyone I know, but none of them would be objective."

He gave her a mewling look.

"Even me?"

She turned away.

"Our emotions are so tied together, you couldn't..."

He moved toward her.

"I suppose. B-But I'm not sure I want to share Dr. Stanley with you."

Her eyes hardened as she slumped onto the couch.

"What exactly do you mean?"

He moved to sit next to her. She shot up and moved past him.

"It-It's not what you think," he said.

She frowned.

"And exactly what am I thinking?"

"I-I think maybe, she-she's kinda a mother figure. But it's all professional, non-judgmental."

She retreated.

"Don't you see, that's what *I* need?"

He looked up at her.

"I know it's selfish of me. I just..."

She scooted in next to him.

"What if we went together to talk to her?"

He smiled.

"Would that really help? She's not a couples' counselor, you know."

She tapped her foot.

"Yes, of course. But she could be objective."

"Okay."

His eyes betrayed his doubts. She sighed. She would go with or without him.

The next day, he showed up at her desk to see his father. She felt Frederick's eyes boring in as she and George exchanged pleasantries. After he left, she didn't see him until arriving at his apartment that evening.

As she put down her briefcase, he rushed over and took her hands in his.

"Guess what happened?"

She raised her eyebrows. "You quit?"

He grinned. "I was making my way down the staircase to the library, and on the second set of stairs I absent-mindedly bumped into... Guess."

Her eyes shot up. "Your stepmother?"

"Marcus was making his way up the stairs."

She squared her shoulders and sat down on the sofa. He joined her.

"He told me to watch where I was going. I said I hadn't seen him. He studied me and then asked to speak to me. I hedged, then said I would meet him in an hour."

She grinned and took his hand.

"Go on."

"We agreed to meet in the executive lounge for coffee. It's usually quiet there after lunch time. I was suspicious, but curious."

She squeezed his hand. "So?"

"We made ourselves comfortable near the window in the two red Moroccan leather armchairs."

She smiled at his need to enumerate every detail. "Yes."

"A waiter brought our cappuccinos and disappeared into the kitchen, and Marcus said he thought we might join forces because we each bring different talents and expertise to the table. Me with the law, him with finance and engineering. He said we'd make a good team."

She scrunched up her face. "What's he up to, I wonder."

His brow furrowed. "Exactly. He must be on Father's bad side and looking for some way to finagle his way into his good graces. Two can play this game. I told him it was a brilliant idea. I smiled, sipped my coffee, and said I would mention it to Father at one of our breakfast meetings. Then he said I need not bother Father with anything until we work out the details."

She leaned in. "So what'd you say?"

He smirked. "I said I would never mention our conversation since Father would be cross if he thought someone was plotting right under his nose."

She giggled and shook her head. "You didn't."

His face blossomed. "I did! He backtracked. I got up and slapped his knee and told him I would put in a good word for him, Father really liked him, that sort of thing. Maybe I do have the killer instinct, after all."

He exhaled in victory. Her stomach tightened. He was entering a dangerous game without the weapons Marcus had at his disposal.

When they went to their appointment with Dr. Stanley the

next evening, George seemed eager. M's damp palms and cold feet entered the room and sat down.

"So, how may I help you?" Dr. Stanley asked her.

"I'm losing myself to other peoples' urgencies. I feel *guilty* to devote time to my studies or my music. I eat, breathe, sleep Leibnitz. I adore George."

He beamed.

"I love the work. I even feel guarded affection for his family, especially his father. He has an impossibly difficult job. It's just that I'm feeling pulled from all sides."

Her eyes pooled.

"Have you talked to George about your feelings?"

She avoided looking at him.

"Not directly."

"Why not?"

"It's so complicated. I wasn't sure he'd understand."

"I see. What do you think he wouldn't understand?"

She looked down. "He has the luxury to be able to focus on one or two things at the exclusion of everything else, unlike me. So much hinges on my meeting everyone's expectations. On top of that, Mr. Leibnitz is the only person who knows about us, so I always have to be on my guard. I've almost slipped up a few times, forgetting to hide my engagement ring at work."

Pent-up frustration set her mouth.

"I think you've held it together remarkably well. This time six months from now, if all your wishes came true, describe your life."

M's eyes widened. "*All* my wishes?"

"Where would you be, what would you be doing, with whom?"

For the first time since sitting down, M's eyes embraced George. "We would have all the details of our wedding set. I'd have my Ph.D., I'd be pursuing an international business opportunity, I'd be singing gospel music in a church, giving three to four concerts a year, and making my first CD."

"You have a clear sense of what you want." Dr. Stanley turned to George. "What do you think?"

His eyes enveloped M. "You are a decisive wonder."

She smiled. "You see my dilemma, don't you?"

He frowned. "Not really. You can quit your job any day you want. I will explain to Father..."

Her back stiffened. "No! I can't have you..."

"Father must be anticipating you will quit, all things considered. That would solve your problems."

"Yes, but I can't just up and leave him and Frederick in the lurch. Besides, I need to earn an income."

His eyes widened. "No, you are my responsibility now."

She frowned. "No, I'm not. Everyone will say I'm marrying you for your money, not because I adore you and can't imagine life without you. Besides, I want a meaningful career. I want to make a real difference. And you said you want to be on your own without the LE safety net."

His lips pursed.

Dr. Stanley interjected, "You've been living on your own for a long time, haven't you?"

M nodded.

"It can be hard to let go of independence. The fear of being diminished, even extinguished." She paused. "One might say that being vulnerable is the greatest act of love."

M's eyes pooled. George squeezed her hand.

"It doesn't matter what other people think as long as we know who you are," he murmured. "It would honor me greatly if you would let me take care of you."

Her eyes bathed him in love. "Thank you, *chéri*. That means a lot."

He smiled. "You shouldn't quit tomorrow. We should sit down with Father and discuss an exit strategy, even discuss some future role in the company. I need to figure out my role, too. I might be able to do something more worthwhile under the Leibnitz umbrella than on my own. I'm not clear on that yet. I know I told Father I want to start my own business, but then he dismissed me, and I just went along with..."

M screwed up her face. "That could be dangerous. He will sense your lack of direction and channel you where *he* wants you to go."

Her eyes implored Dr. Stanley, who turned to him.

"Indeed. Where do *you* see yourself six months from now?"

A pool of doubt flooded his eyes. "You're the only two with whom I feel completely free. I need to become the leader *Gran'maman* wanted me to be. I know why she chose me. I don't have the right to be selfish. However, I want no part of intrigue and plots. I want it to end with me. I will operate under a different kind of ethics."

He looked at both of them in turn. "I need your help."

They smiled.

"M, we talked about discovering who you are and not living in the image someone else has created for you. I've been trying to please my family my whole life. They have saddled me with a role that doesn't fit who I am."

Her eyes encouraged him.

"I know so little about how our business runs or any business really. Father is right. LE needs both Marcus and me. If I can only get him to see that."

He stared into space, then turned to her. "I feel guilty that I have so much without doing anything to earn it."

She took his hand. "Why should you feel guilty? It's not your fault you were born into wealth. You should be proud that you don't want to rest on the laurels of what your family developed."

"But I *am* living off what *they* created. I have contributed nothing. The only reason I wanted to lead LE is to beat Marcus."

She squeezed his hand. "Are you jealous or do you think

he doesn't *deserve* to have it?"

"I-I'm not sure. He has always beaten me at just about everything that matters."

"Matters to whom, your father?" Dr. Stanley interjected.

George turned toward her. "Yes. But also to me. I'm not built like Father, or Marcus, or maybe even Uncle Guenther. I don't have the-the emotional energy, or-or the drive to fight Marcus for power the way Father fought Uncle Guenther. Now, I'm the heir apparent. But I'm not really sure I want it. I have no vision for LE's future. But the real issue is I don't want to be ruthless and ruin everything."

M touched his knee. "I'm not trying to talk you in or out of anything. You can run a family business without being cut-throat or destroying lives. But having no passion for it will destroy you and LE. If you can make your mark by steering it toward what you value, then you could pull it off, right?"

She looked at Dr. Stanley, who nodded.

"Maybe you have to make your mark on something you create. At the very least, you need to find your purpose."

He laughed. "You sound just like Dr. Stanley."

M blushed. "Well, I don't know about that."

"Seriously, I haven't been able to think much beyond school and passing the bar. I've lost the big picture in the process. My purpose has been to fulfill *Gran'maman*'s expectations to run her empire without even understanding what that entails."

Dr. Stanley interjected, "Now, you see, you said *her* empire. What do *you* want?"

"I-I don't know."

He stiffened, and his fingers straightened the crease in his slacks.

"That's a raw spot for you, isn't it?" M asked.

"Uh-huh."

"You went from being excited about the possibility of doing something authentic, and then became engulfed in someone else's vision again."

He laughed.

"I have to stop doing that. I really need your support to chart my own course."

Her heart quivered. "What do you have in mind?"

His eyes sought purchase. "I need both of you to help me."

M brightened. "What do you want us to do?"

"Help me flesh out a direction. I have vague notions of advocating for individuals with disadvantages and conditions that hold people back through the foundation. I could probably convince Father to support some programs for marketing and publicity purposes. But I need to understand the ins and outs of LE first. It will take years to make something happen even when I know exactly what I want to do. Then I will be ready to lead LE."

M smiled. "Don't doubt yourself or let years of expectations hold you back. Just the idea of wanting to change the ethical framework of leadership at LE is a dream. I'll help you."

His eyes pleaded. "Will you really?"

She squeezed his hand. "Of course."

He looked at Dr. Stanley. "What do you think?"

"You've taken a big step tonight. Of course, I'd be pleased to help. You don't need all the answers now. I'm sure your father has much to teach you if you approach him correctly."

He smiled at her. "I think I understand. I remember you told me that I would need to leave my comfort zones and grow *into* the person I want to be. I'm really uncomfortable. Just a few moments ago, all I could think about was the crease in my pants being off-center. Order gives me a feeling of safety and control. The thought of charting a new direction enthralls me, but scares me."

He slapped his knees and laughed. "Now I could care less about my trousers."

Dr. Stanley smiled. "That's wonderful. M, how do you

think you could best support George and not lose yourself in the process? That's why you came tonight."

M cocked her head. "I see a role for me in George's vision. I've wanted to be more than a college professor and *artiste*. I like the idea of becoming involved in the foundation or being the ambassador for his future initiatives. I think there could be a place for me, and I'm thrilled at the possibilities. Somehow, just knowing we'd work together helps."

"That's wonderful. I think you'd make excellent partners."

George grimaced. "But how do we do this and at the same time lighten your load so you can complete the requirements for your doctorate and not put your music on the backburner?"

"W-e-ll, I need to tell your father my schedule must change."

"What if we tell him that once your degree is completed and you are my wife, we would like to explore a role for you within the foundation, as a start?"

She frowned. "Until we have something clearly defined, he will override our thinking with his own agenda. You know how he is."

He nodded.

"If I might make a suggestion," Dr. Stanley interjected.

They turned toward her.

"Focus only on M's immediate need to have the time to complete her degree and maintain her concert schedule. If you approach Mr. Leibnitz with too much, he may misunderstand what you want and think he's helping by making preemptive decisions. I don't think your father's trying to hurt you, George, but he sees his company and your future differently than you do."

"I get your point."

"In fairness, he has many years of experience, an entire group of companies, plus his family to think of. Giving him the most urgent need rather than the future plans you haven't fully worked out should elicit a more straightforward response. He's a problem solver, so don't give him too many problems to solve."

M nodded. "She's right. The level of responsibilities he has is mind boggling. There's far more going on than meets the eye."

George squared his shoulders. "Go ahead and talk to Father."

Chapter 16

The next day M waited on tenterhooks to speak to her boss. The opportunity arose at the end of the day. When she told him she needed his advice, he suggested she join him for dinner, as he was staying in town. They often ate dinner together in his office when he stayed at the UN Plaza Hotel.

They arrived at the Quilted Giraffe at seven. The hostess whisked them in front of the waiting patrons to a table in a secluded corner. The scrutiny of other diners followed them to their banquette. Mr. Leibnitz ordered a bottle of *Dom Pérignon*. M hid her surprise at his wine selection for their meeting. He broke her musing by regaling her with details about the Pavarotti concert he had attended at *La Scala* on his recent trip to Italy.

Abruptly he changed the subject. "Enough of that. When do you and George plan to marry? A year, year-and-a-half from now sounds about right. I assume you will rearrange your schedule as the date approaches."

She masked her pique with a smile. "Actually, I need to discuss my schedule. We would like to have the wedding within six months, but first I need to complete my Ph.D., which I cannot accomplish working seventy hours a week. And I can't prepare properly for concerts."

His eyes narrowed. "What do you propose?"

They were interrupted by the arrival of the champagne.

He turned toward the waiter. She looked down at her taut

hands and relaxed them on her lap.

"There we are. First, a toast to the loveliest, most talented future daughter-in-law on the planet," he said with a flourish of the fluted glass.

She blushed.

The *maître d'* recited the specialties.

M breathed in to gather her nerves and exhaled slowly.

"To complete the requirements by May, I can only work 9:00-3:00, no weekends, no trips. I will train an assistant to fill in and take over my position in about five months."

Her eyes fixed his. He frowned.

"It will totally disrupt my life for you to scale back so much and to then lose you to George. I would be bereft without you."

His lips pouted. Her eyebrows shot up. She smiled.

"I realize it will be quite a sacrifice. Naturally, I will understand if you would rather replace my position right away instead."

He threw her a charming smile. "There is nothing I can do to induce you to alter your plans, then?"

"No."

"May I ask how you would survive without George to support you if you were not in my employ?"

Her eyes shot bullets and her spine straightened. "I've always found the resources to independently support myself since I was sixteen. I will adjust, I assure you."

He chuckled and unfolded his napkin. "Yes, I rather think you would. You are good for George. Pity I did not win you over first."

The faintest flicker of disgust turned her mouth as she glared.

He eyed her coyly. "My dear, does George know where you are tonight?"

She leaned forward with daggers for eyes. "Why wouldn't he?"

He smirked. "I might warn you, M—may I call you M?—

that some could view this evening in a, shall we say, suspicious light."

Her lips trembled as she melted into the banquette. "Excuse me?"

"No one knows you are George's fiancée. People can be quite vicious when provoked."

Her eyebrows shot up and she grinned. "Mr. Leibnitz, I imagine a formal announcement of my engagement will solve that nicely. Of course, all your secrets are safe with me."

His face fell.

She took inventory of the names of mistresses for whom she had been instructed to buy gifts and make bank withdrawals for his driver to deliver. She was privy to deals that his brother would love to know about and arrangements that would ruin his chances of any reconciliation with his wife.

He laughed. "*Touché*. I was only testing you. I would *never* ruin George's happiness. I am rather fond of you, in a fatherly way. I would never deliberately hurt you. It will give me great pleasure to fend off the character assassins."

Her eyes smiled and her hands unclenched. "Yes, you may call me M."

The waiter approached, ready to take the order. As she considered the options, Mr. Leibnitz said, "Mademoiselle will start with the oyster bisque, and then the pistachio-crusted halibut, the mushroom risotto, and the garlic asparagus, followed by the *salade frisée*."

She hid her rising pique.

He turned toward her. "I want you to finish your degree and share your lovely voice with the world. We can manage a way for you to do everything. Hire an assistant and change your hours. Let us say, when I am gone for a week or more, you work half days. For example, I will leave next Thursday for Jakarta for four days, so work no more than three hours. When I am in town, come in at 10:00 instead of 8:00, because I am usually not in the office until 10:00, and leave at 4:00. No

Saturdays or Sundays except in emergencies. When you travel with me, either Frederick or the new assistant comes along to assist you. Carve out enough time to work on your dissertation while traveling. You are free to work on personal projects on the job as time permits. Of course, reserve time to prepare for concerts."

She sighed and folded her hands. "What do I tell employees about my engagement? I don't want them thinking..."

He nodded. "...that you are receiving special favors? If *anyone* makes you feel the slightest bit uncomfortable, come directly to me at once. I will not tolerate it."

She smiled despite her annoyance at his making every decision for her.

A bright light flashed. Through pulsing light and darkness, she detected the shadow of a well-dressed man with a professional camera edging away. Mr. Leibntiz jerked up and knocked against the man's elbow.

"Damned paparazzi!"

The *maître d'* and two burly waiters surrounded the photographer. She watched with horror as her boss snatched the camera, opened it, and exposed the film. The *maître d'* apologized while the waiters forced the photographer to the exit. The buzz of the diners filled the air. She swallowed tears and closed her face like a fist. Her enraged employer berated the *maître d'* and brandished words like *salaud*. He threw his forefinger under the *maître d'*'s nose and returned to the table.

With a stoic face he muttered, "Call George to come at once."

She fought back tears.

"Do it now."

Retrieving her mobile phone from her briefcase, her fingers quivered as she dialed. Hearing George's voice calmed her nerves, but being a public spectacle dampened her appetite.

Mr. Leibnitz sighed. "I am very sorry this has happened. If

I had had any warning of this-this breach of privacy, I would never have brought you here. I must speak to Robert about security."

She looked down at her lap.

"The Quilted Giraffe has lost a customer tonight."

She whispered, "Can we just drop it?"

"Certainly. Do try to eat something."

She looked up at him. "I see what you're trying to do with George coming."

He grinned. "Indeed. Let tonight be your unofficial announcement, and we will leave as a happy family after dessert."

She knew that once the story was out she would be scrutinized and labeled. Anger rose in her throat that he had brought her here instead of ordering from the Oyster Bar or asking his chef to prepare them a meal. When George arrived twenty minutes later with an extra bodyguard tightly at his heel, M had eaten only four or five bites.

George fumed, "Father, what is going on? A mob scene of reporters and photographers are camped outside. Robert and Sebastian had to push their way through."

His father gave him his seat on the banquette and a chair instantly appeared along with a rack of lamb with garlic mashed potatoes and grilled vegetables. Hearing Mr. Leibnitz recount the details made M queasy.

"The two of you should take a few moments alone. I will go to the men's room. Remember, all eyes are on you," he added, vacating the chair.

Her head nestled onto George's shoulder, warmth spreading through her chest. As he stroked her hand, his father engaged in a heated conversation with Robert, who spoke to Sebastian to stay at a discreet distance from the couple while he followed his boss. By the time he returned to the table, her stomach was settled.

He enthused, "Now, we really should celebrate your

engagement."

A quick nod to the *maître d'* produced a large chocolate soufflé and a side dish of English cream with fresh raspberries. The *maître d'* and wait staff started singing "Congratulations to you" to the tune of "Happy Birthday." The buzz of diners' voices turned warm and favorable. George and M basked in the approval. She could see Mr. Leibnitz's mind working. Who had sent the paparazzi?

*****

When she arrived at the office the next morning, the buzz about her engagement and the previous night's dinner surrounded her. Concentration eluded her as her thoughts veered to parsing insincere compliments from genuine congratulations.

Frederick's reaction was endearing. "Dah-ling, I am overjoyed for you. I suspected as much. George is a lucky devil. Now, how can I help you? It's going to be a zoo around here for you."

She gave him a bear hug, and they set about to plan out the day. After a hectic morning, Mrs. Belinda appeared around noon, wearing a demure dark grey Nina Ricci satin pantsuit and silver silk shell. Both executive assistants knew their boss loathed unexpected interruptions. Frederick was starting to explain that her husband was unavailable when Mrs. Belinda turned to M with biting eyes.

"I'm sure, Mz. Staunton, or eeze it M now, has a *certain* influence to persuade my husband to see me. At least, zee papers seem to zink so."

M's back bristled. "Mrs. Belinda, whatever do you mean? George's father kindly hosted a small dinner for us last night. I assumed he told you that George and..."

Belinda aimed her index finger at her. "Vhat my husband does or does not tell me eeze none of your concern. Do not pretend innocence vith me, *Fraulein*. You don't know who you're dealing vith."

M smiled. "Mrs. Leibnitz, I believe I do."

Frederick's eyes met M's. He pushed the silent button to alert their boss. Mr. Leibnitz emerged within seconds from the sitting room that adjoined his office just as his wife was finishing her tirade.

"...slut who may be able to fool zee press *und* zee fools around here," she said glancing at Frederick, whose face remained a stone, "but not me. *I* have gotten rid of more..."

"Belinda," Mr. Leibnitz commanded as he walked into view, "we do not talk to our future daughter-in-law in that manner."

He put her elbow in a firm grip. She squirmed.

"Apologize at once," he growled in German.

She wrenched her arm from his grasp, scowled at M, then turned on her heel and marched down the hall out of sight, her head held high. M and Frederick had understood every word.

Their boss's grimace disappeared as he turned.

"Mr. Metz, if you would kindly excuse us for a moment. I am sure the scene you have just witnessed has already been forgotten."

"Of course, Mr. Leibnitz."

M knew Frederick was dying to find out the scoop from her and then tell his partner, Leo, all about it when he went home.

"Ms. Staunton, would you be so kind as to join me?"

He directed her with an open hand toward the sitting room.

She followed in silence, her heart pulsing. Once they were inside, he turned, his face soft.

"I cannot express my profound sorrow for my wife's conduct. I cannot make her apologize, but I humbly ask forgiveness on her behalf."

He put his hands over his chest.

"Is there anything at all I can do for you to make up in some way? Would you like to take the rest of the day off?"

She smiled. "Thank you, but really, it isn't necessary."

"You are not just being brave?"

She chuckled. "Oh, as a performer, I've been attacked many times. Believe me, I have pretty thick skin."

His head cocked. "Sounds fascinating. Do tell."

Her eyes widened. "Are you sure you have time?"

He grinned. "Who would not make time for what is surely a delicious story? Please. Would you like some refreshment?"

Her palpating heart stilled. "Water, thank you."

She accepted a glass of water poured from a pitcher he retrieved from the small fridge hidden behind the wooden paneling in the wall. She sat down on the beige suede couch and took a sip.

"Well, two particularly difficult moments, one when I was much younger on tour with a group of musicians and the other in January when I sang for the benefit concert you funded for Save the Children Foundation."

His eyebrows shot up. "Oh? What did I miss?"

"The first story is fairly typical. Jealousy that I had the starring role."

A knock on the door interrupted. Frederick's head appeared.

"Excuse me, sir. So sorry to interrupt. The gentlemen were just wondering..."

Fritz frowned. "Yes, yes."

He glanced at his Rolex. "Tell them it is time for a lunch break. Send them off to the executive lounge. Alert Chef they are coming. Ms. Staunton and I will join them shortly. Oh, and, Mr. Metz, please have Chef whip you up something while he is at it."

Frederick smiled. "Thank you kindly, sir. I will attend to everything at once."

As he closed the door behind him, Fritz turned to M.

"You will join us for lunch? I would like the executives to have the opportunity to offer you their congratulations."

Her mouth turned up. "Of course, if you like."

He nodded. His face darkened.

"I am anxious to hear who attacked you at my benefit. Anyone I know? Someone close to me, no doubt."

Her neck pulsed as she dove in. "You may recall, Raul drove Frederick and me to Bowling Green early to oversee final arrangements with the caterers and musicians, and for me to rehearse with the chamber ensemble before guests started arriving in the Great Hall."

He nodded with a warm smile. She gathered her courage.

"I had just met with the caterer, changed into my evening gown, and was making my way through the rotunda when Raul appeared. He said you were looking for me. I put on my coat and followed him outside down the stairs to you."

He nodded. "Yes, yes, you were wearing a long suede coat. I gave you last-minute instructions and went off with Raul to find Frederick. Go on."

She rushed on. "I was thinking about what I needed to do next. When I turned to go back up the stairs, I literally ran into..."

His lips curled. "Belinda?"

Her eyes widened. "How...?"

"On the way home that evening she said you were meddling in family affairs—being chummy with George, Marcus, anyone you could charm. She went on about you not remembering your place."

His eyes narrowed. "What did she do, and why did you not tell me about it?"

M's cheeks flamed. "Sh-she accused me of trying to seduce you after she had already warned me, told me she would ruin me if I did not leave..."

His back reared. "Already warned you?"

His eyes sharpened. M's stomach flopped.

"W-Well, she had warned me on the trip to Florida when..."

"I remember your face looked particularly uncomfortable. Go on."

"At Bowling Green, she tapped my face with her gloves and called me a couple of choice words I wouldn't repeat in polite company."

The fierceness in his eyes unsettled her stomach more.

"What did you do?"

"I said, 'Mrs. Belinda, you have *nothing* I want,' and pushed past her up the stairs."

A glimmer of a smile surfaced on his face. M's pent-up muscles relaxed.

"She is afraid of you, you know."

She cocked her head. "Wha-Whatever do you mean?"

"Your strength. You cannot be intimidated. You are bright and talented, but modest and unassuming. She assumes you would do what she would do in your place—actually, what she did."

Her face flushed. "Oh."

He smoothed his pant legs. "She respects you but would never admit it. She is jealous and running scared. She knows she is losing me and needs someone to blame, someone to attack. I think you understand, but I regret it has become you."

Her eyebrows shot up. He smiled.

"And yet despite that most upsetting exchange, you performed beautifully." His eyes were butter. "Is there a reason you did not tell me? Does George know?"

She looked down. "I-I didn't tell anyone."

He stroked his chin. "You were being noble, I am sure. You thought you were protecting us."

He smiled. She looked up.

"Frankly, I did what I thought you would have wanted."

"Thank you," he said softly. "I can always count on your

discretion. But in the future..."

His voice trailed off, and his face closed up. All the warmth left the room. He arose to leave.

Chapter 17

The next few days M had little time to concern herself with the whispers swirling through the office. Mr. Leibnitz tasked her with an extensive research project on Indonesian politics.

As she was searching for books in the library, Marcus sauntered in and brushed his hand lightly across her arm.

"Well, if it isn't Ms. Staunton, or should I call you M, as your intimates do? If I'd known you were playing father against son, I might have made it worth your while to stake your claim on this side of the family."

He sniggered and screwed up his face. Her eyes shot bullets.

"Careful. We wouldn't want Uncle Fritz to hear that you're manhandling George's merchandise, now would we?"

He put his hand over his heart. "You wound me."

She laughed and turned back to the thick books spread out in front of her.

"Here on some business or just trying to upset the hired help?"

He smiled, winked, and moved closer. "You're *very* clever, aren't you? Congrats and all that. Welcome to the family, however short your stay may be."

He threw her a sly smile and turned to leave. Her pride seethed, but she ignored him. He left her to her work.

Near the end of the day, she slipped her boss a note while he was dictating a memo. At the end of the meeting, he asked her to join him in his sitting room. Once inside, he directed her toward the beige suede couch. She avoided the couch and chose one of the dark-brown leather armchairs that faced each other across the long bronze table in front of the couch.

"Something is troubling you."

He sat down on the end of the couch closest to her. Despite her efforts to remain calm, as she related the incident with Marcus, her voice cracked and her eyes pooled.

"You are *really* upset."

When he reached over to touch her arm, she pulled away.

"Why do they all hate me so much? What have I ever done to any of them? I've been polite, deferential, professional, discreet. I've gone out of my way to be kind and understanding. I've..."

He handed her a box of tissues from the bronze side table.

"My dear, it is what you represent. But you already know this."

She nodded her head and pulled out a tissue.

"Of course, you have been a complete professional and done nothing wrong."

She sniffled and pressed the tissue against her nose.

"You and George should go to the Vineyard for the weekend and put all this behind you. Take Monday off. The weekend will put matters in perspective. Then, we will devise a plan."

Her eyes smiled. "That's very generous of you, but there's so much to do before your Indonesian trip."

He grinned. "Yes, well, Frederick will..."

"But it's not fair to leave him with..."

"You might be surprised at how delighted he will be to be indispensable."

His face opened up. "Now, off you go. My son is probably starving, waiting for you to come home."

He patted her on the knee, stood, and gave her the paternal French *bise*, kissing the air on either side of her cheeks. She left with a light step.

When she told George what had happened over a dinner of wilted spinach salad, orange bay scallops, and a bottle of Chardonnay, his eyes hardened.

"Belinda and Marcus are completely out of line. What's Father going to do about it? He does have a plan, doesn't he? He always has a plan."

Loyalty prevented her from divulging every detail. George might be sympathetic to his stepmother and cousin if he knew of his father's affairs, his callous disregard of his wife's feelings, his keeping Marcus off balance, and the ways in which he orchestrated everyone's life.

George polished off the last scallop. "I think we should visit Uncle Guenther before we head to the Vineyard."

She put down her fork and looked up. "Oh?"

He turned towards her. "I don't think he would allow anyone to treat you with less than the utmost respect."

Her lips turned down. She squeezed his arm. "But how will your father feel about us talking to your uncle? He may lose the upper hand."

He stroked his chin. "But what if we ask Uncle Guenther to keep it just between us?"

She shook her head. "Don't you think he might like to have an advantage over your father?"

"Maybe. But I think Uncle Guenther is fond of me and would be touched, flattered even, if I asked for help. Besides, I might need him on my side someday."

She pursed her lips. "But what will happen if your father finds out we've gone to his rival for support? We need to be careful."

He nodded. "Perhaps, I should go alone and not involve you. I don't need a reason to visit my uncle."

"Don't you think your father will...?"

He laughed. "Disown me? Not likely, unless he thinks I'm plotting against him. Obviously, Father doesn't want Belinda's brats involved with LE, and I doubt he's excited about Marcus as CEO. He wants me to lead the company one day unless I prove unable to meet his expectations."

She frowned and picked up her fork. "That may be true. Just be careful."

He sat up straight and patted his lips with the cloth napkin. "I will."

She said between bites, "And remember, *chéri*. Your uncle may not *appear* to be power hungry, but if he sees an opportunity, you might awaken the lion within him."

He pulled in his lips. "I will. But we need him right now. Trust me."

He flashed his irresistible smile. She sighed. He had no idea what might be unleashed. Mr. Guenther was, after all, Rainer Leibnitz's son.

Part 3

Only those who will risk going too far can possibly find out how far one can go.
—T.S. Eliot

Chapter 1

George entered the private elevator leading to his uncle's Park Avenue penthouse with a clenched stomach. He balanced the fear of going behind Father's back to asking Uncle Guenther for help regarding M's sullied reputation. He steeled his resolve to fulfill his mission. As he entered the foyer of the duplex apartment, his palms dampened. Inside the entrance hall, he spied a large round table covered with a colorful cloth of muted rose and green flowers on which a red star-shaped Baccarat crystal bowl filled with Werther's welcomed him. As he reached to put one in his pocket, his aunt approached.

"Please, take as many as you like. They are your favorites, *ja?*"

His nerves relaxed. He smiled.

"Yes. Thank you."

They embraced and chatted for a moment. He followed her lead through the large sunken living room up the wide spiral staircase into the library. They continued through the full-length French doors to an oversized patio framed by a perfectly manicured lawn, a variety of flowering bushes, and an herb-vegetable garden. His uncle was seated at a cozy oval teak table with matching chairs. He stood to greet George and asked his wife to send Hildegard to take George's breakfast order. The warmth of his aunt and uncle's greeting overcame his anxiety.

"*Ach, Georg,*" his uncle began in German, "to what do I

owe the honor of your long overdue visit?"

George blushed. "Yes, sir. I meant to come sooner, but with one thing and another, I-I never took you up on your offer."

Uncle Guenther smiled. "Not to worry, my boy. My brother would not have approved. Does Fritz know you are here?"

George's face reddened a shade darker and the irises in the garden instantly fascinated him. "No, actually, I-I... Why, should he?"

Uncle Guenther chuckled. "You *are* your father's son. I expect you did not drag yourself out at 7:00 on a Saturday morning to spar with your uncle, now did you?"

George frowned. "No. I need your advice. I cannot think of anyone else who can counsel me."

His uncle's eyebrows opened up. "You do not still see that doctor of yours? What is her name, Stan...?"

George's back stiffened. "Dr. Stanley. How do you know about her?"

Uncle Guenther smiled. "Fritz mentioned her. He says you do not make a move without consulting her."

George placed his hands on his thighs.

"Actually, I have not seen her recently. I feel comfortable asking your advice instead, sir."

His uncle's face opened up. "Well, then, tell me what is on your mind, my boy."

The maid appeared at George's elbow within moments. He ordered a croissant, blueberries, black tea, and orange juice.

After she left, he continued, "As I am sure you have heard, Father's assistant, Ms. Staunton, and I are engaged."

"Indeed. Congratulations. I am thrilled for you. Ms. Staunton is a fine, talented young lady."

"Yes, she is."

He proceeded to describe M's dilemma.

"Members of this family have suggested that lovely creature would deign to stoop to such base motives? Shocking!

What can I do to help? And why has my brother not set things right?"

Within moments the maid appeared and placed his breakfast on the place setting in front of him. George thanked her and quickly took a sip of juice to calm the butterflies batting his insides.

"I was hoping you could advise me. She doesn't want any special favors, but she has been treated badly. She does not want to quit. She is quite independent and fiercely loyal. The whole affair is just a mess. Father suggested I take her away for a long weekend while he devises a plan, but I am not sure he can control all the players, and I thought perhaps I should come up with a plan with your help."

He fidgeted with his croissant. The delicate folds of the buttery bread separated as the parts of his life now divided.

Uncle Guenther's face became stern. "Who is showing Ms. Staunton such disrespect?"

George's face turned a light shade of pink and his fingers became more frantic in separating each fold of the flaky crust of the roll.

A shadow crossed his uncle's face. "Marcus? I would rather hear it from you than from Fritz."

George nodded his head.

His uncle's eyes darkened. "I appreciate your honesty. I will handle my son."

"But..."

He patted George's arm. "Not to worry, my boy. Marcus will never know you said a word, I assure you. He is ambitious. Much like your father at that age. And I. But I changed, thanks to Mother and Tani. It is unwise to let ambition overpower love."

George's mind blanked.

His uncle's voice softened. "You are different. Your heart is tender. I have always seen that. And it is obvious to anyone who has met Ms. Staunton that hers is too. Her problems are only the tip of the iceberg, yes?" He paused. "Marcus is not the only one acting out of jealousy and fear."

Before George could formulate a reply, his uncle added, "Belinda, no doubt, has had her hand in this. Not Racquel, I hope..."

George shook his head.

"Mummy does not know yet."

His uncle nodded.

"Wise, wise indeed. Be careful, my boy, of Racquel, Belinda. And especially Fritz."

He chuckled as George's expression betrayed annoyance.

"No, my boy, I am not trying to turn you against him. Fritzie is a good man, but he will sacrifice many things, even people he loves, to ambition. He has taken LE to a level I never imagined. I admire his prowess. We have all benefited from his business acumen. Tripled our personal net worth. But I fear his Achilles heel is working against him, and by extension, Leibnitz Enterprises."

"Uncle Guenther, what are you afraid of?"

He pulled in his lips. "I am no longer afraid of my brother. Fear made me act stupidly when we were young. I knew he was far more intellectually gifted. I disappointed Papa time and again because I could not get the better of Fritzie on my own. But it was wrong to pit us against each other."

His shoulders slumped.

"Our course was set from the beginning. Mother alone was able to bring healing after Papa's death. And now we have our own distinct roles, ones for which we are well suited."

He sipped his coffee.

"But to answer your question, I fear Fritzie has set cousin against cousin. This pains me."

George cocked his head.

"What do you mean?"

Uncle Guenther placed his cup in the saucer.

"Even while Mother was alive, she encouraged Marcus to

think that one day he could be chairman of LE if you did not show yourself, shall we say, up to the demands of leadership."

George's face bristled.

"I am sorry to break this news to you, my boy, even though I am sure it is no surprise. I am quite fond of you. However, I cannot provide the advice you seek without being candid."

The truth slapped George's face.

"Go on."

"Mother encouraged both Fritzie and me to prepare both of you for leadership. I was delighted that he invited Marcus to intern in the corporate office during the summers in graduate school. I, likewise, sought to invite you to the engineering and machinery divisions to broaden your perspective. He said you were not ready, discouraged any contact with you, and disinvited Marcus. I deferred. A mistake. Certainly, Mother thought so. But I felt he knew what was best, though I suspect he did not want me to influence you. Honestly, I was tired of fighting."

He sighed a pained breath. "I love my brother and would do anything for him. I was not ready for another battle. I am truly sorry. In hindsight, I should have. For you."

Anger rose in George's throat. "I am sure you did what you thought was best. Father never told me of your overtures."

His uncle visibly shrank for an instant.

"I am not surprised. Fritzie would not want you to contact me. I suggest you not mention this meeting. He would feel threatened."

George drew in his eyes.

"Of what, sir?"

"Of what he does not know, I suppose, and, therefore, cannot control. He is still the warrior fighting for territory. He has yet to admit he has won and I am not his enemy. Not here, at least." He thumped his chest. "If I may be so bold, how does Fritz treat Ms. Staunton?"

George's face hardened.

"W-What do you mean?"

Uncle Guenther examined his eyes.

"I am sure she would have told you of any untoward advances."

George's ears reddened.

"Wh-What?"

"I am sorry. It is indelicate of me to ask."

George straightened in his chair and eyed his uncle.

"What are you implying?"

Uncle Guenther's eyebrows shot up.

"My dear boy, are you even vaguely aware of your father's reputation?"

George's face fell. He felt naïve and foolish.

"W-What? I-I am afraid I do not understand."

His uncle's face screwed up.

"Oh, dear."

George leaned forward. "Tell me."

His uncle looked down.

"He has been known to develop, shall we say, intimate liaisons with some staff mem..."

George shrunk back.

"Are you implying that M would...?"

Uncle Guenther shook his head.

"Not at all, not at all. I am sure your fiancée is above reproach. Fritz, on the other hand..."

George's stomach dropped to the floor. His uncle reached out his hand and squeezed his forearm.

"I am sorry, my boy. I thought you knew."

Tears welled up despite George's efforts to squelch his emotions.

"That is behind the rumors about M? People assume she...I-It is so unfair. She is so genuine and pure of heart. And to think..." He couldn't bring himself to say it. "And what about Belinda? You would know, would you not, sir?"

His eyes sought confirmation. His uncle nodded.

"Yes, it is common knowledge that Belinda accosted Ms. Staunton just before the Bowling Green reception earlier this year and in the office within the last few days. But I am sure you..."

George's eyes drew in. "What are you talking about?"

"If Ms. Staunton has not told you, I am sure it was to protect your image of Fritz, or he may have forbidden her to tell you."

George's hands became fists.

"Well, she must quit right away. Damn him!"

He retreated.

"S-Sorry, sir, I-I did not mean to..."

"No, you have a right to be angry."

His heart hardened.

"Sir, will you help me? I will not rest until Father regrets ever trying to sully M's name!"

His uncle's face fell.

"I am afraid you misunderstand me. I have not been looking to throw Fritz over. As I said, he is a good man."

George's back stiffened. His voice grew hot. "No. A good man does not use people. A good man does not throw away his family. A good man does not do exactly what *Ol'papa* did for control. A good man does not compromise a woman's reputation. You are too kind, sir. After all these years, I see clearly. You are the better man."

Pink rose in his uncle's face.

"You misunderstand. There are rumors. I am sure if Fritz had any designs on your young lady, she squelched them. But your stepmother, well..."

George's eyes pleaded. "Will you help me?"

The creases in Uncle Guenther's face deepened.

"I will do what I can. First, I think you need to talk with Ms. Staunton and know the truth so you will understand what you are up against. We must not act rashly."

George sucked his teeth.

"Of course. And, sir, I am not against Marcus. I never have been."

His uncle smiled.

"I know, my boy. If I thought you were, this would be a different conversation."

George moved the folds of the bread around on his plate.

"But I cannot let him hurt M. If he will not work with me, I cannot have him work against me. You understand?"

He sipped his tea.

"Certainly. If we can bring Marcus back to us, it is the best way."

"Of course, Uncle Guenther."

His uncle rang a small silver bell engraved with the letters, RGL. The initials caught George's attention the way the sunlight burned them into the sliver of his heart. Rainer Guenther Leibnitz. He was glad his uncle was called by his middle name.

He looked at his nephew.

"Would you care for more tea or croissants?"

George shook his head. "No, thank you."

"Then before you go, your aunt would like a word."

George smiled. "Certainly. Thank you. I am forever grateful."

His uncle reciprocated, "My pleasure, my boy."

As his aunt arrived, the men rose to greet her. She took George's hands in hers.

"*Georg*," she said in German, "I would like to host a small party for *Fraulein* Staunton. Would it be acceptable to call her myself to extend the invitation and discuss the details? She should feel welcome in our family. Does this meet with your approval?"

His face blossomed. "Of course, Aunt Tani. I am sure she would like that. Thank you."

As Tatania led him down the stairs and out to the elevator door with her husband following behind, she inquired about the wedding plans and what she could do to help.

"I will leave that to M. I do not know if Mummy will want to be involved."

"Of course. I just felt it was important that we take her under our wing and make her comfortable..."

His eyes softened. "I understand perfectly, and it is really quite thoughtful."

She smiled. "*Güt, liebchen.*"

She drew him to her, hugged and kissed him on both cheeks. Uncle Guenther reached out both hands for a bear hug and a pat on the back.

"I will wait for your call, then, my boy.

George nodded. "Yes. I will call early next week, sir."

As he descended the elevator, anger flooded his thoughts. Would he ever escape his father's control?

Chapter 2

When he arrived home, M peppered him with questions and cornered him at the door.

"How did it go? How was your uncle? Did you see your aunt? Will he help or did he just offer advice? You were gone such a long time."

"Let's head for the airport," he said, moving toward the bedroom to gather his weekender bag. "Father has the Hawker standing by. I'll call the pilot so he can file his flight plan, and I'll share everything once we're on the Vineyard. We're behind schedule."

She dogged his heels.

"And leave me hanging?!"

He turned and gave her a winning smile, then proceeded toward his dressing room, where his bag was already packed by the housekeeper.

His voice trailed behind him. "Please, trust me. We need to leave right away."

When they reached his Vineyard home in the late afternoon, they settled in for a delectable meal of clam chowder, peasant bread, and salad that the housekeeper had prepared. He squelched his pique that M pushed for answers and never commented on his house. He put her off until they retired to the bedroom suite. They settled on the loveseat with bowl-sized sniffers of Courvoisier, fresh raspberries, and an assortment of Teuscher champagne truffles.

She pressed into his side.

"Okay, tell all."

As he provided a detailed account of his meeting, an earnest look framed her face. His face hardened.

"We are pawns. You, Marcus, me. Father moves us around on his chess board. I've been a fool, and you've had to pay for my artlessness."

She tucked her legs under her and turned his head toward her.

"I'm not sure you want to hear this. Have you asked yourself why your uncle shared so much information with you about your father?"

His head cocked in her direction.

"What do you mean?"

"What Mr. Guenther said is probably true. But *why* did he tell you? Remember, the brothers have always been rivals. And why would he choose to help you over his own son?"

He moved as if to stand.

"No," he barked.

Her eyebrows scrunched.

"You need to be careful. Don't take everything at face value."

Arguments volleyed through his mind. "So it's all true, what Uncle Guenther said about Belinda attacking you, and Father's infidelities?"

She grimaced. "Yes."

He frowned. "Has he ever... I mean... with you, has he ever...?"

His throat constricted.

She smiled. "Your father has always been a perfect gentleman with me."

His vocal chords relaxed, and he put his arm around her shoulder.

"So in light of everything, I think we should sleep on it and then formulate our own plan. Otherwise, other people will determine what's best for us, and neither of us will be happy with that."

She nodded. "I think your father and your uncle are decent men."

He started to protest and withdrew his arm. She put up her hand.

"But they have their own agendas and believe they know best. Your grandparents schooled them in a particular mindset. They can't help being influenced by the methods and *morés* of their upbringing. But you don't have to fit in their mold and neither do I. Look at your stepmother. I imagine she was a b-i-t-c-h before she met your father, but now she's scared. She's studied the power plays in your family. I'm sure she doesn't want her children to be afterthoughts in your father's financial legacy, and..."

His face hardened. "I really don't give a you-know-what about Belinda, her children, or what she wants."

He stood and faced her. "Look at Aunt Tani. She's warm, caring, nonjudgmental. She's genuinely reaching out to you because no one has."

She nodded. "I agree. Mrs. Tatania does exude authenticity and graciousness, and I *will* call her. Perhaps, that's the starting point. But I don't trust your uncle. I've had only limited dealings with him. He's gracious, but I wouldn't accept everything he says without looking at the whole picture. There's a lifetime of experience between him and your father."

"And you trust Father more?" he countered with sarcasm.

He crossed to the French doors that led to the balcony overlooking the ocean.

She called after him, "I trust him to be exactly who he is—a man with an agenda, carving out his place in history. He will orchestrate, manipulate, even charm or bully to have his way."

She stood and moved toward him.

"I don't have illusions about your father. But he loves you and he also has his mother's strong desire for you to be the next CEO. His methods may be wrong. His ego surely gets in the way, but he thinks he sees the bigger picture, which he probably does. I'm sure he's doing what he believes is best. Maybe I don't trust your uncle because I don't know him as well as I know your father. I just have a hard time accepting his sudden interest in you, that he'd be so willing to thwart his son's ambition."

He turned toward her. "But it isn't sudden. I remember several occasions in the last few years when *Gran'maman* encouraged me to get to know him and he tried to help me, but Father immediately forbade it. I think this is another attempt to do what she asked him to do."

"Oh." She sat down. "Still, what does he gain by helping you? He's a Leibnitz, after all."

His back stiffened. "What's that supposed to mean? I'm a Leibnitz, too, in case you hadn't noticed!"

He walked toward the balcony, her voice trailing after him. "I-I'm sorry, I didn't mean it like that."

He heard her footsteps approach.

"It's just that, looking in from the outside, your grandparents have bred into this family a strong need to rule. If your uncle can weaken his brother's power, why not? You were right when you used the word pawns. I think you and Marcus *are* pawns. It probably was fueled by your grandmother and..."

He pulled away and raised his voice. "How dare you bring *Gran'maman* into this? What can you possibly know about what she did or didn't do?"

He gazed out at the choppy ocean, foam lapping up against the shore. Invisible crystalline birds flitted their wings just above the dancing water. Moonlight dappled the air and took flight through the tails of the waves. Now the ripples moved out in undulating fingers across the expanse of water. His mind painted the picture beyond the window, withdrawing into his own world.

M's hand on his back interrupted his reverie. "I'm sorry. It may be hard to accept, but in trying to reverse the damage your grandfather did, your grandmother may have perpetuated a model that works for business, but not for a healthy family."

The truth slapped him, but his bruised heart rejected it. He tried to recapture the ocean's ballet but it eluded him.

"The sins of the fathers bestowed upon the sons," he whispered.

Her ear cocked. "What?"

He turned toward her. "Just something Father Thomas used to say."

She touched his arm. "Tell me about it."

His gaze floated back out to sea, escaping into the eddy currents. Loneliness bore down on him despite the warmth of her presence, which he would wrap around himself like a blanket if he could release his despair.

He withdrew. "I just need some space. I need to go for a walk."

"Want company?"

His face closed up like a fist. "I need to be alone."

He left her at the French doors, proceeding downstairs and out of the house without looking back. He walked down the winding garden path through the descending dunes to the sandy shore a few minutes from the walled-in terrace that framed the back of the house. Within seconds, his extremities numbed with cold. The keening wind whipped his turbulent thoughts. The outside temperature further tightened his heart, which had congealed in the bedroom where the warm light of love awaited him. He faced the darkness of the ocean and his careening mind, despite the biting wind. As he pushed his hands deep into the pockets of his light windbreaker, he stared into the cold truth of his life. Time froze in the frigid air.

With new resolve, he didn't question his feet as they

turned and moved back up the trail toward the comfort of the inviting light. When he returned to the house, he found M in the kitchen in her silk dressing gown and slippers making chamomile tea. He glanced at the antique grandfather clock. 12:30. He had been pacing the beach for an hour.

She looked up from the kitchen island over which she was bending into a cup of steam and smiled. "Join me for a cup of tea?"

His chapped lips parted. "That would be lovely. I'm frozen solid."

She threw him a come-hither look. "Would you like *me* to warm you up?"

He took a gulp of the hot tea, set it on the counter, and turned into her heat. "After the way I treated you?"

She rubbed his hands, arms, and back. "You were upset. You needed time to yourself."

"Thank you. You missed a spot right here."

He pointed to his lips.

Her inviting eyes embraced him. "Well, we can't have that now, can we?"

Their lips melted into butter.

*****

The next morning, the day started with a long swim in the heated pool of the glass conservatory and a breakfast of croissants, scrambled eggs, strawberries, and *café au lait*.

As breakfast ended, she asked, "Do you mind if we go shopping, come back for a late lunch, and then tackle last night's thorny questions?"

His face brightened. "That sounds lovely. If you like, I can give Thérèse the afternoon off and we can eat in town. There are a couple of charming little bistros. It's early in the season so it shouldn't be crowded."

She smiled. "Whatever you decide."

The drive to town was filled with the chatter of two lovers enthralled with each other's presence. The bodyguard, Sebastian, drove discreetly behind them. As the cars made their way through the narrow streets, George eyed a parking spot in front of a small gift shop. They ambled out and headed for a bookstore fronted with iron steps stacked with discounted books. After thumbing through a few, M wandered inside to look for stationary supplies while he opened a copy of *Architectural Digest*. His eyes widened. He added the magazine to her few items and paid the bill.

As they exited the store, he turned to her. "Guess who's in *Architectural Digest* this month?"

Her face bubbled with curiosity. When she tried to take the magazine out of the shopping bag, he grabbed it.

"You have to wait," he said with an impish smile.

She threw him a seductive look. "When?"

"At lunch."

"Can we have lunch now?"

"I thought you had more shopping to do."

When she reached for the magazine, again he pushed her hand away.

"Can't we shop after lunch?"

"You said shopping, then late lunch, remember? It's barely 12:00."

She pursed her lips into a pout. "Alright, if you give me payment first."

"Payment?"

"A kiss, of course."

She grabbed him by the shoulders and smushed her lips hard against his.

"Not that kind of kiss, silly," he laughed.

"You'll get a proper kiss *after* you've shown me the magazine."

"I can give you a hint or, maybe, you should guess."

Her eyes glinted.

He drew her closer. "Right here on the street?"

"Hint, schmint. I want the real deal, Georgie, Porgy. Now, give."

"Are you sure you want everyone to see?"

She grabbed at the bag.

"Okay, lady-like, now."

He pulled the bag back. She stuck out her tongue.

"Ooh," he said, "right here, right now?"

She scrunched up her face at him. He slowly pulled out the magazine. She rushed to see.

"*Nous voilà!*" he said with a flourish, his face beaming.

Her mouth gaped open, then shut. "It's your house!"

"*Our* house, *chérie, notre maison.*"

Her face opened up like a bloom. "It's sooo exquisite in print. When did all this happen? Wait. *Our house?*"

He smiled. Months earlier Frederick had told him that a crew would be taking pictures of the house. She devoured the magazine. The article showcased elegant snippets of the 4,600-square-foot beach house. Four large bedrooms with baths and an over-scale master bedroom suite featured breath-taking views of the ocean through mullioned windows from the second floor balconies. The expansive kitchen was a cook's delight, with ample Italian basalt countertops, Elmwood cabinetry, a Wolf range, and built-in Sub-Zero refrigerator. Limestone flooring with oriental carpet graced the first floor. An airy gathering area featured a Delaware stone fireplace flanked by built-in bookshelves and cushioned reading benches. Two toile couches were blended with four rattan chairs with built-in plush linen cushions. Floor-to-ceiling windows and a series of French doors took advantage of the spectacular vista beyond the stone terrace and dunes. A cozy cook-caretaker's cottage and a small pool house abutted the garden path that began at the base of the terrace and wound down to the beach below the dunes.

George broke the silence. "Why not get married this year

instead of next? You quit next month and work full-time on finishing your degree and we plan a fall wedding. It's March now, so there's time to plan. What do you think?"

Her face lit up. "Are you sure?"

He embraced her with his eyes. "I've never been more sure of anything in my life, except asking you to marry me."

"Then, why not?"

He dropped the magazine into the bag, pulled M against him, wrapped his arms around the warm curves of her body, and melted his lips into hers.

As they headed hand-in-hand down the street to find a romantic restaurant, George had perfect clarity about what he would do. Since she had so quickly followed his lead, he knew that together they would be able to chart their own course. He had no illusions that his father would make it easy for them. They drove home at dusk. As the sun waned, they snuggled together on the cozy loveseat in the master bedroom's sitting room with bowls of popcorn, sliced veggies, grapes, popcorn shrimp, and a bottle of *Pouilly-Fuissé*.

M chuckled. "Well, *chéri*, we're going where no Leibnitz has gone before."

They both chortled as their happiness glowed in the fireplace light.

George grabbed a bowl of popcorn. "It will be an exciting trek, I promise."

She reached for the veggies and burst into cackles of delight.

Chapter 3

M readied herself for battle upon her return to LE on Tuesday. George insisted that a driver take her to the office each day. She would rather have taken the subway as usual, but he insisted. She called his aunt early in the day to accept her offer to host an engagement party, and the women arranged lunch for the following week. When George's father arrived at the office at 10:05, she handed him a letter, which informed him that she would work 9:00 to 3:30 Monday through Thursday and would stay on for only two more months. She also handed him a note from George requesting a meeting to discuss wedding plans, his position at LE, and a joint meeting with his uncle. As Mr. Leibnitz read the communications, his eyes hardened.

"Obviously, the two of you made plans without consulting me or taking my wishes into consideration. I will not allow it. And the overture to Guenther is unacceptable."

He turned to Frederick and barked, "Mr. Metz, call George to appear in my office within half an hour. Cancel all my appointments. M, my office, now."

Frederick left the room.

Her chest tightened. As she sat across the conference table from him, the intercom buzzed, and he touched the speaker button.

"Sir, George said it is physically impossible for him to arrive before 12:45."

His eyes impaled M.

"Do not play games with me. I want to know why it will take George more than two hours to arrive since you two returned from the Vineyard last night."

"George had a meeting this morning. He didn't mention where."

The intercom interrupted. "Mr. Guenther requests an audience."

Mr. Leibnitz shot her a contemptuous look.

"You do not know what you are doing."

She looked at her future father-in-law without expression.

"You could not wait for me to take care of matters? Is that it?"

She scrunched up her face. "I'm afraid I don't follow."

"When George arrives, I will expect some answers."

She smiled. "Certainly."

His voice hardened. "I thought we had an agreement. You have as much explaining to do as he does."

"Of course."

He shooed her away with his hand and she rose to leave. George's uncle entered just as she was stepping through the door.

"Oh, excuse me, Mr. Guenther."

He moved to let her pass, saying,"Oh, no, please. It was entirely my fault. You look aglow. Your engagement, no doubt."

She smiled. "Yes, I'm quite happy. And how are you this morning, sir?"

He touched her arm. "Oh, I am as much a curmudgeon as ever. Business dries up the soul."

Her grin widened. "Then, a distinguished-looking curmudgeon."

He chuckled, his eyes twinkling. "I assume I may enter?"

"Of course."

She smiled and moved out to her desk.

Slack-jawed, Frederick asked, "What was that all about, if you don't mind my asking?"

Her face went blank. No idea."

His lips pursed. "In all my years of working for Mr. Fritz, I have *never* seen Mr. Guenther show up without an appointment and just be ushered in. Something big's afoot. Mark my words. I'd like to be a fly on the wall, wouldn't you?"

She suppressed a smile. "Indeed."

"Shame the room is soundproof. Otherwise, we could stand at the door..." He paused. "Nah..."

He eyed her. She chuckled. "I'd be right next to you."

His pinched face broke into a wide grin.

The rest of the morning was consumed with organizing the transition of her departure, the process of finding an assistant for Frederick, and catching up on the piles of work still to be done. By 12:00, he had eyed the clock several times.

"What're they doing in there so long? They haven't come up for air or even asked for coffee. Most unusual."

She smiled. "It's certainly odd."

"It's a good thing Mr. Fritz had me cancel his other appointments. Today is turning out to be rather different."

He frowned. "I don't like it. I don't like it at all."

She had no time for chit-chat. She was in the middle of editing a long letter in French that Mr. Leibnitz had written to the head of Frantel, a French telecommunications company with whom he was negotiating. At 12:15 her intercom buzzed.

"Please ask Chef to send up five poached salmon with essence of cucumber, truffle and arugula salad with walnut vinaigrette, three liters of Evian with lime, no bread, fresh berries with *crème fraîche* at exactly 1:15. When George arrives, the two of you will join us for lunch. And have Mr. Metz call Marcus to arrive at 1:10 sharp."

"Very good, sir."

She suppressed a smile. The next half hour dragged on despite busying herself with the work at hand. Her nerves vibrated in fear that their well-laid plans would fail. By 12:50, anticipation was crowding out logical thought, but she resisted the urge to call George. The intercom interrupted her musings. Mr. Leibnitz barked at her because George hadn't arrived. She called his cell phone. No answer.

George arrived at 12:55, ten minutes behind schedule, beads of perspiration dotting his forehead and upper lip. Sebastian trailed behind, a mustache of moisture framing his upper lip.

"Accident on Park Avenue South at 34th Street. Traffic was at a standstill. It's a good thing we started out early. We ended up power walking the last six blocks. I'm a bit moist, but I'm here. I'll just go to the Executive Washroom."

She called after him, "But your father..."

He disappeared around the corner with Sebastian two paces behind. At 1:05, they returned a bit more composed and dry. George and M were heading to his father's office door when her intercom buzzed.

"Where is my son?!"

"He just arrived, Mr. Leibnitz."

He barked, "Send him in. I will call for you momentarily."

"Of course, sir," she replied, shooting George a worried look. "You first. I'm to come later, probably to serve lunch."

He smiled. "Not to worry. Just Father's usual posturing."

"Off you go, then."

Frederick gave her a curious look but said nothing. She focused on typing a letter to keep from fidgeting. Mr. Leibnitz buzzed her to come in just as Marcus arrived. As she opened the door, she had the pleasure of hearing Frederick tell him to wait until he was called. The men immediately stood as she entered the room. George met her with a kiss on the cheek. He squeezed her hand and directed her to one of the soft leather swivel chairs around the large, oval, burnished cherry table that filled the center of the spacious office. The brothers sat on opposite sides of the table. She sat at one end, and George alongside his uncle, an arrangement suggesting that Marcus would sit opposite him.

"Since this is a family meeting," Mr. Fritz began, "I hope you will not mind if we are on a first name basis, M."

"Certainly. What would you like me to call you? Fritz, Father, *Pater*, Papa, *Père*," she added with a grin.

"I think Fritz will do nicely," he responded with a smile.

She turned to his brother.

"Guenther is fine," he said, acknowledging her silent inquiry.

George's mouth turned up. "*Chéri* works for me."

She suppressed a giggle as the intercom buzzer sounded.

"Have him wait outside. I will let you know when we are ready for him. No, not in the sitting room, outside!" Fritz snapped.

His face morphed to pleasantness as he turned to M.

"Before Chef and Marcus arrive, I would like to say how delighted we are that you are becoming part of our family."

"Here, here," his brother added.

She lowered her head.

"Thank you."

"And I will not tolerate anyone treating my future daughter-in-law with disrespect."

Guenther added, "We will see to it. And, for my part, I would like to apologize for my son's behavior. It was totally unacceptable. He will regret it."

She put up her hand. "Please, not on my account. It will just make the situation worse and..."

Guenther reciprocated. "I must insist that he apologize to you."

"But..."

"I agree," Fritz cut in.

George touched her hand and interjected, "I think M's concern is valid. Creating an adversarial relationship with him is not good for anyone. Once he apologizes, that should be the end of it, agreed?"

The brothers looked at each other and then at him. They nodded. Fritz smiled.

"George has asked to lead the discussion over lunch, and I have agreed."

The intercom buzzer announced the arrival of the food.

"Yes, have Marcus wait until lunch is served. Send in Chef now," Fritz growled.

The couple exchanged knowing looks. Eight minutes ticked on the grandfather clock. Finally, Fritz directed George to open the door.

"Hey, cuz, there you are. Good to see you. Come on in. Hope you're hungry. I know I'm famished." George held the door open and extended his hand toward the table.

Marcus frowned. You made me wait long enough, didn't you?"

"Sorry about that, ole chap. The powers that be, you know..."

Marcus glowered at him.

Fritz called out to his nephew, gesturing with his hand. "Come sit by me. You know George's fiancée, of course."

Marcus nodded in her direction. His eyes shot up when he saw the display of food.

"Didn't start without me, I see. Salmon for everyone, is it? Good thing I *like* fish."

Fritz snarled, "Lose the attitude if you know what is good for you."

"I expect your best behavior," Guenther barked.

Marcus bristled. "Yes, *sirs.*"

Fritz turned away.

"Thank you, Chef. That will be all for now. Everything looks delicious."

He gestured to his guests. "Please, everyone, begin."

Chef murmured as he and the sous-chef exited. After everyone had eaten a few bites, Guenther turned to his son. "I believe you have a few words to say."

He looked down at his plate, picked out the delicate truffles with his fork, and laid them to the side.

"Ms. Staunton," he began, his face tight.

Her eyes warmed. "Please, call me M."

"I'm truly sorry if I've said anything that would give the impression that I hold you in anything less than the highest esteem."

Guenther's face bristled. "That will not do. You want to say more, *ja?*"

She put up her hand. "It's alright."

"Excuse me, but it is not alright," George interjected. "Everything should be out in the open? Father and Uncle Guenther have cleared their calendars, and I believe they deserve full disclosure. Marcus, we are the next generation to lead LE. We need to start off on the right foot if we're going to work together."

Marcus frowned. "*Really?* Everyone at this table is steeped in intrigue and subterfuge."

M shot back, "I humbly beg to differ."

"So, according to you, you did *not* worm your way into my uncle's heart and then my cousin's?"

Her face paled.

George shot up, his eyes daggered. "How dare you! You will take that back at once!"

Fritz interjected, "Sit down. Let us hear what Marcus *thinks* he knows."

Marcus's neck blotched. "Well, when Aunt Belinda shared her outrage..."

Fritz's eyes steeled. "What did you say?"

Marcus's eyes frowned. "I'm sorry, Uncle Fritz, but George said we should lay everything out on the table."

Fritz growled, "Out with it."

"Aunt Belinda told me that M made a..."

His eyes shifted to his lap.

"Made a what?" Fritz demanded, putting up his hand to silence George.

Guenther's eyes hardened.

Marcus fumbled, "Well, she, uh, implied..."

Fritz interrupted, "I want to know exactly what she said. M, if you do not want to hear this-this slander, you may feel free to go into my sitting room."

She sat up straight. "I'd like to know what I am being accused of."

Fritz glared at him. "Very well. Continue."

Marcus' eyes implored. "I'm sorry, M. I'm sure I've been wrong about you. Aunt Belinda was so distraught, I naturally believed..."

Fritz pivoted his head. "Exactly what did my wife say?"

Marcus turned to him. "She said she was first your mistress and then you pawned her off on George to try to make a man out of him."

All the blood drained from M's face. Both Fritz and George issued a curse one on top of the other. Guenther rose and went to put his hands on her shoulders.

"I am so terribly sorry. Shall we go next door into the sitting room?"

She looked first at him, then at George, but couldn't move.

George bellowed, "How could you believe such claptrap? Do you hate me that much?"

Marcus tried to defend himself. George accused him of being Belinda's puppet. Their voices rumbled. M's eyes locked on Fritz. All the blood rose to his face, which was contorted in rage.

When he recovered, he thundered, "Enough! Stop it. Both of you. Sit down!"

The cousins' mutual scowl spoke volumes.

Fritz turned to M with buttery eyes. "I have no words to express how deeply sorry I am. I fall on my sword. This is my fault for not having taken matters in hand sooner. We will understand if you wish to go home."

Guenther patted her arm. "Yes, my dear, I will take you."

Her eyes brimmed with hot tears, but she stanched her hurt. "Thank you, Fritz—Father—if you don't mind."

He smiled.

"U-Uncle Guenther," she continued softly.

His face opened up.

"I-I never knew my father."

She looked at Fritz.

"I would like to think of you as a father. And I never had an uncle."

Her eyes met Guenther's.

"Or a cousin—a blessing and a curse."

Marcus looked away from her penetrating stare. Her lip trembled.

"I-It was always just Grammy and Pop-Pop, who loved me with a fierceness that formed who I am. I see how your family intrigue sets everyone against each other. My opinion may not mean much, but if you all spent more time loving each other instead of manipulating and plotting, you'd be much richer. If we shared in each other's strengths and weaknesses, we could do great things together."

George opened his mouth, but she put up her hand.

"I appreciate each one who has come to my defense. I'm sorry, Marcus, that you didn't."

She pinned him with her gaze. He looked down.

"But it isn't really necessary, because I know who I am. But it *is* important to you."

She looked in turn at each man. "It's probably asking too much, but I would like you to end this longstanding war, agree to forgive, and learn to trust each other. Isn't there enough power and all those other things you value to go around?"

She turned to Fritz. "I know you're not responsible for Mrs. Belinda's lies. I think she's acting out of fear. She doesn't really know me. I never told you this before, but she once warned me, early on, that the bedroom belonged to her."

Fritz and Guenther's eyebrows shot up. Marcus smirked, and George's mouth curled.

"She has no idea who I am. Marcus, you don't either. It's easy to believe lies about me."

He looked away.

"Why not work with George instead of against him? You can benefit from each other's strengths. Father, Uncle Guenther, why not ensure that the next generation of leaders are partners instead of rivals? Why not bury the hatchet?" She paused, her face hopeful. "I'd like us to be a close family."

Seeing no reaction, she finished. "I'm done. I think the rest is up to you."

Pent-up tears trickled tremulously down her cheeks, resting on the shoulders of her silk jacket. Each man in turn came to hug her. Marcus apologized and promised to make up for his behavior in any way she deemed appropriate.

"That's up to them," she said, pointing to the others.

She smiled and rubbed her palms together.

"I don't know about anyone else, but I can't wait to have raspberries, *crème fraîche*, and *café au lait*. Shall I serve?"

"Let me," Marcus piped up. "I insist."

The mood brightened. The family chitchatted during lunch. As coffee was served, Fritz suggested that he and Guenther outline how Marcus and George would gain leadership experience over the next several years as the older men prepared for retirement. Marcus suggested M be excused.

Her shoulders straightened. "I'd like to offer my own ideas about a future role for me within LE, with everyone's permission."

Fritz grinned. "That sounds intriguing."

Guenther smiled. "Indeed."

Fritz nodded to his brother. "Alright, then, Guenther, would you like to start?"

Guenther described a timeframe of eight to ten years with

increasing levels of executive responsibility. First, the cousins would divide their time among the legal, engineering, and executive departments. Over the next several years they would both gain experience assisting the senior vice-presidents for the various divisions. By the sixth year, they would each become senior vice-presidents, based on ability, interest, and performance, with the possibility of branching out or changing divisions.

Marcus squirmed in his seat. "So, when will we receive CEO training to decide who will become chairman?"

Fritz folded his hands. "That remains to be seen. We will assess both of your leadership abilities over time. One of you could become CEO and the other President. If we need to look outside the family to fill the positions, we will."

Marcus eyed him. "So you're saying neither one of us is guaranteed a position."

"Correct," Fritz clipped.

Despite Marcus's inscrutable demeanor, M knew he was planning how to outmaneuver George. She sized up the Leibnitz brothers. They would go through the motions of cooperation, but neither would likely cede power. She hoped George wouldn't allow his family's priorities to subsume his own. And she had her own ideas.

Marcus's voice broke into her musing. "I believe M wanted to tell us her ideas for contributing to the Leibnitz family fortune."

Fritz's eyes brightened. "I have no doubt M will make a great contribution. Please."

She sat erect. "I would like to expand the Leibnitz Foundation to include education initiatives that I would lead."

"No one can accuse you of modesty," Marcus scoffed.

Guenther flashed his eyes at him. "That will be enough."

"I am sure you have worked out the scope and budget for this new initiative," Fritz said.

"Yes, it would start rather small. We would provide seed

money for innovative approaches to help economically disadvantaged children and those with disabilities and giftedness. The first three to four years would be small pilot projects, and possibly, the start-up of a few schools for the learning disabled and the arts. The initial investment would be fifteen to twenty million, and then, as we expand our initiative in years four through six, in the range of fifty to eighty million, with international pilot schools at this stage. Within ten years, the foundation would contribute roughly two hundred million or so each year toward the realization of our dream."

At the mention of each set of numbers, Marcus rolled his eyes.

His father smiled. "You have given this a lot of thought."

"Indeed, George and I have."

Marcus leaned forward. "How do you suppose the funds would be raised for this foundation?"

She smiled. "We have a plan for that."

His face dropped. She turned to George.

He smiled. "The tax savings from expanding the Leibnitz Foundation will be substantial. I can show you the numbers and the details. The first order of business, of course, would be that Marcus and I would work together to identify ways to increase LE profits with innovative approaches to the current book of business and develop new areas that will provide additional market share over time. Some of that revenue would fund the foundation initiatives."

Marcus put up both hands. "I don't see..."

Fritz interrupted, "Splendid idea. Working together, building foundation revenue to expand. What do you think, Guenther?"

"I like the idea of them working together toward a common purpose. It sounds exciting. Right, Marcus?"

His mouth tightened. "It sounds rather ambitious, but we can pull it off, right, cuz?"

George smiled. "The final piece is that each of us would donate the first five million dollars from our inheritance to the foundation."

Marcus almost choked on his coffee and floundered. "Wha-? Surely, you don't expect me..."

Guenther and Fritz frowned at him.

"W-Well, of course, I would *consider* it, if Father and Uncle Fritz think it's a good investment."

Guenther's face broadened. "Son, it is an excellent idea. I am sure you will flesh out the details with George. I would be delighted to see you make a small sacrifice..."

Marcus's eyes flashed. "Small? Five million is a lot of money, right, Uncle Fritz?"

Fritz nodded. "Of course, but considering your net worth, and with an eye on the public good, it is a gesture of good will that puts the family's interests above your own. It will send a powerful message to the public about the philanthropic tradition of the Leibnitz family. I think it is well worth your consideration."

M watched Marcus's face shrink. She suspected that five million would not have much impact on his financial wherewithal. He could still be the playboy in his tony Upper West Side three-story brownstone and fleet of antique cars. Like his cousin, bodyguards, personal staff, and access to worldwide family properties and limos, aircraft, and yachts framed his everyday life. She suspected he was thinking that if five million dollars paved the way to being CEO one day, it was a small price to pay.

Marcus shot her a penetrating look, then turned to George. "Well, cuz, I guess we're in business."

Chapter 4

The following week the cousins collaborated as their fathers assigned them projects across several areas to deepen their knowledge base of LE global operations. George's head spun. Marcus already understood far more about finance and business than he did, so he felt ill-equipped to compete with his cousin. He couldn't burden M with his problems. She had a full plate with her duties at LE, working on her dissertation and music, and planning the wedding with his aunt. He vowed that he wouldn't lose sight of his future plans and devoted most of his time to collaborating with Marcus and restoring their childhood friendship and trust.

As the week was winding down, his father invited the couple to dinner in Wilton. George had no illusions that his father could strong arm his stepmother into treating M with the respect she deserved.

They rode in the silver Rolls limo since the Bell Ranger was undergoing maintenance. George insisted that M sit next to his father to avoid motion sickness from sitting sideways or backwards on the circular plush seat that wrapped around the side and behind the front partition of the passenger cabin.

"George, perhaps M would like something from the bar. Kindly make me a Southern Comfort Manhattan on the rocks."

She requested a *Rémy-Martin* and ginger ale.

As he mixed their drinks and a White Russian for himself, his father began peppering her with questions. "Where would you like to marry? In Wilton, New York, Paris, Lieb Island, Martha's Vineyard, one of the yachts, in the Falcon, the Hawker, the 737?"

Her eyes popped as she accepted her drink. She looked at George to respond.

"Well, at first we selected Lieb Island, but many people would not be able to celebrate with us."

"I am sure we could arrange for flights for your guests. But what is your preference?"

She blushed and sipped her drink. "Any of those places would be incredible, but I prefer a simple wedding. I want my friends to be able to afford to come and not be inconvenienced."

Fritz smiled. "The cost would not be an issue. Convenience is another matter. So New York or Wilton would seem to be on the shortlist. But I say the grander the better."

George clenched his jaws. Of course, Father could not have his friends, associates, and well-wishers attend what he would consider a shabby affair.

"I think we should let M decide."

She scrunched up her nose. "This is so hard. I love the ambience of Wilton, the grandeur of St. Patrick's, the intimacy of a small country church. I was raised in a small evangelical church, you know. May I think about it?"

Fritz's voice strutted, "Imagine the wedding in St. Patrick's main sanctuary with the Archbishop himself presiding, next to Father Thomas, and a minister of your choice, and the reception at Wilton, catered by your favorite chef. Limo rides from St. Patrick's to Wilton for all the guests. Helicopter for the bride and groom and the wedding party shuttled to the reception."

Her mouth gaped. George's eyebrows rose.

"What do you say? It would make me extremely happy to do this for the two of you."

She looked at George.

"If that's what M wants. Belinda is going to have quite the surprise."

His triumphant grin made Fritz smile and M frown.

She balked, "How are we going to make Belinda feel special? I can only imagine how she feels."

Fritz patted her on the arm. "It would be just like you to worry about her. Leave her to me."

The conversation veered off to a band for the reception and her name didn't resurface for the remainder of the hour-long trip. As the car made its way up the long, winding road past the guarded entrance gate, the wooded hills that led up to the manor house glowed with light. Fritz rang the driver to stop at the circular entrance drive.

He smiled. "We might as well set the right tone."

Hilda, the aging housekeeper, opened the door with bright eyes as they exited the car.

"*Güten abend, Meister Georg,* how vunderful to see you!"

He hugged her with alacrity.

"*Fraulein,*" she curtsied to M, "*willkommen.*"

M thanked her.

"*Herr* Leibnitz," she continued in German, "Mrs. Belinda is in the library for drinks as requested. The children are waiting with Greta to kiss you goodnight before retiring to their rooms."

"*Sehr güt*, Hilda," Fritz responded with a crisp nod. "Tell Chef to have dinner ready in an hour. We will have *hors d'oeuvres* in the library. Be sure the Beluga is served at exactly 59 degrees."

As Hilda nodded and turned right with Fritz's briefcase, he and his guests proceeded left to descend the two steps into the library.

M touched George's arm. "I just need to visit the ladies room."

"Certainly. You know your way," Fritz replied for him.

Her nervousness enveloped George. It galled him that the

problems in this household, which had nothing to do with her and had existed long before she had entered their lives, would engulf her.

They moved into the sitting room as M disappeared.

Belinda stood to greet them. "George, dah-ling, don't you look da-shing. Come say hello to your brozzer *und* sister. They *vouldn't* go to bed vithout seeing you. It has been ages. But vhere *eeze* your friend? Did she stand you up?"

She laughed, her voice tight.

"That will do," Fritz commanded.

George retorted, "My fiancée."

His face relaxed when M joined them, bringing much-needed warmth to the room. He walked over and gave her a squeeze. Belinda frowned as she eyed her from head to foot. George compared Belinda's trendy black Fendi silk flared pants and knit-lace V-necked blouse with M's elegant Paul Stuart suit.

The children scampered to hug their brother and kiss their father goodnight. Fritz patted Claude on the back. "Say your prayers."

"Yes, Papa."

They moved toward M. Belinda frowned. Fritz's eyes flashed.

"Claude, Brianna, say hello to *Fraulein* Staunton."

Almost in unison, the children chanted, "*Güten abend, Fraulein Staunton. Wie geht es Ihnen?*"

M's eyes crinkled. "*Sehr güt, danke.*"

Fritz continued, "*Fraulein* Staunton will soon be your sister-in-law."

"Ooh," Brianna chirped. "*Est-ce que vous allez vous marier à notre frère?*"

"*Oui, avec plaisir.* Does that please you?" M finished, in English.

"Ooh, yes, I—"

Belinda snorted. "Quit trying to show off. It is vell past

your bedtime. Greta, take zem upstairs!"

Fritz frowned. "Surely, it will not hurt them to have a two-minute conversation."

But the children were already scurrying out the door with their nanny.

"That was unnecessarily rude," he snapped.

"It eeze all pretense. Mzz. Staunton eeze not zee slightest bit interested in *my* children."

M's mouth tightened. "Actually, I am."

Belinda's nose flared. "Oh, please. You may have fooled everyone else in zis family, but not me!"

Both men began defending M, who put up her hands to stop them.

"Please. I'm not here to trade insults. I'm sorry for whatever hurt my presence has caused you. As George has graciously invited me to be part of his family, I will make every effort to get along with you."

"You mean, now zat you have vhat you vant," Belinda hissed.

Fritz exploded, "Enough, Belinda! You will apologize at once. We had an agreement."

Her jaw tightened. "Of course. I was rather carried avay vith myself. The children vere quite trying this evening, vaiting for you to come. Late, as usual. I am sure you understand. I am very protective of zem."

She turned to M. "*Fraulein*, it has come to my attention zat I have confided in zee wrong people *und* certain persons have taken me a bit too literally. I apologize for vhatever pain zis may have caused you. In zee spirit of family unity, I stand corrected in my assumptions about you."

Fritz cleared his throat and glared at her. She sighed and screwed up her face.

"I promise to treat you vith respect *und* to-to velcome you into our family. Anyzing I can do to-to help you vould be my pleasure."

M smiled. "I appreciate the apology."

Belinda looked at Fritz, waiting.

"I believe the *hors d'oeuvres* can be served," he commanded.

"*Sehr güt.*"

She picked up the phone and buzzed the kitchen.

George steered M to several 15th and 16th century manuscripts to shift her focus.

"I must show you one of my favorite books."

He pointed to a large leather-bound book. "It's a Bible from the 16th century with original pastels featured throughout. I used to sit with *Gran'maman* as a boy examining the miniature paintings and reading about David and Goliath and Baby Jesus."

"You are so transparent," Fritz hissed in German. "That was no real apology at all."

"You said I had to say it, not that I had to mean it."

"Sorry you have to hear this. Let's go upstairs," George whispered as he led M up the spiral staircase that opened to the spacious mezzanine level.

Raisa, the downstairs maid, and Hilda arrived with refreshments moments later.

"Not a moment too soon. George, M, come join us," Fritz called out. "M, you must tell Belinda about your wedding plans."

She looked at George in a pleading tone as they made their way to the stairs.

"Father, you tell. We will just be a moment."

"The caviar will not wait, George."

Fritz turned to Belinda and launched into a description of the wedding and reception while the couple walked down the stairs to join their hosts. "It will be the talk of the town."

Belinda choked on her drink.

"No, no, Belinda. Why did you order a martini when you know we are opening a bottle of *Dom Pérignon*? Raisa, here, take this back."

He snatched Belinda's drink from her hand. Her pupils shot daggers. He turned to George and M.

"Ah, here is the happy couple. Let me do the honors the proper way."

He glared at his wife. "It turns out the Quilted Giraffe was not the best place to toast the engagement."

Contempt filled Belinda's eyes.

He removed the bottle of champagne from the ice bucket and loosened the cork until the dramatic pop heralded the celebration. He handed Hilda the bottle. She poured the bubbling liquid into four crystal champagne glasses that were etched in a delicate rendering of a couple's hands entwined, then passed him the tray.

"Now, these glasses," he murmured, "are very special. They were part of my mother's dowry when she married my father. They were made in Russia for my grandmother's wedding reception, a set of twenty-four. The set is still intact. They were shipped to my grandfather's brother for safekeeping when the troubles in Russia started. My parents toasted their engagement with these goblets. They were passed on to me for my engagement to Racquel. They represent the legacy of my ancestors."

George glanced at Belinda. Pain darkened her eyes.

Fritz beamed. "A toast to George and M. Good fortune, happiness, and grandchildren."

Everyone sipped the *Dom Pérignon* as Hilda and Raisa brought around the tray of *hors d'oeuvres*—caviar and sour cream on thick, chewy pumpernickel, eel on thin slices of cucumber moistened with cream cheese and chives, baked brie spread warm over fig nougat on thin crisps, and *gougères*.

"I won't be hungry for dinner with all this," M exclaimed, eyes wide.

"Oh, I zink you vill keep your figure. It vill be another hour at least before dinner eez served. Fritzie never dines before

9:00. I zought you, of *all* people, vould know zat."

M smiled.

Fritz interrupted, "What are you two talking about?"

"Just guessing Chef's recipes," Belinda snapped.

"Ah, yes, he is the best," he crowed. "I stole him from the Donald, you know."

George looked down at his shoes.

The next ten minutes, food captured the discussion.

George squeezed M's hand.

"M is quite the gourmet cook herself. We should invite you to dinner."

Belinda bristled, "Oh, I am sure Mzz. Staunton eeze much too busy to..."

Fritz smiled. "Why, we would be delighted, right, darling?"

She grimaced.

"So I was telling George and M they must decide which band and singer they want for the reception. I am sure I could get Sting or..."

"Father, I think Billy Joel or Harry Connick, Jr. would be more our style."

M's face flushed. "It's not really necessary."

"Yes, it eez a bit too much, vhat vith St. Patrick's, zee cardinal..."

"The archbishop," Fritz corrected. "I hope you will humor me, M. I really want to do this."

"Oh, please. Do you really need to show off zat much, Fritzie? Whom do you need to impress zat you haven't already, some politician, a new paramour, perhaps?"

Fritz's eyes daggered her. "No, dear, it is because I *can*, because I *want* to, because my son and his bride-to-be deserve it. What you or anyone else thinks matters little to me. Now, if you want to be useful, tell Chef to serve dinner precisely at 9:15."

Her face flushed.

George thought of grabbing M's hand and fleeing. He was

sure she was dreading the next fifty-five minutes as much as he was. Unhappiness permeated the room.

"Whatever you and George decide, Father, will suit me."

"How touching," Belinda spit.

Fritz glared at her. M ignored her.

"Would it be alright after *hors d'oeuvres* if we gather in the music room for some frivolity—singing, dancing, perhaps, before dinner?"

"What a splendid idea!" both Leibnitz men chimed in together.

Belinda harrumphed. "I vill check on zee children after speaking vith Chef."

"I pay the servants for that. I am sure they do not need your help," Fritz growled.

"I vill only be a moment."

"Be quick about it."

She sashayed out of the room as the trio chattered about the Golden Oldies and sipped their champagne. The maid appeared within moments.

"Hilda, please tell Chef the Beluga was exceptionally good this evening and bring the rest of the champagne to the music room."

"*Sehr güt, Herr Leibnitz.*"

Frtiz led the way out of the library down the hall. When they were inside the music room, he suggested that M play the piano and sing.

"Why don't we all sing? I'll start us off, okay?" she suggested.

She started playing and singing "Ain't Misbehavin'" in a gutsy mezzo.

"Come on, you two."

At the end of verse one they finally joined her in their faltering voices, and soon the mood brightened. As the song ended George glimpsed Belinda entering the room with a frown. Fritz turned and laughed.

"Do come join us."

She grimaced. "I'm happy to vatch you make fools of yourselves from here, zank you very much."

Fritz turned his back.

"Ain't Misbehavin" was followed by "My Funny Valentine," "Somewhere Over the Rainbow," and "Wind Beneath My Wings." The men barely sang beyond the first few bars of the Bette Midler hit, listening in rapt attention. When M had finished, they both clapped. Belinda glowered. George bent over and put his head on top of M's and rested his hands on her shoulders.

"Would you sing that at our wedding reception, *chérie*?"

She smiled. "Of course."

"I know," Fritz jumped in. "We can hire Bette Midler for the reception as well as Harry Connick, Jr. You can sing it together!"

"You zink zose two divas vill share zee stage?" Belinda cackled. "One famous, zee ozzer a vannabe."

M broke in, "Do you really think you could get Bette Midler or Harry Connick, Jr.?"

He nodded. "I will do everything in my power."

George's attention shifted to Hilda at the door. She waited a moment and then cleared her throat.

"*Herr Leibnitz, essen ist fertig.*"

"Capital. Then let us make our way into the Rembrandt Room, shall we?"

Belinda scowled. "Actually, I took zee liberty of arranging dinner in zee conservatory, Fritzie. I zought it vould be less stodgy for our guests."

"I specifically said the Rembrandt Room. Hilda, if you would be so kind as to see to it at once," he commanded.

She nodded and scurried out of the room.

Sadness washed over George. Belinda seemed to go out of her way to annoy Father, and he treated her as a servant or hired hand. George determined not to allow the palpable contempt between his parents to ruin his happiness. He took M's hand as they walked into the galleried hallway feeling blessed to have her as his partner. When they arrived in the dining room, the maids were busily putting the final touches on the place settings. Fritz smiled.

"*Danke shön*, Hilda, Raisa."

His outstretched hand beckoned to George and M. "Make yourselves comfortable. M, George, on either side of me. Belinda, next to George, *bitte*."

Everyone sat in the appointed chairs. For the first time George noticed the contrast between the plush, wing-backed, upholstered chairs and the massive, cold oak table. It was obvious why Belinda had selected the intimacy of the conservatory. Bottles of wine had been decanted into two cut crystal wine flasks, one of which Raisa now brought to the table and poured into the large crystal wine goblets at each place setting.

"Chef suggests the Cabernet will go nicely with dinner: wild mushroom bisque, roasted pheasant, wild rice, chargrilled vegetables, and *salade frisée*."

"Capital!" Fritz caroled.

George started describing a round-the-world honeymoon trip when Belinda interrupted, "It eez zee vorst time of year to travel around zee vorld. You really should vait until spring. If I vere..."

Fritz countered, "But you are not. I have thought of everything."

Raisa appeared from the kitchen.

"Ah, here is the soup now. M, you will be astounded at Chef's wild mushroom bisque. It is outstanding."

Her face brightened. "I love mushroom bisque."

As everyone began their meal, served on delicate Limoges china, the mood lightened. Belinda said little unless the conversation was directed to her and kept her remarks terse.

George watched M try to draw his stepmother into the

conversation and warmed to her kindness.

"We will take our dessert and coffee on the terrace. The crisp air will do us good," Fritz instructed the staff as the last salad plate was removed. "And bring a bottle of Courvoisier and brandy snifters with dessert."

"*Sehr güt, Herr Leibnitz.*"

"I have asked Chef to prepare a special celebratory dessert. Frederick has done some research on your favorite foods, M, as you might have noticed."

Her face broke into a smile. "Indeed. You needn't have gone to so much trouble."

A snigger escaped Belinda's lips. Fritz glared at her.

"The pleasure is all mine."

"George, if you would kindly take M for a short walk through the gardens, I would like a word with Belinda. We will join you in, say, twenty-two minutes on the terrace?"

George obeyed. "Certainly, Father. We would love a romantic walk."

As they walked hand in hand on the cobblestone path that wound through the flower gardens, he released the tension his body had been holding.

"I'm happy to be by ourselves for a while."

She nodded. "It *is* a bit intense around them."

"I apologize."

"No need."

His mouth tightened. He replied, "I hope he's giving her bloody hell."

The peacefulness of the water drew his attention. The illumination from the underground lights along the winding path brightened their way through the parterre and out to the gentian lake. The cool spring air was redolent with the mingling odors of tulips, hyacinths, daffodils, and roses. The water danced in the reflection of the moon and the lights that surrounded the lake. Light dappled the air and took flight through the cattails that surrounded the lake. Now the ripples moved out in undulating fingers across the expanse of water. Pink and white blossoms hugged the distant shore in welcome, and the fingers stilled.

M's voice interrupted his reverie. "I suspect they both deserve what the other's dishing out."

"I thought this was to be a romantic walk."

"Sorry. We should leave them out of it and enjoy each other these few moments alone."

He turned to embrace her.

"Sorry about my family. I hope my love is enough."

"You're all I need!"

As their buttery lips touched and their arms entwined, the problems inside the mansion moved light-years away.

Dessert was moist chocolate soufflé served with raspberries swimming in white chocolate sauce.

"The soufflé is perfection," M enthused after the first bite. "The texture and flavor are exotic. I wonder what Chef's secret is."

Fritz smiled. "So glad you approve. I will have Chef tell you all about it, but first, Belinda has a gift."

Belinda's transformation astounded George.

"Raisa, *bitte*," she said, directing her gaze to the maid.

"*Sehr güt, Frau Leibnitz.*"

Raisa disappeared through the French doors of the conservatory and returned moments later with a large package wrapped in royal blue paper and an explosion of color ribboned the four sides, blossoming on top in the shape of a piano. The maid transported the package on an oversized round silver tray to Belinda, who took the package and handed it to M with a broad smile.

"As a gesture of a-affection *und* velcome to our family, uh, I, uh,..."

M's eyes smiled. "Thank you. You're very kind."

She set the package on the table.

"You're not going to open it?" Belinda asked.

"Oh."

M proceeded to remove the ribbons, preserving the artistic creation at the top.

George wondered what this could be. Most likely, Frederick had bought the gift at Father's instruction. He knew M had often bought Steuben vases, Tiffany crystal paperweights and bowls, and first edition books at his father's behest for him to present to a favored friend, political figure, or family member for special occasions. She even had selected presents from Belinda's children to their mother. Thus, the irony of receiving a gift from Belinda delighted him.

M blushed and looked at him.

The package gave nothing away. His anticipation increased. As she lifted the top flap of the box, a large royal blue square velvet case with rounded corners and ornately carved gold hinges emerged. The suspense built. Her fingers trembled. As she lifted the lid of the case, she gasped.

"Well, put it on. Let us see how it will look on you," Fritz crowed.

Belinda scowled, then chirped, "Let me help you."

"I-I don't know what to say."

A mirror appeared instantly as she helped M put on the silver tiara inlaid with diamonds.

"This is *Gran'maman*'s," George gushed. "How...?"

"Yes. She bequeathed it to you for your wife to wear on her wedding day. She hoped you would find your princess, and you have," Fritz murmured, his voice trembling. "I wish she were here to give it to you herself, M."

M's radiating joy embraced him.

Fritz smiled. "There is a long story behind this crown, but I think some brandy is in order first."

M started to remove the tiara, but stopped with tremulous hands.

"No, I think you should keep it on. It becomes you," George said, steadying her fingers.

"Indeed," Fritz agreed and glared at Belinda.

"Lovely, brings out your eyes. It vill look perfect vith a vhite vedding dress."

Her voice congealed, then thawed. "Who eez designing it—Valentino, perhaps?"

M blushed. "I-I hadn't thought of a couturier. I-I am sure I'll find..."

"Oh, no, Belinda is right," Fritz insisted. "You must wear something exquisite, designed just for you. We should have Tatania introduce you to..."

"Vhy not let *me* do zis little favor for you," Belinda cooed.

M looked from George to his father.

George chimed in, "Aunt Tani's already offered to help M with the wedding, and she has accepted. It would hurt Aunt Tani's feelings if..."

His stepmother grimaced. "But it eez okay to hurt my feelings."

Fritz shot her a threatening look.

"...Vhat I meant to say eez perhaps I can help. I can speak to Tani and make some introductions..."

M smiled. "Of course, lovely."

A hint of sadness tinged her eyes. Everything was being planned for them. She had planned to use her own meager savings for the wedding dress. The wedding, the reception, now the dress. A simple, elegant wedding wouldn't happen. George's musings were interrupted by Fritz's voice describing the history of the diamond tiara with a few embellishments from the version his grandmother had told him.

"...And legend has it that the tiara was handed down from Catherine the Great through the family line. The tiara was the spoils of war in Catherine's campaign against the Prussians and had belonged to a young princess whose suitor fashioned it from silver and diamonds extracted from his sword. Expert appraisers have valued the crown at more than five million and have dated it from the 18th century."

M gasped.

"But the extraordinary part of the story is how the crown came to this country. Mummy was afraid it would be stolen on the voyage, so she had her jeweler in Vienna remove all the diamonds and her seamstress sewed them into her corset, which she wore at all times. Imagine how uncomfortable, fifty diamonds pressing her ribcage. The silver tiara without the diamonds looked rather ordinary, so no one was interested in it. Once we were established at Auntie's in New York, the diamonds were returned to their treasured place. Mother wore that tiara only four times, I believe—once in celebration of Papa's homecoming party and at three presidential inaugural balls."

George's eyes moistened.

"And *I'm* going to wear this priceless heirloom? I couldn't. What if it is dislodged from...?"

"Not to worry. We will make sure it is firmly attached," Fritz reassured her.

M's eyebrows scrunched. "But what if a thief should...?"

"...crash the party and steal it? Be assured we will have sufficient security in place. You are the new owner of this diadem, not just the pretty head on which it will sit."

Her eyebrows shot up. "I-I am the... Forgive me. Did I-I hear you correctly? I cannot accept this. It is too valuable."

Belinda glowered, spitting out her disgust. "Oh, please."

Raisa appeared near the patriarch's chair.

"*Ja*, Raisa?" Fritz asked, impatience lining his face.

"Excuse me, sir," she interrupted in German. "Chef was wondering if you will need him any further this evening."

"Of course. Send him out."

He turned to M. "Yes, it is yours. It is my mother's present to you, and you cannot refuse."

Her mouth opened, then closed. She looked at George, who gave her a reassuring smile and squeezed her hand.

Raisa excused herself.

Within moments, a swarthy, haggard-looking gentleman dressed in a white chef's apron and toque stepped down onto the terrace. He must have been waiting just inside the conservatory door for some time.

"*Comme d'habitude, Chef, le dîner était somptueux,*" Fritz caroled.

"*Merci, monsieur.*"

Fritz continued, "*Vous vous souvenez de Mademoiselle Staunton, la fiancée de mon fils.*"

Chef moved toward M to shake her hand and offer his greetings.

"*Enchantée, Mademoiselle Staunton. C'est un plaisir comme toujours.*"

Fritz motioned to George.

"*Comment allez-vous, Monsieur Georges?*"

George beamed. "*Formidable. Et vous, Chef?*"

The Frenchman smiled. "*Parfait.*"

After a few moments of chatting about food and recipes, Chef said goodnight. The evening wound down as the couples sipped their Courvoisiers.

Fritz turned to M as he arose from his chair. "Your tiara will be placed back in the vault for safe-keeping until you need it. I assume your dress designer will want you to wear it to fashion a suitable gown. Just let us know when you require it."

"Certainly. Thank you ever so much for going to so much trouble to make me feel welcome." A tear trickled down her right cheek. She looked first at Fritz and then at Belinda. "I hardly know what to say."

George knew she was relieved to relinquish the tiara. The massive 17th century hand-crafted grandfather clock in the long hallway chimed midnight. He was more than ready to leave. As if reading their minds, Fritz suggested they stay in one of the guesthouses. They declined. Sebastian was waiting just outside the front door to escort the couple to the limousine and drive them to the city. M's head rested on George's shoulder as he leaned back into the recessed headrest. They talked over each other in astonishment at receiving such a priceless gift. Belinda didn't figure into their conversation, so complete was their happiness.

Chapter 5

Over the weekend, the couple discussed how to wrest control of their wedding and honeymoon from Fritz. Only his sister-in-law could brook his will. M lunched at the Carlisle Hotel with Mrs. Tatania mid-week to discuss the engagement party and the dress designer. Mrs. Belinda had shared her contacts at De Laurentis, Ralph Lauren, and Valentino, but Aunt Tani suggested that M would be happier with a younger couturier like Vera Wang. She explained that M would need to be firm about what she wanted and not back down. By the time dessert was served, M felt more comfortable.

She couldn't resist asking, "Do you see much of Mrs. Belinda?"

A look of mild disgust crossed the kind face of George's aunt.

"No. She is, uh, a bit difficult. Why do you ask?"

"Well, I..."

M fidgeted.

"Let me be frank, M. May I call you M?"

"Please."

"Belinda is suspicious of every woman, and every Leibnitz is a threat to her aspirations. Mother Aleksandra did not welcome Belinda with open arms. She adored Racquel, as do we all, and then the pregnancy."

M hid her shock.

"I suppose we have not made it easy. I have tried to be

polite and treat Belinda and the children kindly. If she had not been so manipulative, she might have won over even Mother. One can feel some sympathy for her position, after all."

M screwed up her face. "But she makes it hard to like her."

"Yes. She has behaved badly toward you, even convincing my son..." Aunt Tani paused and looked down. "In any case, we all know what a lovely and sincere person you are and will do what is necessary to help you. You are part of our family now."

"You're very kind."

"I understand Mother left you something precious. This gift has created feelings of... Well, it is no secret that Aleksandra favored George. I cannot say it has not caused me pain, but we, on our side, have all been blessed with far more than we can ever use. Each grandchild has received very generous gifts besides a sizable inheritance. I should say at least George and my children. I think Claude and Brianna did not receive quite what Belinda expected. So, despite Mother's keen business mind, I fear she may have created extra problems for Fritz with Belinda. You understand?"

M nodded.

"Aleksandra saw into the heart of things more than others. Perhaps, she knew best."

She tapped her chest as she spoke. "George has a sensibility that endears him to us. Except, perhaps, Marcus."

Her eyes crinkled. "But it is normal for boys within a family business to vie for control. We just seem to have a heightened sense of rivalry and, uh, intrigue, in this family."

A weary look crossed her face. "Mother was a stabilizing influence. Without her now..." She spread out her hands. "Perhaps some miscalculations on her part. And boys will be boys."

M frowned. "When girls behave like that, we call them names and excoriate them."

Aunt Tani chuckled. "Unfortunately, in this family

Aleksandra has followed some of Rainer's methods."

She sighed and shifted the conversation to the party and wedding plans. The afternoon disappeared in the blink of an eye.

M warmed to Aunt Tani's attempts to mother her. She couldn't wait to tell George all about her afternoon and the juicy bit of news that Claude would have been a bastard if his father hadn't married Belinda. She found him reading in the library when she returned to his apartment.

"No wonder *Gran'maman* never favored Belinda, trapping Father like that."

"No wonder your stepmother is always plotting. She's trying to secure her children's future. At least that's what your aunt thinks. Your father wouldn't dare write them out of his will, would he?"

"Of course not. However, *Gran'maman* probably left as little as she could in their trust funds. Of course, that could still be millions. It's not like they'll starve."

Her lips pouted. "I think it's a matter of degree."

"Maybe. Legally, she would have little recourse if *Gran'maman* left my cousins and me the lion's share of the estate. I have a sizable fortune, but I've never bothered to ask how much."

Her eyebrows shot up. How would he survive without his fortune?

"*Gran'maman* and Uncle Sergey made sure Father's houses and properties would be owned by corporations, even the Wilton estate. So, if Belinda is looking to get out of her marriage with a killing, she may not be able to punish Father as much as she thinks. She would still have a lavish lifestyle if they divorce. She would never have to work, pay a mortgage or car payment, or care for her own house. Her life would remain mostly what she's accustomed to. There were prenups she had to sign limiting any settlement, but she'll make out just fine."

She squirmed. "Speaking of prenuptial agreements, do I need to sign one? I'm happy to."

He cupped her face in his hands. "That's one of the many reasons I love you. Actually, I don't know. I'll ask Parker. He and Father oversee my trust fund. Parker told me that if I decided to make it on my own, the fifty million or so shouldn't all be spent in one place. But since Father *gave* you a tiara worth millions, I can't imagine we would need something like prenups. *I* don't think it's necessary."

Her eyes bulged. She swallowed a tingle of excitement.

"I find it hard to believe that Fritz Leibnitz would just..."

"Father adores you. He's very generous to those he loves. Look how much he gave my mother when he divorced her."

Her eyes widened. "Then why did he divorce her?"

"He loves her, but didn't want to live with her anymore." His eyes twinkled. "Don't underestimate my father's generosity."

She fell silent. She knew Fritz Leibnitz better than George did. He was generous, sometimes to a fault, but there was a limit if he couldn't control someone.

The conversation shifted to more pressing matters, like choosing a Matron of Honor, bridesmaids, and ushers.

"I thought of asking my friend Laurence, but maybe it's a gesture of friendship to ask Marcus instead. He wouldn't expect it. What do you think?"

She pecked his cheek and smiled. "How thoughtful. He doesn't deserve the honor, but it's a good tactical move. I'm sure it would please your uncle and aunt. I think we should get to know them better."

"I agree. Well, let's sleep on the choice of Best Man, shall we?"

"Whatever you say."

"And your Maid of Honor?"

She cocked her head. "Maybe my voice coach, Joy. I'm closer to her than anyone else. Frankly, my friends are no more than acquaintances, and it might be overkill to ask your aunt if you're asking Marcus. But I *did* think of your aunt first. She's helping me arrange everything, so she's unofficially my Matron of Honor."

He smiled. "She would be thrilled, but don't women normally pick someone they've known a long time?"

He yawned. She laughed.

"How many women are wearing a priceless headpiece for their wedding? Nothing about this wedding will be *normal*."

He sighed. "You decide. I'm ready to doze off, no offense."

"None taken."

He started snoring as soon as his head touched the pillow while her mind tumbled around the tricky business of becoming his wife. His father was deciding everything. One of the prices to pay for marrying a Leibnitz. For now.

Chapter 6

Over the next several days George delved into the family business with a passion, relieved that Aunt Tani was helping M juggle the wedding details with her other duties. He no longer felt the need to consult Dr. Stanley as he settled into his new responsibilities. He was determined to conduct comprehensive research to outpace his cousin's knowledge of LE business.

For M's last official day at LE, he and his father planned a luncheon party in her honor. Chef prepared an assortment of *hors d'oeuvres, crudités,* and a multi-layered chocolate fudge cake for fifty guests, and champagne capped the festive mood.

As the celebration got underway, Frederick handed M a gift card from the executive staff for two days for two at the Greenbrier Spa and Resort in West Virginia.

George beamed as her eyes moistened.

"How very thoughtful. Thank you so much."

She hugged each staff member.

"Song!" erupted from every corner of the room.

"Oh, please, sing for us," Frederick pleaded.

She grimaced. "Don't expect my best after champagne."

His face opened up. "Oh, posh, your worst will be outstanding."

She stood with her back to the entrance door, closed her eyes, and breathed in. George's eye caught his father entering the room and slipping off to the side.

"My grandfather's favorite song is mine as well. I share it

with the hope that it will bless you as you have blessed me."

She began with closed eyes, *acapella,* in a low earthy tone, "Amazing grace, how sweet the sound that saved a wretch like me..."

With each successive verse, she moved into a higher key. By the final stanza, "When we've been there ten thousand years, bright shining as the sun," she had reached coloratura range, building momentum and volume. She topped off the song with a final "Amazing Grace" that reverberated around the room.

Applause erupted. George's face beamed with pride.

"What a way to cap the celebration," Frederick murmured.

Her eyes embraced him. "Thank you. I can't tell you how much I've enjoyed working with each of you. How much I've learned, especially from you."

She kissed him on the cheek. His father approached as George was threading her arm through his.

"It will not be the same in the office without you."

Before she could answer, he turned to leave. First one, then another, gathered round to say their goodbyes, and she was finally alone with George and Frederick.

"Frederick, call me if you need me," she murmured, tremulous.

His eyes moistened. "Thanks. I might just take you up on that."

She embraced him with another kiss on each cheek.

"See ya round," he caroled as he left.

George squeezed her side. "Leaving all this responsibility behind must be a load off your mind."

"I guess."

She looked down. "I'll miss the hum and rush of activity. But it's for the best."

He rubbed her shoulders. "You're worried they won't think of you in the same way, aren't you?"

Her eyes pooled. "I'll miss the relationships. They'll

change." She sighed. "But I'm moving on. Change comes with the territory."

He smiled, although her emotional connection to the staff puzzled him.

"True enough."

Her eyes pleaded. "Well, I'm free now, so let's head out. I can take the weekend off, but then I'll need to work non-stop on my dissertation. I'm planning to graduate in June, so that means finishing by May 5th and sitting before my committee by May 20th."

His eyebrows widened. "But that's less than two months away. Is it enough time?"

"I think so. I'm past the halfway point already. I know I can pull it off, but I can't be distracted. After next week's concert, I won't schedule any concerts until the fall. I still need to meet with dress designers, but your father and aunt are handling the rest of the arrangements. I really wish I could get out of the whole designer thing." She frowned. "It's so much trouble."

He laughed. "Tell them what you want, insist on a set schedule, and think of it as recreation. Or ask Aunt Tani to choose for you. Father's not going to back down."

"Yes, everything is about how it reflects on him," she groaned. "And I think your aunt wouldn't just choose for me."

"Tell her what you want then."

"I hate to impose."

"What else does she have to do that someone else doesn't do for her?"

"She *has* had a lot of experience with designers. She showed me her closet. It's full of Chanel, Valentino, St. Laurent, Prada, and all kinds of names I don't recognize."

"So she's an old pro. Use her. She'll love it."

M sighed. "Alright. If you say so."

He shook his head. Some women would love to have such a trivial problem.

Chapter 7

Over the next month he barely saw M. She was working on her dissertation all day and through much of the night. He stayed out of her way and immersed himself in every aspect of the projects assigned to him.

To his dismay, he could see that Marcus was outpacing him. His drive to master every detail fueled his every move.

He came home around 8:00 exhausted every night and chatted with M over a hurried dinner about each other's progress. Then she headed to her desk, and he painted in his studio until he dragged himself to bed.

His dreams were disjointed. He was running the company with Marcus as Senior Vice President of Marketing. Then he was president, facing Marcus, the CEO, who was berating him about a failed project and suggesting that M help him. His father and uncle looked down from their portraits on the wall behind Marcus.

"George, my boy, I am sure you did your best. You were in over your head. We understand."

"Son, how could you embarrass me like this? You need M. She has the ambition you lack."

He awakened with a start, drenched in sweat, mumbling, "No, I promise I will do better. Give me another chance, please!"

M turned over to hug him, half-awake.

"Sh-sh, it's only a dream. Go back to sleep, *chéri.*"

"I have to see Dr. Stanley," he muttered.

He fell back into a deep sleep.

When he awoke at five he was convinced Marcus would always outmaneuver him. M yawned and turned toward him.

"*Chéri*, you were talking in your sleep. What's troubling you?"

"Oh, did I?"

She snuggled up to him. "It's okay. Would you prefer blueberry pancakes after our run or a vegetable omelet?"

"Either is fine with me," he barked, feeling hemmed in.

He disentangled from her embrace and arose to get dressed for a five-mile run to clear his head and rid him of the nagging fear that lingered from his nightmare. She insisted on joining him, to his dismay. When he beat her time by 2:54, his confidence returned. He decided not to call Dr. Stanley. A tinge of guilt washed over him. He brushed aside the feeling as his thoughts shifted to Uncle Guenther and Aunt Tani's engagement party the following night.

"I thought this was going to be a small, intimate party," M whined as she set down her teacup.

"I know. Father asked Aunt Tani to invite some of his friends and associates. I'm no happier about it than you are," he added between bites. "At last count seventy-five people were on the confirmed list."

"My point exactly.

He moved his food around the plate.

"Look on the bright side. We both love art, so we can walk around their house, sip champagne, and eat *hors d'oeuvres*."

She smiled. "Who do you think will be there? The invitation says, *Black Tie Optional*."

He picked up his glass of orange juice. "All the muckety-mucks; my mother, whom I'm dying for you to meet; her new beau; I feel sure my cousins and step brother will bring dates; my friend Laurence, whom you have not met, and his wife; two friends from Exeter—John and Anthony—and their dates;

a few guys from the office and their wives; Father Thomas, of course, and you know the people you've invited."

Her fork thudded on the plate.

"Yikes!"

He sighed. She frowned.

"Anything I need to know about your mother or your friends? I don't want to make any *faux pas*."

He grabbed his fork. "We'll talk tonight. I'm running late. I'll be home by 7:00, I promise," he said as he wolfed down the rest of his omelet and coffee.

She beamed. "Great! I'll prepare a special TGIF meal."

He smiled. "Yum! How's your thesis coming along?"

"It's all coming together. I've maybe a quarter more to finish. Professor Béjart has approved all the chapters I've submitted so far."

"Wonderful!"

She frowned. "Of course, the rest of the committee can shoot the whole thing down, if they want, by the time the final draft is handed in."

He fidgeted. "The likelihood of that?"

"Béjart assures me it can't happen on his watch, but I dunno. There are two departments involved and..."

He pushed back his chair. "Then, have one of the Russian profs read what you have so far."

She frowned. "Béjart wouldn't hear of it. Turf, you know."

He stood. "So that's why you're worried."

She patted her mouth with the cloth napkin. "Absolutely!"

He shifted his feet. "Can you do it without him knowing?"

She flattened the napkin. "In that small world? Not likely. That's why I'm trying to beat my deadline."

He was now even more pressed for time. He kissed her, excused himself, and dashed off to the office. He arrived at 9:15, half an hour later than he had planned. He still needed to put the finishing touches on his proposal for the 10:00 meeting. It would be the first independent assignment he had completed. He rubbed his fingers together like rosary beads.

George's secretary had the latest draft ready for his review as soon as he walked into his office. He delved into the twenty page document with a critical eye. Feelings of inadequacy shingled his thoughts, tempting him to wash his sweating hands. He ignored the urge, took a deep breath, closed his hands into tight fists, thought "open hand" as he squeezed harder, and finally released his grip with a long exhale. Then he resumed his punctilious examination.

At 9:45, he alerted his secretary to make copies while he prepared himself.

Deep breaths in and out.

At 9:58 sharp, he made his way to his father's conference room, instructing his secretary to bring the copies of the report to Frederick in ten minutes. George arrived at 10:00, and Frederick directed him to the waiting room. When he entered, Marcus was standing at the window. He turned toward George.

"Quite a view down Park Avenue South. Unless one is afraid of heights. How about it, are you afraid of flying high, stepping out on the edge?"

George's vocal chords tightened. "A little, I guess. You?"

Marcus sniggered. "You're too honest, Georgie. I would never show vulnerability in front of a rival."

George smiled. "I'll take that as a yes, then."

Marcus chuckled and stepped forward. George advanced as well.

"I thought we put that rival business behind us."

Marcus tilted his head. "I wouldn't say *that*."

George pinned his cousin with his eyes.

"One of the ways we're different."

Before Marcus could formulate a pithy retort, the door to Fritz's office opened and Parker motioned the cousins to come in.

"Good that you're both on time. Mr. Leibnitz doesn't like

to be kept waiting."

Marcus started muttering behind Parker's back as George motioned him ahead.

"Don't," he whispered. "Parker takes no prisoners."

Marcus' lips tightened. "Thanks for the warning, cousin, but none needed."

George shook his head. He would relish seeing Parker put Marcus in his place.

"Why are we traipsing through Uncle Fritz's office to the conference room, instead of using the hallway?"

Parker sliced him with a look.

"I brought you *here* before joining the others so that no one is embarrassed."

Marcus's mouth curled. "What's that supposed to mean?"

"You will learn, young man, that manners are of primary importance to the owners of this company. If you want to lead, I suggest you learn to respect your elders."

Marcus puckered his lips. "Yes, sir."

Parker sharpened his voice. "Right words, wrong attitude. You still have much to learn. You could follow your cousin's example."

Marcus's nose flared with taut, blistering eyes. George savored the moment. Parker fixed his steely eyes on Marcus.

"When we go in, speak only when you're spoken to. Answer, 'yes, sir; no, sir.' Be attentive to the subtleties. You both have presentations to make."

"We do?" the cousins asked in unison, their eyes wide.

"Yes, and I expect you to be polite. Keep your cool. Be mature. Learn from the questions."

Marcus rolled his eyes.

"I'm trying to help you, son. If you want to run this company one day, you'll learn the fine art of diplomacy."

Parker turned to George. "I'm sure you don't need to be reminded, but show what you know in there."

"Thank you, sir."

George grew two inches.

Marcus threw him a scowl.

"When you go in, greet each man and thank him for coming, starting with Mr. Fritz and Mr. Guenther. Today, you're not heirs, but employees. I expect you to act accordingly. Understood?"

The cousins nodded. Marcus walked ahead of George, cutting off his entrance. George took the moment to relax his muscles. As they went through the door, conversation fizzled.

"Ah, there you are," Fritz caroled, motioning to them to sit in the two empty middle seats on either side of the expansive table.

They barely had time to greet anyone as Fritz called everyone to take his place. He sat at one end and Guenther at the other. The room fell into a hush. George detected a slight twitch in his cousin's right eye as he looked at his father, who radiated warmth.

"I believe you all know my son, George. You have met Guenther's son, Marcus. Take a good look, gentlemen. You are going to see a lot of these young men. The future of Leibnitz Enterprise rests with them. It is our job to prepare them, pruning and shaping as well as helping and encouraging. So gloves are off today, gentlemen. I know both of them will take your comments, suggestions, and criticisms to heart."

His eyes fell on each young man. "I am sure you will not disappoint Guenther and me."

He turned to the others. "Now, to business. We will hear first from Leonardo, who is reporting on the progress of the negotiations with the Italians on..."

George's attention shifted to the formal agenda in front of him. His presentation was not until just before lunch. Marcus was last on the list, at 4:00. He relaxed his tense shoulders.

At the first fifteen minute break, he asked Frederick, who was taking notes, to bring copies of his report five minutes before he was scheduled to present.

The morning progressed. George didn't understand the intricacies of much of the discussion and took copious notes to study later. He didn't know enough to ask more than what were surely the most inane inquiries. Marcus, on the other hand, seemed to know a good deal. His questions, while incisive, at times seemed too pointed, as though the executives reported to him.

After one sharp exchange, Fritz threw a question back, "So, Marcus, tell us how *you* would handle the Nigerians?"

His voice strutted. "Well, I would play hardball."

Fritz's eyes narrowed. "Meaning what, exactly?"

George couldn't help but notice smirks on the faces of several executives.

Marcus crowed, "I'd sue the hell out of them for starters."

Fritz's voice hardened. "Let us dispense with the colorful language, shall we? How would that help us, exactly?"

Marcus stammered, "Well, they'd, uhhh, have to ante up, wouldn't they?"

Fritz turned to George.

"What do you think?"

He was caught off guard.

"Well, th-this dispute would fall, uh, under international law, which is less enforceable than U.S. laws. The International Court of Justice has no real power to enforce a contract a government wishes to violate."

"Go on."

If looks could kill, Marcus had shot him through the heart.

He remembered meeting the tribal chief most responsible for securing this pulp deal and his senior wife of four at a reception in Wilton a year ago. At the time, he had asked his father many questions about the local culture and the jobs the pulp mill was creating. Now, two years after the completion of the last phase of the project, only the third of four payments had been made by the Nigerian government, although local Nigerians trained by LE engineers had begun running the facility six months earlier. The current crisis centered on the fact that LE employees had been barred from the premises and lives were at risk, a situation which George had surmised concerned the men around the table as much or more as the long overdue payment.

"Legal action may be in order, but it would not really accomplish the goal of getting our nine million and our men to safety. Moral suasion would have greater effect. Negotiating directly with the local chiefs would be our only real hope of recovering the dollars, in my opinion, given local customs. But I think Parker is much more knowledgeable about the matter than I. I defer to his judgment."

He looked at his mentor, who concurred. "Indeed. This will be a tricky business. We cannot antagonize the Nigerians or we will surely lose our investment and, of course, our engineers."

Fritz nodded, then turned to Guenther. "Your thoughts? Your engineers are the ones in harm's way. They have been in Lagos now for how long?"

"Yes," Guenther said, rubbing his chin, "I would have to agree with George and Parker. Pieter, Amos, Julian, and Pau moved to Lagos from the mill site about two months ago. Johanne here can explain. I believe they will have to pull out. There is talk of revoking their visas; even violence."

A stir of voices was quickly dampened when Fritz spoke. "At this juncture, we should bring our boys home. I will make overtures to Chief Mombatabu. George and Parker, develop a proposal with Guenther and Johanne to accompany me to Athens. We will seek an audience while we conduct further negotiations with the Greeks."

George basked in his cousin's glowering face as he scampered to make notes of the research he would need to undertake. He almost failed to register the sound of his father's voice as the conversation moved to the project George had been investigating for several weeks.

"...as George will bring us up-to-date on the latest until about 1:00, when lunch will be served. George?"

He quelled the anxiety rising to his throat and focused on his presentation. He directed the executives' attention to page one of the document Frederick had delivered to each member only moments earlier. He provided introductory information about the resource recovery field and stated that the public relations and legal nightmare that the company would have to face would be too risky. He then referred to figures on page ten of his report that provided statistical data about dioxins and other PCBs that would be prohibitively expensive to eliminate through filtration systems currently in use. He suggested LE would do better to invest dollars in technologies that would decimate toxins from the vapors and other emissions of burning garbage before they left the plant.

"As you will see on page fifteen, the research literature suggests that insufficient dollars have been dedicated to creating a viable technology solution to scrub the filtration systems or, even better, convert the emissions to a different clean product. The possibilities in this area are more palatable and even intriguing. Using newly developed scientific studies in the mixed use of algae and enzymes would emulsify the toxins. Another idea would be to create wood pellets from the emulsified toxins. We could form them with the waste products of pulp mixed with resin that is low in CO_2 emissions. It would be less than one-third of pulp and oil. The pellets could be formed in high-pressure vats and presses and be ecologically more viable than traditional products like coal and wood."

"This is all speculation, of course," Marcus interrupted.

George smiled. "Indeed, as was considering a resource recovery project at all."

Marcus sneered. "It seems to me you would have done more research before presenting such incomplete information and wasting everyone's time."

"George has provided interesting proposals to consider," Guenther offered. "He has done his homework. The objective was to determine if resource recovery makes sense for this company, and from where I sit I think he has made his case. Data in his analysis support his recommendations, which, of course, we need to examine more closely. But I, for one, would vote to explore his proposals for an innovative filtration agent and wood pellets in more depth and bring a scientist on board to study such products' feasibility before we decide to enter this field."

Fritz stroked his chin. "Interesting idea. The floor is open for discussion and questions."

George basked in his uncle's immediate show of support. He fielded a number of questions and comments that helped clarify his thinking and outlined the additional research he would need to do. By 1:00, he felt energized that the proposal had been approved for further study. The group agreed that building resource recovery plants was risky, but further discussion in the afternoon would shed more light on the matter.

The wait staff wheeled in the lunch trays, loaded with veal saltimbocca, poached salmon in dill sauce, Caesar's salad, an assortment of cut fruit, cheese, pastries, coffee, teas, and soft drinks.

Parker approached him. "I'm very proud of you. To be honest, a year ago, I wasn't sure you would be able to come up to speed this quickly. I apologize for underestimating you."

George's head lowered. "That's very kind of you. It's important to me, in working on this project, to prove myself to you."

Parker grunted. "I'm sure it is. Was I that transparent that you realized I had doubts about you?"

George looked up. "I recognized I was a rather late starter, so I knew I'd need to prove myself."

Parker smiled. "Well, you certainly have. And your

suggestions on the Nigerian matter—capital, my boy, capital!"

George glowed.

As the men moved about to fill their plates and socialize, Johanne approached him.

"I like your idea very much. *Und* I will enjoy working with you on the Nigerian problem."

"Thank you. I appreciate your suggestion that one of our engineers work with a scientist to study the dioxin problem."

Fritz interrupted by coming up behind him and patting him on the shoulder.

"Good show. You handled yourself very nicely."

Although pleased, he worried he would not pass the next hurdle set for him.

"I am anxious to see how your cousin will handle criticism this afternoon after the grilling he gave you. I am sure you will give him as much cheek, if not more."

Fritz slapped him on the arm and headed toward Parker. George surmised that Marcus *had* infuriated Fritz by refusing to let up on his questions and suggesting George was wrong. Getting even would be sweet. But it didn't feel right. That kind of behavior would not earn the respect of the other men around the conference table, even if it would delight his father. He remembered the disgusted looks of a few executives before Guenther had suggested Marcus cede the floor to someone else.

Absorbed in thought, he barely registered his cousin's voice.

"...hot stuff, don't you?"

George looked up. "Hmm? Sorry, what?"

"Don't think I'm fooled, Georgie. You know what I said. You think you're the rising star at LE. Just wait. I'll make you look like the schoolboy you are this afternoon." Marcus's eyes threw knife blades.

George smiled. Marcus moved off when his uncle approached and asked him about wedding plans.

"We are very grateful for all the help Aunt Tani is giving her. It is all a little overwhelming for her."

Guenther grinned. "To be sure. But undoubtedly she is up to the challenge."

George nodded. "Yes, she is quite amazing, the way she can juggle so much and maintain her cool."

The conversation was cut short when Fritz called the meeting back to order. Everyone returned to his appointed place within moments. The afternoon proceeded with reviews of the current workflow of the many pulp mill projects underway in Europe, Africa, and Asia. As the meeting approached the three-quarter mark, he glanced at his cousin, who seemed absorbed in thought. Empathy floated across his mind, but the need for revenge squelched it.

Fritz's voice broke into his thoughts. "As the last item on our agenda, no reflection on the importance of the presentation, to be sure," Fritz said, eliciting grins from several, "Marcus will enlighten us about new markets and their viability."

Critical eyes followed Marcus's every move. He straightened in his chair, leaned forward, and began with the confidence born of privilege.

"Fantasy films, online learning portals, and resource recovery facilities are the hottest tickets in the marketplace today, gentlemen. As you will see in the report before you, the revenue stream from these industries has grown steadily over the last five years and is expected to expand exponentially over the next ten to fifteen years, despite what others may suggest."

The lightbulb went off. George's research countered Marcus's rosy picture for technology solutions. He hadn't matched the level of research George had done and had missed key details. George examined the smug face of his father, who obviously had given the cousins a similar assignment, pitting them against each other in a very public way. Was his uncle part of this plot? George's face smoothed into a blank. He sat with rapt attention to Marcus's presentation about the film industry. He half-listened, his mind racing as he flipped through his cousin's handout to the section, Technology Solutions for Tomorrow, in which online learning portals and resource recovery solutions were detailed. He needed to formulate the questions he would ask and the criticisms he would throw at his rival.

He realized within moments that Marcus had done a lot of work, but he had stopped just short of proving or disproving his research hypothesis. He hid a smirk. His obsessive-compulsive nature had served him well on this project. He *had* to prove both sides of his argument in order to make a decision about what to recommend. Marcus should have done likewise. He no doubt regretted his lack of thoroughness and was trying to use smoke and mirrors in a glib tone to prove he was right and George was wrong. George's father had been warning him at lunch. His eyes threw daggers at his cousin, while he searched for holes in Marcus's case. He bided his time, letting others throw the first volleys. He didn't have to wait long. Parker clobbered Marcus with legal questions that were not answered to his satisfaction. The engineers questioned the research. The financial VPs didn't agree with the numbers. The information technology specialist had technical questions about the systems requirements to develop the learning classroom he hadn't addressed in his presentation or report. Guenther asked how the garbage plants would differ from those developed by Waste Disposal, one of the big players in the field. Fritz wanted details about producers and screenplays. Marcus's patrician jaw faltered.

When the cards were most stacked against Marcus, George entered the discussion.

"I would agree that the film industry is volatile, and fantasy films—while intriguing—are risky. Perhaps, in the near future, we can pursue these possibilities. Online portals seem to have the real potential."

Then, his voice softened and he looked down at his notes. "I do have some questions, if you don't mind? What was your research method for the technology projects?"

Marcus bristled. "What do you mean? This isn't a classroom. I don't have to describe how I..."

"Actually, George has a point," Guenther said, stroking his chin. "How you reached your conclusions is important for our understanding of the validity of your projections. You are right, this is not a classroom. It is the real world. We are not going to put money on the line for an idea that has not been thoroughly vetted and researched."

George watched Marcus swallow the sword thrown at him and reach into thin air for an answer.

"Well, I-I talked with scientists, engineers, and investment bankers. I researched our library and checked the information."

George interrupted, "Were the people you talked to in the industry already, or did you also seek expert opinions from those who have nothing to gain if LE pursues these projects?"

He watched his cousin squirm.

"So, you're saying your sources are better than mine."

George shook his head. "Actually, no. I should have thought to talk to Dr. Lascaux and Mr. Toamli. They bring a unique perspective. It's just a pity they work for companies who would be our direct competitors if we enter the fields in question. Scientists from the EPA, epidemiologists, and computer engineers from IBM would have provided critical information we would need."

Marcus's hands tensed.

George savored the moment. The golden boy, the whiz kid who was quicker than lesser mortals whom he could dominate, was faltering in front of his eyes.

Marcus straightened in his chair.

"I congratulate you, George. You have done your homework well. I can certainly learn from you." His voice dripped with graciousness. "Perhaps, we can work together. Between the two of us, nothing should escape our attention."

A shrewd move, George calculated. His face broadened into an inscrutable smile.

"Yes, capital idea," Guenther enthused, looking directly at his son. "You can learn a good deal from your cousin."

Marcus lowered his eyes. "Of course, Father."

"If you can exchange your animosity and arrogance for pragmatism and humility, I think you could make a fine leader one day," Parker added sharply.

Aleksandra's old and trusted confidant could be a sharp dagger without Uncle Guenther needing to defend his son, George surmised. He observed Marcus, whose eyes betrayed him. He misinterpreted his father's silence as weakness and despised him all the more. His gorge must have been rising with the taste of humiliation and castigation from those he most wanted to impress. Retribution would be uppermost in his mind. George turned his gaze to his father who was teaching Marcus a lesson in humility.

"None of us is against you. We are for your growth, your development in this company. The criticisms are meant to show you areas to improve. George would be the first to tell you, I am much harder on him than anyone here today has been on you."

George nodded.

"Rainer Leibnitz was hard on us."

His hand swept toward Guenther, who nodded.

"It comes with the territory. You want to play with the big boys, you have to have thick skin."

"Of course."

George watched his cousin's mouth twist. He had obviously come expecting to increase his power. Instead, he had been lectured to like a child. He wore the smile of a victor despite his apparent defeat.

As the meeting drew to a close, Marcus approached him

about formalizing the arrangement to further explore technology ideas. They arranged a block of time for the following week. The closer they worked together, the better he could find out what Marcus was plotting, and he could achieve his long term goals.

As the executives started leaving the conference room, his father tapped him on the arm and waited until they were alone.

"Do not trust your cousin, George."

Before he could protest that he had no illusions about Marcus, his father continued, "His ego suffered a serious blow today. A fox is most vicious when he is wounded. He has no choice but to make nice. He has not had a change of heart. Rivals do not change their spots that quickly. If you are going to be CEO one day, you will need to learn how to read people and listen to your gut. What does your gut tell you?"

George sighed. "One part of me feels bad for him. Everyone *was* really against him."

Fritz shook his head. "Sympathy is an emotion you cannot afford, son. Marcus will play you, mark my word."

George nodded. "I did sense that he wanted to outshine me, but was it necessary for Parker to embarrass him in front of everyone?"

Fritz nodded. "He warned the two of you, did he not, before the meeting?"

"Y-yes, but still..."

"Parker did exactly what I instructed him to do. You came out of this unscathed only because you rose to the challenge. The meeting was designed to bring out the worst and best in both of you, and you were the better man."

George's chest swelled. "Thank you, Father."

Fritz touched his arm. "Let me be honest. I am rooting for you to run the family business one day. But if Marcus proves to be better suited for the job, I will choose him over you in a heartbeat. Guenther feels the same way. Despite what I may feel about my brother and he about me, each of us will ensure the long term success of Leibnitz Enterprise."

George scrunched his eyebrows.

"Uncle Guenther would choose me over his son? Why?"

Fritz sighed. "It is complicated. Sit down."

They chose the two closest leather chairs and sat facing each other.

"I am sure you know about our rivalry when Papa was alive."

George nodded.

Fritz's mouth curled. "Father instigated it, fueled it, sought to keep us off-balance."

George's eyes widened.

"It was all about Rainer maintaining power, and we both fell for it. But when he died and Mummy took over, she chose how we would work together. Some might say she picked me to lead because I was her favorite. Others would say I cheated my brother out of the lion's share of power. I am not saying there is not a kernel of truth in that. But Aleksandra steered us into the roles for which she knew we were best suited. Both of us believe she was wise. She did it in such a way that we, well, we came to respect what we both bring to the business. Do I trust my brother completely? No. Do I want him to influence you? No. If he had handled his son correctly, we might have a very different Marcus. It has not been easy. There are problems. But, overall, we put our personal feelings aside and make decisions based on what is best for LE. We care about what happens to LE when we are gone. Aleksandra was not shy about telling us that you were her choice as CEO. She saw ruthlessness in Marcus that was too reminiscent of Rainer. Guenther had to admit she was right. She wanted both of you to be mentored with equal fervor to help you reach your potential, ensure the company's growth, and protect the family's financial future."

George's forehead frowned.

"Why would Uncle Guenther not come to Marcus's defense today."

"At one time he would have defended him. But he offended his parents' sensibilities. He does not show proper respect. Guenther feels you have qualities Marcus lacks and has not yet shown that he can develop. If he does, things could change. My brother is pragmatic. To be honest, you remind him of himself, and Marcus is more like a younger, but less mature me."

George's chest sagged under the responsibility that came with his family's expectations.

"I am very touched by your belief, Uncle's belief in me. I will try my best not to let you down. But what about Marcus?"

Fritz touched George's forearm.

"We will do what we can to help him, but you should not let him distract you. Work with him as you can. If he can grow, encourage it, but do not trust him. Parker will monitor you both."

"Don't you think he learned his lesson today?"

Fritz's brows frowned, his jaw tightened.

"I do not, and neither does Parker. Guenther still holds out a small bit of hope, but even *he* sees how willing his son is to break a code of conduct neither of us would ever have broken. Rainer, yes, but not us."

Hatred seeped from his eyes. George cocked his head.

"What do you mean?"

"Marcus is Rainer Leibnitz all over again. He seems to take pleasure in hurting someone innocent and pure, like Papa did."

He straightened in his chair. His voice diminished to barely a whisper. "Your grandfather provided for his paramours generously in his will to hurt your grandmother even from the grave, because she would not cede majority interest in LE. A company started entirely with her very considerable fortune and her able guidance. He was willing to disown us if we did not do his bidding. Your cousin..."

George's eyes widened.

"You really think...?"

Fritz nodded. "Yes. I see Marcus trying to be like me, but he does not know my reasons. He only thinks he understands me. Aleksandra always saw in me, in you, something Marcus seems to lack—heart. I have scruples. There are certain codes I will not break. I am not so sure about your cousin."

George wore his shock like a heavy coat. Now he understood his father's need to control.

"Guenther and I have to know you are tough enough. It is the one attribute you need to develop. The one that concerns us most. Today, you were respectful, but on point. You calculated the right moment to attack, but you were a gentleman. I am proud of you."

George's frame straightened, his cheeks pinked.

"Father, will I ever *not* feel uncomfortable forcing the issue?"

Fritz shrugged.

"You will get used to it, but you may never enjoy it. I hope you do not. That is ego, a kind of hubris that can be dangerous. Marcus does not understand that, but you do. I have crossed the line, and it is costly. I hope never to repeat that mistake."

A pained look crossed his face. An uncomfortable silence ensued, as George looked down at his fingernails. Fritz stood, signaling the end of the conversation.

"Well, I have an appointment in fifteen minutes. I am sure M will not mind if you are home a bit early for a change."

George stood.

"Yes, I think she will be thrilled to eat at a decent hour."

"I assume the wedding plans are well in hand?"

"Yes, she has selected a designer. She has been fitted and approved a sketch of the gown and the wedding parties' attire. Aunt Tani has been helping."

Fritz's face lit up. "Capital. They are getting on, then?"

George nodded. "Quite. She is actually thinking of asking

Aunt Tani to be her Matron of Honor, since she has helped so much." He looked for a reaction.

"Intriguing."

"And I thought I should ask Marcus to be Best Man to set the right tone."

"Very clever, George, very clever indeed."

His jowls lightened. He patted George on the arm.

"I must go. And if you are looking for my approval, Tani, Marcus, capital."

He bathed George in approving eyes.

"I will see you tomorrow night at the party, and then I am off to Paris on Sunday."

"See you at the party, then, Father."

Fritz extended his hand. They shook ceremoniously and then he uncharacteristically pulled George into a firm embrace, quickly released him, and headed into his office.

George's body grew a foot. For a moment, Fritz Leibnitz had become the father he had longed for. His mind returned to his performance at the meeting. He savored the look in his cousin's eyes, even if it had been only momentary. He ruminated on what he would tell M about the day's events. He looked at his watch. 5:45. He scampered to his office to stuff papers in his briefcase for review over the weekend. As he was making his way to the elevator, he caught sight of Marcus heading his way.

"I was hoping to see you before you left," George called out.

The flicker of a frown crossed Marcus's face.

George walked up. "I have a favor to ask."

Marcus's eyebrows rose.

"Would you do me the honor of being my Best Man?"

He watched the wheels of Marcus' scheming mind spin. Marcus smiled.

"I-I don't know what to say. I'm flattered, of course. Why, I'd be honored, cousin. Thanks for thinking of me."

George clapped him on the shoulder.

"I guess I thought you'd ask your best friend. Laurence, is it?"

"To be honest, I only thought of you," he lied. "You and I grew up together. Our future is tied together. You're like a brother."

Marcus seemed nonplussed. "Well, I must say, I-I wouldn't have thought you felt that way. We haven't always been on the best of terms. I will admit, though, that we had a lot of fun as kids."

George smiled. "Yes, we did."

The sting of guilt flitted across Marcus's face, then vanished. His eyes telegraphed that George must have an angle.

"I know we have had our differences, and I apologize if I came on too strong today, but my intentions are genuine."

A glimmer of belief passed across Marcus's eyes.

"All right, Georgie, I accept your gesture of friendship. I'm sure our parents will be pleased to hear you trust me enough to have me on your team."

He laughed a little too forcefully.

"Let me guess. It was their idea."

George's face was blank.

"Actually, the only one I spoke to about it was M."

Marcus raised his eyebrows.

"Oh? What did *she* think?"

"She is enthusiastic about you."

"I'm sorry, George, ole boy. You had me there for a minute. But M? Come on. I mean, I even know my behavior has been despicable."

George kept his gaze on Marcus.

"It may be hard for you to understand, but she is a very forgiving and caring person. You have misjudged her badly."

"I suppose."

He paused and peered into George's eyes. "I guess this

means I need to throw you a bachelor party and perform some other boring duties," he said with a sly grin.

George returned the smile.

"Well, that's the general idea."

The elevator door opened as if on cue.

As the cousins traveled down to the ground floor, Marcus asked, "So, we're on for 10:30 Monday morning, then?"

"Absolutely."

George paused.

"Any plans for the evening?"

Marcus grinned.

"I'm meeting my girlfriend. You?"

"I think M is preparing dinner and we might watch a movie. New girlfriend, or Christie, was it, the last one I met?"

Marcus shook his head.

"Naw. Got tired of her. New one. A bit brainier than Christie."

George's feet shifted.

"I look forward to meeting her. I hope it's alright to announce you as Best Man at the dinner party tomorrow night."

Marcus tilted his head.

"Oh, the party."

George peered into his cousin's eyes.

"You're planning to be there, right?"

He paused and looked down.

"Uh, it was just the question of a date, but I think I have that worked out." He lifted his head. "Of course. Best Man and all."

George smiled. "Good. We'd really like you to be there."

Marcus scrunched up his face.

"May I ask, why are my parents hosting the engagement party instead of Fritz and Racquel, or Fritz and Belinda, or all three?"

George laughed.

"Exactly. Belinda hates M's guts, as you know, and Mother hasn't even bothered to meet her, so that seemed a bit of a stretch. So your mother graciously offered…"

"Of course. But your mother and stepmother will be there, I suppose."

He wondered what Marcus was plotting.

"As far as I know."

He held his gaze.

"That ought to make it interesting."

"Hopefully, not. We don't need anything else interesting, if you know what I mean. I doubt Father will allow anything interesting to occur, anyway."

"Probably not."

The barest hint of a chuckle escaped Marcus's lips, but his face remained inscrutable.

"You sound disappointed."

"Oh, not really. I admit, I love a good cat fight, but I wouldn't want anyone to spoil your special evening."

He would have liked to believe his cousin, but his optimism faded. Marcus would enjoy an argument erupting.

They reached the ground floor, emerged into the lobby, and said their farewells. Marcus started to walk away, his bodyguard emerging from the shadows.

"I'm heading down through Grand Central Station to meet my new friend at the Trattoria. See you tomorrow."

George smiled. "Have a good time. And, Marcus, I genuinely want us to be friends."

Marcus stopped with the flicker of regret in his eyes. "Sure, George. See ya."

As he turned away, George headed for the side door out to the waiting area for limos and taxis. Sebastian had been keeping a discreet distance just inside the door. They exited to the limo where the driver was standing at the passenger door, ready to open it. As George slid into the back seat, his face shone with victory. Joy spread through his chest like gold. He put his head back. Today had been the beginning of a long apprenticeship in leadership, but he felt ready. *Gran'maman* would have been proud. With this happy thought, he closed his eyes and let the *Brandenburg Concerto* fill the empty space around him to block out the world beyond the tinted windows.

M greeted him at the door when he arrived home. "So, how'd it go? You only hinted when you called. I'm dying to know every detail."

She moved toward him, taking his hands in hers, and kissing him full on the lips. He smiled.

"All in good time."

"No dinner for you until you tell."

She pushed up against him.

"All right. But first, a glass of wine."

She smiled. "Champagne. It's on ice waiting to toast you in celebration, because I know you were phenomenal."

His face opened up. "How special."

As she went to the wine cooler in the kitchen, he laid his jacket and tie on the arm of a chair.

"So, what's for dinner, *chérie*?"

"I'll tell if you tell," she called back over her shoulder.

"After a drink of bubbly, I promise."

He wanted to hold her in suspense as long as possible to make the news that much more delicious.

She brought an antique silver tray of braised scallops in leek sauce with the Korbel and two fluted glasses, directing him to the couch. She set the tray on the large, low Moroccan wood chest of engraved Berber metal and wood design that served as a sofa table.

"Let's sit where it's comfortable. I can't wait another minute."

They clinked glasses, and he forked one of the scallops. After keeping her in suspense as long as possible, he recounted the day's events between bites. She sat in rapt attention on the edge of the couch. Occasionally, she asked a question, but mostly listened with furrowed brows. When he recounted how Guenther had told Marcus he had a lot to learn from George, she clapped her hand over her mouth. His face gleamed when he recounted how his father had praised him.

"While it felt good, I didn't need it as much as I thought I would. I could tell that everyone was impressed, even Marcus, though he'd never admit it. I felt that I really belonged, like I was among equals."

She squeezed his arm.

"You are. You're still learning, but I bet you know as much as any of them did at your age, except maybe your father."

"Maybe, but it feels good."

He took a sip of his drink and bit into a lukewarm scallop.

"This is quite good, you know."

She smiled. "Why, thank you. So did you gloat? Or did Marcus disappear with his tail between his legs?"

"Not exactly."

He described his encounter with his cousin at the elevator and in the lobby. She assumed a reflective pose.

"And you trust him?"

"Not really, but I might be able to steer him."

She shook her head. "I wouldn't count on it. Your cousin has had a lifetime to develop a particular mindset and a *modus operandi*. Unfortunately, your father has provided a handy model. Marcus isn't likely to cede power without a fight."

He frowned. "I'd like to keep an open mind."

"I'm sure you know what you're doing."

He looked toward the kitchen. "So, what wonderful concoction do you have for dinner? I see you have taken over the cooking. All of a sudden, I feel ravenous."

She grinned. "It's quite simple, really. I hope you won't be too disappointed."

"Anything you cook is wonderful. I'm not worried."

He reached for a kiss.

"Mmm," he murmured, "we could go right to dessert, if

you like."

She pulled away.

"I see. You're keeping my curiosity at its peak."

He pulled her back.

"Sorta. I was going to cook a leg of lamb, but then I wasn't sure I had time to figure out how to do it. So, we're having spinach salad with pan-seared ginger chicken and mushrooms, roasted asparagus, yellow peppers, garlic, and a dollop of baked goat cheese. We also have apricot-raisin bread to dip in walnut pesto and olive oil..."

He smiled. "It sounds wonderful. When can we start?"

"Everything is ready except the chicken and bread. Twelve minutes, max."

"Maybe I'll just nibble on you while you cook," he said, holding her in his arms.

She laughed. "Then we'll never eat, but you can bring the champagne and keep me company in the kitchen." She rose.

"Sure," he responded. "Would you like me to set the table?"

"Please. "Don't forget the pepper mill."

"Right-o."

Within fifteen minutes, they were seated at the antique Chinese Chippendale dining table starting their meal. They chattered about the upcoming engagement party. Then, she looked thoughtful.

"She'll like me, won't she?"

He scrunched up his face.

"Your mother, I mean."

"How couldn't she?"

"That's very sweet, but Mrs. Racquel is your mother. She may not be anxious to lose you to another woman, no matter how wonderful you think I am."

"Mummy hasn't been in my life much to speak of in the last few years," he replied with a disgusted tone. "She flits from one paramour to another."

M's eyebrows shot up. "Oh! So how do your mother and stepmother get along at family gatherings?"

He laughed. "Mummy ignores Belinda and attaches herself to someone like Aunt Tani, or Father tries to make Belinda jealous by giving his attention to Mummy."

She pursed her lips. "No wonder Mrs. Belinda is such a...a..."

"Bitch," he completed her sentence.

She tapped his arm.

"George, really! If Mrs. Belinda always feels like a fifth wheel, no wonder she tries to guard her turf."

He smirked. "She's brought it all on herself."

"You mean because she got pregnant?"

"That's as much Father's fault as it is hers. The problem is that she treated *Gran'maman* like a rival and a senile old woman. She had a haughty attitude right from the beginning. You should hear the way she treats the housekeeping staff. If Hilda and Raisa hadn't been with the family for so long and Father didn't pay them so well, they would be long gone. She's so transparent. Even Aunt Tani, who believes the best in everyone, has found putting up with Belinda's condescending attitude difficult. She hasn't created any allies in this family, except Marcus, but only when it suits him. She's put herself and her bratty kids into the unenviable position they're in."

Disdain tightened his lips. She frowned.

"You really hate her. She must have been really vicious to you for you to think better of Marcus than you think of her."

He looked thoughtful.

"I-I have very strong feelings, but hate is too strong a word. I don't hate anyone."

She put down her fork.

"Well, that's good, because hate blinds you and makes you vulnerable."

He scrunched up his face.

"Indeed. I don't understand what Father ever saw in her."

"I'm sure she acts very differently around him. And it's possible that once she was different."

"Possibly. But you saw the way she acted the other night."

"Why do you think your mother doesn't hate Mrs. Belinda? From what you've said, she seems to harbor no animosity for your stepmother."

"I think Mummy enjoys watching Father struggle with a strong woman. Revenge is sweet."

Her eyebrows shot up.

"But tomorrow night, everyone will be on their best behavior because no one wants to upset Aunt Tani."

"But embarrassing us would be okay," she quipped.

"That would upset my aunt, and I doubt anyone would do that."

"Hopefully."

George masked his apprehension with a question. "So what's for dessert?"

She smiled. "Double-layer dark chocolate cake with raspberries and, of course, cappuccino."

He sighed. "You must have been cooking all afternoon."

She cocked her head and embraced him with her eyes.

"You're worth every minute I spent."

"Come here, you delicious creature."

He drew her toward him and kissed her with abandon, the heat building inside him.

"Tell you what. Dessert later, after getting cozy in the hot tub?"

"Whatever you say, _chéri_."

Chapter 8

The following day, they rose mid-morning and headed out for a run before a light brunch, followed by a trip to the Guggenheim to see a Kandinsky exhibit. They arrived home with two hours to prepare for a 6:15 departure.

M dropped her pearls twice on the dressing room carpet as she fumbled with the clasp. George disappeared around the corner in his tuxedo trousers and shirt, collar not yet secured. He returned with a small rectangular box wrapped in paisley blue paper with a large silver bow affixed to the upper right corner.

"*Chérie*," he whispered, "for you."

He handed her the package and pecked her forehead.

She sighed. "You shouldn't have. I don't have anything for you."

"*You* are all I want."

"Well, you have me," she cooed, eyes moist.

She fumbled with the paper.

"Here, let me help."

She laughed. "I don't know what my problem is."

He helped her remove the tape and paper, revealing a soft leather jewelry case. She undid the snap that held the case together and gasped.

"How exquisite!"

"Shall I help put them on?"

"Please."

He undid the clasps that held the single strand diamond choker in place. A simple design of circular sterling silver rounds, each filled with a five-karat diamond, was strung by silver connectors. With the necklace securely in place, he removed a set of earrings and a bracelet of the same design and fit them on her. The Van Cleef & Arpels jewels perfectly matched the peach taffeta and silk gown. A form-fitting bodice of intricate lace-and-beadwork flared at the bottom into uneven shoots of thin layers of taffeta that trailed down to her feet. A waistband of solid black set off the silk top and sleeves.

"I had our jeweler consult with your designer to create perfection."

Her eyes pooled. She reached for a tissue box, then smiled and kissed him full on the mouth.

"My knight in shining armor."

He smiled.

"Hmm, we'd better get a move on."

"I just need to find my shoes."

Within minutes, they made their way to the elevator. As they entered the lobby, she pulled his hand into hers. A bellman rushed to open the car door. George guided her toward the waiting Rolls-Royce. As they settled into their seats, he squeezed her hand.

"You look stunning. You've nothing to worry about."

She smiled and began humming softly. A look of serenity framed her face. When they arrived at the Park Avenue building, Racquel was waiting in the lobby to welcome them. She walked straight to M and stretched out her arms in greeting.

"So this is the beautiful and talented young lady who has won my son's heart."

M moved toward her warmth with a smile.

"And you must be George's mother. I have heard so much about you."

She eyed George.

"All good, I hope?"

George moved to greet her. "Hello, Mummy."

"Come give your mother a hug and a kiss."

He embraced her and kissed each cheek.

"You look wonderful. Peach becomes you. Did Aunt Tani arrange the color scheme?"

Her face lit up. She was the picture of elegance in a silk tea-length, strapped sheath gown.

"She thought I should stand out in my own modest way, although M will captivate the room."

M grinned. "Oh, I don't know about that."

"Tani arranged everything. Your dress, mine, hers—all the same theme."

M smiled. "How charming."

She touched M's elbow.

"We must hurry. You're not to make your entrance until 8:15. Tani wants you in the first guest bedroom before anyone arrives, which should be in fifteen minutes or so."

The three scurried to the private elevator. Two burly bodyguards flanked the doors and greeted Bill and Sebastian, who followed a few paces behind the couple. Racquel produced three invitations embossed with LE's gold seal. The guard on the right pressed the button that opened the doors. As the elevator made its way to the penthouse, George sniggered.

"I don't suppose Father will be dressed in peach."

Racquel laughed.

"Actually, he and Guenther will be wearing peach cummerbunds."

"Oh? And will Belinda have peach or red horns?" George chortled.

"George!" M exclaimed.

Racquel giggled. "No, I think she's wearing black, poor thing!"

He avoided the frown on M's face.

The elevator stopped and the doors opened. A maid in starched black and white uniform and white gloves awaited them.

"*Frau* Tatania eeze expecting you in zee south parlor, *Frau* Racquel. I vill show *Meister* George and *Fraulein* Staunton to zer suite."

The servant directed the couple with her outstretched hand. They walked slowly down a long, wide corridor of Impressionist, Cubist, and Expressionist paintings lit by recessed lighting. It was tempting to stop and savor each of the dozen oils, watercolors, and pastels that warmed the passage and invited the visitor to linger.

"*Bitte, Meister* George, but ve must be quick about it," Berthe beckoned. "The guests vill arrive momentarily."

"Of course."

As Berthe opened the double doors to the guest suite, M sucked in air, her right hand going to her neck.

"What a breath-taking view!"

The open silk curtains framed a spacious bay window.

George watched as she sat down on the overstuffed toile cushions of the window seat to gaze out over Central Park East and the gardens surrounding the Metropolitan Museum of Art.

As the maid closed the door behind her, he looked around the room.

"Look, *chérie*, some of your favorites. Here are two Picassos and over there Braque, and Dégas, a Brancusi, and a Chagall."

She turned, and the two gazed at the paintings that graced the walls of the sitting room.

"Aunt Tani has *Gran'maman*'s eye."

He sat down on the brocade couch that framed the end of the king-sized bed and watched M flit around the room from one painting to another and back up to the window like a child in a candy store.

A light tap at the door interrupted the mood. She scurried to the door.

"Aunt Tani, please, come in."

Tatania entered just inside the door. George rose and descended the step.

"I don't want to disturb you. I just came to greet you *und* make sure you have everything you need."

"How thoughtful," M murmured. "We're doing just fine."

Tatania frowned.

"But you have nothing to eat or drink. I must speak to Berthe at once."

"Oh, she's bringing refreshments," George replied.

A sharp rap at the door signaled the arrival of Berthe and a helper. Each maid carried two large antique silver trays. One featured a bottle of *Dom Pérignon* nestled inside a glass wine cooler filled halfway with ice, crystal champagne glasses, crystal dessert plates, thick linen napkins with G & M etchings, and tiny silver forks. The other trays featured a tureen of Tsar Nicoulai Estate caviar, a silver dish of sour cream with chives, small, dark pumpernickel bread squares, miniature poached salmon with a dill sauce, bite-sized legs of lamb with truffle sauce, liver pâté with celery shavings, Fiscalini cheddar, bite-sized round wild-mushroom quiche, and coconut shrimp with peanut sauce. As if that were not enough, plump strawberries dipped in chocolate, almond *milles-feuilles*, and an assortment of Teuscher champagne truffles tempted the eyes.

M's eyes widened. "What a staggering amount of food for two people!"

Tani smiled. "You may not have much opportunity to eat once you join your guests. It is just an assortment of your favorites."

George beamed. "How thoughtful."

"Well, I leave you now. If you need anything at all, pick up the phone and dial 1."

She pointed to the phone on the cherry credenza near the

door.

"Berthe is yours for the evening. I will send Fritz to you in, say, half an hour. If you would like to see anyone else, let Berthe know, *ja*? Your uncle may stop in for a few moments."

They exchanged the traditional kissing of each cheek.

After she left, George looked hungrily at the array of food.

"Shall I open the champagne? I'm starved."

He selected a leg of lamb and began eating.

"That would be lovely, *chéri*." She selected a quiche. "I just need to powder my nose. You go ahead."

She stepped up to the bedroom level with the food and disappeared into the bathroom. As George started on the caviar, he heard the rustle of her gown and looked to see her head popping around the corner.

"You won't believe it! Come see. A mirror just like the one Grammy and Pop-Pop bequeathed to me."

She beckoned with her hand. He bounded up the step, across the bedroom, and into the bathroom.

"Yes, lovely, *chérie*."

A sharp rap at the door drew his attention away.

"Sorry, probably Father."

He moved toward the door just as Fritz entered the room with a broad smile and an ornate package in his hand.

"How are my two favorite lovebirds?"

M stepped down into the sitting room, and George drew her in, mouth petulant.

"We are getting on famously, Father."

Fritz chuckled. "I see no one will starve."

"It is very thoughtful and gracious of Aunt Tani to host this party for us."

"Tani has always been on my list of quality people. You are right to recognize how special she is to host this party. It would have been a bit awkward for me to ask your mother, and Belinda was out of the question."

The couple looked at each other with knowing looks.

"Anyway, I have a little something for the happy couple."

M looked at George with curious eyes. He directed her to accept the gift, which she took gingerly. "You shouldn't have."

Fritz's face lit up as she walked to one of the couches in front of the fireplace and set the gift on her lap. The baby blue package was held by a thick white ribbon, forming a bow on top. As she removed the ribbon and opened the box, the men walked over for a closer look. Inside the larger box was a smaller red box. She chuckled.

"Hmm, one of *those* kinds of presents."

Fritz's eyes twinkled. "It makes it more interesting."

She opened a second red box, which contained a smaller green one.

"This is like the Russian Maroushka doll."

"Almost there," Fritz replied.

"George, come help me."

He made his way around the Qing Dynasty cherry coffee table and sat next to her.

"Let me."

He took the package in his hands. As he opened the green box, an even smaller silver box emerged. He shook his head.

"Of course."

Fritz grinned. "You should let M open the silver box."

George's face opened up. "Aha, the present awaits."

He handed her the small silver box. A royal blue velvet pouch with a stringed closing was nestled inside. Her fingers tremulously loosened the silk string and pried open the pouch. As she reached inside, two keys on a gold key ring emerged. Her eyebrows shot up.

"Oh."

What was Father up to? Reaching further, M discovered a card.

"George, you read it."

She handed him a small cream-colored card.

Dear George and M,

I am a proud father today. Enjoy this home away from home on la rue de Luxembourg for many years to come. Perhaps you will invite me to visit from time to time. Much happiness. The world is your oyster.

Love, Father.

"Father, I-I hardly know what to say."

He handed her the note. She shook her head.

"Is this an apartment you have rented for us?"

"No, my dear, this is your very own home—my engagement gift. I know you like the *Quartier Latin*, and both of you enjoy *les Jardins de Luxembourg*, so it seemed only fitting."

Tears welled up in her eyes. She rushed to hug him.

"This is sooo special. You have no idea what this means to me."

She held the embrace a moment longer, then quickly moved toward George, sidling up to his embrace.

"Well, I expect LE business will give you plenty of opportunity to be in Paris for extended periods of time. It works out in many ways." Fritz quickly put his right index finger to his forehead. "I almost forgot."

He pulled a letter-sized envelope from the inside breast pocket of his tux.

"I thought you might want to check out your house next weekend. I took the liberty of arranging tickets on the Concorde. I will need the 737."

George's eyebrows shot up.

"Oh," M said with a sheepish look. "Unfortunately, my concert is next Saturday night."

Fritz furrowed his brow.

"Oh, dear. I am surprised Frederick did not mention it. The new girl is not working out if something this important escaped his notice. He would not deliberately sabotage your gift, would he?"

The frown on his face deepened his tan. Then his face

brightened.

"No matter. He will just return these," he tapped his hand on the envelope, "and you will choose another time at your convenience."

Relief bathed her face. He frowned again.

"But how can I miss your concert? This is not good. Frederick really *must* be on top of things better than this."

She looked at George, who grimaced.

"Well, we will just go to Claude's next game instead," Fritz assured her.

"Oh, no, not on my account," she replied.

Fritz rubbed his chin. "I must admit I was not really looking forward to an entire weekend at Exeter. We will fly out on Friday. Go to part of the game Saturday. Be back in time for the concert."

George's face hardened. How many of his games had Father missed?

"How will Claude feel? And that will cause a row with Belinda," George clipped.

"I will smooth everything over. In fact, I might be able to attend the full game and the concert. I think it is a late morning game. And your concert?"

She lowered her head. "7:30."

Fritz tapped the tickets. "Well, there you are. I am sure I can do both."

George had his doubts.

"If you will not miss any of Claude's game, then," M said, her face showing relief.

"Well, I will be off then."

"Please have a glass of champagne with us before you go," she offered.

"I would love to, but Belinda will be looking for me. I do not need the aggravation, and I do not want her getting into anything. *À tout à l'heure.*"

He kissed each check and then embraced George. Closing

the door behind him, George pulled M up against him, happy for his father's exit.

"Time to celebrate," he said as he kissed her. Then he pulled himself away to open the champagne.

She fetched the fluted glasses. "Aren't these lovely?"

"Just like you," he murmured.

He popped the cork, poured the bubbly liquid into the goblets, exclaiming, "To us!"

He entwined his arm around hers as they put the glasses to each other's lips and sipped.

She broke the silence. "I'm blown away by your father's generosity."

"Father expects really big things from us. He's proud of me for the first time, I think. He adores you, but he always has an angle."

She blushed. He cocked his head.

"As nice as all this is, it comes with strings attached. A house in Paris probably means we will be *expected* to spend more time there, so I'm not sure what Father is up to."

"I failed to consider that."

She sighed. He let out a breath.

"Let's enjoy this evening, and we'll deal with that later."

They drank champagne and talked between bites about what it would be like to have extended stays in Paris.

Another knock on the door interrupted their repast. He arose and opened the door to his uncle, who entered.

"We are so thankful for your hosting this party in our honor."

Guenther beamed.

"My boy, the pleasure is all mine. I must add how pleased I am that you asked Tani to be Matron of Honor and Marcus to be Best Man. You do not know how meaningful the gracious gesture is to our family. It paves the way for unity and harmony, for which I have longed for for some time."

He gave George a warm embrace, then put M's hands

together and kissed them.

"My dear, you are bringing peace to this family. It warms this old man's heart."

She demurred. "Uncle Guenther, you are not old."

He smiled. "In any case, I want to congratulate you. You are a handsome couple, well suited for each other."

George beamed. "Thank you. Would you join us for champagne?"

"I would be delighted."

M reached for another fluted glass and poured the *Dom Pérignon*. Guenther lifted his glass, and they followed suit.

"To the happy couple."

He took a sip and looked at his Cartier.

"I had best be getting back." He set his glass on the antique sofa table. "Duty calls. I must admit, I much prefer being here."

"Thank you so much for coming to share a toast, and for your kind words," M called after him.

As Guenther made his exit, she kissed George on the cheek.

"Your uncle's a gentleman. I really like him."

"Me too. It makes me wonder about the stories I've heard all my life about him."

"You mean how your grandfather and uncle treated your father?"

"You know about that?"

A knock on the door interrupted them.

He pulled himself away and opened the door.

"Marcus. Come in."

George ushered him in. Marcus smiled at M and extended both arms.

"Don't you look gorgeous."

She allowed him to hug her. "Would you like some *hors d'oeuvres*? We have more than enough."

He laughed. "Indeed. No, thanks. I've already been put upon by Mother, so I'm full. Actually, I came to give you a heads up on the doings of the guests and to see if you need me to do anything tonight as Best Man. Father thought I could be of service."

George's eyebrows frowned. "Is there something we should know about?"

"Aunt Belinda is snooty to Aunt Racquel, as usual. But so far, your mother's ignoring her. Let's see."

He brought his right index finger to his brow. "Father's handling Aunt Belinda. The brats aren't around to get into trouble. My brother and sister have brought dates, of all things. Your friend Laurence and his wife—sorry, don't remember her name—and his buddies and their wives have just arrived. Madame Koslowski—Joy, is it?—is here. A bunch of French and Russian professors are looking for M. And, oh, yeah, your mother brought a date, an old rival of your father's. I've never seen Uncle Fritz so unnerved."

His eyes twinkled. George frowned. "You're kidding, right?"

M cocked her head. "You wouldn't be trying to stir up trouble now, would you?"

He put out his hands. "Why ever would you say that? I'm just giving you the lay of the land so you won't have any surprises. You don't trust me?"

Her mouth tightened. "Let's just do our best to keep a pleasant atmosphere, shall we?"

"Absolutely. I'm just your eyes and ears."

"Right-o," said George.

A knock at the door was a welcome interruption. Marcus rushed to open it.

"I'll see you in a few minutes."

He stepped back.

"Uncle Fritz. They're all yours."

A quizzical look enveloped Fritz's face.

Marcus added, "I was just getting my orders as Best Man."

Fritz smiled and made his way into the room.

"What was that all about?" he asked George when the door had closed behind him.

"Nothing, really. Marcus wanted to know his duties as Best Man."

Fritz raised his eyebrows. "Everything in order, then?"

George's face revealed nothing. "Marcus seemed to think I would want to know my mother and cousins brought dates."

Fritz's eyes narrowed. "I had not noticed."

The couple exchanged knowing looks. Fritz paced back and forth.

"Well, are you ready? You should not keep your guests waiting."

"I'll just put on fresh lipstick," M said and headed toward the bathroom.

"So whom did Mummy bring—that real-estate guy, Lucas?"

Fritz waved his hand. "No idea."

"Marcus seemed to think you know the guy."

Fritz frowned. "Did he? We should be going. Go collect M now."

"Yes, Father."

She emerged just as he reached the door to the bathroom.

"He knows," he whispered.

"Mmm."

"Ah, there you are," Fritz said stiffly as she emerged.

"All ready," she replied.

He opened the door. "Shall we?"

Without another word, he led them out of the room, down the long hallway to the foyer and into the great room. The house was abuzz with the happy chatter of voices and the dulcet strains of the chamber ensemble's Debussy. They waited for instructions. George kept his eye on his family's movements. Fritz signaled to Guenther and Tatania. Guenther approached the band leader and whispered. Tatania approached Racquel and murmured. Fritz, Guenther, Racquel, and Marcus formed an entourage around the couple. Within moments, guests started forming a larger circle around them, while Belinda edged her way forward. A trumpet blast sounded.

Fritz's voice filled the room. "Ladies and gentlemen, if you would kindly offer your attention."

He paused while the voices settled down. George watched him shoot Belinda a sharp look. The circle around the couple deepened. As the voices hushed, Fritz smiled.

"On behalf of the Leibnitz family, a special welcome on this happy occasion. I am proud to *formally* announce the engagement of my son, George, to the captivating Marianne Staunton, whom we affectionately call M."

A round of applause erupted. Wait staff began circulating, offering glasses of *Dom Pérignon*. He smiled. "Please join me in a toast."

He accepted a fluted Tiffany glass from one of the maids, waited until everyone had been served, and raised his glass in the air. George's eye caught Belinda, on the periphery of the inner circle, affecting her most plastic smile, eyes stinging with what he imagined was bitterness and envy. With a nod to his father, he thanked the guests for coming and introduced Marcus as his Best Man. The crowd applauded. He turned to M, who announced her choice of Matron of Honor. Belinda almost choked on her champagne, which she was now guzzling, he observed. When the applause died down, Fritz beamed.

"George's mother Racquel and I would like to thank Guenther and Tatania for graciously opening up their home and their hearts to us all."

He bowed his head slightly to his brother and sister-in-law, who acknowledged his remarks. Belinda's face blistered as she pushed through the onlookers and strutted next to Tatania, where she was out of her husband's reach.

"Yes, Fritz *und* I do so-oo much appreciate Guenzer and

Tani's hosting zis vonderful party, as I am sure does George's *mütter*, as vell."

George watched with fascination as Guenther took Belinda by the arm.

"Belinda, thank you, indeed, for those kind remarks," he said in a mollifying tone. "George, M, please start the first dance for us and, Belinda, you will join me, yes?"

He nodded to the band leader, who had been waiting on the side near the chamber ensemble for the cue. Jazz music filled the room. The hand-woven Isfahan carpets had been removed from the spacious great room's teak parquet floors to make an ideal dance floor. The music muffled the murmurs surfacing through the crowd. Couples began dancing and well-wishers approached the couple. George moved off to keep an eye on Belinda, fearful of her next move.

Fritz danced with Racquel. Belinda wriggled from Guenther's firm hold on her waist and right hand. George's attention shifted to his aunt's pinched face. She danced with her son, Wilhelm, toward Belinda and expertly guided her in the direction of the spiral staircase that led to the mezzanine. His attention turned to M, surrounded by their friends. The movement of his parents caught his eye, and he slipped within listening distance.

"Racquel, I understand Philippe is with us this evening. I do not believe I have had the pleasure of his company."

She waved her hand. "Oh, I'm sure he's checking out the ladies until I need him. Tell me, Fritzie, do I need him?"

He gazed into her eyes. "You tell me."

She looked away. "No, I don't think so. It was gracious of you, mentioning me like you did. I appreciate it. Probably won't earn you any points at home. No skin off my nose. I just don't want anyone to ruin George's happiness. You know, a woman scorned."

His back stiffened. "How very perceptive of you, and I must say I am rather touched. I can handle Belinda."

She smirked. "Don't be so sure. She has many weapons at her disposal."

His eyes narrowed. "I am quite aware of her tricks. I know what I am doing."

"Whatever you say. Ah, there's Philippe now."

She motioned to the Frenchman, who moved in her direction. Fritz moved to approach one of the other guests, but a touch of her hand on his arm stopped him.

"Philippe, you remember Fritz," she called out.

"Ah, but, of course. Fritzie, *mon ami*, eet has beeen too long."

He reached out his hand, which Fritz shook.

The scene captivated George.

"*Mais oui*. Indeed. How is Paris treating you these days? Or are you still tucked away in that *provençal* bank in Nice?" Fritz sneered.

"Ah, what a memor-ie. And I thought you would not remember. *Non*, I am here in New York with ma *chérie*."

He pulled Racquel to his side.

George's face grew hot.

Fritz forced a wan smile. "How delightful. Well, if you will excuse me. I see that I am needed. *À tout à l'heure, hein*?"

He quickly stepped aside and approached George before he had a chance to retreat.

"George, good to see you. A word?"

"Sure. What is it?"

He looked around. "Are you and M enjoying the evening?"

George followed his gaze. "Yes. Thank you for asking. And you?"

"Well enough. Ah, I see Father Thomas. You should make a point to spend time with him. I need to speak to him, so I will leave you. And be sure to make your mother feel special. She is missing you, you know."

George smiled and joined his friends. He wanted to hear about Laurence's meteoric rise to a senior position in Goldman

Sachs. He picked up on the conversation just as Laurence was regaling his audience with the story of how he had amassed a book of clients. M's face darkened as Laurence let out an impish laugh.

"So, you basically stole those clients from executives who had worked tirelessly to bring those accounts on board," she accused.

"Well, I don't know about that."

He turned to George. "George, there you are. Tell M what an upstanding gentleman I am."

George looked at her set jaw and scalding eyes. "What did you do, Laurence, try to sell her the Brooklyn Bridge after you'd sold it three or four times to some unsuspecting clients?" He chuckled and clapped his buddy on the shoulder.

Laurence laughed. "Not exactly, but I get your point. Can't fool you anymore, can I, ole boy? She's wised you up, I see."

George put his arm around her shoulders and squeezed.

"Well, I still want to go over numbers with you, ole pal. Your father's on board. I just need two more investors. I'm sure I can count on you."

George's back straightened. "I'll talk it over with Father."

Laurence's broad smile faltered. "Well, we're gonna circulate and meet a few more folks before heading out. Great party. Congrats and all that."

He and his buddies moved in the direction of Guenther and a small group of men with whom he was holding court.

M frowned. "Maybe you should warn your uncle about Laurence. He's a shark and a user."

George's eyes narrowed. "That's strong language!"

Her mouth set. "Didn't you hear him gloating about breaking into his boss's office and pilfering security codes and then stealing clients from guys who had nursed accounts for years, guys who had put in a good word for him to their boss?"

George's head spun. "He actually admitted that?"

She stiffened. "No, but he bragged about accessing client

codes in his boss's office without approval, and he targeted the clients of executives who were less aggressive in their investment advice."

"That's not theft," George insisted.

She threw him a flabbergasted look. "He saw a weakness and exploited it after stealing the information."

He frowned. Surely Laurence would have a rational explanation.

"M, *que vous soyez belle!*"

His thoughts were interrupted by Professeur Béjart, who was accompanied by his wife, a petite, elegantly appointed *Parisienne* in a Chloé tea-length silk dress and heels.

M's face lit up. She introduced the couple to George, who recognized the Frenchman as her thesis advisor. The foursome had a pleasant conversation in French. After a few moments of vacuous chit-chat, M's voice coach joined them. Joy spoke a halting but passable French, and George quickly lost interest as the conversation veered toward comparisons of Jesse Norman and Kathleen Battle. Out of the corner of his eye, he spied his father and stepmother in the foyer in an intense conversation with Marcus. He apologized and headed in his cousin's direction. He approached, unnoticed, behind one of the columns that framed the entrance hall and keened his ears.

The three were conversing in German.

"I was only fulfilling my obligations as Best Man, I assure you."

"But you were following me and listening to my conversations," Belinda protested.

"As well he should," Fritz quipped. "You were trying to stir ill feelings among George's friends."

George cleared his throat and stepped into view. "Father, might I have a word with you?"

Marcus's face flushed. Belinda smirked.

"Of course. We were just talking about you." Fritz's steely

eyes glanced first at his nephew, then his wife.

Her lips pursed. Marcus bit his lip. The air pulsed with the stench of guilt. George's eyes flared.

"Something I should hear?"

Belinda smirked. "Actually..."

Fritz put up his hand. "Marcus was sharing with me how Belinda and Racquel were having a heated exchange about you."

He glared at his stepmother. "Oh? Tell me. What did you two talk about?"

Fritz began to answer, but George interrupted, "No, I would like to hear it from her."

"I told her you were so lame you had to practically pay the State Boards to pass the bar exam. She told me you were smarter than Fritz was at your age and nicer, too, or some drivel."

"Is that all?" he hissed. "I would have thought you could have come up with something better than that."

Her loathing eyes pinned him.

"Now is not the time," Fritz interjected in a low, commanding voice.

"But I suppose it *is* the time for the three of you to plot behind my back," George retorted, his face hot.

He turned on his heel and headed in the direction of Guenther, who was talking with a colleague on the terrace. Fritz caught him by the elbow.

"A word, please."

He stopped but did not turn.

"George, let me..."

"What do you want, Father? What do you *really* want?"

He threw Fritz a look of contempt. Fritz faltered with a stricken face. Silence jelled around them. He relished this unprecedented sign of his father's vulnerability.

"There are things you do not understand, things I am shielding you from for your own good. I am preparing your future."

George smirked. "Really?"

"You may not feel you have reason to trust me, but you are the future I want for LE. You may not like my methods, but until you have had my experiences, do not judge me too harshly."

Sadness clouded his face. George's heart lurched. He wanted to say he was starting to understand, but a surge of deep-seated anger at always being controlled silenced him.

A voice interrupted his thoughts. "Fritz, there you are. I would like to introduce my son, Fleming."

"What is it?" he glared at the interloper, then turned. "Father, I will catch you later."

"Sorry to interrupt."

George broke away and sidled up to his fiancée for some much needed sunshine.

She whispered, "Is everything alright?"

"Later."

They were interrupted by a tall, striking brunette.

"Oh, *bonsoir, Madame* Forrestier. *Comment allez-vous?*" M exclaimed.

She became lost in conversation with one of her professors, and his gaze fell upon Racquel and Philippe. As he was moving in their direction, Marcus stepped in front of him.

"Georgie, there you are."

He bristled. "Don't call me that."

"Listen, what you overheard. I know it doesn't look good, but I had to play along in order to help you."

George shot Marcus with his eyes. "Really! What are you worried about? Afraid you will report to me one day?"

Marcus wore a contrite expression. "Good comeback. I know you don't trust me, and you have plenty of reason not to, but just hear me out."

George sighed. "Okay. Five minutes."

"Fair enough. Uncle Fritz called me into his office some

time ago and told me he had an important job for me. He knew I was chummy with his wife and he was counting on me to help the family. If I were successful, he said he'd give me more responsibility."

He had George's undivided attention.

"Of course, I was curious to find out what Aunt Belinda was up to, gain her confidence, and get in your father's good graces. And then with your engagement party, everything took on a sense of urgency."

George frowned. "Go on."

"I worked to gain her trust. Actually, she was easily fooled. She despises you and especially M and Uncle Fritz, though she probably won't leave him. She might have to give up too much. Or maybe she just wants to make him miserable. Anyway, I found out she dug up Philippe, your mother's old boyfriend."

George's eyebrows shot up. "So that's how he turned up out of the blue!"

"I feel bad for your mother. She has no idea. She thinks Philippe's in love with her."

Gorge rose in George's chest. "You don't mean he was hired to...?"

"That's my impression."

"Of course, Belinda would love to see Father squirm."

"There's more. She found an old flame of M's and invited him to the party."

"What?"

George's eyes darted through the crowd, then at M, who was chatting with one of her professors.

"Don't worry. I got rid of him."

George frowned. "How did you know who he was?"

"The guest list. Only two men were among Belinda's invitees, so it was easy enough to figure out. No one can get on the elevator without an invitation. I instructed Robert to have his men call me when the guy showed up."

"What did you do?"

"I went downstairs and I told him he wasn't on the master list and I couldn't allow him in."

George grinned. "You didn't."

Marcus smirked. "Yes, I did."

"What did he do?"

"He was all huffy, showed me his invitation, insisted he was invited. I told him it was a fake because it didn't have my mother's seal on the bottom right-hand corner."

"Ingenious. Then what?"

"He walked off spitting mad with Robert and Tomas on his heels, said he'd be back with Belinda, who had invited him. Well, of course, I knew she wouldn't dare be seen with him. But just to be on the safe side, I told the boys to throw him out if he returned. It was quite exciting."

A grin stretched across his face.

"I really appreciate what you did. But what did you do when Belinda found out? I assume he called her right away."

Marcus shook his head. "I don't think she answered her phone because she was with Uncle Fritz. Anyway, I didn't tell him who I was, so..."

"But she must have had her suspicions when he didn't show up."

Marcus nodded. "Certainly, my eavesdropping made her suspicious, but I think I smoothed that over. After all, she needs an ally, and I might still be useful. At least, Uncle Fritz thinks so."

George raised his eyebrows. "Oh?"

"Look, I'm trying to do the right thing, here. We're both going to be leading our family's business, and it seems high time we were on the same team, like you said. I'm sick of being played back and forth. When you asked me to be your Best Man, you took a risk. At first, I was suspicious. But then I realized it's just the kind of thing you'd do. You've opened up a way for us to have a new beginning. If you're willing, I'm game to break the old Rainer Leibnitz tradition. Whaddaya say?"

He put out his hand.

"I'd like that."

Without a second thought, George reached out and embraced him. As he pulled back, he backed into his father.

"Hmm, partners in crime, eh?"

He turned around, his face pink.

"Uhhh, Marcus has a few ideas about expanding the Bachelor Party, right?"

He shot his cousin a conspiratorial look.

"Indeed. I hope you don't mind. I thought we might have the party at thirty thousand feet on the Boeing 737, where we could have *complete* privacy. With your permission, of course."

Fritz's face relaxed. "Is that all? I am sure that could be arranged. Sounds like *some* party. I suppose I am not invited."

"It would not be a proper Bachelor Party," Marcus replied.

George suppressed a smile.

Fritz smiled. "Of course. Capital idea. You should save Best Man talks for later and attend to our guests. George, I am sure you have not greeted everyone. Marcus, I assume you have duties to attend to."

The cousins quickly parted, throwing each other furtive looks.

George moved with confidence through the crowd. He quashed the distracting thought of M's old flame. He stopped to chat a few moments with guests and made his way over to his mother, who was just interrupting a *tête-à-tête* that Philippe had been having with a voluptuous blonde. Racquel brightened when he approached.

"Sweetie. Where *have* you been all evening? I was starting to think you were avoiding me, like everyone else."

She sent a pained look in Philippe's direction. George turned to him.

"I understand my stepmother and you are friends."

Racquel's jaw dropped. Philippe's eyes shifted.

"*Non, uh...*"

"Don't bother to deny it," she quipped. "It seems clear enough that you're not here for me. Go along and find your mistress. I'll be sure to send your things to Fritz's apartment. He'll be *delighted* to have a chat with you, for old times' sake."

Philippe pouted. "*Non, ce n'est pas comme vous pensez...*"

"I'll save you the trouble, Mummy. I'll go ask Father now. In fact, come with me. I feel sure Father and Belinda would both love to chat with you."

Racquel gave Philippe a withering look and turned on her heel.

He protested, "*Georges, ce n'est pas nécessaire.*"

"*Mais oui.* It *is* necessary, *mon vieux.* It'll only take a moment, and then you and Belinda can leave together to commiserate on this unfortunate turn of events."

They approached Fritz and Belinda, who were outside on the veranda deep in a heated argument, the air between them congealed. Belinda turned to the approaching men, a guilty look hooking her face. She moved to make a quick exit, but George stepped in front of her. Fritz put up his hands.

"This is not the time to introduce..."

"Oh, Philippe and Belinda know each other quite well, right, Belinda?"

Her cheeks reddened. "Vhatever do you mean? I..."

Fritz smirked. "Well, well."

George sniggered. "Philippe is here at Belinda's invitation. It seems they see *quite* a lot of each other, *hein*, Philippe?"

"*Non, uh,...*"

Her face contorted. "How dare you? I vill not stand here and take zis abuse."

Fritz grabbed her arm as she moved to escape.

"Philippe, I think it best that you wait for Belinda downstairs. She will be along presently," he barked. "George, have Marcus call security to escort Philippe out at once."

George turned to see him already heading in their direction. While Marcus threaded his way through the crowd, Fritz guided her through the crush toward the bedroom wing. George overheard her protests as they reached the hallway. His eyes trailed behind his stepmother once he had handed over Philippe. Satisfied that everything was in order, he headed toward his mother, who had joined his aunt and fiancée. Triumph framed his face.

"You look rather pleased with yourself," M said as he entered the family circle.

Racquel's head cocked. "Oh, George just rid me of a nuisance."

"Really?" M and Tani asked in unison.

"It's quite delicious," she chirped. "George just confronted Belinda and her lover in front of Fritz and unveiled her plot. I've never seen either of them so lost for words. And to think it's his old rival, Philippe. As I said, quite delicious."

M's eyebrows shot up. "Astonishing."

"Shocking!" Tatania uttered, her voice laced with disgust. "She brought him here, to my home!"

George smiled. "We have Marcus to thank for uncovering her plot to ruin your party."

Tatania's face relaxed. "How nice. Tell us about it."

"I would love to, but you will forgive me if I keep an eye on the foyer to make sure she leaves," he replied, his eyes darting to the front entry.

Fritz and Belinda appeared near the elevator. Her cheeks were lined with mascara. He exchanged words with Robert and Marcus, who joined him. Then they escorted her into the elevator. Fritz's lordly demeanor resumed as he began mingling with guests. George turned. His entourage hadn't missed any of it.

"I guess the happy couple isn't so happy anymore," Racquel said with a malicious grin. "She's had it coming, and Fritz is reaping his just desserts."

"Now, Racquel, do not dwell on the past. We do not want to spoil this special celebration. M will have the wrong impression."

"No, Aunt Tani. Tell me, Mummy, what do you mean?"

"Oh, it's just..." She looked quickly at Tani, who gave her a withering look. "Now isn't the time. I must leave you lovebirds and go find Father Thomas. I promised to introduce him to one of my friends."

George wished she had said more, but in deference to his aunt, he let the matter drop and kissed his mother on the cheek before she turned to leave. The sting of bitterness grabbed his throat. M squeezed his hand.

Tani sighed. "*Liebchen*, do not blame Fritzie too much. He is Rainer and Aleksandra's son, after all. He has always tried to overcome that legacy."

George frowned. "I'll try to remember that."

"Shouldn't we go talk with Dr. Stanley and introduce her to your family?" M interjected, a distressed look across her eyes.

George's face brightened. "I didn't realize she's here."

He scanned for Dr. Stanley. He spotted her near the French doors that led to the terrace talking to a distinguished looking silver-haired gentleman and a couple whom he didn't recognize. He and M moved through the crowd, stopping as guests congratulated them. When they finally approached, Dr. Stanley's face broke into a smile.

"Dr. Stanley, how good of you to come," he gushed.

She smiled. "M, you look ravishing this evening."

M's eyes smiled. "How very sweet of you to say. And this handsome man is...?"

"David Stanley. *Enchanté*," he said, taking her right hand and kissing it.

She blushed. "Aren't you the gallant one."

The couples started chatting about the details of the wedding. After a few moments, George tired of small talk.

"I would love to introduce you to my family if you don't mind."

Mr. Stanley smiled. "We'd be delighted."

As George turned, Racquel appeared at his elbow with Father Thomas. George's face lit up.

"Mummy, Father Thomas, just the two people I wanted to introduce to Mr. and Dr. Stanley. My mother..."

He put his right arm around her, certain her intention had been to pass off Father Thomas because she thought the priest was seeking her support for yet another children's fund for which she couldn't have been bothered. She immediately warmed to Dr. Stanley's aura of good will and attentiveness. George watched Father Thomas key into another potential patron, and the conversation turned to business.

After several minutes had elapsed, M whispered, "Why don't you grab your uncle or aunt's attention and rescue the Stanleys."

He nodded. "Good idea."

He scanned the room for Uncle Guenther, who was close by talking to a company executive. He slipped away and interrupted him.

"George, my boy, you remember Giles."

"Yes, of course. How are you?" Without waiting for a reply, George continued, "Would you come meet someone important, Uncle Guenther?"

"Of course, lead on. Excuse us, Giles."

George smiled. "So sorry."

He escorted his uncle to the little group around the Stanleys and interrupted his mother by touching her elbow.

"Mummy, I would like to introduce Uncle Guenther to our guests."

She frowned and threw him a bitter laugh. "I was just trying to find out all the dirt on you from the good doctor."

Dr. Stanley's mouth dropped.

"You're kidding, right, Mummy," he exclaimed.

"Of course. She wouldn't tell me anything anyway." The petulant look on her face hung in the air. "Well, I really must be off to the ladies room. Will you walk with me, M?"

"Of course. I'll be back."

M threw him a pleading look as Racquel took her hand. Once he had introduced his uncle, he approached his mother and M.

"...and *you* can tell me why he's been seeing this attractive doctor. They seem quite close, don't you think?"

"I believe Dr. Stanley has helped George develop more effective study strategies."

"Oh, I think it's much more than that. Don't be naïve. You'll find that Leibnitz men have a certain charm that women find irresistible. I'd watch that one if I were you."

George's ears burned.

"Thanks for the warning."

M looked above her head. "Oh, there's my voice coach. I haven't had a chance to say hello. Do you mind?"

George quickened his pace just as she was making a bee-line to Joy. He overheard their conversation at his approach. M was describing the family situation as he walked up.

"Oh, hello, George," Joy said, seeing him.

M took his hand. "I'd love to share stories, but I promised George to bring his aunt over to meet someone. I'll catch you later."

Joy frowned. "Ta-ta. Do relax a little. It's okay to be a *prima donna* sometimes, you know."

M looked at George and winked. He smiled as she went off to find his aunt, who was instructing one of the maids. He went back toward the Stanleys, who were conversing with his uncle and father. George stepped toward them just as his aunt and M walked up.

"Well, however you developed your method, I applaud you for it. George has matured by leaps and bounds," Fritz enthused.

Upon seeing them, he reached out and pulled M's hand toward them.

"Of course, M has been good for my son. I am sure the two of you have much to talk about. But I think you have not had the honor of meeting our captivating hostess, the divine Tani."

She warmly greeted the Stanleys and complimented the doctor on her exquisite diamond and emerald necklace. Fritz moved toward David Stanley and Guenther, who were beginning an intense conversation about corporate aircraft. Mr. Stanley piloted his own Beechcraft King Air 250, which traveled at 270 knots. He had been looking at a Cessna Citation Jet, with speeds up to 375 knots, versus the new Learjet 45 at 463 knots, he said. As the men continued to banter about aviation, the ladies discussed wedding plans.

"You mean, Bette Midler might perform at your reception. I'm impressed," Dr. Stanley exclaimed.

"That's Fritz Leibnitz. Only the best. And he knows how to get it," M gushed.

Tatania raised her eyebrows.

M sighed. "Yes, well, that is part of his charm."

George and the ladies all laughed.

Within moments, several guests came to bid farewell, and the group broke up as more party-goers followed suit. Within an hour, only a few remained. George's parents were deep in intimate conversation in the library. Guenther and Father Thomas were relaxing with bowl-sized sniffers of brandy in front of the dining room fireplace, where two comfortable overstuffed chairs had been set out for them. George, Laurence, and Marcus chatted about pork-belly futures. George glanced at his aunt, who was sending off Willie and Georgina to the family drawing room with their friends. The musicians broke down the set as the strands of Mozart filtered through the Bose house speakers.

"Smashing party," Laurence said as he clapped George on the back. "And your Best Man here has quite the charm of your father, I dare say. Why, Rebecca is totally taken with him."

He winked at his wife, who blushed. George grimaced.

"I'm glad you enjoyed it."

"Say, let's have lunch soon. I'd like to get your input on something rather unique."

"Indeed. Well, I will be pressed for time for the next few weeks."

George looked at Marcus.

"We have the Paris and London trips coming up, George. You know how your father gets."

He acknowledged Marcus's help with a grateful look.

"Yes, yes, of course." He turned to Laurence. "I'd be delighted to see you again before the wedding, if we can fit everything in."

"You won't regret it. A number of your guests are in on the deal, and your father and uncle, so I think you'll want to take a look at my offering. Shall I call your office, then?"

"Sure."

Laurence and his wife said goodbye, leaving George with Marcus.

When the other guests were out of earshot, George said, "I thought he'd never leave. Thanks for helping me out."

Marcus smiled broadly. "Glad to help. What are cousins for? Besides, he's a bit too pushy for my taste."

"Quite. So, how are things on the Belinda front?"

"All quiet. I think Uncle Fritz put the fear of destitution in her, because she's called it a day. But she won't give up."

Marcus furrowed his brow.

"Yes, of course. What's to be done? I hate to see her with her hooks in Father."

"Your father has a plan."

"Of course. Father *always* has a plan."

They laughed.

His weary brain couldn't give any more thought to his parents' scheming. He bid Marcus goodnight, relieved that the party was finally over. He and M still needed to say goodnight to his aunt and uncle.

He found his uncle sitting with Father Thomas in front of the lit Italian marble fireplace reminiscing about the old days. He knew a fascinating story awaited him if he joined his elders, but he was ready to find M, who had now gone off to talk with his aunt.

"George, do join us for a cognac," Guenther enthused, extending his hand. "I will have another chair brought out for you."

"I would love to, Uncle Guenther, but I really need to get M home. She's exhausted. She would never let anyone know, of course. I'm sure you understand. It's almost midnight. Where is she?"

He looked around for an excuse to leave.

"Oh, she is probably with Tani."

"I will just go collect her, then."

He moved in the direction of the kitchen.

As he approached the swinging wooden doors of the kitchen, M and Tani were just coming out.

"There you are, *chérie*. Ready?"

"Aunt Tani and I were just discussing details about the wedding reception menu."

He screwed up his face. "I thought you would be tired and anxious to head home."

Her eyebrows frowned.

"Well, it has indeed been a long *und* enjoyable evening. I am ready for a hot bath and a cognac."

M gave her benefactress a tender hug. "I'll call you next week, then. Thank you so much for your gracious and generous hospitality, and your friendship."

"My distinct pleasure."

Guilt washed over George's face. "Aunt Tani, I won't forget your many kindnesses to us."

He embraced her. She grinned. "Well, you might rescue

your uncle so he can retire for the evening."

His cheeks flushed. "Of course. How thoughtless of me."

He led M by the hand in the direction of Guenther and Father Thomas.

"Your aunt and uncle are the best!" M whispered. "We need to make sure they know how much we appreciate them."

"Of course."

His right eye twitched and his body stiffened. As they made their way to send his uncle off duty, he pulled away his hand. As they approached, Guenther looked up.

"Let me have two more chairs brought."

George shook his head. "No, thank you. We must be heading out. Aunt Tani is waiting for you in the family wing and has asked us to escort Father Thomas home. It has been a wonderful evening, and we are forever indebted to you for this special evening."

Guenther rose, arms extended. "I cannot imagine a more deserving couple. Come, let us say goodnight, then."

They each embraced him.

"I am off to a nice long shower. I think you know your way out, *ja?*"

"Father Thomas, come, we'll drop you off on our way home," George offered. "Where are you staying this evening?"

The priest smiled. "The Jesuit rectory. Thank you. That will give us a chance to talk for a few minutes about the..."

"Not tonight, Father, another time, perhaps," George barked.

Father Thomas lowered his head. "Of course."

Shame tugged at George's heart. "Can I meet with you one day next week?"

The priest smiled. "I'd like that."

The three made their way down to the lobby and walked to the waiting limo under a star-lit night.

Chapter 9

The ringing of the bedside phone woke George from a deep sleep.

"H-Hullo."

"I need to come over immediately. Put on the coffee."

Before he could utter an objection, Fritz hung up. George groaned and lumbered out of bed.

M yawned.

"Who was that?"

"Who else? Father's on his way here!"

"Now?" she bellowed. "Do we ever get a break?"

"Not if you want to be a Leibnitz," he snapped.

Every muscle in his body rebelled as he made his way to the bathroom. He stepped into the oversized shower to wash away his exhaustion and pique, but his father's intrusion shattered the peace. When he emerged from the bathroom, coffee was perking and M was preparing vegetable omelets, fruit bowls, and cinnamon-raisin toast. The wafting smells improved his mood.

"*Chérie*, what did I do to deserve you?"

She smiled. "Aren't you sweet!"

He grabbed her and gave her a juicy kiss.

"No time for that. I'm afraid your father will be here soon, and I need to shower as soon as we eat.

His mouth turned down.

As they sat down to eat, the conversation shifted to Fritz's imminent visit.

"Father could be divorcing Belinda and giving us a heads-up."

She frowned. "No, this has a sense of urgency about it. Of course, Fritz Leibnitz can make a big deal about anything if he's unhappy."

"Father *can* find the tiniest imperfection and blow it up into a major disaster. Why does he have to control *everything*?"

He pouted. She put down her fork. "It's probably tied to your grandparents in some deep psychological way that Dr. Stanley could explain. He's probably insecure about being loved and needs to control everything because he doesn't trust anyone."

He fidgeted in his seat. "Why do you say that?"

"I-It's just how he treats everyone. Sometimes, he lets his guard down, but then he pulls back and exerts control. And he seems to have things to hide, things he's ashamed of, or ambivalent about, or afraid of. He's a perfectionist. He doesn't want anyone to see the real him. That's what I think."

He cocked his head and scrunched his face. "I wonder what Father has to hide. What would he be ashamed of? I don't suppose you would know anything?"

She looked down at her plate. "No idea. Your aunt and uncle really outdid themselves last night, don't you think?"

"Wha-? Oh, yeah."

His face relaxed as he finished chewing a mouthful of omelet.

"I'm glad to know them better. Father's made a point to keep me away from them."

She looked at the Venetian grandfather clock against the dining room wall.

"Oh, my gosh, look at the time! I still need to shower."

She gave him a peck on the cheek. Before he could protest, she rose from her chair.

"*Chéri*, please put the dishes in the dishwasher and make the kitchen presentable before your father arrives."

She scooted out of the room. Irritation rose in his throat with the acid of the recently digested fruit, but he swallowed it. Surely she knew Father's secrets but wasn't telling him. And she should have timed getting ready better so he wasn't left with cleanup duty. He busied himself with the remains of breakfast and was pouring a cup of coffee when the phone rang. Dread swept over him.

"I do not want to be kept waiting. I will be in the lobby in five minutes. Tell the doorman to send me up at once."

"Sure, I..."

His father had already hung up.

The acrid taste of every scintilla of control wrested from him stung. He poured the new cup of coffee into the sink. The urge to wash out his mouth became overwhelming. He made a hasty trip to the bathroom only to remember he had forgotten to call the doorman. He rinsed his mouth and ran out to the intercom in the kitchen. He almost knocked over M in his haste as they crossed paths in the hallway. He informed her that his father was on his way up. They rushed to the kitchen to prepare for his arrival. He started toward the elevator just as Fritz bolted inside. She rushed to the couch with an antique black lacquered tray filled with a mug of coffee and a plate of almond biscotti as the men stepped into the living room. Fritz gave her a peck on both cheeks.

"How lovely you look this morning. I see my coffee is just as I like it. Ah, and my favorite treat. Sit down," he commanded with a flourish of his right hand. "George, join us. I apologize for barging in so early after a late night, but this could not wait."

George shot her a quizzical look as he sat next to her on the toile couch and took her hand in his. Fritz positioned himself across from them. He took a sip of coffee and a small bite of biscotti that had been dunked in the creamy liquid.

"Now, to business."

George squeezed her hand.

"I am going to spend a fair amount of time in Europe over the next several months. You will both join me. Guenther and I will be working closely together, he in New York, me mostly in Europe. M, I realize you will need to be in New York for your studies, concerts, and wedding arrangements. Frederick will assist you. Tani and Guenther will make themselves available as needed."

She started to protest, but he put up his hand.

"It has all been arranged. You will take possession of your new home in Paris and shuttle back and forth between Paris and New York on the 737, as necessary. I realize this is all quite sudden, but it is necessary to keep you from the immediate reach of, uh, certain individuals."

Anger rose to George's cheeks. "Y-You c-can't come here and take over our lives. What is the meaning of this?"

"I am not at liberty to say. You two are my top priority. M, you will find a welcoming staff in the Paris office to assist you with whatever you need. Frederick will help you from New York and coordinate with the Paris office."

Her eyes flashed. "Forgive me, but could you explain why we should change everything about our daily lives on such short notice without any real explanation? Why should we just pick up and move to Paris?"

"I agree," George chimed in, his jaw set.

Fritz sighed. The lines in his tanned forehead telegraphed frayed nerves. The set jaw spoke of heavy responsibility. His darkened eyes said he would brook no argument. Yet changing M's life overnight gave George stubborn resolve.

"Why should we?"

Fritz smiled. "Of course, you both have every right to know. I did not want to burden you."

He looked from one to the other. "Belinda and I are, shall we say, not on the best of terms. Her Machiavellian plots are worse than I had realized. She seems to have uncovered every indiscretion I have even thought of committing."

He scowled. They glared at him.

"I can handle that. But, no surprise, she has such loathing for both of you."

His eyes softened. M leaned forward. "So, what are you saying?"

George's voice stiffened. "Father, we want to know *everything*."

Fritz frowned. "I have known for several weeks that Belinda wanted to disrupt your party but did not realize to what extent. Fortunately, I put the security staff and Marcus on the alert when I realized how serious it was, to thwart her. She has been looking to discredit M in front of our family. She hired a private investigator and discovered..."

"Donald, of course," M said matter-of-factly. "He's capable of saying anything to get even with me."

His eyes widened. "Indeed. Your old boyfriend was set to crash the party and claim you were still seeing him off and on, that you were only marrying George for his money, he was still your one true love, or some such drivel."

"What?" George yelped.

"That is not all. Belinda threatened to tell the press that M attempted suicide and had an abortion some years ago after a fling with a professor at NYU..."

George's face contorted with rage. "She did not!"

M's mouth twisted. "I really get around, don't I?"

"Belinda is desperate. Such rubbish is simply blackmail, pure and simple."

George's heart overturned. The bottom of his world vanished beneath his feet. Warmth left his hand.

"What professor?"

"Professor Béjart, who else?" she snapped.

"B-But you told me nothing happened?"

Fritz's face darkened. "Is it true? Here I have been

defending..."

She glared at them, her face taut. "Of course, it's not *true*," she yelled, with blistering eyes. "Don't you know me better than that? She wants you to think that. Obviously!"

Silence congealed the air. She burst into hot tears. She looked at George, then at Fritz.

"I can't believe you jumped so quickly to the conclusion that if I'm accused I must be guilty. She's won then?"

Fritz's face colored, his eyes softened. "Of course we believe you, right, George?"

He looked down.

"A-Absolutely."

He looked up.

"I-I know you said Béjart has quite the reputation as a ladies' man. I just..."

She jumped up and hurled herself out of the room down the hall to the bedroom suite. The sound of a slammed door reverberated.

His eyes beseeched his father.

"Well, we have made quite a mess of this, George."

"She's right. Belinda has won," George muttered, his heart crushed with guilt.

"Not if I have anything to do with it," Fritz said, his eyes afire. "Now you understand why I must act as I do? Do you see why I need to protect you?"

George's heart ached, and shame trapped his voice in his throat.

"Now, run in there and make her believe she is all that matters. Leave the rest to me."

George collected his courage as he approached the bedroom door. He straightened his back and burst through the door to find her a heap on the floor.

"M-May I come in?"

"If you must," she barked.

He watched her face close shut.

"I wouldn't blame you if you never wanted to see me again, but I hope you'll give me another chance. I'm so sorry."

She buried her head in the lush carpet.

"I have no excuses. Not trusting you was a reflex action. To waver one millisecond in trusting you was pigheaded and wrong. I *do* know you better than that. And I love you with all my heart. I hope you believe me, *chérie*. Please."

His voice cracked. She slowly turned up her face. The bud opened, and she launched herself at him. The dam of emotions burst down her cheeks, and she melted into his opening arms.

Part 4

If thou couldst empty self of selfishness
And then with love reach out in wide embrace
Then might God come this purer self to bless;
So might thou feel the wisdom of His Grace,
And see, thereby, the radiance of His face.

But selfishness turns inwards, miry, black,
Refuses stars, sees only clouded night,
Too full, too dark, cannot confess a lack,
Turns from God's face, blest, holy, bright,
Is blinded by the presence of the Light.

-Lines after Sir Thomas Browne

Chapter 1

As Fritz stepped off the elevator, Guenther's face opened. The brothers embraced. Necessity swallowed the pride that limped into Guenther's home. Fritz followed his brother down into the living room. They sat across from each other in wing-back chairs.

"I know we've had our differences," the younger brother began in German, looking into his brother's eyes.

Guenther shook his head and smiled. "Fritz, it's been years since I have vied for power. I've been content in my own modest sphere."

Fritz's eyes widened. "Content?"

Guenther frowned. "You doubt me after all these years of faithfully carrying out my assigned roles."

Fritz held his gaze. "I assumed you would connive to insure Marcus's position."

Guenther chuckled. "Fritzie, *you* have plotted and schemed, not I."

Fritz's mouth twisted. "I beg to differ."

Guenther shook his head. "I was deluded by Papa telling me that I would rule over you one day. But Mummy showed me otherwise. I didn't fight you after Papa's death."

"I thought that was Uncle Sergey's doing. And with George, you were trying to..."

Guenther's face hardened. "Be a good uncle. To give that gentle boy the kind of attention he didn't receive from you."

269

Fritz's eyes shot bullets, his back stiffened. "How dare you?"

Guenther put up his hands. "Fritz, be honest. You were always too hard on him."

"And you too easy on Marcus."

The vapor of sadness crossed Guenther's eyes.

"I refused to be Papa. I wanted my children to love and respect each other, not like us."

"Forgive me, Guenther. It was wrong of me."

Fritz squirmed in the overstuffed wing-back chair.

Guenther sighed. "No, you're right."

Fritz nodded. "And *you* are right. I've been too hard on George. But it was important to prepare him against the sharks out there."

Guenther's eyebrows shot up. "And within our family?"

Fritz leaned toward his brother. "Both. Our most immediate concern is within our own ranks. I had no idea Belinda could be so vicious. It's one thing to get back at me, but to take it out on George and M is beyond the pale. I'm sorry, but Marcus hasn't been completely trustworthy. He seems to lack, well..."

Guenther took a deep breath and pinched the bridge of his aquiline nose. "Scruples."

"I haven't helped much. I've involved him in my attempts to keep Belinda in check and thus fueled his ambition."

Guenther patted his brother on the arm. "Marcus is very much like you."

Fritz let out a long sigh. "Which has encouraged me to take him under my wing, but I've gone about it the wrong way. Truly, he is more like Papa than I am."

Guenther's brow furrowed. "You may be right. But you're your own worst enemy."

Fritz's head tilted as he looked down the bridge of his nose. "And you're not?"

Guenther chuckled and spread his hands out palms up.

"Indeed. It's time to turn over a new leaf."

Fritz crossed his right leg over his left. "That's why I'm here. I must know whom I can trust."

Guenther smiled. "And you want to know if you can trust me?"

"Yes."

"Above all, I want what's best for the children. You and I have had a good run, but we must do right by our children and LE. I want that understood up front."

Fritz flinched at the sincerity in his brother's eyes. "Agreed. But it will take time."

Guenther puckered his lips. "So, then, what's best for LE may not be what's best for our children. *All* our children."

Fritz's eyes narrowed. "Are you suggesting I'm ignoring my other children?"

Guenther's mouth drew in. "Why do you think Belinda is so determined to ruin any happiness George might have? Not just out of spite or hatred for you? Surely, you see that."

"What are you saying?" Fritz barked, twisting in his chair.

"If you don't mind my saying, it appears that your wife and her children mean very little to you. George is all you care about."

"After all I've done for them!" Fritz hissed.

Guenther frowned. "Be honest. Have you even suggested a future for her children in LE?"

"It has never come up nor would I entertain such an asinine thought," Fritz spit out.

Guenther sighed. "My point exactly. And you wonder why a mother would not be ferocious in trying to secure her children's future, especially if she feels she's merely an appendage and your affections lie elsewhere."

Fritz's face flashed with anger. "How dare you?"

Guenther cocked his head. "I'm only a mirror."

"I-I, well, Belinda is impossible. She has no sense of propriety. She's only in it for what she can get, as she has made perfectly clear."

As Fritz shifted his legs, he noticed a nearly imperceptible smudge on his Italian loafers.

"Perhaps, Fritz, it would have helped if you had listened to Uncle Sergey years ago."

Fritz's eyes shot daggers. "What do you know about that?"

"Belinda was never genuine, but that's water under the bridge, as they say. However, it's also possible she once loved you very deeply, but she's been hurt for reasons you can't admit, and her love has turned to a kind of vicious hate that could consume all of us."

Fritz waved his right hand in the air. "She knew the rules from the beginning."

"You can't expect her to like them. And then there are your children to consider. Try to think from her perspective."

Fritz stroked his chin. "Hmm... a woman spurned, protecting her pups."

Guenther narrowed his eyes. "Really, Fritz, they're *your* children, too."

Fritz's eyes blazed. "Of course, they are! I want what's best for them, despite what you think. Even if I don't see their future in the same way I see George's."

Guenther nodded. "My point exactly."

"Give me some credit, Guenther. Claude and Brianna have no interest in anything to do with the business."

Fritz waved his hands. "Claude has his heart set on becoming a doctor this week. The week before it was a pilot. Who knows what next week? He loathes business. And Brianna is too young to know what she wants. She's more interested in being swept off her feet by some dashing young man. And, frankly, it would be for the best. If I have learned anything from George, it's to let my other children make their own paths instead of carving one out for them. Obviously, Belinda doesn't see how much I love our children. It pains me to think she would assume they are-are disposable objects."

He turned his head to squelch the tears forming in his eyes.

"And, of course, Mummy was clear that either George or Marcus would succeed us."

Guenther frowned. "True, but Belinda senses that she and her children are not as secure as ours."

Fritz glared at his older brother. "Because I'm grooming George? Haven't you done the same with Marcus? Do your other children feel less cared for?"

"Not at all. Like Claude, Willie doesn't know what he wants. He has no strong interest in anything. And Georgina is so young. There's plenty of time for her to find herself. Both will eventually discover what they truly love. Yes, Mother said..."

Fritz squared his shoulders. "Exactly. Belinda has no reason to think I would slight Claude or Brianna. Of course, Mother made provisions for George she didn't make for my other children. She had rather strong feelings about Belinda."

Guenther patted his thighs. "Exactly. Belinda knows George has always been the favorite. Frankly, we've all known that," he clipped.

Fritz frowned. "Really? Aleksandra left your children a sizable fortune and property, artwork, jewels, automobiles." He waved his hands in the air. "I've made genuine overtures to groom Marcus and have told you that I will support whoever is the better man to lead the company."

Guenther puckered his lips. "Oh, Fritzie, don't be so thickheaded. Mummy treated George differently than Marcus. She was more than generous and kind and benevolent to all my children, but she barely tolerated Belinda's children. She had little patience with Marcus. You know what Mummy thought of Belinda, and she was right. Still, she might have been able to bring her along. Instead, she set up a chain of events that fed Belinda's jealousy."

"With predictable effects, I might add." Fritz's face

softened. "I never really gave it any thought."

Guenther's mouth turned down. He crossed his arms and stared at his brother. "Excuse my bluntness, but you can't expect her not to be suspicious and jealous of anyone you show a special affection for, like M. You've certainly given her cause..."

Fritz's eyes flared. "I have not! M is George's fiancée. To imply otherwise is ridiculous. I'm just trying to make up for Belinda's behavior, and Mummy bequeathed the tiara to George's future wife. You've known that for years."

Guenther stared at Fritz. "To be sure, she gave other valuables to Marcus in turn. But don't be so thick. Surely you can see how certain actions can be misinterpreted if one has an envious, devious mindset."

Fritz rubbed his thumbs with his index fingers.

"It may be too late now to undo things. However, you might think of showing some sensitivity to your wife. If nothing else, as a tactical move. In the meantime, we need to devise a plan."

"I'm open to suggestions."

Guenther stroked his chin. "Professional assistance is in order."

Fritz gasped. "You don't mean...?"

"Yes, I do."

Chapter 2

Marcus's head spun at the rapid turn of events. His least favorite supervisor, Parker Gibson, was in charge of the New York operations and Marcus's assignments. Fritz took Belinda and their children to Lieb Island for an unexpected two-week vacation. Marcus' parents and siblings left for their Viennese estate. George and M flew to their Paris home for an extended stay.

Just as Marcus was starting to get his bearings, Belinda called him from the island, but he declined to answer. Getting what he wanted required thinking carefully about which alliances to nurture. He made his first move the day after his family had departed, strutting into Parker's office at 8:00 am with a baronial air.

"Good morning."

Parker glanced up over his glasses perched on the bridge of his nose. "Why, good morning, Marcus."

Marcus stiffened his face. "I have a number of important things on my agenda for us to do. First of all, we need to get cracking on the resource recovery project. I've made some discreet inquiries."

Parker glowered at him. "Young man, our course over the next month was well laid out by the Leibnitz brothers before they left. There will be time for your little projects in due time. For now, you have your hands full doing the research we need to resolve the Nigerian mess. I have prepared a list of requirements and a timeline for you to follow. I expect your full attention on the matter at hand. Do I make myself clear?"

"Quite," snapped Marcus, squaring his jaw. "But I would watch that tone if I were you. You do well to remember who I am."

Parker glared at Marcus, his body taut. "You would do well to remember who you are *not*, Marcus. Now, if there are no questions, let's get to it, shall we?"

He handed Marcus a thick file.

Marcus simmered. He focused his mind on mastering every detail of the inner workings of the company while he attended to his immediate duties. Proving himself would get him what he wanted. If he were patient.

While his cousin chafed under Parker's thumb, George bristled under the gruff leadership of the Paris division chief, André. The *Chef de Bureau* did not seek his input and shut him out of the decision-making process. George missed working with his mentor, Parker. To make matters worse, M was sailing along working with the French. When she wasn't doing her research, writing, and shuttling back and forth between Paris and New York, she was setting up housekeeping in their Paris home and couldn't help him. She brushed aside his annoyance.

"You need to get used to the fact that not everyone will cater to you. Besides, your father probably orchestrated this arrangement to push you toward leadership."

He frowned. "How can I do that if they ignore me? André treats me like I report to him just like everybody else."

He slumped in the sumptuous rose velvet chaise-longue in their bedroom suite. She barely looked in his direction from her perch on the edge of the bed.

"Didn't you report to Parker?"

His face tightened. "But he made me feel like an integral part of the team. He gave me responsibility and trusted my judgment. André acts like I'm a nuisance."

He toyed with a small loose thread.

"You probably are. Maybe, he thinks your father sent you to spy on him."

He rubbed his chin and broke into a grin. She moved in his direction.

"Have a frank conversation with André and don't let him bully you."

His lips puckered. "He's a pretty forceful guy."

She stood over him. "If you really want to run LE someday, take charge. Or don't. Just don't complain about it."

His eyes flashed. "You don't think I have what it takes."

She sat down in the chair of her baroque secretary, her papers askew, and turned toward him.

"You shouldn't let anyone bully you. People sense ambivalence..."

"Weakness, just say it."

His eyes moistened.

She sighed. "Show you're a team player, but take charge. That's what your father hopes you'll do. What André expects. What I know you can do."

She came over, kissed him on the cheek, sat in his lap, and wrapped her arms around his neck. "You can do this."

She got up and stood over him. "Now, we have a few things to go over before the driver takes me to the airport."

His face relaxed, and he stood up, taking her hands in his. "Why don't I go with you to the airport and see you off. Would you like that?"

"S-Sure, *chéri.*"

M's half-hearted smile spoke volumes.

As they chatted, he helped her organize her papers and put them in her Cole Haan leather briefcase. As they made their way downstairs with her case and a small Louis Vuitton suitcase, the distance grew between them. He came up with an excuse to go into the office instead of to the airport, sick at heart.

Chapter 3

It had been three weeks since Marcus had become Parker's protégé. After their rough start, Marcus had ingratiated himself to the old curmudgeon through his stellar work. The cousins had frequent late-night phone conversations about engineering contracts that left him with the upper hand. He gloated about the new turn of events when a rustling at the door drew his attention away from the papers scattered across his desk.

"My, my, ve certainly are trying to impress Uncle Fritzie, ja?"

Marcus's head shot up. "Oh, it's you! I thought you were abroad."

"Ve returned a few hours ago."

Belinda sauntered toward him. "Tsk, tsk. You've been avoiding your Aunt Belinda."

His face flushed. "Well, I..."

She moved like a snake. "Don't bother to deny it. Changed sides, have ve?"

A muscle in his left eye quivered. "I-I don't know what you mean, Aunt Belinda. I'm merely..."

"Oh, really. Don't take me for a fool."

Sloe-eyed, she narrowed her gaze and simpered. "I'm sure you know how to play both sides, switching as it suits your purposes. Ve are much alike. I understand you better zan you zink."

She leaned over, placing her hands on the mahogany desk, the top three buttons of her Oscar de la Renta ruffled-taffeta blouse open just enough to expose her ample bosom. Then she straightened up and sat across from him in the leather armchair.

He looked her over, put on his most brazen look, and feigned lustful interest.

"Well, one must do what one must to get ahead."

Belinda licked her full lips. "How delicious." Her sultriness turned cold. "I vill get right to the point."

He chortled. "I'm dying to hear whatever that scheming brain of yours has concocted. Are we just going to kill off the competition or let our victim die a slow and embarrassing death?"

She sharpened her gaze. "I have somezing much more devious and entertaining in mind."

"I'm listening."

He enjoyed playing the double-agent. But her coming to him now unearthed contempt for this *parvenue* who thought she could use him like he belonged to her. No wonder *Gran'maman* had despised this tramp—putting on airs when she was nothing more than a grad student/cocktail waitress who had trapped his uncle into marriage. He would enjoy making sure she got her comeuppance.

"First zings first. Ve can't have another fiasco like last time."

He shook his head. "I didn't..."

Her angry eyes shot bullets. "Don't deny it. You left me hanging in zee wind. And I am *Aunt* Belinda to you."

His eyes blazed. "I had no choice, and you know it."

"If you say so. But zis time, ve vill have assurances in place. You von't like the consequences if you double-cross me again."

Her steely eyes bit. He suppressed a flinch, his antennae finely tuned.

"Do whatever you must, *Aunt* Belinda. You know as well

as I do that I will *not* allow my spineless, inept cousin to outmaneuver me."

She smiled. "Very good. There eez promise in you yet."

She rose from her chair and turned to leave. "I vill be in touch."

He frowned. "You're leaving, just like that? You come in here, mess with my brain, and take off without giving me any idea of our plan?"

He pushed papers in all directions. "Count me out. If you don't trust me, I'm not interested. Find yourself somebody else who can do what I can do, has my access."

She turned. Frigid eyes melted to sugar. "Marcus, dahling, of course, I trust you. I just needed to know vhere you stand. *Du verstehst, ja?*"

Of course, he understood. Far more than she knew.

She sat down and leaned back in the sumptuous Italian leather chair, eyeing him.

"If I cannot discredit zee bitch, who seems to have vormed her vay into everyone's affections, but yours, of course, dahling..."

He smirked. "Obviously, someone with her looks and talents would only be interested in my cousin for..."

"Oh, please," she sneered, "I get it. You vould like to have her for yourself. But for now, you and I vill focus on bringing down your cousin. You are up to it, *ja?*"

He snarled, "And how do you propose we do that?"

Her eyes smiled. "Let's just say zat someone in Paris owes me a big favor. The vheels are turning as ve speak. Vhat I need you to do eez keep Fritz *und* Guenther from interfering *und* put some documents vhere zey should not be."

He leaned back in his chair and smiled. "My, my, we do get around, don't we?"

She threw him a scathing look. "Vatch yourself, dah-ling."

"Of course, Auntie."

He sat up straight. "I had no idea you knew so much about

the inner workings of LE."

"I'm not some air-headed blonde. You must remember zat vhen I met your uncle, I was completing my MBA." Her eyes flared. "I know a helluva lot, enough to ensure my future and my children's future."

She stood up and looked down her nose. "Right now, vhat you need to know eez zat you vill receive instructions next veek. Memorize its contents, zen destroy zee evidence, and report to me on my cellular number zat you vill not divulge to anyone—*anyone, ja?*"

She handed him a folded piece of paper, which he took without opening it. He pursed his lips and glared. "Yes, ma'am, loud and clear."

Her face closed. "And vatch your tone. Zis is *my* operation. Remember zat," she hissed. "If you do your part, you can be assured of running LE. That's vhat you vant, *ja?*"

He suppressed his loathing. "Absolutely. If you can assure me of that, Aunt Belinda, I can tolerate your condescension. But be careful. I am a Leibnitz, after all, and I will hold my own."

"Of course," she purred, the ghost of disdain crossing her face as she rose to leave.

*****

"Hi, cuz. There's a snake in your office. Call me right away."

As Marcus waited for George's call, he paced. His mind flitted from spinning webs to entrap Belinda to berating himself for ever thinking she would advance his goal. Something was odd. The accent.

He would be the one to unravel her plot, but he needed his cousin's help. Uncle Fritz would see that George, the golden boy, the one who would grovel to him one day now that *Gran'maman* was gone, didn't hold a light to his prowess. He lay down on the bed, savored the thought, and waited.

Chapter 4

Energy electrified George at the thought of protecting his family. He didn't dare share his thoughts with anyone until he checked out his suspicions about André, the Paris office *Chef de Bureau.*

He arrived in the office early, knocked on André's door, and entered without waiting for permission. *"Excusez-moi, mon vieux,"* he began in French.

André winced.

"Sorry for the intrusion. I have just been on the phone with one of our African agents, who has reported disturbing news about the Nigerian negotiations. But if you're busy, I can deal with this myself."

He turned to leave.

"No," André replied in English. I'll have my secretary clear my schedule for,..."

"Oh, I think half an hour should do it."

He waited while André alerted his secretary, savoring the *Chef de Bureau*'s discomfort. Sitting down at the end of the burnished rosewood conference table and placing his portfolio in front of him, he waited for André to complete his call. A 5:00 am conversation with Marcus, followed by a conference call with François—a trusted employee in Abuja—had left George both unsettled and motivated. Plotting with Marcus centered him. The cousins had agreed that unraveling Belinda's plot would impress their fathers that they could work well together. They dared not fail.

None of the Paris staff could be trusted, and they suspected that feeding André false information would flesh out the traitor. The documents Belinda had talked about seemed connected to the Nigerian tribal alliance, since the Paris office had coordinated the engineering work on the Lagos pulp mill.

André hung up the phone and walked around his desk to the conference table with a frown. "*Uh, il faut que Monsier Leibnitz...*"

George glared at him. "If you want to be responsible for earning my father's ire, call him. But he has put me in charge, so I think the first order of business is for us to discuss the matter."

André squirmed. "Well, if you think it is for the best."

George smiled. "Tell me what you know about the negotiations with Chief Mombatabu?"

"He's a second-class chief who has been rising in power. Rumors are that he had one of his rivals killed, but it was never proven. I thought negotiations had stalled after he came to Connecticut in April and it didn't go so well. Is there some new development?"

"Yes, Belinda offended the number one wife by having one of the secretaries take her shopping in New York instead of going herself. Quite a fiasco."

The Frenchman's eyebrows shot up. "Oh!"

"In any case, apparently some documents are floating around with evidence of unaccounted large bribes. Which would put the company in a very bad light with the Nigerian government. I was wondering if you knew..."

André's eyes faltered. "What are you suggesting?"

George's heart leaped. "Nothing. I know so little about the goings on in this office. I wondered if you could help me sort it out and see if the staff knows anything that would shed light on the matter. Engineers talk. You know how rumors are. They so easily get out of hand. I wouldn't want anyone to think *you...*"

André's face tightened. "I can assure you that no one in this office was involved. Your source is mistaken. A-Agents in Africa? Who, might I ask, has put forward this-this inane rumor?"

He flailed his right hand in the air.

"Our man will be here by the end of the week, so you can meet him yourself. For now Father would appreciate your investigating the staff. I'll be investigating everything with one of the New York lawyers, who will arrive tomorrow. I'm sure we will get this matter cleared up immediately and have a report on Father's desk in a matter of days."

George maintained a perfect equilibrium and relished the look of sheer panic that crossed André's face.

André's voice cracked, "*Monsieur* Leibnitz, I do not believe eet will be necessary to do all that. We can handle everything internally here."

George smiled. "Well, if you think we can get to the bottom of this, I'm willing to entertain the notion."

André put his palms together. "*Milles remerciements.* Y-You w-will not regret eet, I-I assure you."

"*Pas de problème.* I will leave it in your capable hands, then."

George rose from his chair with a soaring heart. The wheels of his mind formed a path for his future.

Chapter 5

"A snag in our plan? What do you mean?"

Marcus smiled and put the phone a few inches away.

"Someone in Nigeria has preempted us," Belinda hissed.

"What happened?"

"As if you didn't know!"

"Aunt Belinda, I have no idea what you're talking about," he barked.

"Did you know zee company has agents in Africa?"

"Really?"

"Someone in Nigeria has gotten André and Michel fired. George is Acting Chief of zee Paris office. Parker's left for Paris to make a complete investigation. Surely you knew zat since you vork directly vith him," she bellowed.

"What?! I-I knew Parker left for Paris, but, as you well know, he treats me like an underling and tells me only what he wants me to know," he snarled.

He relished the memory of the phone conference with George, Uncle Fritz, and Parker two days earlier in which his cousin had given him the credit for uncovering a serious plot and in which a plan had been hatched to subvert the perpetrators.

She cackled. "So you didn't know Fritz is making you Chief Liaison to the European division?"

He barked, "And Uncle Fritz told you before he told me? I can't believe I'm always the last to know everything."

Her voice dripped with delight. "My, my, so you didn't know? How delicious."

He savored the deception. "Chief Liaison has a nice ring, don't you think?"

He would have loved to have been a fly in her private boudoir watching her unravel.

She hissed, "Pleased vith yourself, are you? You haven't even given one zought to me, how zis affects me, y-you little prick!"

He smirked. "Really, Aunt Belinda, your language."

"How dare you!" she screeched.

He sniggered. "Alright, don't get your hackles up. Give me at least a moment to bask in the knowledge that my hard work has finally been rewarded. I'm sorry if this sets back your plans, but it's all news to me."

Her words clipped, "I zought you made it your business to be in zee know about everyzing your sorry father and his brother do. Not as clever as you think, are you, dah-ling Marcus?"

"You wound me," he yelped.

"I vill be in touch. As they say, don't call me. I'll call you."

The line went dead. There was definitely something wrong in the accent.

He put the thought aside and let out a belly laugh, savoring victory.

✶✶✶✶✶

George's voice captured Marcus's full attention.

"Belinda is planning something truly nefarious."

He sat up in his king-sized bed, moved the phone from his left ear to his right, and grabbed a pad and pen. These regular, late night calls with his cousin invigorated him.

He chuckled. "I haven't heard from her in two weeks. I thought we'd done her in."

"Hardly. Noël, one of the French agents, has just left for New York. Father believes she knows you double-crossed her and you're in danger."

He threw back the covers. "H-How could she know?"

"That's Noël's job to find out. And to protect you. Father will fill you in later this morning. Be alert and do what he says, no matter how bizarre."

"S-Sure, whatever you say."

His mouth went dry. "I-I just can't imagine how Belinda would know. Or go this far. This is really serious. You must be in danger, too."

A tug of concern and love for George caught him unawares.

"Father thinks so. Maurice has been my shadow since last night. And another thing, if you have a girlfriend sleeping over or that sort of thing, send her home. Father's having M brought back to Paris today, with two escorts, just in case."

His face grew hot. "Listen to what you're saying. Why doesn't Uncle Fritz just get rid of her? I mean, if she's capable..."

"Father may be many things, but he's not a murderer."

His eyebrows shot up. "Really?

George's voice bristled. "What do you mean?"

"Forget it. I just think it would be easier if she disappeared."

"Out of the question. And another thing."

He couldn't wait to hear. He loved the thought of plotting against *someone*.

"M can't know anything about this. She's flying back to New York in three weeks to defend her dissertation to complete her doctorate. She doesn't need any distractions. Promise."

"Sure."

He felt a prick of his conscience at the thought that he would take advantage of the situation. He brushed it aside and stroked his chin. It was time to worm his way back into Belinda's affections.

*****

"Vhat to you vant? You haven't called me in ages *und* now all of a sudden you call my private number, at zis hour?"

"Aunt Belinda, what can I say? I've had to be on my best behavior. *Everyone's* watching me."

"A likely story. Vorking both sides, zat's all you're doing," she clipped.

His voice pinched. "You pierce my heart. You know as well as I do that I'm merely a pawn on my uncle's chess board. But not for long."

Her voice sharpened. "Is zee child becoming a man? Tell me, Marcus, what do you have in mind?"

Newfound power wrapped around him like fur.

"How well do you know the New York security staff?"

She stumbled. "V-Vhat-vhatever do you mean?"

A frisson chilled his spine. Had she wormed her way into the affections of a bodyguard?

"Well, I was just wondering if there would be a way to, you know, strengthen our position, more directly."

She laughed. "My, my, I had no idea you had such a Machiavellian mind."

He smirked. "I learned from the best."

"You play a dangerous game, Marcus. I know far more zan you zink I do. You're playing vith zee big boys now."

He hid his disgust. "Of course, Aunt Belinda. I'm thinking of how to level the playing field. Any ideas?"

She spit, "Don't vorry your *entitled* Leibnitz head about zee competition. Aunt Belinda is taking care of everyzing."

He purred, "How intriguing. I'm game for anything you think I could do to help."

She clipped, "Don't mistake me for a fool. I've been in zis

family long enough to know zee players extremely vell."

He bristled. "What do you mean?"

Chills inched down his spine.

She let out a hollow laugh. "Don't zink I don't know you Leibnitz men. You vould do anyzing to keep *your* precious empire in zee *first* family? I vatched every move your supercilious, *royal Gran'maman* took to ensure her favorite grandchild vould succeed his father, not even considering another heir? And zee poor, disfavored Marcus," she whined, "trying to imitate Fritzie, get in his good graces, zinking you vould outmaneuver zee master himself? And now, trying to play *me, me* who knows you like a book, zinking you vould trick *me*? You have no idea who you're dealing vith. I assure you, you will *never* be the successor. *Never!*"

Shame slapped his face hard. The joy and excitement of winning dissipated. The family was in danger. He knew what to do.

No answer.

What voicemail could he leave without tipping off Belinda if she were with Uncle Fritz?

"Hi, it's Marcus. Sorry to call so early, but you said you wanted my analysis as soon as possible. Uh, I'm going to be unavailable soon, so call as soon as you can."

He dialed George next, swallowing his pride.

*****

Fritz exited the shower and toweled off, annoyed at the ringing phone. He brushed his teeth and let the call go to voicemail. He padded around his spacious Trump Tower penthouse bedroom, glad Lorraine had left before midnight. Belinda may have been ensconced in Wilton, but her presence hung in the air.

Sighing, he listened to the message. He frowned and called his nephew.

"I assume you have a good reason for interrupting what I am sure would have been a pleasant..."

Marcus broke in, "Uncle Fritz, thank God you called."

All his mental faculties sharpened.

Marcus's fear palpated his voice. "She knows everything. She threatened to kill me!"

"Slow down. Tell me everything."

Fritz slumped on the bed, the weight of his family sagging his shoulders. As he listened to Marcus relay his conversation with Belinda, his blue-blood jaw hardened. She had become far more trouble than anticipated. Guenther's plan had better work.

Chapter 6

"But why is he bringing them *here, now*?" M wailed, throwing up her hands. "Doesn't he know I'm defending my thesis in less than three weeks? *Do* something. Don't just sit there. I can't keep changing everything every time I turn around because of your father's latest whim! I just can't!"

Her eyes swam with searing tears.

"I'm sorry, *chérie*. I know it couldn't come at a worse time, but it can't be helped. I didn't want to worry you, so..."

He started pacing across the bedroom.

"What? George, out with it!"

Her thoughts tumbled like the papers on her secretary. The words on the laptop screen jumbled. She rued the day she had stepped into Leibnitz Enterprises. Her life would have been so much simpler. She would have her doctorate already and be making her *own* way in the world.

As he detailed the impending danger, her face blanched, then changed to puce, and finally to ashen resignation as she slumped in her chair.

"I'm afraid it gets worse. You'd better tell Liza to prepare the guest rooms."

Her eyes impaled him as she stood up. "Four unwanted people! You'll let me know when we can get back to our own lives!"

"Six, actually," he muttered, looking at the floor.

"Six?! What are we, a hotel?"

She threw up her hands and launched herself down onto the damask couch, bawling.

"I'm as upset as you are, but the governess and Chef are coming to help you."

"That's supposed to make me feel better?" she blubbered.

He touched her arm, which she threw off.

"Father's trying to minimize the disruptions to your schedule. We already have a housekeeper, and if you don't have to do anything except smile sweetly and occasionally pop out of the bedroom for nourishment, he thought it would not be *that* bad."

She lifted up her head, sat up, and exhaled slowly, her mouth set. "Alright. But make sure the kids stay out of my way."

"Sure."

He hugged a stiff, cold body.

A sting of disdain for him and his family enveloped her. She looked at herself in the mirror. Hairs out of place. Makeup smeared. Her life was unraveling before her eyes.

*****

When Fritz, Claude, Brianna, Katya, and Chef arrived, M had folded up her feelings into the protective cocoon on the shelf behind her heart. She greeted them as they entered, switching back and forth from French to English.

"*Chef, quel plaisir*! I haven't been able to get your chocolate soufflé out of my mind. I do hope you'll make it for us while you're here."

His face opened up. "*Bien entendu.*"

She turned to the children. "Brianna, Claude, my, how you've grown. Claude, you're gonna break some lucky girl's heart. You're quite the handsome young man. And Brianna, *jolie, comme toujours.*"

"*Merci, Mademoiselle,*" the children said as one.

"Let me show you to your rooms." She gestured to follow her upstairs.

Fritz interjected, "I will be staying at the *Champs-Elysées* flat, so no need to go to any trouble for me."

She ignored him. "Children, Katya, Chef, let's get you settled in. Liza here," motioning to the housekeeper, "will see to anything you need. Of course, Chef, I'm sure you know your way around Paris, but if you need anything from the neighborhood markets, Liza can show you."

He beamed. "*Formidable!*"

She smiled. "Katya, we've arranged for a liaison from the Sorbonne to contact you about tutors for the children in their subjects. *Vous parlez français, n'est-ce-pas?*"

"*Oui, mademoiselle.*"

She nodded. "*Bien.* You'll find clothes, toiletries, school supplies, everything the children and you will need in your rooms."

She paused, looking first at one, then the other. "*Alors*, I'll escort you to your quarters. I'm sure everyone will want to rest a bit before an early dinner."

She led the way up the stairs with the children whispering to each other. With Katya watching their every move and three burly men standing guard at the door, the children must know their mother couldn't contact them.

As soon as her guests were settled, she would hide in the third floor loft and return to her fast approaching dissertation defense. Professor Béjart had assured her she had nothing to fear, but her mind had been divided in so many directions that she had lost the thread of her arguments.

She turned her guests over to Liza, who brought up the rear, as they reached the second floor. She returned to the first floor landing to remind George of her need for solitude for the next few hours. Hearing father and son whispering stopped her approach.

"How long will the children be here? What are you doing

about...?"

"Not now, George. We will discuss it later. I have matters to attend to. We will meet in the morning. Marcus will be over later tonight. Two of our most trusted bodyguards and a trained, uh, specialist, are just outside the door, so you have nothing to fear. In the meantime, go help M with the children."

He excused himself, leaving her with the disquieting feeling that he had left his children here because he was still figuring out what to do.

Chapter 7

Fritz's mind flitted between his responsibilities and a sense of dread about the purpose of his visit to Uncle Sergey's *l'Isle de la Cité* home. The sage, old spy would know how to handle errant Belinda. Yielding to Guenther's judgment soured his mouth, but protecting the family required it. By now, Frederick would have notified her about his unscheduled trip with their children. He was counting on her wanting to know where he had taken them. Coming to his uncle was step one in keeping her off balance. In the meantime, if guards on the security staff had fallen under her spell, he needed to ferret them out. Noël might need to have another persuasive talk with André.

*****

Sergey Zerbst waited for his nephew, reflecting on Aleksandra and his childhood escape from the Russian authorities. It had been good training for his role in World War II. As a spy in the French Resistance, he had survived countless attempts on his life through wiliness, treachery, and creative genius. While his family didn't know the extent of his deeds, he had no regrets about his coldblooded tactics. The thought of yet again helping his sister's favored son secure the Leibnitz Empire thrilled the 92-year-old widower. He had outlived his usefulness to his daughter, five grandchildren, and sixteen great-grandchildren—all perfectly happy to let the loyal and aging staff of valet, butler, housekeeper, and gardener keep the patriarch company in his spacious *manoir* while they enjoyed the fruits of his labor.

Since his wife had died and he had handed over his manufacturing empire and *Provençal* estate to his daughter and son-in-law and the vineyard properties to his grandchildren, Sergey had seen less and less of his progeny over the years. Thankfully, he remained mentally keen, if not physically agile, and kept himself busy advising the French Minister of Interior as the need arose, infrequently as the years had passed.

He found himself at times eyeing the man in the mirror as a stranger. The years had not been kind. He remembered when his commanding presence had unnerved the bravest, most elite spy. Now, he resembled an over-sized frog, with buggy eyes, leathery, scarred skin, shaggy eyebrows, pronounced jowls, rotund middle, and thick legs and arms. Only his patrician carriage and perfectly tailored, silk after-dinner jacket exuded position and power. He grunted.

He welcomed Fritz into his embrace over bowl-sized snifters of *Courvoisier*. He pursed his lips and keened his ears as Fritz described recent events. The two Romanov descendants sat in over-stuffed cordovan leather wingback chairs in front of a roaring fire that blazed in the gargantuan walk-in stone fireplace of Sergey's well-appointed study. He had always found Fritz far more like Rainer in his callousness and ambition than Aleksandra would ever admit. The current situation proved him right. Fritz should have heeded his advice years ago when he had uncovered Belinda's identity. But Fritz had to have his own way. And now he came to his uncle humbled and afraid. The thought of securing Aleksandra's empire once again energized the old warrior. Guenther and Robert had been right to keep him informed.

When Fritz told him that he had brought his children and

nephew to George's Paris house, he smacked his lips and rubbed his hands together.

"*Merveilleux*. Totally unexpected. Insured protection. Yes, yes. I take it you have no love left for this woman, *non?*"

Fritz's eyes flashed. "None whatsoever."

"*Bon, alors*, I can arrange for a quick and painless end..."

"You are not suggesting..."

Sergey glared at him. "That makes you squeamish, *hein?* I would think after the way your father died, zat would be no *problème.*"

Fritz's eyes flickered. "Wh-What do you mean?"

"Fritzie, remember who I am, *hein?*" he countered in a wilting tone.

"Get on with it. What are our options?"

"*Bon*, we must take this vixen off-balance yet again."

He fingered his slightly askew Yves-St.-Laurent silk cravat. "I have something in mind. Better you don't know the details, *hein?* Just do as I say. Everything will turn out as you would wish."

"Hold on. You cannot decide what is going to happen and leave me out."

Fritz's privileged jaw was set.

"You're better off not knowing. That way, you can act naturally, and she won't know what hit her, shall we say, until it is too late."

"You are talking about a-a hit?"

"*Pas de tout*. You have already ruled that out. Do you trust me, *oui ou non?*"

His cold eyes penetrated Fritz's defenses. The younger man looked away with clenched fists.

"*Oui*, Uncle Sergey, of course. But..."

"You don't like being in the dark. *Je le sais*. I don't blame you. But some things are better that way. Do you want my help, *oui ou non?*"

"Of course."

"Then, leave everything to me, *d'accord*?"

Fritz nodded.

Chapter 8

George paced as M burrowed herself in her study as he waited for his cousin's arrival. Clearly, he had to take charge or the situation would overrule his intentions.

Within moments of Marcus's arrival, a knock at the door interrupted his recounting of instructions.

"Who could that be at this hour?" George muttered. "You were just saying that Father ordered us to stay put. Do you think we should answer it?"

"Open the damn door. Noël or Michel or that other guy, Boris, I think Uncle Fritz called him. He would have called if we were in real danger."

"Fine," he huffed. "Obviously, I'm the last to know everything."

He opened the door to Noël, flanked by Michel. Another giant with a pug face and claw-like hands lurked to the side.

"*Monsieur Georges, Monsieur Leibnitz m'a commandé de vous emmener, avec Mademoiselle M et Monsieur Marcus, au bureau tout-de-suite.*"

"Oh," he exclaimed. "Why are we going to the office at this hour?"

"*Je suis désolé, Monsieur,*" Noël replied. "A change in plans. Maurice is waiting to collect us. We'll just wait here while you bring the others."

George ascended the stairs two at a time to collect M, whose flaring eyes telegraphed her feelings.

Noël delivered the trio to Blaise, Noël's backup, who escorted them to the *Chef-de-Bureau*'s third-floor office of LE's stately 17th century building on *l'avenue Montaigne*. The shadows of four swarthy sentinels on the property loomed large beyond the expansive windows, before Noël closed the heavy silk drapes and stood guard at the door.

"Sorry for the change of plans and the late hour," Fritz began with a furrowed forehead.

He motioned the three to sit around the rosewood conference table. George glanced at M, whose face was screwed up. Marcus's taut face flitted in his peripheral vision.

"I have just come from Uncle Sergey's home, and we have..."

"Uncle Sergey?" M interrupted.

"Ah, yes, of course, you met when Aleksandra died," Fritz responded. "You may recall that he is her brother, a leader in the French Underground during the war, and a highly respected consultant for the French government..."

She threw up her hands. "Oh, is that all? Matters have escalated to the point that we need an ex-spy to handle a disaffected wife?"

He put his hands together. "We are fortunate to have Uncle Sergey put a stop to all the nonsense we have all been through. Of course, you are upset by all that has been happening."

Her eyes pleaded with George as she replied, "I'm just a bit overwhelmed right now. In the last month or so I have been carted off to Paris away from everything familiar and now I have numerous houseguests, two of whom hate my guts. Our lives are in danger from a vindictive, paranoid, jealous wife who'll probably show up at my door with a knife with my name on it. And in, let's see, seventeen days, I'll need all my wits about me to shuttle back across the Pond, overcome jet lag, and successfully defend my dissertation and my doctoral project so I can earn my Ph.D., which I've sacrificed and slaved for, for more than five years now. And now you tell us that some high-level James Bond-type pro is on the scene, just like in some god-awful James Cameron movie. So, pardon me if I'm just a teensy-weensy crazed."

Her eyes spit fire.

He reached over to squeeze her hand, which stiffened.

"Father, this whole thing has gotten out of hand! We need answers now!" George exclaimed.

"I agree," Marcus piped up. "This is really serious. We need to know exactly what the hell's going on."

Fritz looked at his hands. "Yes, it is serious. Otherwise, Guenther and I *never* would have brought in Uncle Sergey. I-I have managed things rather badly. So it is up to me to set things right. I have tried a number of approaches that have not worked. I had no choice but to seek his assistance."

George huffed. "And what exactly is Great-Uncle Sergey going to do? It sounds nefarious and immoral. Is that what you want on your conscience? I won't stand for it!"

Fritz sighed. "Not at all. I was very clear that Belinda is not to be harmed."

"Well, that's a relief," George said, letting out the breath he hadn't realized he'd been holding.

Marcus cleared his throat. "Uncle Fritz, what *is* Uncle Sergey going to do?"

He looked down. "I have no idea."

Three audible gasps filled the room.

His shoulders sagged. "As difficult as it is to admit this, he would not tell me. He asked me to trust him."

George glared at him. "You cannot be serious."

"I trust him implicitly. He will not let anyone harm any of us or jeopardize the empire his sister built."

His voice hardened and increased in volume. "As you have all pointed out, this has gone too far. Belinda is no match for the likes of Uncle Sergey. I-I need you to trust me that I have made the right decision."

So Fritz had relinquished control to Great-Uncle Sergey.

He must live up to every bit of his reputation. The stories of his great-uncle's daring-do were legendary. He glanced at Marcus, whose smug face telegraphed his delight at this rare moment of witnessing Fritz Leibnitz humbled by Belinda and subject to someone more powerful. If Marcus had entertained any mutinous thoughts, George knew the thought of their great-uncle had quashed them.

He glanced at M, whose face was closed. A frisson ran down his back. He couldn't find the woman he loved in her hard eyes.

His father's voice rescued him from the dread in the pit of his stomach. "So, I need each of you to tell me if you trust me to take care of you. No more plotting on your own, Marcus. I know everything you have done."

His ears reddened. "Of course, Uncle Fritz."

"I need to know I can trust you. Your father and I are united on this. Can I count on you to be honest and put our family first?"

His face wilted under his uncle's scrutiny. "You can count on me. Family absolutely comes first."

"Good. George?"

His father's eyes bore into him.

"I cannot say I agree with your methods. Frankly, I am offended."

"Now,..."

He put up his hands. "No, Father, you said to be honest. I'm appalled. You had a big part in my stepmother becoming a-a monster. I...well, I will put that aside because family comes first. And right now my family starts with M. I will *not* see her goals derailed. I will not see our plans for the future destroyed." He looked beseechingly into her eyes. "But, I will do what needs to be done to protect the Leibnitz family."

"Thank you." Fritz turned to her. "M, can I count on you? Do you trust me?"

She locked eyes with his. "Can you count on me? Yes. Do I

trust you? I really don't think that's a fair question."

"Point taken. This is what we need to do until I get the next set of instructions."

Chapter 9

Belinda paced back and forth across the plush carpet of her Wilton bedroom suite, heart racing, incensed that Fritz had taken her children. The muffled sound of her private cell ringing from her vanity safe interrupted her rage. She quickly went to her dressing room and opened the safe, but in her panic she couldn't remember the combination. She slowed her breathing, fingered the lock, and finally remembered the numbers. She checked to see who was calling, frowned, and let voicemail pick it up. She couldn't tip her hand yet.

*****

André turned in the lone chair in the center of the half-dark conference room toward his interrogator.

"*Voilà!* I told you she wouldn't answer. No matter what you think, *je ne sais rien*. Threatening me changes nothing."

"*Ah, mais je ne pense pas que vous compreniez, Monsieur Bouillot*. There's someone here who is very much looking forward to a conversation with you," Noël hissed.

André Bouillot carried himself with aplomb, sure that his six-foot-four, muscular frame could handle any opponent in a fight, if it came to that. Besides, the refined Leibnitz family wouldn't allow the towering bodyguard to lay a hand on him. Guilt seared his stomach. His little fling with Belinda had been a big mistake. Sharing confidential information would cost him a prestigious position that hadn't been worth the indiscretion. He cringed at the thought that a nice severance package would do nothing to bolster his bruised ego. How could he tell his wife he had been fired? The vague outline of a man crowded out that depressing thought.

The shadowy figure projected his raspy voice into the room, "*Monsieur Bouillot*, have you checked your bank account in the Caymans today?"

"Wh-What do you mean? What bank account?" André's voice squeaked.

"There's nothing there, so it's of no concern to you. Perhaps Mrs. Belinda Leibnitz, or your wife, Lisette, had a need for some insurance. I would say 428,000 in U.S. dollars and 200,000 French francs would be sufficient insurance for even an aggrieved wife. Or mistress? Do you think your mistress, Camille, will need insurance? Eh?"

All the blood in André's face drained into his sweaty palms.

"We might be able to find it for you, even scrape up enough to add a tidy sum to it, with the right information."

He remained mute and stared into the bleakness of his life.

"Pity you don't believe me. Noël, perhaps you can trigger Mr. Bouillot's memory. Show him his bank statement."

He watched as the bodyguard retrieved two pieces of paper from a briefcase. When he saw the numbers, his face became ashen. "What do you want to know?"

*****

It had been three days since Belinda had received a message from Paris: *Game over.*

Her heart fluttered waiting for the next call. An hour elapsed. Two. Four. A frisson ran down her back. She calmed herself with the thought that tomorrow her plan would be executed. Unless Fritz suspected. She called his cell.

No answer.

Maybe Marcus could still be manipulated.

No answer.

Frederick.

Nothing.

London office. No one knew anything.

Why didn't she think of it sooner? He would have taken them to Paris with George and M. She called her man in Paris.

No answer.

Unfortunately, Sebastian was in New York, not Paris, so he would be no help.

She pushed aside the feeling of emptiness that choked her. She couldn't afford distractions. Divorce wouldn't give her what she wanted. It had gone way beyond that now.

She shook off her fears and called Sebastian with the next set of instructions. Then, she called the maid on the intercom to prepare the hot tub and bring a bottle of *Pouilly Fuissé* and extra spicy buffalo wings to her suite. Power was so delicious.

Chapter 10

George kept his distance from M to avoid the chill that permeated their relationship. He knew she was at a critical time in her life. She was so close to completing her doctorate that he didn't want anything more to stand in the way of her having a clear head when she flew to New York to sit before her committee. Now that Belinda's plot had been uncovered, he could spend long hours in his office to research and make plans for his future with M, with or without his father's blessing.

He had long lunches with his cousin to try to uncover whether Marcus had good ideas for the future of LE, or if he wanted the chairmanship to take it away from George or secure power for power's sake. Finding the measure of Marcus's heart would help him make some critical decisions.

*****

The only way M could compartmentalize her emotions so that she could focus exclusively on the imminent oral examination was to freeze everyone else out. She pushed down the guilt of ignoring her dear, sweet George, telling herself that he deserved it for being a Leibnitz. His father had ruined everything he touched because of his overarching ego. The adrenaline that pushed her through sleepiness and exhaustion had no time for George's needs. She brushed aside the thought that percolated at least once a day that her life was deeper and richer, and her future had endless possibilities because she had set foot off the Pan Am building elevator into LE for the interview that had changed her life, her perspective, and her future.

She would make it up to George one day, if she ever forgave him for being Fritz Leibnitz's son.

Chapter 11

Sebastian finalized his reservations and called the LE security office with the pretext that his sister in Los Angeles needed him. Then he left a message for his contact in Paris to set plans in motion while he waited for the car service to take him to the airport.

At JFK he checked in at the Air France counter and made his way through the security checkpoints and onto the shopping promenade. As he ambled along, he sensed the presence of someone whose steps were closely aligned with his own. His training prompted him to turn his head slightly. He observed travelers making their way through the busy terminal. Directly behind him walked a tall, striking woman with a multicolored silk Ferragamo scarf stylishly wrapped around her head, a tailored navy pantsuit with pearl choker, and a Louis-Vuitton carry-on bag slung over her shoulder. She maneuvered to pass him. He smiled and let her advance. She returned the smile and asked if he knew the location of a ladies room. Looking around, he pointed to the nearest sign.

"How obtuse am I," she said in an East-European accent.

"Let me help you with your bag."

"Zank you, but I zink I can manage. But it eez very kind of you to offer."

As she patted his hand, a small child ran into her legs, and she brushed against Sebastian's side.

"So sorry."

He watched as she dodged her way through the crowd into the ladies room. He continued ahead, savoring the lingering odor of her perfume. When his flight was called, he noticed the Ferragamo lady boarding ahead of him into first class. The large diamond ring on her right hand captured his attention as she adjusted her scarf, looked his way, and threw him a flirting smile. He returned the gesture. Someone was well kept, he thought. He reminded himself of his mission and held back in the first-class line, making sure not to rub shoulders with the intriguing stranger.

Once he was seated in 3B, he relaxed. The exotic woman occupied a seat in the row behind him. Again he rejected the idea of talking to her and turned his attention to a magazine.

When the blue-eyed, blonde-headed stewardess with the lilting French accent offered him a glass of champagne, Sebastian happily accepted, surprised he didn't need to pay for the drink. He smiled, basking in newfound luxury. The good life awaited if he accomplished his mission.

*****

"Belinda, I saw you called."

"Fritz," She answered in German. "Where are you? And my children?"

"I brought them with me to Paris. Frederick didn't call you?"

"That was more than a week ago," she snarled.

"I don't spend enough time with them, as you've mentioned repeatedly. So I surprised them by bringing them for a combination business-holiday trip. They've been enjoying themselves. Marcus and George have been most entertaining. And a team of tutors has been instructing them. Now we're heading off to the Greek Isles for some sailing on the Aleksandra."

Her voice pouted, "And you didn't invite me?"

"In our last conversation you made it quite clear that you're happy to have my fortune but not me, so no. Besides, I want to get to know my children better. They're absolutely delightful. They've matured so much over the last six months. All is well with you, then?"

"Oh, lovely. I don't suppose I could speak to them?"

"Of course. I'll collect them from their studies. I'm sure they'd love to say hello. Shall I call you back in a couple of hours?"

"Fine. And then you'll be back at the Champs-Elysées house, no doubt with a friend."

He laughed.

She hung up the phone, loathing her husband even more than she could have imagined half an hour earlier. Her only consolation was knowing that his world would fall apart in less than twenty-four hours.

*****

Fritz hung up the phone, victory expanding his chest. The children were relaxing downstairs in their cabins, and he was enjoying a Southern Comfort Manhattan on the deck of the Feadship Aleksandra. Uncle Sergey had informed him half an hour earlier that Belinda's ability to cause any harm to the Leibnitz family had been thwarted. Within another few days, she would be asking for a quiet divorce settlement, and his marital problems would disappear.

Chapter 12

Marcus paced while George wrapped up a phone conversation.

"Wonderful. Thank you, Father. Talk to you soon."

George hung up and turned to him. "All is well. We can leave Paris and get back to our lives, at last."

Marcus' face relaxed. "So what happened? Is Belinda dead or what?"

"Of course not!" George bellowed. "The situation has been resolved, that's all. We're safe."

He would have loved to know the unsavory details of what had transpired, but self-interest focused his mind. His best course of action would be to partner with George and continue proving his mettle. His conscience overrode the desire to get the better of his cousin. Living in close quarters for the last two weeks with him and M had changed his opinion. They were either great actors or genuine in their desire to work with him. He sloughed off the feeling and prepared to make his next move.

The next morning, as he and George were preparing to leave for the office, their usual chauffeur Maurice didn't show up, and Noël and Boris were stomping about outside. When he overheard Noël tell Boris to stand watch at the house with M while he drove the cousins to the office, the hair stood up on his neck.

Later that morning the buzz traveled throughout the office

that Maurice had been in a car accident around midnight Tuesday. Then just before noon, Mrs. Bouillot's sister turned up to inform them that André had been in a scuba diving accident off Grand Cayman and had suffered a heart attack. His female companion was injured but on the mend. Mrs. Bouillot had sent her sister to inform the office staff and ask for help. He offered to represent the family at the funeral, since George had planned to accompany M on her trip to New York in three days as she made final preparations for her thesis defense set for the following Friday.

Great-Uncle Sergey had not lost his touch.

*****

George braved the chill of approaching M as she was getting ready for a shower to let her know that the danger was behind them. She smiled, sighed, and barely acknowledged the good turn of events. He wanted to engulf her in his arms in the hopes of easing the tension that had built between them but pushed aside the thought as she turned away. The sudden fear that she would never come back to him from the safe place in which she had ensconced herself surfaced in the strong need to wash his hands. He moved instead to take out the legal pad on which he had been laying out future scenarios of their life once her exam was over and they could return to some semblance of normalcy.

Chapter 13

Belinda paced. None of her accomplices had responded. The previous night's conversation with the children had enraged her as she learned they'd been on the yacht somewhere in the Mediterranean for several days. Fritz had led her to believe they were still in Paris. They hadn't spoken to their brother or cousin for days, but Sebastian still hadn't checked in.

She called Frederick. "I've been trying to reach my children. I believe zey vere staying vith George and zat voman in Paris. You vouldn't happen to know...?"

"Mr. George called earlier today and mentioned they would all be in Paris a while longer. But gosh, Mrs. Belinda, your children, no, I've heard nothing about them yet. The last I heard they were with their father."

"Never mind. I'll find zem myself," she snapped and disconnected him.

The roar of panic reverberated in her ears.

"They're alive—all three of them! My lackeys have taken my money but done nothing to earn it!" she screamed.

Vengeance boiled her veins.

"I've been relying on others when I should have gone to New York and Paris myself!"

She scurried to the safe in the bottom of her vanity where she had squirreled away almost fifteen thousand dollars. First, she needed to check on the funds she had wired to three

Cayman accounts, one for each of her collaborators. She had arranged for each of the wire transfers personally. The numbers were hidden in an envelope on the third shelf of her safe behind the Tiffany diamond necklace and earring set Fritz had given her the previous Mother's Day.

She cocked her head and sneered. "I can withdraw the money as well as deposit it!"

She retrieved the numbers, raced to her study off the master bedroom and called a maid to bring a bottle of *Château-Neuf du Pape* to calm her nerves.

Once the servant had brought the wine and exited the room, she swigged a gulp, set the glass on the desk, and sat down. She checked on the private account she had set up the first year of her marriage. She had managed to build a nest egg over the last fourteen years from the hundred dollars here, the thousand dollars there she had lifted from Fritz's dressing room, what she had saved from the two thousand dollars a week he had doled out for spending money, and the sums she had extracted by claiming the weekly allowance had fallen short of expenses. She had always been amazed that he kept thousands in his pockets but never paid for anything himself. He always had some lackey pay his expenses.

Gall rose in her throat.

She called Matthew Springer, manager of First National Bank of Wilton.

"Hello, Mrs. Leibnitz. So nice of you to call. How may I help you today?"

"I vould like you to check somezing."

"Of course."

"I have a question about my personal account?"

She gave him the account number.

He asked her a couple of verification questions and said, "Very good."

She paced while he retrieved the information.

"Excuse me, Mrs. Leibnitz. I'm confused. According to Mr.

Barker, you closed your account yesterday."

Her heart stopped. "Vhat? Zat is absurd!"

"I-I'm sorry, but he said you came in yesterday and closed it."

"I did no such zing," she growled.

"Let me put Mr. Barker on the phone."

Her mind raced through the possibilities.

Mr. Barker's voice interrupted her thoughts. "Good afternoon, Mrs. Leibnitz. You came in yesterday around 2:00. I remember exactly what you were wearing. A lovely Ferragamo scarf of navy and gold wrapped exquisitely around your head. I even commented on it. Those wonderful Gucci sunglasses. A beautifully tailored navy pantsuit, navy kid gloves, a pearl choker, pearl-diamond teardrop earrings, navy stiletto heels. You even remarked about the ridiculously expensive Prada crocodile shoes."

Her lips quivered. "Vhat? You let someone else come in *und* take my money. I'll sue you for everyzing you're vorth."

"But you signed the documents yourself. Your signature was a perfect match."

Belinda's mental gears turned. "Uh...fine. S-So I've changed my mind. I vant to transfer zee money back from zee Cayman account and re-open my account vith you. You should have no problem vith zat."

"W-Well, of course. I would be more than happy to. Give me a moment to retrieve the wire transfer document and the account number."

She drummed her long ruby fingernails on the desk.

"Alright, Mrs. Leibnitz, I'm back. I'm typing in everything. I don't suppose you remember the password you used to access your Cayman file?"

"*Mein Gott, nein!*" she gasped.

"No? Well, let's see."

The pause was deafening.

"Good. Here it is. Alright. Let's put it in. Hmmm... Surely, you know that account no longer exists. Mrs. Leibnitz, what game do..."

She disconnected him, slung the phone across the room, and erupted in scalding tears. She collapsed into the luxurious carpet, feeling every bit a pauper, despite being draped in a Givenchy fur-and-velour tracksuit and wearing her favorite Mikimoto pearls, Fendi pumps, and the Cartier three-stone diamond ring and diamond Rolex Fritz had given her for their twelfth wedding anniversary.

The blood rushing through her head deafened her ears. Tiny hammers pounded out the zeros of her reality. She stared into the exquisite Austrian crystal goblet, drained of any hope of punishing Fritz. She toppled the glass and lay on the floor in a fetal position. Minutes ticked like hours.

Her anguish spent, she righted herself into a sitting position, surveyed her sumptuous suite, and scrambled for her phone. She dialed her in-laws' home number.

"*Güten tag.* Leibnitz residence."

"Tell Tani I'm on the line," she barked in German.

"Mrs. Belinda. I shall inquire if Mrs. Tatania is home."

"Make it snappy."

She licked her lips.

"*Es tut mir leid, aber Frau Leibnitz ist nicht verfügbar.*"

"What do you mean she's not available?" she yelled. "Are you saying she's there but won't speak to me or that she's out?"

"*Frau* Leibnitz is not available. Shall I take a message?"

"Of course! Tell Tani to call me at once!"

She launched her phone across the carpet.

"Fine. So she's taking sides. Guenther won't."

She scrambled for her phone, which she discovered under the overstuffed floral chaise-longue next to the window. An acrid taste reminded her of her loathing for this house's furnishings. Even in her private quarters, she wasn't allowed to change anything from the Old World style her mother-in-law had chosen years ago.

As she dialed his office number, she calmed herself.

"Good afternoon, Leibnitz Enterprises. Mr. Guenther Leibnitz's office. Carmen Gutierrez speaking. How may I help you?"

"Belinda calling to speak vith Guenther. He eez expecting my call."

"Hello, Mrs. Belinda. I'm sorry but Mr. Leibnitz isn't taking calls right now. He's in the middle of an important conference. May I take a message?"

"Vhen vill his meeting end?"

"I'm afraid I don't know. These meetings can go on for hours. I'd be happy to tell him you rang. Does he have your number?"

"Uh, give him anozer number since I may be out. But zis number eez not to be given to anyone else. You understand?"

"Certainly."

Another brick wall. After half an hour and no call, she began pacing back and forth, feeling more and more worn down as the hours went by. One hour. Two.

A new idea soothed her nerves.

"Archer Detective Agency, Barbara speaking. How may I direct your call?"

"Bob Hall, please. Tell him Mrs. Leibnitz eez calling."

"I'm sorry. Bob no longer works for the agency. He took another position. Out west, I think."

Her eyebrows shot up. "Oh! Who-Who eez taking care of his clients?"

"Well, ma'am, it depends. If you want, I can check to see who has your file. I'm just gonna put ya on hold. I'll be back witcha in a minute."

"Fine."

The sour dregs of the wine churned the volcano in her stomach as the minutes dragged on.

"I'm sorry, Mrs...."

"Leibnitz."

"Yes, Mrs. Leibnitz. I'm sorry, but we don't have any file with that name. The boss searched Bob's files, checked with Bill and Rudy. Nothin'. I'm really sorry, ma'am. Are ya sure you got the right agency?"

She gasped. Her spectral face dropped as she hung up. Who else could help her?

"Aha! Why didn't I think of it earlier? Gregory!"

She had experienced no problem finding out from Gregory the juicy bit of ammunition about the will. She should have hung on to the young stud. Maybe it wasn't too late. She dialed his number.

"Leibnitz Enterprises, Legal Department, Juris speaking."

"I-I'm looking for Gregory Putter. Isn't zis his number?"

"This was his number. Mine now. I've taken over his duties. May I help you?"

"Vhere's Gregory?"

"South America, or maybe it was South Africa. Sorry, I don't remember. He got an offer from another company, big signing bonus and everything. Some people have all the luck. Sorry, is there anything I can do for you?"

"I-I don't, uh, yes. I need to speak to Parker."

"Mr. Gibson? I don't believe he's in, but I'll check. Who did you say was calling?"

"I didn't!" she barked.

"Ma'am, I'm sorry, but I don't imagine he will take the call if I can't tell him who..."

"Fine. Belinda Leibnitz."

"O-Oh, Mrs. Leibnitz. I'm so sorry. F-Forgive me. I-I'll get him right away."

Her forehead was throbbing.

"Hello, Mrs. Belinda. Parker here. What can I do for you?"

She breathed.

"Parker, dah-ling. Just zee man I need."

"Why, whatever do I owe the pleasure of this call?"

"Some strange zings are going on. I zought perhaps you could help me."

"Oh?"

"People aren't returning my calls. Millions of dollars have disappeared. Fritzie has abducted my children and..."

"Abducted? Surely you don't mean Mr. Leibnitz kidnapped his own children? Missing money? This sounds serious. Perhaps, I should send another security guard out to Wilton right away."

"That von't be necessary."

"Let me assure you that the protection of the Leibnitz family is of the utmost importance to me. I will get on it immediately. In fact, I'll send Robert to you at once. Don't worry about a thing. It was good you called me. I'll take care of everything."

The line went dead.

"The old horse *knows*. *He* has orchestrated all of this. But how?" she fumed aloud, declawed.

Her thoughts scrambled in panic. Reservoirs behind her frantic eyes cascaded down her face. After a few moments of anguish, she collected her crushed frame from the carpet and straightened her spine. She would have one of the private cars brought around and stop by Trump Tower to gather some things. But first, she needed some cash. She opened the safe. She would take all her jewelry as a precaution and fetch the Louis-Vuitton travel safe she had purchased the day before that horrid engagement party had thwarted one of her well-laid plans. She grimaced, then reached deep into the bottom shelf to retrieve her money pouch. As she fingered the bag, she smiled at the new web forming in her mind. She grabbed the pouch and opened it. A one dollar bill.

Her eyes bulged. She threw the pouch to the side and clawed the empty cavity of the bottom shelf. Rummaging through each of the dozen deep felt-lined shelves, she dragged everything out and dumped it in piles on either side of her.

She slumped to the floor, her lips wilting with small gasps. She stared at the void of her life, the broken marionette arms and legs, the temples pulsating defeat. After a few moments, a jagged smile emerged. She would break into Fritz's closet and rummage through his suits as before. This time she would take everything she found. His stash had never let her down before. Her New York lawyer would fix this mess. The hope of revenge picked up her pride from the floor. She flounced away toward his suite of rooms, which she had accessed countless times through the hidden paneled entrance off the hallway between her study and the master bedroom. Reaching behind the brooding Brueghel painting on the wall, Belinda's fingers typed the four numbers she had observed him enter when he had been putty in her hands.

Nothing.

Taking deep breaths, she pushed again, more slowly.

Nothing.

A third time. A fourth.

Apoplectic, she punished the wall with her fists.

"Fine, I have other tricks up my sleeve!" she screeched and turned on her heel.

She muttered as she slung her priceless jewelry into a silk shawl and then ran to her closet—a large room divided into four sections framed in the middle by a sitting and dressing area. Rummaging through a selection of casual Gucci, Versace, and Chloé jeans, pants, and tops and grabbing a Givenchy embroidered silk dress, a Ralph Lauren silk pantsuit, an assortment of Gucci, Fendi, and Ferragamo shoes and boots, and her short Olivieri sable fur coat, Belinda stuffed her ample Louis-Vuitton travel bag with clothes and jewels. Frantic, she sprinted to the intercom phone and called for the Bentley.

"*Es tut mir leid, Frau Leibnitz. Niemand ist heir ausser mir*," a tremulous maid responded.

"Fine, you're by yourself. Come upstairs at once. I'm going into the city," she hissed.

Within moments, she heard the sound of the elevator doors.

"Finally!"

She inhaled the rush of power.

"Get my suitcases and be quick about it."

Hearing no reply, she exited the dressing room and gasped. Her legs buckled. Parker and Robert were standing not more than twenty feet away.

"Hello, Mrs. Belinda. You remember Robert."

Robert tilted his head.

"Vh-Vhat eez zee meaning of zis? But you were in New York moments ago. I-I'm outraged. You-you..."

"Mrs. Belinda, I'm truly sorry for all this." He spread out his hands. "I believe you're starting to discover that all your accomplices are nowhere to be found, and all avenues have been cut off. It's time to go."

"G-Go? Vhat do you mean?"

She glowered, a caged animal searching for a means of escape. Two hundred thirty-five compact pounds of toned muscle and sinew moved off to her right.

"It's time for a trip. You wanted to see your children, right?"

Words strangled in her throat.

"I feel sure you're ready to go. There's nothing left for you here."

Robert picked up her luggage. She lunged for it.

"No! Mine! All mine!" she screeched.

Parker smiled. "Yes, of course. Robert will carry it for you as we make our way to the car. All your belongings will come along shortly. Everything has been arranged."

"I demand to know vhere you are taking me."

"You are in no position to demand anything. The pilot has already filed his flight plan. We will be at Westchester in less than an hour. Shall we go then?"

"My lawyer will learn soon enough about zis-zis

kidnapping."

She held her head high as she strutted behind him with Robert at her heels.

*****

Belinda made her way halfway down the 737's exit stairs. An unnerving sight awaited her. A swarthy 300-pound linebacker with a pock-marked face and toady eyes in a fitted black silk suit and turtleneck stood on the red carpet that shot out from the bottom of the stairs next to a tall, blonde woman in an Armani navy pantsuit, Ferragamo navy and gold scarf, navy Prada stiletto heels, and diamond Rolex watch.

"*Mein Gott!*"

Raw terror chilled her spine as a bitter gust of wind sliced through her. She looked up at ominous clouds scudding across the early morning sky. She turned back toward the Boeing Business Jet 737.

"Don't worry," Parker called behind her. "You're in good hands. Boris and Aliana will escort you to the Leibnitz estate. I understand this will not be your first visit. You'll find everything you need upon arrival. The family will join you soon. I regret that Robert and I are needed elsewhere. Sorry we missed a chance to chat on the flight. Enjoy your stay."

Her fuzzy brain tried to piece together her arrival in the Austrian countryside. When it had become clear that neither Parker nor Robert was going to answer her questions, and she was confined to the master stateroom, she had plopped on the king-sized bed. She had tossed and turned on the mattress where she had first tasted the thrill of possessing her enemy. Bemoaning her nasty turn of fortune, memories of her sister Jenny had flooded her mind. She had failed Jenny by falling in love with Fritz and forgetting her promise. But with every mistress and flirtation, she had laid her plans carefully to make Fritz writhe in the pain he deserved. Mocking self-loathing had lain next to her. He had outmaneuvered her.

The sound of the retracting stairs brought her back to the present. No customs officer. A thug and an imposter stood in front of her. The hair on the back of her neck vibrated.

She reluctantly accepted Aliana's handshake as the menacing Boris directed her to follow Aliana into the pristine silver Rolls Royce. It vexed her that Aliana took a seat next to her instead of sitting up front with Boris. Although the elegantly appointed woman didn't even attempt to converse after her initial greeting in High German, she seethed to share the same space with the woman who had impersonated her at the bank. She peered through the window pane at the verdant Alpine woods, rattled by her defeat.

Bringing her to Guenther and Tani's Vienna estate puzzled her, but her brain couldn't wrap itself around the thought as sleep overtook her.

She awoke with a start, seated on a stiff winged-back chair in a large semi-dark room. Her last memory was dozing off in the car within moments of leaving the private airfield. Her neck stiffened with pain. The dim light obfuscated much of her surroundings of walls of book-lined shelves, library ladders, Old Master paintings, a large table, reading chairs and couches, and dark floor-length curtains. As she widened her gaze upward, she detected the shadow of a tall, large figure in black staring at her from the mezzanine level. A chill ran through her.

The man spoke in German. "How very nice of you to join us. I hope you were comfortable during your journey."

"Who are you?" she retorted, also in German. "Why have you brought me here? No doubt Fritz's idea," she spat. "Trying to scare me? It won't work, you know."

The man's cold, guttural laugh scalded her skin. "Why would I do that when I have exactly what I want?" the gravelly voice replied.

"What would that be?"

"You know what I want. You are quite the schemer, after all. But, first, let me assure you. Mr. Fritz has no idea you're here. As far as he knows, you're safely tucked away in Wilton, Connecticut."

"You expect me to believe that."

"I have what I want."

She quailed. A cold sweat began a path down her back.

"Why would you want me?"

"I think it's time to enlighten you on how your plans have fared."

Her bones rattled.

"I don't have the slightest idea what you're talking about."

A short, cold cackle reverberated in her solar plexus. "*Monsieur André Bouillot*, dead of a heart attack while scuba diving with his mistress off Grand Cayman Island."

She gasped. "You wouldn't..."

"His poor grieving wife is mortified to learn that her sweet husband had a mistress. But she is comforted that her dear André provided for her and their children. A million francs, was it? No need for her to know that her husband was fired for revealing secrets to his erstwhile mistress—Belinda Leibnitz. And then there is the poor distraught mistress with a hundred thousand francs magically appearing in her checking account. How her dearly departed André loved her."

"I don't know..."

"Then, there is poor Maurice. You remember your second accomplice. Tragic accident with a Mercedes truck, I believe. Pity. But his grieving mother is enriched by almost two hundred francs."

Her hands gripped the arms of the chair as terror silenced her tongue.

"Sebastian. Ah, yes, I almost forgot. A heart attack en route to Paris. The poor Air France flight attendant was in hysterics for hours. Not to worry. His dear sister is so gratified for the quarter million deposited into her account in his name. What a generous brother."

She couldn't scrape a voice out of her constricted throat. Breaths labored to escape her burning lungs.

"Then there is Gregory. You must be thrilled for him. A seventy-five thousand signing bonus from a prestigious firm needing an attorney, where was that? No matter. And Detective Bob. Another lucky devil. A fifty thousand dollar signing bonus to join an elite agency out west."

She clamped her hands over her ears and swallowed thickly. "No more! Please, no more!" she yelped like a beaten dog.

"Heard enough? That pretty much covers it. Just one other matter or two. Your identity, for example."

Her head shot up to glare at her veiled accuser, her fingernails digging into the cherry claws of her chair. "What do you mean?"

"I don't think Belinda Metternich Leibnitz has quite the right ring to it. No, Belinda Moore Leibnitz, that suits you much better. Yes, indeed. Belinda Moore, Jenny Moore's younger sister. You remember Jenny? You know, your husband's first love, the one Rainer Leibnitz seduced to prove she was not the 'right sort,' I believe he called her, the one he paid off. The anorexic Jenny who eventually took her own life when no one would have her. Cut her wrists, I believe. What was it, six, eight months later? Broke your parents' hearts. Yes, the dead sister on whose grave you swore revenge."

Her face blanched. Blood oozed from her bitten lower lip.

"A glimmer of recognition, I see."

Two fingernails broke as they dug deeper. Cold sweat trickled down her armpits.

She screamed, *"ENOUGH,"* but no sound escaped her constricted vocal chords.

"Yes, you see all too clearly," the steely voice tamped down.

Finally, the tigress within her growled, "Who are you?

Fritz's man?"

"You sully the Leibnitz name," he hissed, "by even speaking it. I assure you, no one in this distinguished family shall ever know your real identity, the details of your sordid plan, the people who have died because of you. This is a family of royal blood. Not a word shall be breathed of your vile and filthy misdeeds," the dark figure bellowed. "Especially not the fact that you're not who you claim to be. Fake name, fake accent, fake passport. A fake through and through. Shall I go on?"

"I get it. You know who I am. So what?" she hissed.

"Let me tell you who you *really* are. For all your so-called 'noble' motives, you betrayed your family, your sister's memory, your own promising future. Just like your sister, you were seduced by power, money, and position. You both went in with your eyes wide open."

"How dare you?! She was not!" she uttered a barely audible, piercing howl. "She was innocent, sweet and vulnerable."

Tears tumbled down her cheeks. "Sh-She j-just became confused. He took advantage of her. You know nothing of who my sister was!"

"Hmmm, perhaps, not. But I know *you* well," the shadow snarled.

Her head drooped onto her chest.

"Let me spell it out for you. You're the lowest kind of power-hungry, social-climbing harlot. Do you think Aleksandra Zerbst Leibnitz wouldn't know who her son was marrying? Do you think she wouldn't have you watched, wouldn't have her most trusted confidant keep a close eye on her family and follow her instructions, even after her death? Wouldn't have his successors lined up to watch over her family? Wouldn't insure that no one would *ever* hurt any of her progeny, touch any of her fortune, imperil her empire? You may think you're clever, but you have no idea what I'm capable of. That knowledge would curdle your blood."

"That witch! Hidden cameras? Watching my every move?"

The dark figure cackled.

She cringed, all her venom spent.

"I misjudged him. He loved me. I-I loved him."

She licked her lower lip, savoring the memory. "B-But he betrayed me. He-He forced me to fend for myself, to-to curry the right favors, to wait for the perfect moment to have my revenge. But now it's all ruined-ruined because of you! Who are you?!"

A dark cackle answered.

An acrid, dulling sensation covered her tongue with the accumulated bile of vengeance denied. Her eyes narrowed. Her jaw tightened its grip. She would see the revolting man in the shadows get his due. Her eyes strained to decipher his identity. But despite her show of bravado, she shriveled in the stiff chair like a crumpled doll.

The grotesque voice softened. "I can be generous to those who do as they're told. There's a row of papers on the table to your right with places for your signature. I highly advise you to sign in each marked line where indicated. The first paper is the signature page of the settlement agreement. This agreement stipulates that you will receive a large, exclusive chalet property in the Swiss Alps. Since you are an expert winter sportswoman, you will surely find it pleasurable to make the Alps your permanent home."

Hope blossomed in her chest.

"Obviously, I could send you to the most remote region of the world, should I so desire. So you would be wise to accept your fate graciously. With this estate in the mountains you'll have household staff, your choice of the finest furnishings, two vehicles of your choosing, yearly upkeep, at no cost to you. It's a large private estate in your name. You'll receive a million per annum to use at your discretion, far more than you deserve."

She breathed a sigh.

"Your children will continue their private education in America and visit you as their father sees fit. Mr. Leibnitz will retain sole custody. No negotiation is permitted. Finally, you will never step foot outside of Switzerland. Obviously, any contact with the press in any country is forbidden and punishable to the utmost extreme."

She launched from her chair, vehement. "How dare you? I will do..."

Her captor growled, "You will do exactly as I say. Make no mistake. The other option is final."

"You wouldn't!" she spit.

"Yes, I would."

She collapsed into the chair.

"The next document stipulates that you will never attempt to seek any money from any Leibnitz or Leibnitz holding or Leibnitz company. Even from your children. You give up all rights to anything beyond what's spelled out in the agreement, and you will abide by it. The next document confirms your name of birth and that you agree to never use it again. You will continue to use the false name Belinda Metternich Leibnitz. The next document states that you will never contact any member of your family of birth. The last document confirms your payment arrangement with each of your accomplices."

Her temples screamed.

"Your husband will never see any of these documents except the settlement agreement. Once all the documents are signed, you'll never see me again. Unless, of course, you should renege on any promise you make today by signing these documents. Surely, you know the result of such a foolish move."

She quailed.

"No Leibnitz will ever know the despicable acts you've committed. Other than the settlement agreement, I will hold the other documents in a safe place as insurance that you'll fulfill your part of the bargain. Of course, there's always a final solution should you choose to brook any of my instructions."

She glared at the shadow. "You won't always be alive to menace me," she growled.

"Someone will."

She pulled in her broken claws. "Fine. When do I give the settlement agreement to Fritz?"

"You'll sign now. Aliana will be in momentarily to assist you. Your children will be joining you in a few hours. I'll have Mr. Fritz's signature before the day is out. I'm sure today you're turning over a new leaf. You understand me, yes? I believe our business is concluded."

"Who are you?" the tigress bellowed.

A cold, hard cackle replied.

She did as instructed, her energy drained into the cold, clammy sweat that seeped from her pores. The thought of wrapping her arms around her children soothed her spent nerves. Someday somehow she would have her revenge.

*****

Sergey limped off and sighed under the weight of his years. Even if the last many days had been exhilarating, his energy flagged. This encounter had drained him.

"It's time for Robert to take my place."

*****

"I see. Capital! Hmmm... Very good. I will alert Robert at once. Thank you, Uncle Sergey."

Guenther hung up the phone and licked his lips, savoring the elixir of power.

Chapter 14

M set foot in George's Fifth Avenue apartment, relieved that life was returning to normal. To everyone's surprise, Belinda had agreed to a divorce and was permanently relocating to Switzerland. As soothing as the end of the drama of the last few months was, the looming thesis defense before her doctorate committee in two days left her utterly enervated. She needed every ounce of determination to muster her courage and focus. Her goals had been almost completely subsumed by recent events. The irony of writing a dissertation on the grotesque and the sublime in the midst of the Leibnitz family feud struck her. The one shining bloom among the thorns was George's genuineness and growing self-confidence in the face of the turmoil. She wanted to relax in his love but needed every ounce of strength to finish what she had started.

"M, do you want me to disappear tomorrow, so I won't distract you?" George asked as he handed his travel case to the housekeeper to unpack. "I have quite enough to keep me busy all day at the office."

"How sweet of you to ask. I-I need to return to my apartment to collect my thoughts."

He looked down at his hands. "I thought you weren't going back there anymore."

"I don't mean to keep shutting you out. I-I just need to be alone."

He bit his lower lip. She handed off a dress and took his hands in hers.

"Please do this for me. Remember how you needed your own space before sitting for the bar?" Her eyes pooled.

"Of course."

Flooded with guilt, she drew his face to hers and kissed him full on the lips, her mouth butter.

"I really appreciate it."

She went back to her suitcase.

"Would you prefer I go to the office now?" he chirped, his face brightening.

She smiled. "You must be tired. Don't you want to relax? Let's spend the rest of the day unwinding. Then tomorrow I'll head over to my apartment when you go into the office."

Relief washed over his face. "Lovely."

Turning to the housekeeper, M asked her to give them some privacy. As soon as she had exited the bedroom, M turned into him and tried to put his mind at ease about their relationship, even though she felt disconnected and distant. She went through the motions of tenderness, even though her mind was consumed with thoughts of fleeing.

As the evening unwound, he disappeared into his studio to paint. She busied herself with her notes, barely noticing when he went to bed. She waited for the sound of heavy breathing before joining him. She turned toward his peaceful face, a blade of remorse tearing at her throat. She shut her heart's door and turned away. She tossed and turned and finally arose at 5:15, being careful not to awaken him. At 6:05 she pecked his forehead.

"*Au revoir, chéri. Tu me manque déjà.*"

She would miss him, but she needed to find her own way without him. The constriction in her throat stopped her. Picking up pen and paper from her nightstand, she wrote a note next to his watch on the nightstand.

Chéri—and you are every bit dear to me, I can't imagine life without you. Love, M.

Her cheeks flamed. An emptiness filled her heart. False hope would make it harder when she didn't come back.

Chapter 15

Fritz reviewed his life as he looked around the state room of his custom-fitted 737 business jet, sipped a Southern Comfort Manhattan, and smiled. A master bedroom suite with two medium-sized state rooms, an ample lounge, private office, and a state-of-the-art kitchen made the 737 a comfortable home-away-from-home. Fiber-optic/acrylic ceiling lights, built-in pecan cabinetry, plush leather furniture, Bose speaker system, original paintings and sculptures—a rich elegance that had never failed to impress even the most jaded guest.

He had seduced Belinda into his bed on a business trip to London when he had grown tired of Racquel. He felt an uncharacteristic lack of confidence in himself and the strong desire to feel the power of a strong woman succumbing to his charms. He tried unsuccessfully to shrug off the thought.

His mother had warned him Sergey had discovered disturbing information about Belinda, but he had refused to listen. He regretted not heeding her warning. He needed another drink and motioned to the stewardess. More galling was having been duped. He quashed the thought, relishing instead the memory of watching the father who had stolen his first love gasp for his last breaths and refusing to help him. He slugged down the alcohol. Uncle Sergey had refused to explain why Belinda had agreed to his terms so quickly, and he no longer cared to know.

He shifted his focus to his two youngest children. Watching the two adolescents at war in a game of chess diverted his brooding. He had seen no sadness in their faces at saying goodbye to their mother when they joined him for their return to New York. He smiled and ordered another whiskey. Empty power stared at him from the bottom of the crystal. He could have wept for the idealistic, loving young husband and father who had tried to please Papa. But that man had vanished the day he had looked Rainer in the eye and said, "Go to hell where you belong." He motioned to the stewardess to refill his glass. He sucked the mantle of responsibility through his teeth. He did not have the luxury to ruminate about the past when he had his family's future to think of and a wedding to orchestrate.

Chapter 16

M fidgeted outside the conference room of the Romance Languages Department on the sixth floor of 13 University Place. She couldn't just sit down and wait, as Professor Béjart had suggested. The professors had seemed impressed, although some of the questions had been totally unexpected. She thought she did well, but doubt plagued her.

While the committee deliberated on whether or not to grant her doctorate, she couldn't quash a growing uneasiness. The seven men and two women at the conference table held her future in their hands. The suffocating feeling that she would always be controlled by someone squeezed her chest. She exhaled her disgust. She had made the right choice to revisit her apartment to find herself again. Some of her devotional books faced her on the bedside table—Frederick Buechner's *The Hungering Dark,* Madeleine L'Engle's *A Stone for a Pillow,* C.S. Lewis's *Mere Christianity.* Reading sections she had once highlighted had settled her mind and restored her spirit. Then she found the *Bible* Pop-Pop and Grammy had given her for her tenth birthday. Opening to the dedication page, the inscription had smacked her in the chest:

To our precious Marianne
August 27, 1973
Whenever you're in doubt, remember:
"Be still and know that I am God."
"Above all else, guard your heart, for it is the wellspring of

life."

Remember who you are.

Love, Pop-Pop and Grammy

A scalding tear slipped down her cheek. Who had she become? Had she sloughed off innocence for risk only to be transformed into someone she wouldn't want to know? Several more of her favorite books laid in boxes next to her reading chair. Thumbing through, she had spied the writings of Kathleen Norris, Henri Nouwen, Madeleine L'Engle, and Philip Yancey, among others. Dozens of leather-bound journals in shades of blue and purple had brought back a flood of unwanted memories of Donald's betrayals. She had needed to find her own identity and beliefs apart from his rejection of God. Another smaller box of religious accompaniment CDs and cassette tapes had transported her to the songs she used to sing. *People Need the Lord* and *Amazing Grace* had brought tears of conviction.

She had left part of herself behind when she had been swept into all things Leibnitz. Ignoring her conscience had come with a price. Being who others wanted her to be and giving in to others' agendas would never satisfy the longing in her heart. She found she was not so different from George, who was trying to find his own voice and unique path.

She went back to the verse "Be still and know that I am God." She had stopped listening to the quiet voice that had always stilled her heart when she sang, when she prayed, when she wrote. Coming to the end of the self that others projected onto her was the path to finding her way home to her true self. In the quietness of her tiny apartment, she read through some of her journal entries and poems as the tears fell with the memories. The nudging in her heart beat loudly.

"Marianne. *Mari-anne!*" Prof. Béjart's voice interrupted her musings. *"Venez. Nous vous attendez."*

His face beamed.

She tucked away her memories, regained her composure,

and followed him into the conference room as the fog dissipated and her path became clear.

Chapter 17

George's heart somersaulted when his phone rang.

"Hello, *chéri*. Doing anything special tonight?"

"Of course," he replied. "I'm meeting you at *La Bibliothèque* for a private dinner."

"Then, I guess I'll need to wear something special. Problem is, that certain outfit is in the Fifth Avenue apartment."

"Should I leave, or did you have something else in mind?" he asked.

"Hmmm... I think we should keep the suspense going as long as possible. Let's say that *Doctor* Staunton, soon-to-be *Doctor Staunton Leibnitz,* needs two hours of privacy between 4:00 and 6:00 and will join her *beau* at 7:00 at *La Bibliothèque.*"

He smiled from ear to ear. "Sounds perfect to me. We have the restaurant all to ourselves from 6:00."

"Then, *à tout-à-l'heure, chéri.*"

He pranced around the apartment. As he made his way to the bedroom, his pocket rang. The caller could wait.

*****

George took in the breathtaking view of the East River to quell the butterflies fluttering through his stomach. Reflecting on his earlier lunch with Father Thomas, whom he had sought out for counsel, he smiled. He embraced newfound confidence that the vision he would cast would resonate with M.

The *maître d'* interrupted his thoughts by announcing that the silver Bentley had arrived. He galloped toward the door just as M exited the car. She scintillated in a royal blue tea-length silk dress with a wide, woven, dark-blue, cinched waist and scooped neck, which her shoulder length blonde hair touched seductively. She was wearing the Van Cleef & Arpels diamond necklace, earrings, and bracelet set he had given her before their engagement party. As soon as their eyes locked, she launched toward him. He enveloped her, holding her close as she kissed him full on the lips.

"I've missed you," she murmured.

His heart bloomed. "I've missed you more."

She snuggled her head into his shoulder. He held her close, luxuriating in the certainty of their love. After a few moments, she lifted her head and giggled.

"I think we're embarrassing the wait staff. Maybe we should continue this later."

He purred, "I don't care about them. Only you."

"Well, *I'm* starved. And we have much to catch up on."

"We most certainly do."

He released his hold and led her to their table. A bottle of *Dom Pérignon* rested in the wine bucket next to the table. Propped on a chair sat a small wrapped package topped with a bow and a larger, thick rectangular package.

As soon as they sat down, he motioned for the *maître d'* to open the champagne and turned to her. "I have asked the chef to prepare several of your favorite foods, which will appear in a staggered fashion."

Her face opened up. "How thoughtful."

"So, tell me all about your exam."

She threw him a grin. "They hated me, of course, but signed off on the degree anyway."

He chuckled. "Naturally."

Her eyebrows knitted together. "It was intense. Naturally,

the Ruskies had to look good in front of the Frogs, so there was a bit of showboating. But at the end, they all gave me a kiss on both cheeks. It was rather nice."

She took a sip of her champagne.

He stared into her limpid eyes. "I have important news, but, first, two gifts are dying for you to release them from their boxes."

He handed her the silver carton in front of her place setting.

She grinned. "I love presents."

As she popped open the box, a small navy-blue velvet case emerged. Hands trembling, she removed it. As she opened the case, her eyes moistened. A small 24-karat gold key encrusted in tiny diamonds with the initial M was tucked into a 24-karat gold lock laid in tiny emeralds with the initial G. Underneath the lock and key was a small note with the words, *M, you are the jewel that has unlocked the key to my heart. All I am and all I have are yours, now and always. Je t'adore toujours, George.*

Her eyes glistened. "How exquisite."

He took her hands in his. After a moment, he grinned. "I know you're famished and some food is in order."

She smiled. "Sounds great. But you said presents."

He cocked his head. "Well, just to keep the suspense going, I thought we'd wait until dessert for the second gift."

She shook her head. "You really want me to suffer, don't you?"

He signaled the *maître d'*, who disappeared. Within seconds, two waiters appeared with the first course.

As they dipped the escargots into melted butter, they talked about the final fitting of the wedding gown, a bridal shower her friends had scheduled in July, and the Leibnitz Foundation.

As the courses continued, she became agitated.

"Do you think we could change the wedding date to late

summer? I'd like to get married as soon as we can."

"Fun-y you sh-ld a- tha-," he mumbled while chewing a bite.

"I didn't catch that."

He swallowed. "Sorry. I said, funny you should ask that. I was thinking along the same lines."

Her eyes brightened. "We think so much alike."

He smiled. "I love it!"

"What do you have in mind?"

"I have a plan."

She glowed. "I can tell this is gonna be good."

"I thought we'd move everything up to your birthday, August 27th. That gives us almost three months from today. Father will object, but this is *our* wedding. Where do *you* want to get married?"

She tapped her forehead with her right index finger. "Hmmm... St. Patrick's a wonderful place to have a wedding. And all the people I care about could be there."

"But is that where you *want* to be married?"

"Part of me prefers a small church like what I grew up in, but it's more convenient for everyone in the city, and it's important to your father."

He smiled. "Leave him to me. Next, the ceremony. What do you think of Father Thomas?"

"That would be really nice. I'd like that."

She glowed as she put a bite of black sea bass in his mouth. "Next question?"

He swallowed. "The reception?"

"Wilton's fine. Now that your stepmother won't be there. It's a gorgeous place for a reception, and it's your family home."

"Wonderful. And singers?"

"A really good band is all we need."

"Done. And the honeymoon. Father wants to send us on a round-the-world trip on the 737 or the 737 and the

Aleksandra. Or would you prefer Lieb Island, or...?"

Her eyes widened. "Who wouldn't want a round-the-world trip? To see places I've only dreamt about, why not? Unless..."

"If you want it, it's settled."

She grimaced. "But, George, what do *you* want?"

He cupped her chin in his hands and locked into her eyes. "We both want the same thing. Amazing, isn't it?"

Her earnest eyes smiled.

"Finally. I'd like to share my vision for our future. But first, where do you want to live, and what are your dreams?"

She scrunched up her face. "Well, I don't think we need so many houses and cars and servants, and that sort of thing. I'd like us to make a home together, just the two of us. Not quite so grand. We could help so many others if..."

He patted his mouth with the linen napkin. "We have the same dream, to make our own way, to make other people's lives better, to..."

"Yes," she cut in. "I'd like to be able to sing, for you to pursue your art, too. What do you think?"

He nodded. "Exactly! But before I describe what I have in mind, you should open your second present. I hope you like it."

"I'm intrigued," she gushed as he directed the *maître d'* to place the chair with the rectangular box next to her.

She tore off the wrapping. When the last piece had been removed, she started to open the box.

"Here, let me help you."

He lifted the top of the box and she gasped. A tall blonde wearing a flowing, navy silk gown was standing with one hand on a grand piano and the other hand extended toward an unseen audience. Her expressive face captured the radiance of music, her mouth partially open in song.

Her eyes widened. "*My* portrait. It's-It's stunning!"

He smiled. "Do you really like it?"

343

Her face beamed. "I love it."

"I've worked on it for awhile."

"*You* painted this?"

He nodded.

"I had no idea how accomplished an artist you are."

He blushed.

"I'm surprised you haven't been showing in galleries."

He sighed. "I wanted to when I was younger, but *Gran'maman* would never agree. Your portrait is the only painting I've worked on in a while. Like your singing, painting is a part of who I am. But I want to do far more than paint."

She put her hands on each side of her face. "I'm all ears."

He laid out his plans over dessert. As she placed the last bite of raspberries and sabayon in his mouth, he sighed. Father would be displeased, but the future of the Leibnitz family would be better for it. Even Father. If he chose to see it.

Chapter 18

Fritz smiled as the maid set a cup of cappuccino in front of him.

"*Ach*," Tani began in German, "what do you think? I don't usually make requests regarding business, but I believe Mother Aleksandra would approve, yes?"

He nodded. "Yes. Thank you, Tani, for your obvious affection for my children. As you know, I've handled my affairs badly. It's a credit to both of you that you haven't taken advantage of the situation. Tani, you've always been genuine. Mummy saw that. She had a keen sense about people. What has occurred recently has shaken me to the core. I'm mortified."

His jowls darkened. "But we are Leibnitzs. We don't let setbacks deter us, do we, Guenther?"

He studied his brother for a sign of contempt or perverse pleasure in his predicament, but kind eyes met his own. He blushed.

"No, Fritz, we don't. Tani and I stand by you. In everything. Tell us how we can help."

He struggled to accept Guenther at face value. He cleared his throat. "Of course, we need to keep things pretty much as they are. Agreed?"

Guenther nodded.

He smiled in relief. "Then, we'll meet with Marcus and George and make things right."

*****

The next few days rushed by. Before George could meet with his father to inform him of his new plan, Fritz summoned a family meeting in Wilton. George and M arrived with anticipation to find Father Thomas, his brother and sister, his mother, his uncle and aunt, and his cousins already there.

The Wilton library overflowed with trays of *hors-d'oeuvres* and drinks. After refreshments, his father directed everyone to find a seat. They ambled to the south end of the great room, where an expansive wrap-around blue and white toile couch built into the large bay window and several padded Queen Anne armchairs were arranged to take advantage of the view of the flowering gardens outside. George helped M to a seat and waited while the others sat down. Fritz sat in one of the armchairs next to Guenther.

Fritz began by thanking everyone for coming on short notice.

He nodded to Father Thomas, who stood. "Let us remember who we are in God's eyes. Accept this blessing as a sign of a new beginning for the Leibnitz family." He smiled at each one. "Let us pray. Father, God of the universe, we pray for unity and a sense of purpose and conviction. As I reflect on the many years You have called me to serve this family, I am reminded of the mercies You have shown, the prosperity You have allowed, the responsibility You have imparted. I pray that You will remind us whose children we are. May we love one other well. May we put aside enmity and personal ambition to embrace love. May You receive honor and glory through all that is accomplished today. In the name of the Father, the Son, and the Holy Spirit. Amen."

George crossed himself and looked at Father, who was gazing at Marcus, seated on Guenther's right.

"Let me begin with a confession. I apologize that I have put this family in danger." Pain crossed Fritz's face. "Suffice it to say, ultimately, I am to blame. We may not like Uncle Sergey's tactics, but he is the reason we are all safe."

George looked at Marcus, who flinched.

M blanched.

Fritz sighed. "Mummy arranged for her brother to take certain precautions long ago, and only recently have I seen the import of what he discovered. Without going into details, let me just say that if I had been a better husband..."

He turned to Racquel.

"And father..."

He turned to his children.

"And uncle..."

His eyes fixed on his niece and nephews.

"Much tragedy and pain could have been avoided."

A haunted look crossed his face. "I am humbled. I know, some of you believe that is impossible, but I have been brought to my knees. I pride myself on the ability to predict and orchestrate events, to the betterment of this family. Yet, I have been blind. I apologize to all of you, and to my brother most of all."

George's attention shifted to his uncle, whose eyes smiled.

"Guenther, I have always seen you as my rival, not my equal. But after much soul searching and long talks with Father Thomas, I realize, you are the better man. I am afraid I have carried on Rainer's tradition far too long."

His hand threaded through his thick, graying hair.

George's heart bloomed.

Fritz's eyes moistened as he looked at his children. "I understand what Papa thought he was doing. You children may not have the perspective of history that Guenther and I have. Some of you do not know that Leibnitz Enterprises was born out of great peril from hard and treacherous times. Mummy, Papa, and Uncle Sergey had to make hard choices to protect the future of our family's survival. It seems inconsequential to you, who know nothing of *real* struggle.

But your grandparents knew firsthand the compromises that had to be made to protect future generations. They were far from perfect. Rainer was unfaithful, ruthless, cold-hearted, treacherous, and cruel. He started a tradition that must stop. Right now."

He scalded Marcus with hot eyes. Marcus blinked and looked down.

"But we can understand why he did it and love him, despite his faults. 'From cog to cog in three generations,' Winston Churchill, another man of my parents' generation, said. What we do not struggle with our blood to produce we do not treat with the same fervor. Mummy saw that, but she also saw that brothers and cousins could complement each other."

He locked eyes with Marcus.

"Rivalry helps, but only to a degree. Collaboration, in the long run, is the key to meaningful survival. Guenther and I will say, today, that the only way Leibnitz Enterprises will survive and prosper beyond us is for the next generation to work together, not against each other."

"Here, here," Guenther caroled.

George's heart leaped.

"Guenther and Tani tell me that Wilhelm and Georgina have no desire to work in the company."

Both nodded their heads.

"Claude and Brianna's interests lie elsewhere. Which brings us to George and Marcus."

George blushed as his father looked first at him, then at Marcus.

"Both Guenther and I would like to know how you see the future of Leibnitz Enterprises and how we can help you make your dreams for this family's future a reality."

George sat back, extended his hand in Marcus's direction, and gave him a deferential smile that signaled only one thing.

Marcus's eyes stung with hot tears.

Epilogue

George's heart fluttered as the bells resounded.

The massive doors opened on cue, the heavenly orchestral strains of Mendelssohn's *Wedding March* resounded, and the rustle of six hundred guests came to their feet as the bride and distinguished tuxedoed gentleman with gray temples floated into the cathedral. George's face glowed as M and his father began the march down the long aisle. As the butterflies in his stomach took flight, his heart burst with the sweet honey of love. His face flushed with pride to observe how the bonds of love had brought his family together in this sacred sanctuary. Marcus to his right stood tall and confident. From the front pew, the remainder of his family radiated affection.

He could almost see *Gran'maman* smiling on the waves of antiphonal sound. Life had come full circle. He was his own man at last.

About Atmosphere Press

Atmosphere Press is an independent, full-service publisher for excellent books in all genres and for all audiences. Learn more about what we do at atmospherepress.com.

We encourage you to check out some of Atmosphere's latest releases, which are available at Amazon.com and via order from your local bookstore:

Saints and Martyrs: A Novel, by Aaron Roe

When I Am Ashes, a novel by Amber Rose

Melancholy Vision: A Revolution Series Novel, by L.C. Hamilton

The Recoleta Stories, by Bryon Esmond Butler

Voodoo Hideaway, a novel by Vance Cariaga

Hart Street and Main, a novel by Tabitha Sprunger

The Weed Lady, a novel by Shea R. Embry

A Book of Life, a novel by David Ellis

It Was Called a Home, a novel by Brian Nisun

Grace, a novel by Nancy Allen

Shifted, a novel by KristaLyn A. Vetovich

Because the Sky is a Thousand Soft Hurts, stories by Elizabeth Kirschner

About the Author

Karen M. Wicks holds a doctorate from New York University and has taught in middle and high school and at the college level. She has served as director for curriculum and instructional development at the College Board. She and her husband Les co-founded a supplemental education company and the K-12 public school, Royal Live Oaks Academy of the Arts & Sciences Charter School, in South Carolina, where Karen has been the Executive Director/CEO since 2012. Her creative pursuits include writing, singing, cooking, and gardening. Les and Karen have traveled widely and feel blessed to have made many long lasting friendships.

CPSIA information can be obtained
at www.ICGtesting.com
Printed in the USA
LVHW051600041021
699491LV00004B/782